Room 119

The Whitby Trader

T F Lince

In memory of

Diane Lince who passed away during the writing of this book, when she smiled the room smiled with her. She will be sadly missed, always.

Foreword

I'm new to this book writing malarkey. Did you know a foreword (which, incidentally, is foreword, not forward or foreward) is meant to be written by someone else, maybe someone famous to draw you guys into buying millions of copies?

Well, I don't know anyone famous. So I am going to break form and write my own foreword. Obviously my second book will be forewordeded by Stephen Fry, or by whoever plays Dean in the film. I'm thinking Tom Hardy, but he's unaware of this fact right now. So if you are Tom Hardy – or Martin Scorsese looking for your next script, for that matter – drop me an email.

OK, back to the book. About three years ago now, I had a sequence of dreams. When I told someone at work about my dreams, she said I should write a book – which couldn't be more absurd as English wasn't your best subject.. However, I wrote bullet points of the dreams down in MS Word and left it there. That was that, I thought.

In January 2017 and approaching fifty, probably hitting a mid-life crisis, I set a New Year's resolution to write the book. Why not? Some 90,000 or so words later, here we are.

I hope you enjoy the twists and turns the story will lead you on. If you like to buckle into a rollercoaster, I promise to take you on a memorable ride. Please comment on the book, letting me know your thoughts on the Twitter or Facebook pages, and tell all your friends – especially if your friends are Martin Scorsese or Tom Hardy.

I have lots of people to thank, but I will thank them at the end where the acknowledgments are meant to be. I will thank my wife Claire here, though. How she put up with me through this obsession I will never know.

Trev Lince.

Part One – Crash and Burn

Chapter 1 – City Boy

How did he end up in the City, a leading trader at Falconer International? From his humble background in Whitby, a fishing town on the North Yorkshire coast, to the dizzy heights of his office towering over the river, one of Canary Wharf's finest. Mr Hawthorn from High Grange School would be so proud if he could have seen him right now, two GCSEs to his name and one of Falconer's trading stars.

Mr Hawthorn didn't like Dean, thought he was a waster. Talented, but could not be bothered, always just doing enough throughout his schooldays. But Dean's enough was not Mr Hawthorn's enough; they were worlds apart. He was probably right, though; Dean was too busy pulling scams in the playground, conning kids out of their dinner money, to worry about getting grades. A northern kid from a poor family needed life skills rather than qualifications, and life skills had got him to where he was today, punching well above his weight and stepping up the ladder of success twice as fast as any university could have propelled him.

He was sitting in his office overlooking the Thames, six plasma screens on the wall alive with dancing red and blue trading candles, his eyes bouncing from screen to screen, noticing any bearish or bullish moves across the trading boards. He called them 'the boards' – his boards. He knew where every stock, share and FOREX currency should be, and if it wasn't there, why not, and what was going to happen next. The trick of trading is not just knowing what is happening now, but what is going to happen next. He was good at reading tomorrow's news, and if you know what's happening tomorrow, today is a nicer place to be – which was why he had his own office in Canary Wharf, a lavish apartment round the corner and a beautiful wife and daughter in a flash house in Hampshire. As well as his beloved Porsche 911.

Life was good for Dean right now. He was at the top and in control of just about everything. He had two motivational paintings on the wall that he had commissioned from an up-and-coming London artist, Theo Wallgate, at a cost of £100,000 each. The one on the right depicted the sun setting over the Thames with Tower Bridge closing its gates, its strapline being 'London is closing, the rest of the world is in control, BE AWARE'. The one on the opposite wall was Tower Bridge opening against the rising sun with the competing strapline of 'London is opening, TAKE CONTROL'.

Dean looked at his paintings, so proud of them. *I wonder if Mr Hawthorn used to have a painting in the staff room in Whitby*, he thought. Maybe Dean would send him a picture of one of his, or a photo of his fantastic view with the caption 'Remember Me?' Dean started to laugh, realising that if it hadn't been for the efforts of Mr Hawthorn and the other teachers back then, he probably wouldn't be sitting in this office right now.

He took a bottle of whisky out of his bottom drawer and poured two measures into crystal tumblers. It was Johnnie Walker Blue Label, Ryder Cup limited edition – a present from his wife and daughter, along with three days in Gleneagles with the boys watching Europe defend the Ryder Cup, with his name engraved on the front: 'Dean Harrison, love you always, Sarah and Jodie x x'. He was expecting Dexter, and they always shared a drink on a Friday, although Dean's glass barely had enough whisky to discolour the water it was topped up with. It was more of a tradition than a drink, but Dean nevertheless raised his glass to the paintings.

"Mr Terrance Hawthorn, sir, one of your boys did good."

Just then, Dexter Falconer walked in. Dexter was Dean's boss, but Dean had him wrapped around his little finger, being far too streetwise for him. All of those cons and card games in the playground many years ago had sharpened Dean to a point, and the natural wit and sarcasm of a northerner had kept the point sharp throughout the years.

Dexter was nearly sixty. He wore a suit like it had never wanted to fit him, like it was being rejected by his DNA. You couldn't knock him for trying, though, as he had a different one for every day of the month. Dean, on the other hand, looked razor sharp with minimal effort. Some people can and some people can't. Dean could; Dexter couldn't.

"What's up, Dex? Have you seen today's figures?" Dean knew Dexter had seen the figures; he'd always seen the figures. He also knew that a knock on the door at 4pm was a good sign. The 1pm knocks were the bad ones.

"How do you do it, Deano? You're dragging this company up on your own. You're just about the only one anywhere near this month's targets. I mean, how did you call CAD vs NOK would go bearish when it's been bullish all week?"

"I can't give my away my secrets, Dex old boy." Dean's intention was to appear smug, but he was aiming for the not-too-smug variety.

"I know, I know, it's not about what's going on today, it's about what's about to happen tomorrow." Dexter's tone was very much 'we've been here before', and he was right. Dean had a knack of performing well when others didn't. Yes, he had the odd slump or two, but they were infrequent. Dexter's praise was justified and they both knew it.

"You got it, Dex."

"Mind you, you had better watch your back, Deano. The new boy is well up there on the figures; he's just behind you, actually. Got something about him, that kid. He reminds me of a young man I met in here fifteen years ago." He picked up a framed picture from the desk of a nervous looking Dean standing shaking hands with a much younger and slimmer Dexter.

"Fifteen years – has it been that long, Dex? What's the new kid's name again?" Dean already knew his name. He'd seen him around the office, flicking his annoyingly disobedient blond hair out of his eyes what seemed like every other second; he just wanted to sound like he wasn't bothered.

"Oliver Steadman-Fisher, a twenty-three-year-old whizz kid. Remember the name, Dean. He'll be the next of Falconer's shining stars."

Dexter placed the picture back down on the desk.

"Let me guess, Dexter, Oxford graduate?" Dean was paying a little more attention now. Although Dexter was getting a bit long in the tooth, he could still spot talent. If Dexter had his eye on Oliver, Dean could do with an eye on him too.

"Yep, you got it, Deano. He comes highly recommended from Oxford's top financial academy. Oliver majored in financial statistics." Dexter lifted his leg and swung it back and forth, half sitting on Dean's desk with the other leg still on the floor.

"Well let's see what Oliver's like when it's real money. It's easy to make tough calls on a real time simulator but I doubt he'd be so cocky with the company's…sorry, *your* money, Dexter."

"We might find out soon. I'm thinking of letting him loose into the real world."

Dexter looked for a reaction from Dean, but didn't get one. The 'your money' comment seemed to have done the trick. While Dexter was saying the word 'might', Dean knew he really meant 'might not'.

"Anyway, Dean, it's a Friday and you know what that means. All the boys are going to celebrate at Gino's. It looks like you are all going to hit the bonus at the end of the month. So I think you'll be getting a couple of beers paid for. Only right as most of it was your doing, bonnie lad." Dexter clearly didn't realise 'bonnie lad' was a Geordie term, and Newcastle is nowhere near Whitby. Dean let him get away with it, though. At the end of the day, Dexter was the boss.

"I can't tonight, Dexter. It's Jodie's birthday tomorrow and I've not made it home in the last two weeks as I've been working." Dean started to pack up what papers were left on his desk and put them into the drawer.

"No, you haven't, Dean, you've been on the razz with the boys. Barcelona last weekend, wasn't it?" Dexter chuckled and got off Dean's desk, taking Dean's paper-rustling as a hint to leave.

"Yes, but Sarah doesn't know that, does she, Dexter? She thinks it was all business, and she'd better not find out, either. Tell the boys I'll pop down for one or two, but then I'm off. It's an important day for Jodie tomorrow. You're only fifteen once, Dexter."

"I wish I was fifteen again, Dean. I would love to do it all again. Fifteen. Wow."

This was Dexter's parting comment as he left the room, dreaming of being fifteen again.

He must have a good bloody good memory, Dean thought as Dexter disappeared out of view.

Chapter 2 – Gym Bunnies

Friday was the day Sarah could be late picking Jodie up from school. Dean had taught Jodie how to play chess last year on holiday and she had not looked back since. She had still not beaten her dad, but she was getting closer, and the main reason for that was Jodie's Friday after-school chess club.

This meant for Sarah that Friday afternoon had turned into Body Pump Friday in the gym, followed by coffee in the health bar. After a tough workout today, Sarah was in the changing room with the girls, talking about the last hour of lifting weights, squatting and general body abuse. Sarah did not have much time for the girls, but she hardly saw Dean nowadays with his job being so chaotic. So from being a once or twice a month thing, the gym had turned into an everyday event for her. She was quietly proud of her body, not like some of the other girls who treated Friday like they had to do some annoying work before earning a coffee and cake reward. It showed.

It was very much about status in this gym. You had to have matching gear and it all had to be this season's latest trends and colours from Nike or Sweaty Betty. When the girls had all showered, they changed into clean designer gym gear so that when they eventually left the gym, everyone could see they had been. Otherwise what's the point?

Sarah was always first out of the changing room and into the health bar. She was naturally beautiful and did not need the war paint that some of the others required; she was quite happy to towel dry her blonde locks and throw them back into a ponytail.

It made a lot of sense to turn up for Friday's gym session. Whoever failed to show would generally be the topic of conversation. Sarah sometimes wasn't sure if it was a gym club or a gossip club. It was probably a bit of both. When everybody turned up, like today, the conversation would go round and round in a circle until one of the girls showed a sign of weakness and let their deflector shields down.

Today was Sarah's turn to be caught off guard.

"So, Sarah, where is Dean this week? Working *away again*?" Doreen said. A couple of the other girls lifted their coffee cups to their lips, more to mask their smiles than out of a need for caffeine. The question was not delivered with venom; it was as if Doreen was in a boat on a still summer's afternoon, casting a fishing rod into a pool, the float bobbing along the surface, the bait underneath waiting for a dumb ass fish to swim by. Sarah knew she should have sniffed the bait and swum away, but Doreen had been casting away for what seemed like weeks now, and wherever Doreen headed, the rest of the girls normally followed.

How dare that bossy bitch try and drag Dean down? Sarah not only took the bait on the hook, but devoured the line and sinker in the process.

"Well, Doreen, Dean has been working really hard. Not like your Tom who sits at home on his backside living off his mother's inheritance."

Doreen was thick-skinned. She knew that Tom was a lazy bastard.

"This isn't about Tom, Sarah. Look, I'm sorry. Forget I ever mentioned it. Obviously you don't trust Dean. Maybe things aren't as perfect for you as we all think they are."

The other four girls got comfy. Doreen had got a bite and it was a good one. Now she was playing with Sarah before reeling her in for supper. They all had seats at the back of Doreen's boat to see the action unfolding without really supporting her. They had all experienced being on her hook before, but that didn't mean they had Sarah's back. Backing someone up against Doreen would mean rocking the boat, and that could have the consequence of deflecting the conversation onto them. So they maintained a watching brief, keeping as still as possible.

Sarah knew she was on her own for now so went on the attack. "For your information, Doreen, I do trust Dean implicitly and we are extremely happy."

"Have you checked Dean's credit card bill recently? That's how I caught my first husband out." A couple of the girls gave a nod in Doreen's direction and murmured their agreement.

"I check my Brian's," one of them said. This got Sarah's back up even further.

"I don't have to. I trust and love Dean, he would never cheat on me." As the words tripped out of her mouth, Sarah felt like she was at a dead end. There were much better ways of saying what she meant.

Doreen spotted the weakness and slowed the conversation down as if she was lecturing a schoolkid.

"No one said he was cheating, Sarah. That's all your own supposition. We didn't mention anything of the sort, did we, girls?"

The girls all nodded and muttered like Members of Parliament in the House of Commons when the Prime Minister is in mid speech. Doreen smiled, knowing another fish was safely in the basket.

"Whatever! I have to go to pick Jodie up." Sarah was doing her best not to show how upset she was feeling inside, but she also knew it wasn't worth arguing anymore. "See you tomorrow, girls, at Jodie's party with your kids. Two o'clock start. Don't be late." She could not have been more cheery as she reminded the girls about the party. Giving Doreen a stare on the way out that would melt ice, Sarah knew she would get her own back one day, but today was about dignity and class. Sarah had them both in abundance, and had the best life of them all, and the girls knew it. Thinking she was not actually perfect gave them all a little bit of hope. Jealousy is a strange and not very beautiful creature.

Sarah left the gym through the front door, giving a wave as she did. For the next hour, she and Dean would be the hot topic of conversation, the girls picking their whole lives apart, convincing themselves that it would be awful to be them and have their sad life. The truth could not have been more different.

Chapter 3 – Gino's

Gino's was an Italian bar among many bars in Canary Wharf. Although trading was a cutthroat environment, different companies had different loyalties to different bars. Gino's was Falconer International's chosen establishment; it was classy and had all the top wines and champagnes. When guys down this end of town got a bonus, it was up to the likes of Gino's to encourage them to spend it as quickly as possible. A couple of smaller trading firms used it too, but there was definitely a pecking order, and in Gino's Falconer's ruled the roost. So there were a set amount of prime tables empty for Falconer International, not reserved by signs but by respect.

Some of the smaller firms' traders were already lurking in the shadows before the Falconer boys turned up. Jack Smith was first to the bar, as he always had been ever since Dean first met him. Dean liked Jack, a fellow northerner from Burnley in Lancashire. Lancashire and Yorkshire people are not meant to get on, but Jack befriended Dean when he first came down south to work.

"Us northerners stick together, Yorkie," he'd said, and to be fair, Jack had always had Dean's back from that moment on. As far as the Lancashire versus Yorkshire thing went, they both knew about the Wars of the Roses, but neither of them knew which side had won.

Jack did his usual, buying everyone in the gang a drink. Dean tried refusing as he was driving back to Hampshire tonight for his daughter's birthday tomorrow and there would be hell to pay if he missed it, but Jack got him one anyway. Dean had just taken his pint and had a gulp – London Pride was not John Smith's, but long gone were the days when beer was garbage down south – when his phone vibrated in his pocket so he headed outside.

It was already 6pm and getting cooler. April was not the summer or the winter; April was April, and the temperature was very April indeed. Dean lit a fag and phoned Sarah back, not looking forward to the call.

"Are you in your car yet, Dean?" Sarah delivered this opening gambit with barbed wire wrapped around every syllable.

"Just having one drink with the boys, honey. Setting off in a bit." Dean shrank his head into his shoulders and prepared himself for the barrage.

"I can't believe you, Dean! It's Jodie's birthday tomorrow – you don't give a shit. Can you even remember what we have got her?"

Dean moved the phone away from his ear and gave it a stare as the rollicking continued. Sarah had an uncanny way of blunting Dean's natural sharpness. His wit got him nowhere; she knew him too well. So he did as any self-respecting man would do in his situation – he went on the attack.

"Sarah, I love you to bits, but do you know how hard it is being in London all week? The mortgage doesn't pay itself, you know, and you don't complain when you're out buying another dress, handbag or Range Rover…"

Beeeep. Sarah had hung up, and a smile broke out across Dean's face. *A moral victory*, he thought. Although he would have to deal with the consequences, he knew Sarah would be OK. She always was.

When Dean got back to the bar, there was already another pint of beer and a Sambuca lined up for him. *Sod it*, he thought, *I'll go first thing in the morning and be home before Jodie gets up.* Anyway, he could not be arsed with the grief he'd get when he got in.

Dean downed his pint in one, trying to catch up with the boys who seemed like they were in for a heavy session. Then he turned the empty glass over on his head as was the tradition, to prove it was empty beyond any doubt. Anyone watching would probably have thought he was a prick – he did look like a prick, but all the Falconer's boys followed like sheep and did the same.

As soon as a pint disappeared another would arrive, followed swiftly by the mandatory Sambuca, often of the flaming variety, alight with sunken coffee beans. Dean started thinking about Jodie and how hard he was on Sarah. He did love her, but sometimes it seemed easier not to be at home with her than to be there, particularly in this last year. He had got an apartment on the river due to the late nights and early mornings he had to work, but to be honest, his commute would only be an hour or so. Would that be too much of a price to pay for seeing his wife and daughter? The more he thought, the more the apartment seemed like a convenience rather than a necessity.

He knew he was out of order. Although he was a little tipsy, while he could still hold a conversation, he phoned Sarah from the quietest corner of the bar.

The answering machine announced, "This is Sarah Harrison, please leave me a message and I'll get back to you as soon as possible."

"Sarah, it's Dean. Sorry about earlier, it's just been a mad week. I'm gonna stay at the apartment tonight as the boys have bought me a couple of drinks. I will be up at six-thirty am and be there for JoJo's birthday. I do love you, you know."

Dean took a second to look around. He should have gone home and he knew it; he was getting a bit tired of all of the fun and games of a trading lifestyle, especially now he was north of forty. *Dean, for Christ's sake*, he thought before heading back to the madding crowd, which welcomed him with open arms.

"Right, it's my round, Jack. What are we all having?"

Jack held out his hand to stop Dean. "No can do. I'm off, Yorkie. Got to get back to the missus on the ten pm train."

Jack had met his wife Holly when they were at school. They had been childhood sweethearts, and Dean knew that if Jack said he had to get back, then he had to get back. There was no point pushing him.

"Ten o'clock? How the fuck did that happen? OK, anyone else want another?"

"We are off to the strip joint, Dean. You're welcome to join us if you want to. Anyway, you'll have to as it's your round – unless you've had enough and need to go to bed."

It was Oliver, the new boy, who delivered this line with confidence, putting Dean down and bigging himself up in the same sentence. Dean didn't like the laughs from his so-called friends.

Little upstart, he thought.

"OK, lead the way, *Olivia*, hope you've brought your ID with you."

Dean got a titter or two from the evening's survivors who could sense an element of dick measuring coming on. He had not been to a strip joint since his stag night in Madrid over eighteen years ago. He couldn't remember much about that night, but was reliably informed that he'd had a good time, mainly by Jack who'd bought every other round as usual but never seemed to get drunk. It was like he was immune to alcohol.

There were only five lads who had lasted this long; the rest had cried off. Dean felt like the outsider; he was the most senior, and the rest were just kids, including Oliver who was gaining such a good reputation with Dexter. Dean only really knew one other by name – Martin. The rest he'd seen hanging around the canteen and coffee area, but they didn't move in the same circles as Dean, or even work on the same floor as him. It was a long way up to the top, and when you got there, you tended not to look down very often. Dean had made a 'we are the best company in the world' corporate speech at Martin's induction, which he'd known was a load of bollocks, and remembered Martin seemed to be scared of his own shadow. When it had been Martin's turn to introduce himself to everyone, his bottom lip had started to shake and he'd gone as red as a beetroot. Dean would normally ask lots of questions during his induction talks to see what the new guys were like under a bit of pressure, but Martin had been such a wreck, Dean had taken the pressure off by allowing someone else to answer his questions.

"OK, are we all h-e-r-e?" Oliver had one of those accents that made 'here' sound more like an animal with big ears.

"Oliver, you sound like you were born with a silver spoon up your arse."

Oliver's disciples again gave out a disloyal suppressed titter; Dean still had a northern twang to his voice. *If you're proud of where you're from, you keep your accent*, was his motto.

Dean thought Bazookas was aptly named. He felt like he was back at a football presentation night in Saltburn or Redcar with a comedian, followed by strippers. This joint was a bit classier than Ruby Street Social Club in Saltburn and there was no comedian, just a stage and a pole. The boys got the best table opposite the pole, which was presumably where all the action was going to take place.

Not forgetting it was his round next, Dean went to the bar.

"I don't suppose you serve beer?"

The barman pointed to the lager pumps and stared at Dean as if to say, "Are you blind?" Dean could not be bothered to explain the difference between beer and lager.

"Six lagers and six Sambucas, please," Dean slurred to the

barman.

"Are you babysitting tonight, sir?" the barman replied.

"Yes, I suppose you could say that." Dean looked around and thought, *what the fuck am I doing here?* That thought only lasted until the drinks were poured.

"That will be eighty pounds, sir," said the barman as he handed across the drinks.

"My God, eighty pounds? They'd better be good." To Dean, £80 was peanuts, but he still tried to keep in touch with his roots. He dropped off the drinks and went to the toilet.

Oliver took out a small capsule from his jacket pocket, broke it open and poured the contents into Dean's drink.

"Let's see if Deano can take his drink, shall we? Olivia, my backside," he said with a sinister laugh that sounded more Dick van Dyke than Dick Dastardly.

Martin pleaded with Oliver.

"Don't, Ollie, he's an OK guy. It's not worth it."

"It's only an E. Anyway, it will help the old man perk up a bit. Don't say anything or you're dead."

Martin's bottom lip started to quiver and his redness went up a notch on the blushing scale. "I won't, Ollie," he said.

Dean returned. "OK, boys, what's happening then? I hear you've been having some very good results on the simulator. Well done – especially you, Oliver." Dean was from the 'credit where credit is due' school. Besides, any healthy competition in this industry kept him on his toes.

Martin's eyes flickered between the spiked drink and Oliver.

"Yes, it's going quite well, thanks, Dean, but it might just have been beginner's luck so far," Oliver replied.

"There is no such thing as luck, Oliver. The markets do what they are supposed to. Guessing is a mug's game. Guessing the market gives you a fifty/fifty chance; you are currently running at 84.7% over 246 trades, so that's not luck." Dean raised his glass to Oliver as a mark of respect and urged them all to take a drink. "The next thing, Oliver, is the timing of when to pull out of the trade. You have pulled out of all of your trades within ten per cent of their peak price, most of them within five per cent." He raised his glass a second time and took another sip. Before Oliver could answer, Dean added, "Between you and me, I think you'll be using real money before long."

Dean raised his glass for a last time and urged his companions to finish what they had left. "Good luck, boys, hope you all have a good career."

They drank their drinks down in one, led by Dean, pouring the dregs over their heads. Martin's shirt was soaked; he'd only got three quarters of his drink down his neck.

"Now, gentlemen, give it up for the lovely Chantelle!" the compère announced.

From behind a curtain, a young blonde in black high heels strutted. She had more vital statistics that Dean had just thrown at Oliver, but calling her a stripper was a misnomer as she barely had anything to strip off. She was wearing suspenders, a black thong and a feeble excuse for a bra which was doing an amazing job at holding in her enormous surgically-enhanced tits.

The boys were fixated, tapping their feet to 'I'm Sexy and I Know It'. Dean was again thinking that he should be at home and wondering how the hell he had ended up here, although there were probably worse things to be doing than looking at Chantelle, who was currently upside down with a pole between her legs. Her bra, meanwhile, had given up the fight.

Chantelle moved off the pole and over to Martin. Unclipping one of her stockings from her suspended belt, she slowly slid it off, putting her foot into Martin's crotch. He went redder than ever and slipped a twenty-pound note into the elastic of her thong. She smiled at him, giving him a look as if to tell him that he was the one. Really she was probably thinking he was a pervert, but still it was the easiest £20 she'd ever made.

The music stopped. Chantelle, now totally naked, took her bows then clumsily retraced her steps in nine-inch black heels, picking up all of her clothes. She gave Martin a wink on her way past, hoping for another twenty quid on her next set.

Dean was losing a little focus as he took a swig of his latest pint. He shook his head and for a second felt OK again as if he'd reset his brain.

"And now on stage, give it up for London's finest – Chelsea."

Dean looked up to see Chelsea, but all he could see was a blurry figure. The music was dull and unrecognisable like it was being played under a pillow, and his head was thudding with every beat. His pupils dilated and his heart felt like it was leaving his body. He could hear it pumping as if it had relocated into his ears. He started to foam at the mouth. Dean had done cocaine a couple of times to join in with the older lads when he had started out at Falconer's, but this was different. He was not in control; it was more like he was an outsider looking at his body. It certainly wasn't a 'high'.

He clumsily got up out of his chair.

Oliver spotted this and said to the boys, "Let's go. We need to get out of here." Dean heard Oliver in slow motion, the words 'we need to get out of here' echoing around his head as if Oliver was shouting in a cathedral.

As they left, Dean headed in the direction of the toilet to throw up. As he did so, he fell into Chelsea who was attempting to mount her pole to Madonna's 'Like a Virgin'. Two bouncers appeared from nowhere and grabbed Dean.

"You dirty fucker," one said as they manhandled him through the strippers' curtain and threw him out into the back alley. One of them followed him out, kicking him in the face and stomach for good measure.

"Pervert," he said, giving Dean a last dig in the ribs as he tried to stand.

Oliver flagged down a London Hackney cab with the other boys.

"Waterloo Station, please," he ordered.

"See you later, boys," Martin said. They could all see Dean lying in the back alley from the cab. "I can't leave him."

Martin walked to the alleyway. Dean was throwing up a mixture of bile and blood; he was barely conscious and on all fours. Martin helped him to his feet and they staggered together to the roadside, looking out for a cab with its light on. Martin threw his arm out to get the driver's attention.

"What's your address, Dean?" he asked as he bundled Dean into the back seat.

"It's 447 Waterfront Wharf Apartments," Dean said on autopilot without opening his eyes. After a short cab ride to the east, Martin got Dean, who had come round a little by now, to his front door.

"Thanks, Martin, I don't know what happened. I've got a lot going on at home at the moment. I think things just got on top of me."

Martin gave him an 'it's not your fault' look, but he was too weak to say anything. He felt at least he had done his part in getting Dean home.

"Are you OK from here, Dean?" Dean definitely did not look OK from anywhere.

"Yep, I think so."

As Martin went to let go, Dean nearly fell over, using the door for support.

"Are you sure, Dean?' Martin let go of him again, allowing Dean to get his balance

"Yes thanks, Martin, I won't forget this."

Dean struggled through the door then up in the lift. Opening the caged door to his apartment, he threw the keys onto the kitchen table and took his phone out of his pocket, setting his alarm for 6.30am so he could get back for Jodie's birthday. Before collapsing, he afforded himself a look in the bedroom mirror. His bruised face and swollen lip looked straight back at him.

"Dean, you're a prick," he said before allowing his beaten-up body to crawl into bed.

Chapter 4 – Jodie's Birthday

Sarah was up at 7am. It was a big day for their daughter – or was it her daughter? Neither she nor Jodie had seen Dean for two weeks, and the one night he should have been there, he wasn't.

She wondered whether she might have given Dean a hard time last night after listening to the message he'd left her. She knew that when he got home, she'd forgive him as she always did. She also knew that he'd make Jodie's day; he could do nothing wrong in his daughter's eyes. Sarah adored him, too; she just wanted Dean to appreciate them both a bit more. It had been all about work for Dean recently, although today was not the day for that fight. It was Jodie's birthday, and nothing was going to spoil that.

At 8am, Sarah thought he should really be here by now, even if he'd hit some traffic. She decided to give him a call; she was still pissed off with him, but she'd better check he was OK.

"Hi, this is Dean Harrison, Falconer International. Please leave a message and your number and I will return your call at the earliest opportunity…

Beep.

"Where are you, Dean? I could use a hand – Jodie's big day, remember? She's only fifteen once. Oh, I nearly forgot – you're still a prick for last night, ha-ha. I've not forgiven you yet. Ring me – we've got thirty screaming kids arriving at two o'clock."

9am. *Beep…*

"Dean, you're taking the piss. You were setting off at six-thirty, I'm a bit worried about you. Let me know you're OK…you'd better not be fucking with me, Dean. Ring me, not joking."

10am. *Beep…*

"Where are you, Dean? You don't come home for two weeks, and now I can't get hold of you. You don't even want to know what's going through my head."

10.30am. *Beep…*

"You know what, Dean, you're an arsehole. Everything is all about you, your work and your pissing life. Dick!"

10.45am. *Beep…*

"Cock!"

11am. *Beep…*

"It's not me I'm bothered about, Dean. I'll get over it, but I'm sick of covering for you with Jodie. She keeps asking where Dad is. What do I say? You're probably shagging some hooker in London – that's what the girls in the gym think."

11.30am. *Beep…*

"Don't even bother, Dean, you've blown it this time. Jodie and I will be fine, we don't need an unreliable prick like you in our lives."

Dean opened one eye. He was in his bed in his London apartment, still wearing what he had gone to work in yesterday, and he *never* did that.

He scrambled for his phone on the bedside table, fumbling it to the floor. "Shit, Jodie's party," he said out loud. Putting his hand under the bed, he fished for his phone, reeling it in and pressing the button to illuminate it.

"Fuck, 12.31. What the fuck? What the hell happened last night?" He shook his head to kick-start his body, then saw the seven missed calls.

"Fuck!" This fuck wasn't the short one he'd let out when he realised the time; this one was a drawn-out fuck – an 'I'm in the shit' fuck.

He bounced out of bed, his body not appreciating the movement – his body was not ready for any 'doing' words at the moment. Then he staggered across to the walk-in shower, stripping off on the four or five strides it took to get there.

A cold shower was what he needed right now. He washed his hair and splashed his face a few times, only allocating two minutes to the shower. He would have loved more, but every minute counted right now as he had under one hour thirty minutes to get home. It might be worth a couple of speeding tickets – he knew he could get one of the kids in the office to take his points at the going rate of £200 a point.

Dean felt like shit, but his body had an amazing way of letting him get away with it for a while – not forever, just for a while. All debts have to be paid eventually, but for now his body was giving him a pardon. He dressed and allowed himself a quick glance into the mirror. What he saw was worthy of another "Fuck!" He had a cut on his nose, a split lip, and looked like he was getting a black eye.

Dean cleaned his teeth, and put gel into his hair before splashing on some aftershave, which made him wince as it hit his split lip. Still in sped-up mode, he grabbed his car keys and headed for the lift.

Dean still felt wrong. His mind seemed to be a few seconds behind his body. *What happened last night?* he thought. He couldn't even recall where he and the boys had gone. He remembered naked women and lots of alcohol. *If that's all I can remember and I'm going to see my wife, my memory could really do with bridging some of the gaps.*

He pulled the cage for the lift to the side and headed down to the car park.

It was his pride and joy, a midnight blue Porsche 911 Turbo S Cabriolet, but today was not the day to admire it. He pressed the button, opened the door and slid into the driver's seat in more or less one movement, grimacing as his body reminded him of the kick in the ribs he'd got last night.

He sped out of the underground car park, his Porsche engine roaring and echoing under to the low roof, opened the gates and launched himself up the ramp into the East End of London. Setting the satnav's touch screen to home, he negotiated the first few bends one-handed.

"Calculating." After a few seconds, the satnav proudly announced, "Route is set. Your arrival time is 14.31pm."

He had thirty-one minutes to gain on Little Miss Know-it-all inside his satnav to be there on time. Technically, he should arrive more than one minute before his daughter's birthday party, but he knew how Sarah's mind worked. If he was going to be late, there would be a world of difference between 13.59 and 14.01 – 13:59 meant Dad at least cared; 14.01 meant Dad didn't give a shit.

The thing was, Dad did give a shit, and most of last night wasn't his fault. His memory just hadn't confirmed this fact to him yet.

London seemed to be in a rush. Dean's car flew past the famous landmarks, upset about the lack of attention they were getting. On leaving the City, he thought he had better phone Sarah, then he decided he'd better listen to the seven voicemail messages first to get a feel of her mood. He never knew, she might just want him to bring some bread and milk in.

He listened. It didn't help that Sarah's tone, getting worse with each message, was being pumped by Bluetooth through some of the best car speakers money could buy. Yep, it was official: he was in the shit. Being late was no longer an option, so he put his foot down on the accelerator hard enough for fire to do a flaming dance out of the Porsche's turbo, if that were possible.

While driving, he tried putting a story together, and after failing miserably to come up with a believable alibi for last night, he thought he would settle on the truth – or at least, what he remembered about the truth. His memory teased him with a few of snippets of information.

1. Falling over on a stripper – *I might not use that one yet.*
2. Feeling like he had been drugged – *That's a keeper. Use that one.*
3. Getting told by Martin in the taxi that the bouncers had given him a good kicking – *That's in as well. It would explain the nose and busted lip.*

He rang Sarah.

"Dean, where the fuck are you?" She sounded pissed off, and busy. "Yeah thanks, put them over there," he could hear her add to a helper. "Well?"

Dean took a deep breath.

"Sorry, Sarah, I got beaten up last night in a club in London. I think my drink was spiked. I've just got up, but I'll be there before two o'clock, promise."

Busy though she was, Sarah still managed to land a blow.

"Dean, I'm so pissed off with you. You're never here, and the one day you couldn't miss, you're going to miss."

Dean forced his foot even closer to the floor of his Porsche.

"I won't miss it, I'll be there. Can't wait to see you, honey."

There was a pause. She was thinking, and that was never a good thing.

"'Don't 'honey' me, Dean. Fuck off; save it for your girlfriend."

Dean pulled an *ouch* face.

"Girlfriend…?"

Beeeeeeeeeeep.

Apart from the girlfriend thing at the end, Dean actually thought that went better than expected.

Dean headed towards Sunbury to pick up the M3 where he could really open up the Porsche. There was a temporary 50 mile per hour zone due to roadworks for 10 miles on the M3, which was where he played his trump card and put the hammer down – 95mph all the way, and give the penalty points to one of the kids in the office. He saw a couple of speed cameras flash but didn't care. As a trader for nearly twenty years, he'd learned that money is power. People crumple to money. The morals and values he'd been taught by his dad had been sucked into the false life of the City, and when in Rome…

His satnav had been recalculating every second, scratching her metaphorical head and wondering how he'd managed to gain time on such a difficult route. He was now due to get in at 14.22pm and the roadworks were over. At 120 miles an hour, he was gaining a minute per minute, his mathematical brain telling him an ETA of 13.56. For the first time today, he felt in control.

His body then let up on his 'how he should be feeling after last night' clause and evoked a 'feeling even shitter' legislation that he was due from earlier. He had to stop on the hard shoulder and throw up. He then had to endure five minutes of getting rid of the unwanted liquids on the roadside, his body apologising to his mind like a cheap lawyer.

"*I held them off as long as I could…*"

Having been ill, Dean started feeling better. He was on his way again, the satnav smugly announcing he was going to be late. *Not if I can help it*, thought Dean. He was doing over a ton before moving on to more responsible roads where only an idiot would go mad. Dean was a lot of things, but no idiot – it could be his daughter crossing the road, so he slowed down.

As he pulled into his home village, he could see kids heading to his house for Jodie's party. He pulled into the drive at 13.58pm, and as he turned the engine off, he gave the satnav a couple of taps as if to say, "I told you so."

His wife ran out to meet him. "Welcome home, Dean," she said, giving him a big kiss and a hug. Dean did not think he really deserved this, but saw it as a bonus until he noticed five or six of the kids' mothers looking on. He recognised them as the Friday

Gym Mafia from the Body Pump Russian Roulette that always followed Sarah's workout. Sarah was not stupid; she could put on a show so she would not be the talk of the town.

She kissed his neck and whispered in his ear, "You are in so much trouble, Dean, and what the fuck has happened to your face?" before she turned to the girls and smiled. "Dean thought he wouldn't make it. He's been working so hard in the City. Isn't that right, Dean?"

The Stepford Wives were watching their every move. Doreen gave Sarah a 'you might fool them, but you're not fooling me' smile before replying, "It's really good you could make it, Dean. Jodie will be so happy you've found time in your busy schedule."

Dean looked at Doreen. She was prickly, always had been, but he normally managed to get her on side and blunt her prickly spikes.

"Doreen, can I just say how beautiful you look today? Have you got a new hairdresser?"

That did the trick.

"Oh, thank you, Dean. Yes – do you like it?"

Dean took Sarah's hand.

"Sorry, girls, it's Jodie's day. If you can excuse me, where is she?'

Jodie left her friends, who were talking on the lawn, and walked over to her dad's waiting arms. Dean picked her up and spun her round, even though she was too old for spinning round. She saw so little of her dad at the moment, she didn't mind.

'Thanks, Dad, glad you could make it. Where have you been?"

Ouch! Dean thought, but he probably didn't deserve a full on welcoming committee. Jodie would have let him get away with it a few years back, but she was fast becoming a young woman. She was growing up right in front of his eyes, and Dean had been too blind to see it. Although she wouldn't let it show, he could tell she was pissed off with him. Sarah and Jodie had obviously had words.

Dean ran the BBQ outside and took care of the music and karaoke, which was set up in the marquee. Sarah looked after the rest of the food and all the parents, apart from the husbands

who occasionally escaped their wives to join Dean outside for a beer or two.

Sarah's mum and dad were doing their grandparents thing. Jodie's granddad even had a go on the karaoke, until he realised that the kids had never heard of Frank Sinatra or 'My Way'. It wasn't quite *X Factor*, but they gave him a cheer anyway before the next budding Katy Perry was up strutting and doing her thing.

Sarah was determined to make sure it was the best party Jodie had ever had, and so was her dad, but neither of them spoke to each other all day apart from through necessity. They were mostly occupied doing independent jobs to make sure their daughter's day went without a hitch.

Jack turned up and helped Dean on BBQ duty for the afternoon while Holly, his wife, helped Sarah inside.

"I think you've done it this time, Yorkie, what the hell happened last night?"

Dean started to flip a row of burgers that were neatly lined up along the length of the gas-powered BBQ.

"That's the thing, Jack, I can't remember much. That Oliver had something to do with it, though – he couldn't stop smirking at me, the little prick."

Dean started on the second row of burgers which were sizzling away nicely.

"Well, all I know, Yorkie, is that you're in the shit. Sarah called Holly this morning, and although I only heard one side of the conversation, I got the impression that you are not flavour of the month." Dean looked at Jack. "Are they ready yet?" Jack asked.

"No, you've just seen me turn them over, Jack!" Dean threatened to rap Jack's knuckles with his flipper. "Well, Sarah and I will be fine, but you know what? I'm sick of this life. Last night made me realise what I have and what I've been neglecting." Dean pointed to the baskets of buns. "Go on, then, I have to test they're ready."

Jack took an already split bun and lined it with ketchup and mustard.

"I don't know how you do mustard, Jack, makes you breathe out."

"What?" Jack replied.

"Makes you breathe out, like…never mind."

Jack accepted the burger which looked the most done and

loaded it into his pre-prepared bun before taking a bite out of it as it got comfortable in its new home.

"I've got a big trade going down next week, Jack, and if it goes well, that's me out. No more London. Going to spend time with Sarah and Jodie, try and prove to them I'm not a complete dick."

Jack looked at Dean while he munched his burger.

"So, Yorkie, you're admitting you're a dick, then? Just not a complete one."

"Name a trader who isn't, Jack. Self-centred pricks, the lot of us, and the worst thing is, we all know it."

Jack tilted his head to one side but thought better of putting up a defence.

"Don't get me wrong, Jack, it's hard work to get on the merry-go-round and you enjoy the ride, but the hardest thing will be getting off. It's like a drug. But if all goes well, next week, that's me done."

Dean was looking for a comforting nod or maybe a few words of wisdom from his best friend. He had to settle for, "Have you got any more burgers ready, Yorkie? Bloody gorgeous, them."

Chapter 5 – The Aftermath

Dean was finishing loading the dishwasher as Sarah entered the kitchen.

"You'd better go and see Jodie before she falls asleep, Dean."

Dean headed upstairs, trying to peck Sarah on the cheek on the way past, but she was having none of it.

Jodie was already in bed.

"Did you have a good party, JoJo?'

"Best ever." She paused. "Mum could have done with you here this morning, Dad."

Dean had words, lies and excuses all lined up, but decided to stay silent. Jodie was right and they both knew it.

"Can we have a game of chess on my new chess set, Dad?" They both looked at the antique Jacques Staunton chess set dating from the early 1900s that Dean had got Jodie for her birthday, along with a new iPad. Even Dean realised that a £1,200 chess set, complete with an English mahogany-framed board and beautifully inlaid squares of alternating rosewood and boxwood, was a bit of an unusual present for a fifteen-year-old girl, but Jodie loved chess and was already one of the best at chess club at school. Dean knew she would cherish the gift and look after it with loving care. She deserved it.

"OK, but we might not be able to finish it tonight, though, Jodie. It's late, and your mum and I need a quick chat. Black or white?"

"Black, Dad, please." She smiled at him.

As Dean was white, he started. They played for thirty minutes, both having a few victories and losing a few pieces each, but more or less cancelling each other out, plotting their way back and forth on the chessboard like fencers looking for an opening.

Jodie looked at her dad, eyes wide. She knew she was only six or seven moves from beating him, and she had practised those moves. She knew where the pieces were right now. Her dad did not stand a chance as long as she concentrated. Dean knew he was in a bit of trouble, but not how much. He'd nearly lost to Jodie before, but had always found a way out.

"You're getting better, Jodie, I'll give you that, but remember what I always say: 'There is always a way. When someone has got nowhere to run, it's better to go down fighting, no matter how futile the fight'."

Dean had a way of saying things. Sarah called them Deanisms. He smiled at Jodie; he had used this particular Deanism to make her feel sorry for him. All is fair in love and war, and Dean was not a 'let her win' type of dad. She would win when she deserved to.

"Right, Jodie, we'll have to leave it where it is for now. I have to go and see your mum."

Dean sat up.

"But, Dad…"

Jodie stopped. She could hardly tell him she was about to win.

"OK, Dad, night. Thanks for today, you're the best."

Jodie yawned and Dean gave her a kiss on the cheek.

"Night-night, JoJo. Your mum and I love you very much."

He had a last look at the chessboard, smiling as he did so before turning the light off in Jodie's bedroom. He got a sleepy, "Night, Dad," from Jodie as he half closed the bedroom door and went downstairs.

Sarah was tidying the kitchen. "Jodie loved it. 'Best party ever,' she said. Oh, and she's about to beat me at chess."

Sarah ignored all of what Dean had just said and dived straight in with what had been bothering her.

"Dean, are you seeing another woman?" There was a tone to her voice which implied that she didn't care if he was.

"Of course I'm not. Don't be daft," he replied instantly without even looking at her.

"Dean, I've had enough. I don't want to shout, I don't want to fall out. It's obvious you don't want to be here anymore. The one day I asked you to be here, you let me down. It can't always be everyone else's fault, Dean."

"Sarah, one – no, I'm not seeing anyone else. I don't really know what happened last night. If I did, I would tell you."

She stopped tidying away.

"Try me, Dean, I'm all ears."

Dean thought talking bollocks would not be a good tactic right now. He'd not seen Sarah like this before and truth was the only way out.

"OK, I had a couple of drinks so couldn't drive. That was a mistake. I should have come home last night…"

"Damn right you should."

"OK, I know, but I only had five or six pints in Gino's. Then it was my round and some of the younger lads were going to a club. Actually, Sarah, it was a crap strip club."

"Really? That's what you do to get your kicks now, is it, Dean?" Sarah was fighting off the tears.

"No! It was where the lads wanted to go and it was my round, so I bought everyone a drink, then I was going to leave after that. I'm not lying, Sarah, someone spiked my drink. All I can remember is the bouncers kicking the shit out of me outside."

She shook her head at him. "They don't kick the shit out of you for nothing, Dean. What the fuck has happened to the man I fell in love with?"

"I honestly can't remember much of last night. All I do remember is Martin getting me home, and then I was out like a light, slept straight through my alarm."

"I don't believe you, Dean." Sarah changed tack. "Where were you last weekend, then?"

"I told you, Sarah, had to work last weekend."

"Really?" Sarah pulled out a credit card statement from behind the bread bin and slammed it on the table. It had Barcelona written all over it. The girls in the gym had put the idea into her head and they had been right.

Dean was cornered. Whatever he said was going to be a mistake, so he had to take this one on the chin. He looked apologetically at her.

"I hope she was worth it, Dean. I gave my life and career up for you and this is how you repay me." Sarah would not give him the satisfaction of seeing her cry. She fought the tears back and added, "You're in the spare room tonight and you can stay in London for a bit. I need some space. I don't trust you, and I never thought I would say this, but I'm not even sure if I love you anymore."

"Sarah…"

"I can just about cope, but you let Jodie down all the time, and because she loves you, you get away with it. I'm sick of picking up the fucking pieces."

Dean tried one more time. "I would never cheat on you, Sarah…"

"Really? You could have fooled me. Night, Dean. Don't even think about coming to our bed."

Dean nodded in reluctant agreement.

"I love you, Sarah."

She gave him a last look, shaking her head as she did so.

"Not sure if that is enough anymore. Maybe you need to try and find the man I fell in love with."

She left the kitchen and headed off to bed, alone.

Sunday morning, Dean was up early, cooking a peace offering breakfast.

"Jodie," he called, "breakfast."

Jodie knew that if she didn't get up now, she would be shaken awake and fireman lifted downstairs by her dad. She was tempted not to get up as she hadn't seen her dad laugh or smile for ages, but she was worried in case this time he didn't bother. She wanted to keep that memory without it being spoiled.

Jodie walked in, giving her dad a kiss.

"Morning, Dad, thanks for yesterday, it was fab."

Sarah then walked in too and gave Jodie a kiss, blanking Dean. Obviously she had not forgotten what she had said.

Dean dished up breakfast, loving being with them both and realising that all he'd been bothered about recently was his work and himself.

"Dad," Jodie said.

"Yes, JoJo," he replied, topping up three glasses with fresh orange from a jug in the middle of the table.

"Are you leaving us, Dad?"

As Jodie tucked into her scrambled egg on toast, Dean looked at Sarah and gave her a 'we could have told her together' stare. Sarah shrugged her shoulders back at him. Dean was sick of telling lies and thought his daughter should know why he wouldn't be around for a bit.

"I might have to go away for a while, just to let your mum have some time on her own, but I love you both very much and will still be there for you. Why do you ask, Jodie?"

"I had a dream last night, Dad. A nasty dream about a clown coming to see me and telling me that you would be leaving in the morning and you might never come back."

Dean again looked at Sarah, who shook her head in a 'nothing to do with me' way.

"That was just a nightmare, Jodie. If that nasty clown comes to see you again, make sure you let me know."

"OK, Dad, but he did say you might never come back." Jodie stared across the table at her parents.

"I will always be there for you, Jodie, whenever you need me. Don't listen to nasty clowns in nasty dreams."

After breakfast, Dean packed a bigger bag than normal and gave his wife and daughter a kiss.

"I've been an idiot," he said to Sarah. "I'll get you back, I promise."

"It's just not good enough, Dean. Make sure you keep phoning Jodie. She needs you."

Dean drove off, fighting the tears until he was out of sight around the corner. Then he could no longer hold them back.

Chapter 6 – Back to Work

Dean got back to the London apartment, thinking about Sarah and how she thought he was having an affair. Nothing could be further from the truth, but he could see why she had jumped to that conclusion. He'd been a dick and he knew it.

He looked in the fridge and shook his head, turning down a beer he'd not even been offered. Instead, he thumbed through the training course he was delivering tomorrow to ensure he was prepared, not really taking much of it in as his mind was on other things. Then he looked up the share price of a steel company up in the north-east on his boards. He'd had a big tip off and was going to make Dexter a very rich man tomorrow, and hopefully make himself enough to be able to jack it all in.

It was only 8pm, but his body felt like it was later. He still felt a bit groggy from Friday night and needed to sort himself out. Tomorrow was where it would all start.

Bed time, he thought, prep done. He texted Sarah *I Love you both to bits… :))* then put his aching head onto the pillow and was out like a light.

Dean's two bed apartment, with its giant kitchen and a breakfast bar that divided the kitchen from the living area, was enormous. The kitchen had all the mod cons, and the living area included two screens above the TV with all the trading data for him to wake up to.

The TV was on *Sky News*, reporting on the Chinese leader's visit to the UK where the Prime Minister was to show him round before a banquet at Buckingham Palace tonight. This was followed by a report on the floods in the north-west, and then came the news Dean was waiting for.

Another steel company in the north going down the pan. It was in Redcar this time, near where Dean had grown up. Some of Dean's school friends worked there, but Dean had a feeling they would be OK. In fact, it was more than just a feeling. Dean smiled at the TV and turned it off.

Monday morning in London was the same as it was in any other major city in the world. From his apartment, Dean was watching people milling around, all with somewhere to go, all of them ignoring everyone else. Their heads down, they were rushing along on the commuter express like they were on tracks. Dean was one of the lucky ones who could walk to work without having to endure a Tube ride from hell where everyone was in a world of their own, elbows tucked in, tackling their Sudokus or listening to their music on full blast in case anyone around them had forgotten their iPod.

Dean looked at his phone. There was no response from Sarah, so he thought he wouldn't push it and would give her the space she'd asked for. He got ready, once again looking razor sharp. The swelling round his lip had gone down and his nose wasn't feeling as sorry for itself as it had been yesterday.

Dean set off on the short walk to the office, having a quick chat with the girls on reception before he headed into the lift. He entered his office and turned on the boards to see how his open trades were panning out. They were up, as usual – well, of course they were. That's what Dean did: make money. Today, though, was all about training other people to do what he did. This was difficult as there are so many variables in trading, and he couldn't really teach intuition. Dean felt intuition; it lived and breathed inside him. This was another reason he was so good at chess – he was unpredictable, and that along with intuition was a lethal combination.

Dean entered the training room, which was empty. He loved training, probably because, like most other things, he was very good at it. He logged in and checked his email to see who the lucky trainees were today.

Martin Samson, John Davies, Oliver Steadman-Fisher, Laura Green, Gary Bond, Steven Spencer, Lisa Hanson.

Not a bad bunch, he thought, although he still couldn't remember much about Friday night and needed to catch up with Martin and Oliver to work it out. He prepped his PowerPoint and went to grab a skinny latte from the Costa franchise in the canteen, again checking his phone. There was still nothing from Sarah, or from anyone else for that matter.

When Dean walked back into the training room with his coffee, most of his trainees had arrived and were sitting quietly flicking through the exercise books that had been left for them on the table. Dean gave a nod to Martin. Martin nodded back just as Oliver strolled into the room.

"Come on, Oliver, you have just broken your first rule of the day. You're five minutes late." Dean tapped his watch and then pointed to the clock on the wall.

"It's not ten am yet, Dean, so I'm not late. Got two minutes."

"Oliver, I start training at ten am, but it's going to take you two or three minutes to log in and I'm sure you'll want to grab a coffee, so by then you'll be late. If you're on one of my courses again, you'll turn up ten minutes before the start, and that goes for all of you."

Dean looked each of them in the eyes, scanning the room like a viper. *First rule of training,* he thought. *Take control of the strongest early on and the rest will follow.*

Oliver stared straight back at him without flinching, thinking better of having a petty argument he wouldn't win. He had to spend the rest of the day under Dean's control and they both knew it.

"OK, a couple of pointers for anybody who's not been in a training room with me before. Listen, learn and join in. You might not want to be here, but you are, so you might as well have a bit of fun along the way. You never know, you might just leave the room today with a little more knowledge than you came in with." He scanned the room again before adding, "And looking at some of you, that should not be too difficult."

Dean got a couple of laughs from his already captive audience.

"So, boys and girls, let's get this party started." Dean used the clicker behind his back to bring in the first couple of housekeeping slides covering fire alarms, toilets, breaks etc., then the fun could begin.

Click. The projector beamed a picture of a statue of the two symbolic beasts of finance, the Bear and the Bull, in front of the Frankfurt Stock Exchange. The Bear and the Bull were fronting each other up, ready to commence battle.

"We all know this is a game between the Bears and Bulls," Dean announced. "Bullish markets are going up and bearish markets are going down. Well." He paused and looked around his trainees. "Well," he said again before continuing, "Well, I hope you know this. If not, there's the door."

Dean let out a laugh and a few of his trainees joined in.

"So how hard can it be to predict a two horse race?" He left a pause, not waiting for a verbal answer but for visible thought. "Well, if it was easy, everyone would be doing it, right?"

Click.

The next slide showed some historic bubbles and crashes with a title of 'Be Aware'. Dean challenged the team on each of the bullets on the slide in turn. If they had been to university, they should know about at least six or seven, and on the whole, they did. It was Oliver who stood out, though. Dean had to give it to him, Oliver knew his stuff, to the point where Dean would ask everyone but Oliver to answer his questions.

Second rule of training – engage your learners with questions and don't speak if you can get them to speak for you, but shut up anyone who is a smart arse.

Dean took the trainees through each of the historic events, picking out the signs that had been there for all to see before they'd happened, and that was the point. The signs *had* been there and nobody had spotted them. Why?

"Lessons learned are important," Dean concluded. "History won't tell us everything, but what it does tell us is that nothing happens without a reason. It's action versus reaction. If you can read the signs, it's all laid out in front of you. Knowing where to look and what to believe is important. It is what makes a good trader."

Dean paused again to let the trainees absorb that statement into their fatigued grey matter.

"Any questions?"

The trainees all looked mesmerised at how much knowledge they had gained from one lesson. It was more than university had taught them in three or four years. Dean was conducting a masterclass and they had free tickets for the show.

"No questions?" There was silence. "OK, see you after lunch. Martin, Oliver, just hang back a sec, will you?"

Martin's lip started quivering as usual. The room emptied with the trainees still engaged, mumbling about what they had just witnessed.

"Did you enjoy that, boys?" Dean said, smiling at Martin and

Oliver who were looking as if they were on the naughty step. Oliver's straight blond hair was flopping over his eyes.

"Yes, great, Dean. What's up?" Oliver replied confidently with a flick of his disobedient hair. Martin was busy looking everywhere but at Dean.

"It was a good night Friday. Can you tell me what happened as I think my drinks may have been spiked in the strip club? Oh, and while we are on the subject, how did I get a bust lip?"

Dean stared through the centre of Oliver's head without blinking. Oliver's body language started to let him down. He was fidgeting and feeling uncomfortable, his fingers occasionally flexing into a fist.

"Well, Dean, as we got up to leave, you went crazy and attacked the stripper."

Oliver smirked at Dean, knowing he could not contradict this statement. If Dean could, he wouldn't have asked the question.

"Oliver, if I find out this has anything to do with you, you'll be making tea in the post room for the rest of your career." Dean focused on Oliver's eyes through the gaps in his hair. Oliver didn't flinch; this was not the time for one of his trademark flicks. He just returned the stare with interest.

"Dean, I don't know what happened to you. I guess, as you say, you may have had a drink spiked. Happens a lot round that area of town. Are you OK now?"

"I'm fine. Mind how you go, Oliver." The 'mind how you go' was accompanied by a cold smile that clearly meant 'watch your back, Oliver'. "See you after lunch, don't be late. Oh, and Martin, thank you. Where I'm from, it's always good to know when someone's got your back."

Martin nodded and said, "Any time, Dean," trying not to draw more attention to himself than was necessary.

Dean watched them leave for lunch. He could read people like a book. Oliver was as guilty as sin, and he knew it. Martin was like Oliver's little brother, who would get a good kicking if he told his mother what he had been up to after school. But it could wait. Dean had to invest some time in putting his life back together.

Chapter 7 – Inside Information is King

Dean picked up his iPhone and ordered some flowers for Sarah. He knew it would not change anything, but did it anyway. He then made a call to one of his contacts in the government offices.

The steel company in the north of the UK which was just about to go bust was going to be saved by the government. Another UK firm would take it over with incentives from the government to save jobs and boost the economy in the area, which was on its knees. History and intuition were all well and good, but inside information took away the guesswork. Dean already had £400 million put aside, signed off by Dexter, which was the biggest trade he had ever had the authority to place. Of course Dexter had taken some convincing, but Dean had a way of making Dexter think that everything he did was a sure thing. And this was a sure thing.

Dean picked Stewart B from the contacts in his phone.

"Dean, let me call you back in two mins. I'll just pop outside for a fag," said Dean's contact on the other end of the phone. A couple of minutes later, Dean's phone rang.

"Stew, what's happening? Is it still on? I've got a lot resting on this one." There was a nervousness to Dean's voice rather than the usual confidence. He had just spent the morning telling his trainees about Barings Bank and a rogue trader called Nick Leeson taking it down on the blind side of the company. But he could take comfort in knowing that he was no Nick Leeson and that his trade was authorised.

"Yes, the rescue package has all been signed off by the PM. It's getting released on the three-thirty pm news conference." Stewart panted as he managed to get the sentence out in one breath.

"Did you take the stairs, Stew? Think you need to lay off the fags." Dean's confidence had gone up a notch or two on hearing the deal had been confirmed by the PM.

"I know, Dean." Stewart panted again and took in enough oxygen for his next sentence. "Killen Steel are being given the site for peanuts if they keep it running with no loss of jobs, so everyone's a winner, Deano. I've seen the paperwork myself."

"OK, Stew, I'll see you alright on this one. I'll meet you in The Barley Mow sometime next week. Thanks again, and love to Karen. Bye."

Dean allowed himself a fist pump as he hung up the phone, then headed off to see Dexter to pick up the authority paperwork to buy £400 million worth of Killen Shares. He'd watch them soar after the announcement that only he and a few others knew about. He had been planning to take a month off after this, but after what had happened at the weekend, he might jack it all in, maybe take Sarah and Jodie somewhere hot and give them some of the time he had been depriving them of lately. With this deal, he could get out for good and start enjoying life with all of its benefits. Life was good, but could be better.

Dean told Dexter the news and received the trading authority code, then headed off to his office. At 13.05pm, he set up the trade to buy £400 million of Killen Steel shares. Looking at the picture of his wife and daughter, he said, "Here goes," and pressed the 'place trade' button followed by the authorisation code Dexter had given him. The trade was confirmed on the screen.

He looked at the boards for a reaction. That transaction was obviously news to the market. In under a minute, the impact of that much money being pumped into a company that had been struggling began to show. Dean could see the Bulls wrestling the Bears to the ground in front of him as the rest of the world tried to catch up and not miss out on the fight.

The shares were already up 10% in the twenty minutes that had elapsed since Dean had pressed the button. The phone rang; it was Dexter.

"Dean, you're a fucking genius. Take the afternoon off. It's going through the roof…twelve per cent up already."

Dean afforded himself a smile. "I'm OK, Dex. I might take some time off next week. Anyway, I've got that training to do. I've got to make you some more trading stars, remember?"

"Fuck the training, Dean." Dean could hear the joy in Dexter's voice. He was ready for retirement and this would probably do it for him.

"No, Dex, I've just bollocked them for being late this morning so I had better go and finish it off, otherwise it wouldn't look good. Anyway, I'm enjoying it. Have a good afternoon, Dex. The announcement's at three-thirty pm and the shares will rocket after that."

"Deano, up seventeen per cent now, woohoo!"

Dex sounded a bit unstable as he hung up. Dean chuckled to himself.

"Crazy old fucker," he said out loud.

Any good trainer knows that the afternoon session is known as the graveyard shift. Everyone has had lunch and the last thing they want to do is sit in a hot room and watch loads of PowerPoint slides.

All the students were early, which always happens after the morning. Dean headed straight for the air con and set it to 16 degrees Celsius. He had a bounce in his step. Today was a good day, and even that little runt Oliver was not going to spoil it.

"OK, everyone up in a circle. This is a mathematical game called Fizz Buzz to sharpen your minds. Anyone heard of it?"

Nobody had…or at least, nobody admitted they had.

"OK, here are the rules. We go round in a circle and count upwards from one. Easy, eh? But whenever we get to a number five or multiple of five, instead of saying the number, we say, 'Buzz.' So it's one, two, three, four, buzz, six, seven eight, nine, buzz. Got it?'

"That's easy, Dean," said Oliver. Martin gave Oliver a stare as he had been about to ask for the rules again.

"Oh, I forgot to mention fizz, Oliver. We say, 'Fizz' whenever we have a seven or a multiple of seven, and the running order also reverses on a fizz so we go the other way. We'll play for ten minutes as a team. The record is 143, but looking at you lot, I think we'll be lucky to get to forty-three. I'll start us off. Moving to my left, one."

In the first attempt, they got to fizz and Martin, still unsure of the rules, said, "Seven." This was met with a barrage of discontent from the rest of the circle.

"Martin, it's fizz, you prick."

"OK, I don't think I've got all the rules."

"Seven is fizz," said Oliver.

Dean did not have to police the game; it policed itself.

"OK, everyone got the rules?" he asked and got a team "Yes".

After a while they managed to get to seventy-seven, which was always tricky as a fizz-fizz-fizz would catch most people out. To Dean's delight, it was Oliver who screwed up.

"OK, last go, guys. Concentrate."

In their last go, the team managed 107 and felt very proud of themselves. If this was the graveyard shift, nobody had told Dean's trainees.

"Well done, guys, not a bad effort." Dean asked for a round of applause, and the trainees obliged. It felt good to work as a team, and yes, even Oliver enjoyed that one.

The third rule of training – have fun. You learn more when you're having fun.

Dean then launched into the afternoon session, talking about risk and reward, followed by the tricky topic of intuition involving a series of real scenarios which were borderline. The trainees chose which way to go: buy, sell or avoid. Dean then explained a live Forex chart on the screen. It was the Canadian Dollar versus Sterling. The Canadian Dollar had been going down now for ages. It had had a small bounce just after the Brexit vote in June 2016, but apart from that, it had had months of going down with feeble resistance lines.

"So stand up if you think this will go down again today."

Everybody stood up.

"Dean, is this meant to be a trick question? We all know it's going down." Oliver led a chorus of laughter.

"OK, let's see how confident you are. I have just put a thousand pounds into your personal live trading accounts and pinged you the link to the live system."

The laughing stopped. This was real money; a real test.

"Dexter wouldn't let us on the live system yet, Dean." Oliver had lost some of the confidence in his voice.

"It's not Dexter's money, it's mine."

They all were now taking notice, until Oliver announced, "It's not much of a risk, though, Dean. It's obvious from trade on the board it will go down one to two per cent, which it's done for the last six or seven months. Easy."

Oliver looked smug.

"Well let's make it interesting. You place your bet with the thousand that's in your account, my little money virgins, and you can take the trade-off whenever you like in the next twenty-four hours. Whoever wins gets ten thousand pounds from my bonus."

The trainees had already clicked the link and logged in.

"OK, it's 2.50pm now. You have until 2.50pm tomorrow. Place your bets, ladies and gentlemen."

Dean split their screens so they were all visible via the projector. They all bet down, down, down. It was surely just a matter of stopping the trade on the most downward spike for a cool £10,000.

After all the screens had turned red, accepting the downward bet, Dean bet the other way. Everyone could see his screen standing out blue.

"Dean, are you an idiot? Guys, he's screwed. Do we really care who wins? Let's share the 10k out – think it's called a win-win situation."

Oliver made a joke of this statement by laughing, but he still looked around, gauging the response from the others in the room.

Dean looked at his watch. It was 2.59 and fifteen seconds.

"OK, boys and girls, you still have lots to learn." He enlarged his and Oliver's screens side by side. "What happens at three pm, Oliver?"

"Err, you lose ten grand?"

"Well, I'll tell you what happens at three pm, Oliver. It's eight am in Canada, and they are a bit pissed off that their dollar is so low. All of a sudden, they have some control. Why?"

"Their exchange opens," said Laura, who had been very quiet all day.

"That's right, Laura. They have been fighting this for months, and it's a futile fight, but watch. It's three pm."

The trading candle, which was already thirty pips down since they had placed their bets, stabilised before fighting back and starting to edge the other way. Before long, it had gone past where it had started from when the trades were placed. Everyone but Dean was losing £1 a pip, their profit turning into a loss. Up and up the Canadian Dollar soared against the Pound. Everyone was amazed, apart from Oliver.

Dean took off his trade.

"But you said we had until tomorrow at 2.50pm."

"You have, Oliver. Good luck with that. You'll make eleven hundred pounds at best."

Dean's phone vibrated in his pocket, and he apologised to the class.

"Sorry, guys, I have to take this. Dex, what's up?"

Dexter sounded in a jovial mood.

"Nothing is up, Deano. Do you want to pop up and watch the announcement?"

"OK, be there in a tick." Dean dropped the phone on the desk as he locked his laptop.

"OK, guys, hope you enjoyed that. We'll take twenty-five minutes as you have all been so good."

Dean shot off to Dexter's office to check on how his monster trade was looking. All the trainees left the classroom for a coffee apart from Oliver. He was making some notes; although he did not think much of Dean, he still knew he could learn from him. Dean was at the top, exactly where Oliver wanted to be, and it would be foolish not to accept a free ride from a master trader.

As Oliver was leaving for a coffee, he noticed Dean's iPhone vibrating next to his laptop on the presenting table. It was Stewart B, whoever he was. Oliver looked around to see the room was empty before he answered it.

"Dean Harrison's phone."

"Hi, is Dean there? It's important."

Oliver thought about this for a second.

"No, I'm sorry, he's busy at the moment. I'm his personal assistant, though – I can get a message to him."

Stewart B was panting and wheezing like he had been running.

"Take this down, son, and tell him immediately. The Chinese leader has scuppered the Killen Steel deal as the Chinese want to monopolise the steel industry worldwide and he's got the PM over a barrel…oh, it doesn't matter. Just tell Dean to pull out of Killen Steel, now!" Stewart's voice was shaking. "The news conference is getting put back at least thirty minutes. I have seen the Prime Minister's new speech." Stewart took a breath. "Have you got that, kid? Say it back to me; it's important."

Oliver had a smile creeping over his face. "That's Killen Steel, the deal is off and he should pull out now. Is that right, Stewart?"

Stewart's voice had calmed down slightly.

"Yes, tell him now, son. Don't fuck about."

"I will do, Stewart. I'll run up and see him straight away."

Oliver looked at Dean's phone. Dean had been digging at him all day, and this was his opportunity for payback. He deleted Stewart's calls from the list and placed the phone back on the desk.

"Good luck, Dean, you fucking prick."

Chapter 8 – What Could Possibly Go Wrong?

Dexter's office made Dean's look like a broom cupboard. There weren't as many plasma boards, but all the broadsheets were spread out on the coffee table and framed posters of the company's highlights were all over the walls. The view was the best one in the building, looking straight down Old Father Thames.

"The TV press conference has been delayed due to the Prime Minister being occupied with the Chinese leader." Dexter looked red-faced and excited. He hadn't got to where he was today without an element of greed; there were enough bad days in trading to make the good ones count double.

Dexter had already poured Dean a glass of whisky. Killen Steel shares were up 40% on the day, and everyone was wishing they had bought early. They were just waiting for the PM to confirm the deal before they went all in.

"I'd better not, Dexter." Dean turned down the whisky. "It's been a good day, though, and don't worry, it's a cert. You might see it go down a bit as people get twitchy, but it will go up two to three hundred per cent when the announcement is made, and then we're out."

Dean delivered this with confidence – what could possibly go wrong?

Back in the training room, Oliver walked over to Dean.

"Got you a latte, Dean. Two sugars, is that right? And thanks for today. I have learned an awful lot."

"Thanks, Oliver, I'm glad you're having fun. OK, we're on the home stretch, boys and girls. Let's look at trends followed by lines of support and resistance. I know what you're thinking – the fun just keeps coming." He looked around the room. "Hey, I admit it, this one is a bit boring, but it's really important, so switch on."

Dean launched into the late afternoon stint like he always did, and before long he had the trainees eating out of the palm of his hand.

Four o'clock came, and Dexter stood at the door of the training room.

"A round of applause for our leader, Dexter Falconer."

Dean led the applause and the rest joined in.

"Dean, can I have a quick word?" Dexter said nervously.

"No problem, Mr Falconer." In front of the trainees, it was always Mr Falconer. "Take five, everyone."

Dean headed into a breakout room with Dexter. Oliver took the opportunity to punch 'Killen Steel' into the trading software and check its shares. The graph showed that they had shot up miles today, but were now nearly back to where they had started. Although Oliver did not know the full picture, he was smart enough to know that if Dean had a trade on and didn't know what Stewart had told him, that was bad.

Oliver connected to *Sky News* online. The Prime Minister was just about to make an announcement about a steel plant in Redcar. He put in his headphones.

In the breakout room, Dexter sat uneasily on the table. "Dean, you're lucky. I trust you and have known you a long time, but I will have a lot of explaining to do if this goes tits up."

Dean reassured Dexter. "Dexter, have faith. I have an insider, he's even seen the PM's speech."

Dexter calmed down a bit.

"But it's almost back to where it started, Dean, back at where we bought in…"

Dean looked at his phone. There were no missed calls or unread messages.

"Dexter, I give you my word. Am I ever wrong?"

Dexter looked at Dean and his face lit up. "No," he replied. "And there are four hundred million reasons for you not to start being wrong now."

"Well, there you go, then, Dexter."

The PM looked more concerned than usual, probably because he was about to deliver a speech that he had not planned to give. This morning he had been going to tell the world that he was saving a northern town's industry and the thousands of jobs that went with it. Now all the PM had had to say how the Chinese were pledging 2 billion investment to coalitions and industry collaborations which would ensure the UK moved forward as a stronger, healthier nation by partnering with one of the fastest growing global markets. No mention of the failing steel plant in the north east.

Dean was still reassuring Dexter in the breakout room. They were laughing as the Prime Minister dropped his bombshell.

The first question came from a member of the northern press.

"Prime Minister, what is happening with the Redcar Steel Plant? We were expecting an announcement today."

The PM moved uneasily in his chair and fumbled for some notes on his lectern.

"Unfortunately, although every attempt has been made and every avenue explored, it has been impossible to agree a rescue package for the plant. I assure you, though, that all the support necessary will be given to the workers to re-skill them. This government will pledge two million pounds as an initial payment to help the Teesside area."

There were follow-up questions followed by follow-up questions. The cat was well and truly out of the bag and everyone knew it, apart from Dexter and Dean.

Oliver looked up at Killen Steel. The shares were visibly bottoming out; he could see the bearish red candle burning the wax away in front of his eyes. Oliver did not know how much Dean had on the trade, but if Dexter was involved, every extra minute they spent in that office was another nail in Dean Harrison's coffin.

Dexter headed back upstairs. Before Dean could finish off the afternoon's training, he was summoned to Dexter's office, and this time the older man was in no mood for joking. The shares had dropped 75%, costing Falconer International getting on for a cool billion pounds. Dean Harrison was not quite Nick Leeson, but he'd had the same effect. It didn't matter how good he was when he'd fucked up.

Dexter told security to give Dean ten minutes to grab a few things from his office. Dean took his Ryder Cup whisky, a picture of Sarah and Jodie and a box full of bits and pieces before being escorted off the premises. On his way out, he saw Oliver standing on the ground floor with Martin.

"Good luck, Dean," said Oliver. "Oh, I meant to give you a message from Stewart B, whoever he is. I must have forgotten."

Martin stared at Oliver.

"Have you got something to do with this, Ollie?"

Oliver smiled at Dean and said, "No, Martin, Dean fucked up all on his own. Didn't you, Dean?"

Dean went for Oliver, only for security to manhandle him to the floor before kicking him out onto the street. His boxes landed next to him, the picture of Sarah and Jodie smashing on the pavement. This was much the same as his life right now – he was destroyed. How did he lose control? How had it all gone so wrong?

Dean picked himself up, dusted himself down and headed for the nearest bar to find the answers at the bottom of a bottle.

A few bars, a few drinks and a good few hours later, Dean seemed to have shared his story with every barman who would listen – which was not hard as all good barmen listen. Then he headed off home. He wanted to call Sarah more than ever, but he could not bear to tell someone who really mattered to him what had happened. She would think about the house, the cars and the lifestyle they led. The truth was, though, if he had made the call, Sarah would have been more concerned about him.

Dean took the easy option and put his phone back into his pocket. Putting the boxes from work in the spare room with the broken picture of Sarah and Jodie perched on the top, Dean sank his head into his hands and tried to make sense of the last few days.

He looked up at the boards and saw Killen Steel still on a downward spiral. He just hoped someone had pulled out of the deal before it could do even more damage than it already had to Falconer's. The company and especially Dexter didn't seem to care about him, they had proved that, but he still felt responsible and had lots of friends at Falconer's. He even felt for poor old Dexter – what would Dean himself have done if the boot had been on the other foot?

Dean watched the red and blue trading candles bouncing up and down in front of his eyes on the screens. For the first time in as long as he could remember, he did not care what the markets were going to do; he didn't even know what he was going to do. He was in an uncontrollable mess.

His eyes did their best to fight off the inevitable before he collapsed in a heap on the sofa.

The next morning, Dean woke up on the sofa and there was no trading on the boards, no broadband, no phone. His subscription must have been cancelled. It seemed that his life had been cancelled as well as far as Falconer International Trading was concerned.

He assumed his company credit cards would have gone the same way. At least he had his car and his flat which were not on the company books, although he would have to work out how to pay for them now. Dean had not had to think about how he paid for anything in the last ten years. Things had taken care of themselves when he had money.

He thought about going to see Dexter and offering to work on a trial for a month or so without salary to pay back whatever had been lost, but looking at how deep Killen Steel had dropped, he knew he would not be welcome. He may even have taken Falconer's under unless someone had pulled the plug on that deal.

Dean looked through the window at the hordes of people all with somewhere to go. He had nowhere to go, and he didn't want to go anywhere. He was just about at rock bottom.

His mind helped him weigh up the situation. When you're down, you have a couple of choices. You can look up and start to climb again, maybe call in a couple of favours at a smaller trading firm. Dean's reputation would surely afford him that. Then he reminded himself that nobody in this city would touch him with a bargepole until the Killen Steel fiasco had all blown over, and nor should they.

The second choice was to look down. If you're just about at

rock bottom, you may as well see what the very bottom is like, have a look around, and savour the atmosphere for a while.

That's what Dean did. He headed for a shop to get the cheapest bottle of vodka he could lay his hands on. Walking along the Thames, taking a swig of his Russian new best friend every few hundred yards, he popped into bars along the way for a couple, staying for more than a couple in The Prospect of Whitby, one of the oldest pubs in London. It reminded him of his home up north. The hangman's noose dangling from gallows attached to the side of the building seemed very apt at the moment.

The next morning, Dean's head was banging. His place was not looking as spick and span as it used to, not that Dean noticed as he threw a capsule into the coffee machine and pressed the button. The machine made a noise like it was sucking the coffee out of the container before filling a glass cup, the air bubbles flying up from the bottom like a waterfall in reverse.

Dean turned on the screens to be presented with the 'No Signal' sign. *Fair enough*, he thought as he turned them off again. He grabbed some tablets from the drawer, popped a couple out of their sleeve, left the rest on the kitchen worktop, and took a sip of his coffee. *What will today bring?* he thought.

Buzzzzzzz.

Dean rushed to the receiver on the wall, more to stop the noise entering his delicate head than from any curiosity as to who was on the other end. Dean wasn't really in the mood for company.

"Yorkie, it's Jack. Are you OK?"

"Fuck off, Jack, of course I'm OK."

"Can I come in? It's freezing out here."

"No. 'Fuck off,' I said."

Dean smiled as he pressed the button to release the door. If he had to draw up a list of people he would want to see when he didn't want to see anyone, Jack would probably be top of it.

The lift cage opened into Dean's apartment; Jack knew the code.

"Dean, what in God's name went on, on Monday?'

Jack never called Dean 'Dean'; it was always Yorkie, so Dean took notice. He grabbed two beers out of the fridge, handing one to Jack.

"To be honest, Jack, not really sure. I had a deal all planned out – signed, sealed and delivered, and from a great source, too.

What I do know is that little shit Oliver had something to do with it."

He pulled the ring pull on the can – *fsssss* – before pouring the beer into a glass.

"Come on, Yorkie, you can deal with the likes of Oliver in your sleep. You got in too deep and fucked this up all on your own."

Jack opened his can and poured the beer, the magic widget delivering the perfect pint experience. He took a sip before the beer had a chance to settle, spoiling the magic somewhat.

"Yes, I know I fucked up, Jack. Did they get out of it OK?"

"Not really. They are still working out what to do. Falconer's will survive, but only just. A few people will be out on their ear. There will be casualties, Yorkie."

Dean looked down at his shoes and then back at Jack.

"Are you going to be OK, Jack?'

"Yes, I'll be OK, but will have to keep my head down for a bit. They've blamed you for the lot. That's why I'm here. I think they're coming after you. For the lot, I mean – this apartment, your car, even your home." Jack took a sip of his beer and carried on. "They are pissed off, Yorkie. They want it back, and you know how it works. You can't wipe out that kind of money and just walk away, you know that."

As Dean looked around the room, the realisation setting in, Jack continued.

"It would have been worse if Dexter hadn't let Oliver put on a reverse trade. You'd have been in for a lot more. You need to thank him really."

Jack looked around at the apartment. It looked a mess. He shook his head at Dean. Dean felt like he was being tried in court by his best mate.

"Thank him? You think so, Jack? He screwed me over. I don't know how, but I do know he failed to tell me the deal was screwed, LITTLE SHIT!"

Once Dean had calmed down from his rant, he added, "Anyway, it was an authorised trade, Jack. They can't get me for nothing."

Jack looked surprised. "Well no one at work is saying it was authorised, most of all Dexter. He's saying you were the typical rogue trader and that he would never authorise that much. He says you were flying solo."

Dean jumped all over this accusation. "Bullshit and he knows it, Jack."

"Really, Dean? That's a lot of dough. Dexter's never even been close to signing that much off before."

"Don't say you don't believe me either."

Dean stared at Jack, who shrugged his shoulders as if to say, "I'm not sure who to believe."

"You don't, do you, Jack? Well, do you know what? Why don't you just fuck off with the rest of them."

Dean headed for the lift and punched in the call code.

"Yorkie, I'm the only friend you have got right now. That's why I'm here."

Jack walked past Dean, shaking his head, and pressed the button. As he slowly disappeared from view, Dean could hear him shouting, "Good luck, Yorkie, you're going to fucking need it."

Chapter 9 – Off the Rails

It's a lot easier for a train to fall off the tracks than it is to get back on them. That was the case with Dean – he was so far off the tracks that he could barely see where they were anymore, and getting back on them was not an option at the moment. Two weeks of getting up late, drinking all day and going to bed when his body gave in were taking their toll – Dean was unshaven and looked like a down and out, blending into the nooks and crannies of London like he belonged there. Gone were the suits and clean cut look; he was well and truly at the bottom now and didn't really care.

He had bought a pay as you go phone and punched in Sarah's number. He'd even practised what he would say to her, but each time he went to phone her, he was too pissed and thought better of it. He did miss Sarah and Jodie, but it was hard to get a signal from the bottom of the earth – much easier to get another beer.

Dean staggered back to his apartment after another day and night on the town. It was not the pristine apartment he had lived in a couple of weeks ago; it was littered with pizza boxes and empty beer bottles and fag packets. He thought, like he did every other night, that he would tidy up in the morning.

The morning came too early, as it always seemed to lately. He staggered out of bed and looked in the mirror.

"What the fuck, Dean? Sort your fucking self out," he said, expecting his reflection to talk some sense into him. It didn't, but at least it listened.

He looked at the phone on the table. He would have to call her sooner or later. Then he saw his box of belongings from work with the picture of Sarah and Jodie and the Ryder Cup whisky. He owed them both a phone call.

He fumbled with the pay as you go brick as his fingers were not programmed for its size quite yet. He didn't have to scroll far down the contacts list as it was the only number he'd put in there. Taking a deep breath, he selected Sarah's name before hitting the green call button.

"Hello?"

Dean paused. He loved hearing the sound of her voice.

"Sarah, it's me." Dean sounded nervous. His confidence had all been drained out of him.

"Dean, where the hell have you been? I heard about your job and I don't know why I'm bothered, but I have been trying to ring you to see if you're OK." Although her sentence was spoken with compassion, the words inside it were not opening the door wide enough for Dean to do any more than peer through a crack. "And don't think I rang because of me. I couldn't care less, Dean. It's Jodie – she wanted to know that her dad is OK."

Dean listened for a change.

"Jack's told me about your job and about the state you're getting into. Well, good luck, Dean. I'll tell Jodie you're not dead." There was a pause. "Yet," she added. "Oh, and keep out of my and Jodie's life. We don't need a prick like you."

"Sarah, I really need to see you both right now. I've been going through hell here." Dean meant it – he was on the boxing canvas in the twelfth round as the referee counted, "*One, two, three, four,*" in his face.

"Dean, if I have my way, you will never see us again. We might even be moving away."

"*Five, six, seven,*" the metaphorical referee counted.

"Moving where? Don't think you'll stop me seeing her, Sarah…"

The boxing referee thrust fingers eight and nine into his face.

"Dean, have a nice life."

Sarah hung up.

"*Ten.*" Ding-ding-ding. "*Knockout.*"

Dean reached for a his Ryder Cup whisky and scanned the fridge, hoping he'd bought some tonic, coke or anything other than milk that he could mix it with. He found some Sprite – that would do. He sipped his drink, thinking about Sarah and Jodie and how things had ended up like this. He realised now what he'd had, and he would do anything to get it back to how it was three weeks ago.

Dean was pissed off, and it showed. "Stop me seeing her? How the fuck dare she? We'll see about that." He left his drink, which he had hardly touched, before grabbing the car keys, the picture and the whisky bottle and heading for the car park.

It was 3.15pm and Jodie's school got out at 4.30pm. Mumbling to himself, "I'll see her whenever and wherever I want," Dean drove, glancing at Jodie and Sarah's picture on the passenger seat beside him. The conversation with Sarah had pushed him over the edge and he was falling into whatever lay beneath.

He raced through London and headed out of town, unaware of his speed. After the last two weeks, he probably shouldn't have been anywhere near the wheel of a car, but he wasn't exactly Captain Sensible right now. At 4.15pm he pulled into a parking place opposite the school, riding up and down a curb while doing so, then opened the door and headed for the gates to see Jodie.

As soon as Dean spotted Jodie in among the hordes of pupils leaving the school building, he shouted her name. Leaving her group of friends, she ran to her dad, screaming, "Dad! I can't believe it!"

Sarah had been coming to collect Jodie from school since Dean left. Despite Jodie's protestations that she was more than old enough to get the school bus with her friends, Sarah could tell deep down that her daughter was comforted by the gesture. Despite her attempts to hide it behind teenage bravado, Jodie had clearly been feeling insecure ever since Dean had left.

Parking up, Sarah noticed through the crowd that Jodie was running towards a man at the gates. Leaping out of her car, she ran across the road, realising as she got closer that it was Dean.

"Dean, what are you doing here? Jodie, come over here."

"She's OK here with her dad, aren't you, Jodie?" Dean slurred his words a little, which did not go unnoticed. The last couple of weeks were still in his system.

"Yes, Dad," Jodie said as if on autopilot.

"Dean, you're drunk. Let Jodie go now."

Dean gripped Jodie tighter.

"For your information, Sarah, I'm not drunk." He then turned his attention to Jodie. "Jodie, you know I will always love you, don't you?" Dean felt a tear trying to force its way out his eye and fought it back.

"Yes, Dad. Are you coming home so we can finish our game of chess?"

Dean looked at Sarah and got a 'not on your life' stare.

"Maybe one day, Jodie."

"Dean, you let her go now, you're scaring me. JODIE!" This 'Jodie' was an order. Jodie made a move to go to her mother.

"I thought we might go for a ride. Would you like that, Jodie?" Dean grasped her tighter still.

"Yes, Dad. Mum, can we go for a ride?"

Sarah walked over and grabbed Jodie's arm.

"Dean, you can kill yourself, but you're not killing my daughter."

Sarah started to walk away before turning on her heels, her ponytail slapping in her face.

"That's the final straw, Dean. Fuck off and don't ever come back. You will never see me or her again, you drunken prick."

Dean fell to his knees at the school gates, a couple of teachers who had come over to find out what the commotion was all about looking at him and shaking their heads. He watched Sarah and Jodie walking off, Jodie turning to get another look at her dad before her mother, in floods of tears, forced her forward again.

"Who the fuck do you think you're looking at?" he said to the teachers who were his judge and jury right now. He jumped up and walked to the car, barging a couple of onlookers out of the way as he took the most direct route.

Dean got in the car and drove. Would he ever see his daughter or Sarah again? He was not sure, but he knew he'd fucked up, and fucked up big this time. He kept looking at their picture on the seat of the car next to the whisky bottle and his eyes filled up until he was struggling to see the road through the tears.

Heading south, he thought he would go and have a chat to the sea. The sea was always a friend to him when he was a kid; the sea was a good listener. Arriving in Brighton, he parked up and took a walk along the pebbly beach with the picture grasped close to his chest. He skimmed stones over the sea, beating himself up over how it had all ended up like this.

"Fuck, fuck, fuck!"

He slumped to the ground, looking at the picture, stroking Jodie's cheek gently with his finger.

"You are both better off without me anyway."

That was it. They *would* be better off without him. He was a fucking mess, and nobody liked a mess, especially a mess of the fucking variety.

He jumped up and headed to the car as if the compass in his head had given him a new direction. It was clear to him that if Dean Harrison was no longer around to fuck everything up, then the rest of the world would reset back to normality. For the first time in two weeks, he knew exactly where he was going. Was he scared? No. The demons in his head had given him a way out and he was ready to take advice from anyone right now.

Dean keyed Beachy Head into the satnav, which announced the journey would take just over an hour. If he put the hammer down, he reckoned he would nail it in forty-five minutes. Even Little Miss Satnav could not annoy him now. He was clear in thought and ready for whatever would come next.

Chapter 10 – All Downhill From Here

Dean parked behind a battered old minibus with *Sweet Dreams Nursing Home for Alzheimer's* on the side.

Sweet dreams? he thought. *I do hope so.* He grabbed the picture, and the whisky bottle as he might need some Dutch courage.

Turning to look at the battered old bus, he muttered, "Well, you can't take it with you," and took out a large wad of notes which he placed under the wiper blade. His dad had had Alzheimer's, and Dean thought doing a good turn just before his own day of judgment might not be a bad thing.

Dean headed up the path, still clear in thought. He was doing exactly the right thing. Everything would be fine in ten minutes' time; Sarah and Jodie would be fine and the world would be a better place.

Oblivious to the world around him, Dean walked up the path, past the phone box put on the suicide hotspot of Beachy Head in 1976 as a lifeline for potential jumpers. It was plastered in Samaritans business cards, but Dean did not even give it a second glance. This was it. When Dean made his mind up, he would always go through with it.

He stepped over a small white picket fence, wondering how that was meant to make anyone have second thoughts about jumping. He could see the edge of the cliff in front of him, and his heart rate increased by enough beats per minute for him to feel a kick of adrenalin filter through his veins.

There were some people near the top of the cliff, probably bloody do-gooders trying to stop jumpers.

They're not going to stop me, Dean thought.

To his surprise, as he passed them, he noticed they were an old-ish couple sitting sharing a flask of soup, tartan blankets over their knees. *They will make people want to jump rather than put them off*, he thought, smiling as he walked to the edge.

Dean stopped as his feet approached the cliff face, briefly looking down. Then he looked back at the couple, who were still drinking soup and not paying him much attention. He released his grasp on the picture he had pulled into his chest and looked at Sarah and Jodie one last time before giving them both a kiss.

"I love you both. I'm so sorry."

Unscrewing the top of the whisky bottle, he intended to take a final drink before jumping into the unknown.

"Well, get on with it. You're spoiling the view," the man behind him shouted.

"Can a man not have his last moment in a bit of peace?" Dean looked over the clifftop to the sea before taking a sip of what was left of the whisky.

"If you're going to jump, jump. Oh, and you know someone has to tidy that bottle up, you selfish bastard."

Dean turned to give the man a stare.

"Don't look for sympathy over here." The man straightened the blanket on his wife's knees.

Dean shuffled forward like a diver preparing for an Olympic dive, his feet now perching half over the cliff edge. He had one final look at Sarah and Jodie, hugging the picture back into his chest, then let the now empty bottle of whisky release from his grasp. It fell, smashing on the cliff face on its way down.

Dean looked out to the sea, closed his eyes and leant forward, feeling at peace with the world while his brain frantically indexed through his memories, trying to find one to stop him jumping. It settled on one from when Dean was ten years old. He was on his dad's 30-foot Yorkshire coble *The Whitby Trader* to go yucking, a northern term for fishing with rods. The coble had left Whitby Harbour even before the milkman was up, steaming to the east to anchor onto one of the many shipwrecks.

After fishing for an hour or so with no luck, Dean had hooked a monster. The rod under his arms kicked twice to indicate the bite, and he struck it hard as his dad had taught him. The fiberglass fishing rod was bent double and nearly pulled him over the side. His dad held on to his braces, laughing as Dean struggled to reel in the fish. Dean knew that it would have been easy for his dad to take over, but landing the fish on his own had been one of life's lessons.

"He's definitely a son of yours, Sam," one of the crew said to Dean's dad.

"And we all thought he looked more like the milkman," another added, laughing.

"I'll fucking sort you out in a minute," said Dean's dad, Sam.

"That's what the milkman said to your Rosie." Everyone laughed once again until one of them got a small fish on the line.

"Ignore them, Deano, you're definitely a Harrison. Come on, keep its head up, son," his dad had urged him.

As the fish broke the surface, Dean's dad grabbed the line and lifted it into the boat by its gills. Dean slumped back onto the seat of the boat, exhausted.

"What is it, Dad?" The fish was thin, and definitely not a cod, haddock or whiting.

"It's a monster, Dean, that's what it is."

"I know it's a monster, Dad, but what is it?"

"It's a ling, Dean, and I've never seen bigger one."

Dean had made his dad so proud that day, and his dad didn't normally let him know he was proud of anything. Dean hadn't ever forgotten that; it had been a special day, and always would be.

Opening his eyes, Dean found himself balanced precariously at the top of the cliff. His dad would be waiting for him on the other side. He smiled and leaned forward to join his father.

"No one will miss you, Dean, you coward," the man behind him shouted. Dean nearly fell, his arms rotating forward to re-establish his balance. Struggling, he managed to get one foot back onto firmer land as his other fell forward over the cliff face. He pushed back with the one foot still in touch with terra firma and fell into a heap at the top of the cliff.

Dean picked himself up and walked purposefully towards the couple.

"What did you say?" He looked at the man, his eyes sharp. "*What* did you say?"

"I said, 'No one will miss you, you coward'." The man shuffled back in his chair. Dean was towering over him.

"No, you didn't, you said *Dean.* You said, 'No one will miss you, *Dean.*' How do you know I am called Dean? What's going on? Do I know you?"

"Listen, my wife and I have Alzheimer's. My memory drifts in and out, but she's more or less gone. That's why she's being so quiet. I don't know your name; you must be mistaken. Look, we're not after any trouble. Anyway, I thought you were jumping." The man made a hand gesture towards the cliff edge. "Go on, if you're going to jump. You haven't got all day."

"I'm no longer in the mood." Dean shook his head, a wry smile on his face.

"But you've come all this way."

"I might come back tomorrow when there is not an audience. I'm not really one for entertaining crowds. But how did you know my name?"

"I don't know what you're talking about, Dean…"

"See, you said it again – Dean."

"Well I'm assuming you are called Dean since you've been accusing me of calling you Dean since you came down from the edge."

"I thought you'd called me by my name."

The man shook his head to plead his innocence.

"What are your names, anyway?" Dean enquired, remembering his manners. Manners seemed important again now he wasn't dead.

"I'm Albert and this is my Betty, Dean. We're both glad you're still here. How did you get into a mess like this?"

"I don't really know. Everything has been going wrong at the moment, Albert – you did say Albert, right?" Albert nodded. "I thought it was the only way out. I'm not sure if it still may be, to be honest. I'm sorry to cause you all this hassle. I'm sure you don't need it."

Dean put out his hand and Albert shook it.

"I don't think you realise what you have done today, Albert, but I appreciate it. If you hadn't been here…oh, never mind."

Dean smiled at Betty. She didn't look as though she was in the real world, and reminded Dean of his dad's final months. Occasionally, a beaming smile would break across his dad's face, so Dean knew wherever his mind was wandering off to, sometimes it was somewhere good.

"Have you been together long?" Dean asked, not taking his eyes from Betty.

"Forty-three years this year and counting." Albert smiled at his wife and took her hand in his. "You really need to get yourself sorted, Dean. I'm sure you have someone who will miss you?"

Dean looked over to the cliff face. "Yes, and to be honest, I'm just happy they're not scraping me off that cliff at the moment. Don't know where my mind was. It was as if I was on autopilot, and yes, I suppose they would miss me."

As Dean said this, Albert took a crumpled old beermat out of his pocket. He smiled as he read the words on it before carefully folding it back up and placing it in his jacket pocket, giving it a respectful tap. He then went into his wallet and pulled out a black and gold embossed business card, the gold shimmering in what little daylight there was left.

"I'm glad we were up here to help, Dean. Give these people a ring. They are good at dealing with people like you. It's where we spent our honeymoon. Make sure you book into Room 119. It's the best room they have."

Dean looked at the card and thanked Albert and gave Betty a kiss on the cheek. "Do you need a hand back down the hill?" he asked, only then noticing the blankets were covering wheelchairs.

"No, Dr Rhodes is coming to take us back to the home."

"Well, I don't know why you were here, but thank you so much for giving me a second chance."

Dean gave the old couple a nod of appreciation then turned to leave.

"Book into that hotel. It will really help. Oh, and Dean? Sorry about the 'coward' bit."

Dean looked back over his shoulder at Albert.

"You weren't wrong, Albert, suicide *is* a coward's way out."

Dean walked down the hill, making his way to the car. He put the picture of Sarah and Jodie back on the passenger seat then took another look at the business card.

"Welnetham Hall, mmm, Room 119, eh? Fuck knows, I need a break."

Dean placed the card under the sun visor and left Beachy Head a lot less dead than he'd expected to be.

Chapter 11 – Putting Things Right

Dean's head was racing with thoughts, but the demons had gone. He felt like he was in Second Chance Saloon, and Second Chance Saloon was a much nicer place to be than Last Chance Saloon. He punched 'Home London' into the satnav and turned the sound off – he couldn't be doing with Little Miss Know-it-all's directions right now as he needed to think. Should he ring Sarah? What would he tell her? He could hardly say, "Sarah, I tried killing myself, but now I'm OK." He had to do better than that.

It was now 10pm and dark. The satnav was taking him down a small country lane, twisting and turning in between two farmers' fields, barely wide enough for one car. But Dean didn't care; he felt re-energised and full of happy thoughts.

He thought about Sarah and how he'd been a prick with her. He'd not looked after the two people he loved more than anything else in the world. Picking up his new pay as you go brick, he rang Sarah. Whatever she said, he could deal with. It wasn't about him, it was about her.

"*Hi, this is Sarah. I can't take your call right now, leave me a message…*"

Beep.

"Sarah, I love you so much and I have so much to tell you. I've been a dick, I know that now. I miss you both so much…I can't wait to see you. I'm going to put things right, Sarah. I know you won't believe me, but I love you to bits. I can't wait for the rest of our lives. Love to you both."

Dean looked at the phone and smiled. Everything was going to be fine – he was going to make sure of it.

He went round a sharp bend and saw two fox eyes reflecting his headlights. He instinctively swerved, skidding first to the left and then to the right before losing control. His Porsche ploughed into a ditch, the airbag deploying into Dean's face. He was out cold.

When Dean woke up, it took a few seconds for his brain to compute what his eyes were telling him. He looked at his watch. It was 3.30am.

"Jesus Christ, bloody fox." He adjusted his position to get a look at himself in the rear-view mirror. He had a cut above his eye which had led to a stream of blood working its way down his face. He reached for some wipes in the glove compartment and dabbed the wound.

"Aghhh, fuck!"

He cleaned up his face and tried opening the door, but it was jammed against the hedge. Crawling into the passenger seat, he decided no bones were broken before opening the door. He crawled out of the car, making sure all his limbs were functioning as they should be.

It was dark, but he could see he'd damaged the front right wing of the car, which was not as bad as he had been dreading. He climbed back into the car and started it up, putting it into reverse and trying to back out of the ditch, but the ditch was having none of it. The wheels spun, so he started to rock the car back and forth, putting it in first and then back into reverse to gain some momentum. That did the trick and he managed to get the car back on the road, although it was making a horrible non-Porsche-like noise. He got out and kicked the wheel arch where it had caved into the tyre.

"What else?" he said out loud, a few more kicks making the front of the car look more car shaped. At least it was drivable, but he'd have to get back home before daylight or he'd be pulled by the police in no time.

Dean got the car back into the underground car park at his apartment at 4.30am. As he got out, he had another look at the damage. *Bollocks*, he thought as he pressed the key, turned on the alarm and punched in the code for the lift.

Dean hit the bed – what a day. The pillow was his friend that night; Dean was out like a light, ready for whatever tomorrow would bring.

Dean woke up late, which was to be expected. It was already early afternoon when he got out of bed, feeling like he had been run over by a bus which had reversed back over him for good measure. His neck was killing him and his head had to move in tandem with his shoulders. The crash must have been worse than he'd thought.

Walking as if he was on glass, not knowing which leg to hobble on, he went to the bathroom to assess the damage. The cut above his eye was not as bad as the blood that had gushed out of it last night had made it seem. It still needed cleaning up, though.

He took some cotton buds out of the bathroom cabinet and put some antiseptic on them. Dabbing it on his eye, he let out a loud, "Aghhh! That hurt."

He could see that he was also getting another black eye – after the episode in the strip club, he had just been getting his looks back. *Back to square one*, he thought.

He came out of the bathroom into what used to look like his living area. "Dean, for fuck's sake!" he said, realising for the first time in two weeks that the place was a tip. He picked up the pizza boxes and cans of beer which had been dumped in every room, the dishwasher, washing machine, vacuum cleaner and even the iron getting an outing as his apartment slowly started to look like his apartment again. Then he made four or five trips down to the basement with the rubbish he'd filled into various bags. Sarah would be proud of him right now.

He afforded a look at his car opposite the bin area and walked over to it. How the hell had he driven it home in that state? In the light, he could see the extent of the damage. The front bumper was hanging off and must have been dragging on the ground, and the wing was a mess, crumpled in and out in equal measure. The 'in' bit must have been the crash impact; the 'out' bit was Dean kicking the shit out of it to get it back into a shape that would make the car drivable. The midnight blue paint had been scratched by the hedge along the whole right-hand side of the car, and the front right alloy was full of mud.

Dean opened the car to find the driver's side airbag deployed and blood and mud all over the seats. He was about to lock up the car again and walk away when he remembered what Albert had said on the cliff top.

"Room 119. Say I sent you."

The card? Where did I put the card? Dean looked in the glove box and central panel before checking the sun visors. It fell onto the driver's seat as the visor was lowered – a black card embossed in shimmering gold.

"Welnetham Hall Hotel. Room 119, you say, Albert? OK, you're on."

Dean headed back upstairs, slid the lift cage open and placed the card on the kitchen worktop before running a much needed bath. He soaked in the bath and had a shave before checking his wardrobe for something suitable for a man on the up rather than a man dossing around the town. Looking in the mirror, he saw he was still a mess, but more of an organised mess.

He phoned Sarah, but there was no answer. Maybe he'd give her a couple of days to calm down. She must have got his message, and she'd come round in time. He would make sure that he gave her every opportunity to do so.

"Right, Albert, they are good at dealing with people like me, you say?"

He took the business card and called the number.

"Hello, Welnetham Hall Hotel. How can I help?"

"Hi, I would like to book a room for tomorrow night, please."

"No problem, sir, can I take your name?"

"Yes, it's Dean Harrison. Do you need my card details?"

Dean walked over to his wallet, which was lighter than normal after his donation to the windscreen of the Alzheimer's minibus. He had forgotten all about that and his face contorted into a smile.

"That won't be necessary. We are strictly cash here, sir." There was surprise in the receptionist's voice that Dean would even offer a card. "OK, sir, that's you booked in."

And that should have been that, but Dean then remembered he was supposed to ask for the best room.

"I nearly forgot, may I have Room 119? I really need a break right now, and Albert said it was the best room."

Dean laughed to himself. God, did he need a break right now!

"Wait there, sir." The receptionist's voice changed in tone, and Dean could hear her mumble in the background, *"He wants Room 119."*

"Tell him it's taken."

"I've already taken the booking now."

"Well tell him you made a mistake, we are full."

The lady came back on the phone. "Sorry, sir, I've checked again and I made a mistake. We are fully booked."

Dean was having none of it.

"What, no rooms at all? I'm sorry, but you have taken the booking now. I will be there tomorrow night and you'd better make sure 119 is free."

There was a pause.

"Can you put on the manager, please?" Dean added.

"No need, sir, it looks like we might be able to shuffle a couple of things round. Are you sure you want 119? We have much better rooms."

Dean looked at his phone as if it was stupid.

"I will be there at six pm, and yes, I want Room 119 if it's not too much trouble?" Dean's tone suggested there would be trouble if it *was* too much trouble.

"OK, sir, we'll see you tomorrow."

Dean came off the phone.

"They're taking the piss! Thanks, Albert, for sending me to a fucking nut house."

Part Two – Welnetham Hall

Chapter 12 – The Journey is Half the Fun

Dean woke up with a lot fewer aches and pain than yesterday. His joints felt like they had been oiled overnight. He rang Sarah again, but there was no answer. She would ring him when she was ready.

He googled Welnetham Hall, which looked nothing special. It was in the middle of nowhere, but at least it was near a train station. His car was out of action for a while, but to be honest, it was only a car and he had bigger fish to fry right now. Dean then packed an overnight bag, had a bite to eat and headed off to the train station in the early afternoon.

The train he boarded from Liverpool Street looked like something from the Dark Ages with corridors between the carriages. He'd obviously been travelling in first class for too long. If nothing else, it would be character building living back in the real world for a while. There was a loud whistle and the train slowly pulled out of the station, and before long the rhythmic sounds of the wheels on the tracks lulled him to sleep, his head resting on his folded arms on the table.

Dean was abruptly woken by a guard with a thick grey moustache and eyebrows to match shaking his shoulder.

"Tickets, please," said the guard with a friendly smile.

Dean lifted his head and as if on autopilot produced a ticket from his wallet, checking his watch at the same time. He'd been asleep a couple of hours.

"You're off at the next stop, sir."

The train slowed and Dean got ready near the door. The guard was still punching the last couple of tickets in the carriage, and said, "You've got ten minutes yet, sir, this station is no longer in use," with a smile as he walked past Dean.

"OK, thanks." Dean gave out a yawn – he'd obviously needed that kip. The train crawled through the disused station, and he saw the sign 'COCKFIELD STATION' with a strapline of 'Part of the Long Melford Branch Line'.

"This station closed down in 1961, sir, not stopped here since," the guard claimed with the authority of someone who knew everything about trains. "You're the next stop – Welnetham Station opened in 1865. You staying at the hotel, sir?"

"Yes, I need a break," Dean replied.

"OK, sir," said the guard with his ready smile. "Go out of the station and turn right. It's about a mile's walk up the lane on the right. You can't miss it."

"Think I'll get a cab."

"I don't think there is such a thing as a cab round these parts, sir. I hope you have comfy shoes on." The guard looked down at Dean's brown brogues. "You should be OK in them, sir. Mind how you go."

The guard moved into the next carriage, shouting, "Welnetham Station, next stop."

The train pulled into the station. Dean had to slide the window down to get to the outside door handle, which reminded him of when he used to go to Saltburn for the day as a teenager. The guard was one carriage up now, making sure everyone who needed to get off did so, and then making sure that all the doors were closed. He gave Dean a last smile before blowing his whistle, and the train slowly disappeared into the distance.

Dean checked the timetable, which was in a cabinet between two advertising boards. There was a train every two hours on a Sunday with the last leaving at 6pm. He made a mental note to catch the 4pm then left the station behind him and headed off up the hill as instructed.

It was a much longer and steeper walk than Dean had expected, but eventually he saw the lights of a large building appearing from the gloom. It was not dark yet, far from it, but it was a gloomy, foggy type of day which rounded off the edges of buildings and made things seem further away than they really were. A large black sign with gold writing proudly announced to all that they were passing Welnetham Hall and it might be a good idea to pop in. Dean had no choice; he was staying there.

No escaping now, he thought as he walked up to the entrance, wondering what was in store for him. He could hear Albert's voice in his head: "*They can help people like you, Dean.*" What did that even mean? Was he going to attend happy-clappy classes where everyone would stand up and admit how badly they had screwed up their lives? How would telling everyone about it make them feel better? Happy and especially clappy were not really Dean's forte.

In a grand Edwardian entrance hall, everything looked and felt like it was a little too big for the space it was occupying. Dean walked over to the reception and rang the bell. He had to hit the button on top of the bell with the flat of his hand, and there was something rather satisfying about the clear ringing that echoed around the hallway. Dean was half hoping nobody would respond – he quite fancied ringing the bell again.

"I'm on my way, I'll be there in a tick." The voice came from behind a red curtain which was draped over what used to be a doorway. The curtain morphed into a body shape as a lady struggled to find the gap in *Morecambe and Wise* fashion. "Oh, there we are!" she exclaimed as she eventually wriggled through. "Right, how can I help you?"

The woman who emerged was wearing a black satin uniform and had wild blonde hair that looked as if it had never seen a comb. Dean thought she looked a bit mad. Her eyebrows were very high up on her head and she looked like she had put her makeup on in the dark, all whites and pastel blues and pinks.

"Well?" she prompted. Dean was still allowing his brain time to absorb her look. "Name?" She opened a book, raising her eyebrows at him as if they could get any higher. Putting on some half-moon reading glasses, she peered over them, her pen poised above the hotel register.

"Errrr, Harrison. Dean Harrison."

"Mmmm, I see you have booked Room 119. Are you happy with being in that room, Mr Harrison?"

"Why? Should I be worried?" Dean laughed as he said this, trying to lighten the tone of the conversation. She again trained her eyes on him.

"You asked for that room, didn't you, sir?"

"Yes." Dean thought he'd leave the funnies out for now. They were clearly not appreciated.

"Well, I trust you will find everything in order, sir. Room 119 it is."

She turned around and pressed on the wooden panelling at the back of reception. A well-hidden cabinet opened. Dean noticed her name badge: *Mrs McCauley, Hotel Reception Manager.*

Mrs McCauley handed Dean the key with explicit instructions

on how to find the room – up the stairs and third room on the right, just past the shoe cleaning rollers.

"OK, thanks," said Dean, taking the key and placing into his pocket. He bent his knees to pick up his bag, then put it down again and asked, "So, Mrs McCauley, what fun have you got planned for me?"

She looked him up and down. "You make your own *fun* here, Mr Harrison. I'm sure you won't be disappointed. Good day."

With that, she logged his arrival time into her book. Dean shrugged his shoulders and shook his head. Mrs McCauley was weird, but Dean liked weird. Better than boring. He wouldn't forget her in a hurry, that was for sure.

Dean headed up the stairs to find his room. He felt an excited nervousness as he stood outside the door. What was all the mystery about Room 119? Why had the receptionist he'd spoken to on the phone not wanted him to stay in this room? Why had Mad Mrs McCauley downstairs asked if he was sure about this room? It was only a room. Dean had lots of questions and as yet no answers.

The key was an old mortise style one, like a typical house key from the 1970s. One turn would only half unlock the door, so Dean had to turn it twice to get in. Click, click – the door was now unlocked. He turned the door handle and entered.

Well, that's a let-down, he thought. It was a nice room, but it was just like any other room. Everything was large, like everything else in the hotel. A four-poster bed sat in the centre of the room, there were a couple of hunting pictures on the wall, and a tub chair was in the corner, next to a writing table. There was also a door that Dean assumed went to an en suite. There was no TV, but to be honest, he would not miss it.

Dean unpacked his stuff into an overly large wardrobe, his clothes looking a bit lonely in such a big space. He looked at his phone – no signal. That was no surprise as he was in the middle of nowhere. *Having* a signal would have been more of a shock.

Dean opened the curtains and looked out of the window. The fields rolled on as far as he could see, undeniably England's green and pleasant land. He opened the en suite door and was pleasantly surprised. The bathroom was half the size of the main room with a free-standing bath and generous washbasin area. He popped back into the bedroom and picked up his wash bag, which he had dumped on the bed while he was unpacking his case, and placed it in the bathroom.

He climbed onto the bed and lay down, thinking of Albert giving him the hotel's card on Beachy Head.

"OK, Albert, you've got me here. Now what is so special about this place?"

Before his mind had time to answer, his thoughts had moved on to Sarah and Jodie and what he had put them through. Then before another thought could interrupt, he nodded off.

Chapter 13 – Big Wheels and Waltzers

Dean woke up with a start as if someone had walked across his grave. He stood up and did the shuddery shoulder type of thing which seems to be the international reset for when a person feels like they've been grave walked, accompanying it with a "Brrrrr."

He could hear dampened down organ music in the distance, along with the odd scream. When he walked over to the window, the view was no longer of lush green fields for miles and miles. The once empty fields were now lit up with fairground rides, a circus Big Top and a hive of activity of the funfair variety.

"What the…" He left the sentence unfinished. Looking at his watch, he saw it was 9.30pm – he'd only been asleep for two or three hours at most, and someone appeared to have built a fairground and pitched an enormous circus tent in what was technically his back yard.

As he was up now and had nothing better to do, he thought he'd go and see what all the fuss was about. When he got outside, he could hear the sounds more clearly. The shrieks were piercing as the rides reached their high points before spinning, twisting and corkscrewing back down to earth, safely delivering their passengers and eagerly picking up some more willing volunteers.

Dean could not see the fairground from the hotel driveway so followed the sounds and the lights which were forming a glow in the night sky. He knew his room was at the far side of the hotel and he could see the funfair from his window, so he set off in that general direction back down the lane he had walked up from the station.

After a few hundred yards, Dean got a sense that he was being followed. Not that he had seen or heard anything, he just had a feeling he was being watched. He turned quickly, hoping to catch out who or whatever it was, but everything was as it should be. If someone or something was following him, they were good at it.

He continued along the lane, the music and screams getting louder and louder. There was a track on the right-hand side with a hand-painted sign pointing off the main road: *Funfair*. The sign wasn't very engaging or convincing, almost as though it was apologising for mentioning the fact. Dean followed it anyway.

The track narrowed as he got nearer to the fair, the trees on either side appearing to have joined forces and interlocked their branches to form a canopy. The sounds of the fair were dampened by this canopy, allowing Dean to hear a *tick-tick-tick* behind him. He felt eyes burning a hole in the back of his head; again he turned quickly. This time he saw a tall, dark silhouette of a man with a silver-topped stick shining in the moonlight.

The man was well over six feet tall and was not in the mood for stopping. His face could not be seen, hidden by a fedora hat with the wide brim angled down. *Tick-tick-tick*. An icy feeling flowed through Dean's body. If the man was following him, Dean thought it would be a good idea to get some distance between them. Falconer International Trading would still be a bit pissed off with him, and Dexter might have sent in the heavies to collect whatever they could from him. If they wanted some kind of payment, he didn't really want to find out what form that payment would take. He wheeled around and continued up the track a little more briskly than before, heading for the safety of numbers in the fair.

Even though he was getting closer to the fairground, he could still hear the ticking of the man's cane on the path behind him, and it seemed to be getting closer by the minute. Dean brushed past a few people and he could now see the entrance to the fair. He took a sneaky look back on the kink of a bend and the man was nowhere in sight. Had Dean lost him? Then he heard the ticking and saw the man's large frame appear from around the bend.

Paranoia was setting in. Dean felt a mild comfort in knowing the man was twenty steps behind him as opposed to not knowing where he had gone. He then started to think rationally – the man might not even be following him. He might be just heading to the funfair like everyone else.

Dean entered the fair through a grand archway which was all lit up by individual bulbs set out in rainbow shapes, flashing in their respective rows. He could see waltzers, bumper cars and numerous other rides with queues of people ready to feed their need for a kick of adrenaline. This was the last thing Dean needed right now; his adrenaline was pumping so fast through his veins it was almost protruding from his temples.

He looked around once more and saw the man gaining on

him. Dean took a sharp right and forced his way through the queue for the waltzer. Behind him, the people in the queue parted to let the man through. Maybe this was in deference to his size, but it seemed more that subconsciously they felt they should not be in his way.

Dean was in no doubt now that the man was focusing on him. While running round behind the whirling seats of the waltzer, he managed to get a better glimpse of his pursuer.

He was thin faced with deep set eyes. The stare he gave Dean said, "*You can run all day, but I've got a lifetime to catch you.*" This made Dean run even harder, but the man was still catching up on him with minimal effort. Everyone in his path was moving to the side. It was like Dean was creating a human jet stream, making life easy for the man who had not even broken into a sweat.

Dean was scared now. "What the fuck is going on?" he said as he bolted around another corner in between a 'hook a duck' stall and a rifle range. To the annoyance of the stall owner, Dean threw some big cuddly toy prizes on the ground behind him, hoping to slow down his relentless pursuer. Glancing back to see what effect they had, he saw the toys move out of the way without the man even touching them.

In a clearing near the circus tent, Dean stopped. *Think, Dean, think.* He saw a door on the left-hand side and entered it. Leaving the door open ever so slightly, he hoped to see the man dash past. The man didn't; instead, he stopped outside the door, trying to figure out which way Dean had gone.

Dean was breathing in slow motion, trying to be as quiet as he could. The tall figure had his back to the door Dean was peering through. He speared his silver-topped cane into the muddy ground and retrieved an old book from the inside pocket of his black coat. Dean could just about make out a map of what appeared to be the layout of the funfair. But that wasn't what shocked him. Dean's name and date of birth were underlined at the top of the book above the map: Dean Harrison – 22 November 1974. On the map, a red dot was slowly fading in and out.

His pursuer was looking around the clearing, confused. He stepped into the centre of the clearing and surveyed the area, slowly moving round in a circle, looking for his prey. At one point he was looking straight at Dean, who was still peering through the crack of the door, motionless and too scared even to take a breath.

The man then shook his head and closed the book, replacing it in the inside pocket of his black overcoat before straightening his hat. Then, slowly and calmly, he walked back past the stalls in the direction from which he had come. People were acknowledging him, and he slid his thin fingers across the rim of his hat to thank them for allowing him through. Dean watched as the man stopped to pick up the two large teddy bears and apologise with a nod to the 'hook a duck' stall owner before paying him a coin for his troubles.

Then the coast was clear. Dean started to breathe at a normal volume and cadence, checking once more that the man was no longer in sight. Preparing to leave, he opened the door a little wider.

"If you leave through that door, Dean," said a voice behind him, "you are as good as dead. You can only run so long before he catches you."

Chapter 14 – Send In The Clown

Dean turned around to see a large clown wearing a multi-coloured outfit sitting in front of a dressing table. He was taking care making up his face, looking in the centre one of three angled mirrors surrounded by bright white lightbulbs. Dean could see in the left-hand mirror that the clown's face was half made up with white foundation and light blue eyeshadow. There was an assortment of brightly coloured wigs on mannequin heads to the clown's left.

"Happy or sad?" he asked Dean.

"A bit of both, to be honest," said Dean. "I have not got a clue what's going on. It all seems a bit weird, and to be honest, this isn't helping me to make any sense of it."

Dean turned to take another peek through the crack in the door. He wasn't sure who was worse – the scary man outside or the scary clown in the room with him.

"I'm not on about you. Should I put a happy or sad face on today?"

"Oh, sorry. Happy, I suppose. You lot are scary enough, you don't need any help." Dean's heart rate seemed to be returning to normal and the adrenalin was levelling off in his veins.

"Happy it is, then." The clown started to apply an upturned mouth to his already busy face.

"What did you mean, I'm as good as dead if I leave?" Dean shut the door and placed a chair in front of the handle. He wasn't sure if that would stop anyone forcing their way in, but he'd seen it in films and it always seemed to do the trick.

"Life's about choices, Dean, and that door does not look a good choice to me right now. What do you think?"

Dean took another look at the door before responding.

"I think he's from the company I used to work for. They might be after me. They think I owe them some money."

Dean turned and looked into the clown's overly large eyes.

"No, you don't think that, Dean. You're saying it as it makes you feel better. He's after a lot more than money, and you know that." The clown was adding the finishing touches to his makeup with a soft brush, applying some rouge to the cheek area. "I like being a happy clown. Good choice, Dean."

"How do you know I'm called Dean?"

Dean remembered the cliff top. He hadn't been sure whether Albert had really said his name as he was standing on the cliff edge, but the clown had definitely called him Dean ever since he'd entered the room.

"Just a guess, Dean. How could I possible know your name? Or that the man outside is not after money?" Without leaving a gap for an answer, the clown looked at the wigs. "Red or yellow?"

"I don't know. Err, red, I suppose." Dean wasn't that bothered about the clown's looks right now. His head was spinning, trying to make some sense of the last hour or so.

"See, Dean, you can make choices when you feel like it. You're good at it." The clown looked proudly into the three mirrors which all reflected a happy face back to him.

"So who is he, then? And what does he want with me?"

Dean wanted a straight answer, but the clown had other ideas.

"Not so much who as what." The clown put on his jacket. As clown-like music came through one of the doors behind the dressing table, he made a move towards it as if he was being drawn in to perform.

Dean said, "I give up," and moved the chair from the door handle. The clown looked at him.

"I told you, Dean, go out of that door and you are as good as dead."

The clown continued moving towards his pending performance.

"Well, at least I'd know what the fuck is going on. You are all fucking mad here. What's the worst that could happen?"

"Did Jodie tell you about me, Dean? Did she tell you that I went to see her and told her you would leave home?"

Dean took his hand off the door and raced across the room, pinning the clown to the wall.

"What the fuck is going on? If you touch her, I'll kill you, weirdo. I fucking hate clowns – always have, always will."

Dean tightened his grip on the clown's neck.

"If you want to see Jodie again, Dean, don't go through that door. You'll thank me one day." The clown pointed to the other door behind the dressing table, just about managing to get his breath out of his mouth. "That way. Go that way."

Dean looked into his eyes. The clown was not scared and his happy face was doing its best to remain happy. He looked at the other door.

"Please, Dean. It's your choice and it might be the last choice you make. I can only guide you. It's the rules." A tear slowly trickled down the clown's face, taking some of the blue greasepaint with it. "Please, Dean."

Dean released his grip on the clown's neck and headed for the door.

"I hope to see you soon, Dean. Remember, it's all about choices, and at least now you might get to make another one."

The clown left through one door to his music; Dean left through the other door, straight into his en suite in the hotel. The changing room had gone and he was back in Room 119.

Dean rushed over to the window, but there was no sign of the fairground. All was quiet; all was how it was meant to be.

"Jesus Christ, what a dream," Dean said out loud, but he knew it hadn't been a dream. He knew it had been as real as day and night.

He splashed some water on his face in the bathroom then looked at his watch: twenty past midnight. He fell onto his bed, fully clothed but still alive.

"Bloody hate clowns," he muttered as he drifted off into a deep sleep.

Chapter 15 – Checking Out

Dean woke up after a great night's sleep. If the fairground had been a dream, his memory wasn't giving it back to him in bits and pieces; he remembered every last detail. He shook his head a few times.

"Good God, Albert, where the hell have you sent me?"

He had a late breakfast just before the hotel stopped serving at 11.30am and could sense the disapproval of the waiting staff. Even though his breakfast was probably not made or delivered with love, eggs are eggs, and they were just what Dean needed. After a few coffees, he went back to his room and had a shower before re-packing his overnight bag and heading off to reception to be greeted by Mrs Happy.

"Was everything adequate for your stay, Mr Harrison?"

Dean resisted the temptation to say he had been chased round a funfair by a madman in a hat and then he'd met a clown who'd probably saved his life.

"Yes, everything was more than adequate."

"Good, that's what we like to hear." She put a line through his name in her book, slammed it shut and muttered, "Good day," as she disappeared behind the curtain.

She was right about one thing: it was a good day. Glorious, in fact, so Dean didn't mind the walk back down the hill to the train station. As he made his way down, he could see the fork in the road where he'd turned for the funfair last night, but there was no apologetic sign, no music, no screams, no circus tent. It was as if last night had never happened.

Dean continued on to the station and stood on the platform, glancing down at his watch. It was twenty minutes to four, and according to the timetable, there would be a train at 4pm.

The train turned up at quarter past four with no apology for its lateness. Inside was the same guard with the same familiar smile.

"Welcome back, sir, do you want me to punch your ticket now so you can have a sleep? I expect you have had a busy night."

Dean fumbled through his wallet for the return portion of his ticket.

"Enjoy your journey back, Dean." The guard turned and headed off down the carriage. "Any more tickets please from Welnetham Station?"

Dean thought for the briefest of seconds that he hadn't told the guard his name before shouting, "Excuse me," to call him back. The guard turned and gave his trademark smile.

"Can I help, sir?"

Dean thought better of it. "Err, it doesn't matter."

The train ambled past the disused COCK-FIELD STATION. Part of the Long Melford Branch Line, and Dean saw the man in the fedora in the waiting room, holding the black cane with the silver top and looking directly at him. Dean got a good look at him this time, which was easy as he wasn't running away, sneaking backward peeks in the hustle and bustle of the fairground. The man was taller than he'd first thought, although he was slightly hunched over, and was dressed all in black. It was the first time Dean had seen his face properly – a very thin face with cheekbones more or less apologising for protruding as much as they did. He did not look like someone Dean would want to meet on the darkest of nights, or even the lightest of days. If Dean had a choice, he wouldn't want to meet him at all.

The man burned a stare right into the middle of Dean's forehead. As the train slowly eased past, he pointed his cane towards Dean before tipping his hat at him just before he disappeared out of view. Had he gone to a disused station just to let Dean know that he was real – very real? To assure Dean that he was still on his case?

Dean was assured.

The next day, Dean was up at the crack of sparrows. He already had a coffee on the go when he decided he was going to try and make sense of the weekend. When in doubt, when all around you seems lost, there's only one thing that will help…Google.

Google's first challenge was *Cockfield Train Station, Melford line.* Dean was not surprised when the top result was *Disused Stations: Cockfield Station* – he'd known old Smiler the Guard would not be wrong. He was surprised, though, when he clicked on the link to explore further and looked at the map. The whole line had closed in 1961, not just Cockfield, Welnetham included. But how? He'd just been there; he'd got off the train there; he'd stood on the station and had his ticket stamped.

Dean scrolled down to see old black and white pictures of both stations. It was definitely the same place. He'd left from Liverpool Street, Platform 19, so he googled a station map. There was no Platform 19; only eighteen platforms at Liverpool Street. It all felt a bit *Harry Potter*, but this was no book. This was Dean's life; he was living and breathing it.

Either someone was playing tricks on him or playing tricks on Google; the former seemed more feasible as no one fucked with Google. Dean shut his laptop and went outside for some air, heading for one of the many coffee shops around Canary Wharf. Sitting outside with his skinny latte steaming in a tall glass cup, the milky vortices visible through the sides, he looked over a waterway which was an offshoot of the Thames. It was very quiet for a Monday with a lot less to-ing and definitely less fro-ing going on than usual.

His mind was doing mental gymnastics, trying to make sense of everything that had happened to him over the last week. He wasn't the type to go jumping off cliffs. He knew he was in the middle of a healing process; he just wished it would hurry up so he could get back on with his life with Sarah and Jodie.

He took a sip of his coffee, thinking about the man with the cane. What would have happened if he'd caught him? As he stared over the water, he tried to make sense of what the clown had said to him. He was missing a lot of information as the clown had spoken in questions and riddles, answering very little of what Dean asked him. Dean's mind was like a detective halfway through an Agatha Christie play where nothing made sense right now. He was hoping it would all make sense in the end. The problem, though, was Dean did not know how the end was going to pan out, and he wasn't really sure if he wanted to find out.

Dean was getting no response from Sarah, although he rang her every day, leaving message after message. It was Friday morning, and his routine for this week had been coffee shops, thinking and walking London's streets, trying to find answers. But it's hard to find answers when you're not sure what the questions are. He certainly wasn't going to find answers at the bottom of a skinny latte.

There was only one place that had the answers he was looking for. It was burning inside him, dragging him back like a magnet. He had unfinished business in Welnetham Hall and Room 119, and until he returned, nothing was going to make any more sense than it did right now.

Dean picked up the phone and called the hotel.

"Hello, Welnetham Hall, how can I help you?" Dean could tell by the lady's voice it was Mrs Cheery Pants McCauley, the reception manager, and decided to play it straight. He recalled that she didn't take kindly to humour.

"Hello, it's Dean Harrison…"

Before he could finish, Mrs McCauley interrupted.

"Mr Harrison, we have been expecting your call. We have Room 119 available for you tonight."

She's in a happy mood, Dean thought.

Dean had never said he was going back so her words felt a bit presumptuous, but hey ho! *Beggars can't be choosers*, he thought.

"Yes, that would be great, thank you, Mrs McCauley. Is the funfair there this week?" Dean enquired.

"Funfair, sir? We have not seen a funfair around these parts for years."

Dean looked at the phone as if it were betraying him. Maybe he had dreamt it all last week.

"All booked in, Mr Harrison. See you around six pm, if I recall correctly."

Dean arrived at Liverpool Street Station to catch a train running on a disused train line and leaving from a platform that did not exist. If Google was right, then both the ticket machine and the station were in on the joke, because Dean purchased his ticket with no trouble at all, and when he got to Platform 18, he could see Platform 19 to the right under an archway, as it had been before. He stopped for ten minutes or so and noticed that although Platform 19 was clearly there, nobody seemed to be taking a blind bit of notice of it.

Why is nobody using the platform? he thought. It appeared everybody was going anywhere but Welnetham Station.

Dean gave a wry smile as he ventured through the archway. The friendly face of the guard was there to greet him and the few other passengers milling around, ensuring they all got on the train OK. Dean looked back at the archway, which still had no traffic coming through it. Who were these people on the platform with him? Where had they come from? None of them had come through the archway with him. Maybe it was just a coincidence. Maybe it was just a quiet train, or maybe he had not observed the archway for long enough. Either way, he was here now, so he took his seat on the train armed with his ticket and his bag, ready for whatever lay ahead in Room 119.

Chapter 16 – Checkmates

Jodie was in her room, staring at the chessboard. The pieces were in the same positions as they had been since the unfinished game with her dad. The blacks could not lose; it looked worse and worse for the whites the more she looked at it. There must have been twenty ways for black to win from this position.

But Jodie wasn't looking for a way to win; she was trying to find any weakness that the white pieces could exploit. Each time she tried, she failed. It was hopeless.

She started to sob, shedding tears on the board as she reset the pieces after her latest failed effort. It was only a game of chess, but it was her world right now. She had been about to beat her dad for the first time, and kept recalling what the clown in her dream had said.

"*You might never see your dad again.*"

Jodie thought back to the incident in the playground earlier, her mum tearing her out of her dad's arms. She blamed herself for everything.

"It's all my fault, Mum," she said as Sarah walked into the room. "He knew I was going to beat him at chess."

Sarah hugged Jodie to her chest.

"Jodie, your dad loves you to pieces. Nothing is your fault. Bad things just happen sometimes."

Jodie could hear her dad's words in her head, the 'Deanism' he had spoken during the fateful chess game.

"*There is always a way. When someone has got nowhere to run, it's better to go down fighting, no matter how futile the fight.*"

"I'm going to find a way for Dad to win, Mum, then he might come back."

"I thought you said there was no way white could win."

Jodie looked up at her mum, her eyes bloodshot. "There is always a way, Mum."

Sarah held her daughter tightly in her arms. "You know what, Jodie, you sound just like your father. You'll find a way, I'm sure you will, and he'll be very proud of you."

Soaking up a bit of sun in the front room of the house, Jodie was using a chess game app on the iPad Dean had given her for her birthday. It had taken her about fifteen minutes to set an exact online copy of her game with her dad into the chessboard simulator. Then she clicked 'Playing as white' and 'Outcome percentages'.

Her heart sank as she absorbed the stark probability figures on her screen:

- White win = 00.01%
- Black win = 98.47%
- Stalemate = 01.52%

There must be a way, she thought in desperation. But she had no reason to believe that the figures were anything but spot-on. Overtaken by a sudden fury, Jodie fled upstairs to her room, threw her head into the pillow on her bed and sobbed her heart out.

The next night, Friday, there was a knock at the door. Sarah looked out of the upstairs window and saw Doreen from the gym with her son, Kyle.

She's the last person I want to see right now, Sarah thought. But Jodie got on with Kyle; he was a friend from the chess club. *What are they here for?*

Sarah headed downstairs, looking in the mirror and straightening her hair on the way down.

"Hi, Doreen," she said, opening the door. "Kyle, Jodie's upstairs if you want to head up."

Kyle didn't need a second invitation.

"I've cooked you this, Sarah, because I bet you're not eating." Doreen presented her with a large homemade lasagne which was accompanied by a baguette-shaped bag letting out the giveaway aroma of garlic. "It needs to go in the oven on about 180 for twenty to twenty-five minutes until the cheese is all bubbling and brown."

Doreen could be quite officious even when she was being nice, but at least she was being nice.

"Thanks, Doreen, I've not really been eating since…well, you know."

Sarah took the lasagne and headed for the kitchen. Doreen followed.

"Sorry about what happened at the gym, Sarah. You know how it gets sometimes." Doreen went to her bag and pulled out a bottle of prosecco. "I think you need a glass of this."

Sarah nodded and took two crystal champagne flutes out of the kitchen cupboard above her head. As Doreen poured them both a glass, Sarah's eyes filled up.

"It's OK, let it all out, Sarah. You're not on your own. We are all here for you."

Sarah looked at Doreen as she took a sip of her drink. "It all could have been different. Why did I look at his credit card statements? I should have trusted him. He's a good man, you know."

Doreen looked at Sarah, who was holding her prosecco glass with two hands like it was a mug of hot chocolate.

"Well…" Doreen left a pause in the air. "You can blame me for that, Sarah. I was the one who put doubt in your head." She prised Sarah's drink out of her hands and topped her glass up. Sarah picked it up again and immediately drew it back into the hot chocolate hug position, taking a sip.

"Doreen, it's not your fault. Dean and I were getting no time together. I know he loves me, but I needed him to start looking after Jodie and me. Not just being happy that we were there."

Sarah could feel a tear slowly making its way down her face. She mopped it up with the sleeve of her white knitted jumper.

"Now that's enough of all that. It's not your fault, Sarah, and the faster you learn that, the better. You have to be there for Jodie and you know that. Don't you?"

Sarah put her glass down and straightened her body to a more upright position on her chair.

"You're right, Doreen, thanks. It really means a lot." Sarah held her hands out and Doreen grasped them.

"It's all going to be OK, Sarah, but you have to be strong right now for Jodie."

Sarah nodded and wiped another tear away with the damp

sleeve of her jumper.

Upstairs, Jodie was staring at the chessboard. She had been staring at the chessboard more or less continuously since her dad left.

"There must be a way, Kyle," she said by way of a greeting when he entered the room.

"We've been through this in chess club, Jodie. We've had twenty games from this position with you playing white then me playing white. There is no way without black throwing the game for white to win."

"There must be a way. Dad said there is always a way, you just have to look hard enough." Jodie motioned to the chair for Kyle to join her. "Let's go again. I'll be white, and play for real, Kyle."

Kyle sat opposite Jodie.

"OK, Jodie, but I think we've done this to death."

"One more time, please, Kyle. You know what it means to me."

Kyle looked at the chessboard.

"OK, it's me to go, Jodie. Good luck – you're going to need it."

It wasn't long before Kyle reluctantly proclaimed, "See, Jodie, it can't be done. White is in such a weak position you only have a few key pieces left. One more piece then maybe it would be possible. But it's a very weak place to start."

The board was carnage. There was hardly a white piece left on it. The king was looking very naked, a couple of loyal pawns were fighting to the end, but eventually they all surrendered. The black pieces were all over the board, flexing their muscles and looking proud of themselves.

"I know, but there has to be a way, Kyle. There just has to be." Jodie stood up and hugged Kyle. Kyle gave her a couple of little pats on the back to let her know that one, he wasn't good at hugs, and two, this hug was going on far too long for a bad hugger to manage. Jodie let him off the hook, releasing him from her grasp.

"Thanks, Kyle, I'll see you in school."

Kyle nodded and gave her a smile.

"I'll have a think, Jodie. Like you say, there must be a way, but white gets beaten time after time. They're under too much pressure from the beginning."

Jodie started resetting the board back to where she'd left the game with her dad. She knew the positions off by heart having reset it so often.

"I know, Kyle, but I can't give in now."

Jodie leant forward and gave him a peck on the cheek.

"What was that for?" Kyle's tone was defensive. She'd caught him off guard and he felt himself going red.

"Just because, Kyle, that's all. Just because. Thanks."

Jodie smiled at him. Kyle had regathered his thoughts and tried to regain some control, giving Jodie a playful punch on the arm.

"Idiot!" he said. Jodie looked at him; she didn't need to retaliate.

"Your help means a lot, Kyle. I can't do this on my own."

"Kyle…" A yell, unmistakable and Doreen shaped, came from downstairs. Although Sarah had just seen her soft side, her default setting was loud, brash and controlling.

"Kyle…" A second shriek was not good, and Kyle did not want to hear a third.

"I'd better go, Jodie. Let me know if you have any ideas." He gave her another sneaky punch as he left, running out of range as he knew he would not get a second free hit without retaliation. Jodie gave him a wave.

"Bugger off, Kyle. Idiot!"

Jodie and her mum had just finished off Doreen's lasagne. It was the first good meal Sarah had eaten for a couple of weeks, and that coupled with her chat with Doreen had made her feel more positive.

"Right, Jodie, no more down in the dumps. We have to get on with this now. When we wake up in the morning, we are going to be positive. Agreed?" Sarah held her hand out for a high five, and got a mid to lowering five. But it was still classified as a five, so it was a start.

"OK, Mum. I'm just trying to find a way for Dad to win. I

need him to win – you know that, don't you?"

"Jodie, I know, but it won't bring your dad back, honey. He's not been in touch since yesterday." Sarah's lips wobbled momentarily. How she wished now that she hadn't been so hard on Dean at Jodie's school; apart from one voicemail message, neither she nor Jodie had heard from him since. Nor did he answer his phone when they called him. "We're on our own for now."

"Yes, Mum, I know. Positive tomorrow, right?" Jodie's shoulders were slumped, but her mother could see she was trying.

"Yes, JoJo, tomorrow's another day. Go on, up you go."

Upstairs in the privacy of her room, Jodie looked at the chessboard again. The blacks glared at the whites, knowing the next game was going to be theirs. Jodie picked up the black queen and stared her in the eye.

"I think you need to back off my dad for a bit and give him a break."

She replaced the queen in her home position. She then did this with all the pieces so they could have a break from the war. The white pieces looked like they had been given a stay of execution; it was as if they let out a simultaneous sigh of relief. The white king could give them a good motivational team talk and prepare for tomorrow's battle. If there was to be a battle tomorrow.

Jodie crawled into bed just as her mother entered the room. Sarah looked at the reset chessboard and smiled. Her daughter was moving on, and God knows, she needed to.

"You know it's for the best, Jodie. We have to keep living our lives, you know."

Jodie was under the covers, facing the wall and trying not to cry. She wasn't giving up on her dad; she was giving everyone a break.

"It's just for tonight, Mum. I couldn't face another night of the black team bullying my dad."

Chapter 17 – Old Friends

Dean did not sleep this time; he wanted to make sure whatever happened was not a dream. After a couple of hours with no funfair activity outside, he popped down to the bar for a couple of drinks.

The room housing the bar was very grand with oak panelling on the walls intersected with paintings of racehorses, some more modern than others. The newer paintings actually looked like racehorses; the older ones looked like something L S Lowry might have painted. They were really matchstick animals with long bodies as if they had been stretched out of proportion.

The bar itself was a lighter wood with a brass footrest. This would not be required today as there was no queue, and footrests were for queues. A young barman was cleaning glasses one by one with a cloth, inspecting each one before placing it back in the row and automatically picking up the next one like he was on a glass cleaning production line. However, the barman, in his early twenties, tall and slim with blond hair and a blond moustache that looked as if it was apologising for being on his top lip, looked quite happy in his work. It seemed a shame to interrupt such a well-oiled machine on the glass upkeep, but needs must.

"What beers have you got, please, David?" Dean had already clocked the barman's name badge, and politeness never hurts.

"Oh, you'll wish you'd never asked, sir."

Dean already wished he hadn't asked the minute David uttered those words. The next five minutes consisted of David reciting a well-rehearsed speech not only listing the beers and lagers, but telling Dean where they were brewed, what percentage alcohol they contained, and the colour and taste they offered.

"…and this one is brewed in Skipton, Yorkshire by the Crafty Dog brewery. It's their flagship beer called Pippin, and it's a light…"

Dean stopped David in full flow.

"That one will do, David. You had me at Yorkshire."

"Good choice, sir."

David pulled out a Crafty Dog Pippin branded glass and

poured the beer with a great deal of love and care. David really liked his beer, Dean could tell. When he wasn't talking about or pouring beer, Dean suspected he was drinking it. Maybe he was the head of the Suffolk branch of CAMRA, the Campaign for Real Ale.

"I think you'll enjoy that. Is it on Room 119, sir?" David rang the price into an old-fashioned till and got Dean to sign a slip of paper.

"Yes, Room 119." Dean didn't bother asking how David knew his room number. There were only another three or four people in the bar, and the rest of them all had a drink, so maybe his was the only room number that hadn't yet been served. "Thanks, David."

Dean went and sat near a pool table, which looked as old as the hotel with beer stains all over the cloth. The pictures on the wall in this area were not of horses, but of dogs drinking, smoking and playing pool. Dean thought the artist must have been on something stronger than Crafty Dog's Pippin when he'd painted them.

"Do you play?" said the man sitting to the right of Dean. A young woman next to him was sharing a drink with him.

"A little," Dean replied, although he played more than a little. Dean was a natural at most things, but at bar games he was very good, especially pool. All the misspent hours in his youth, playing pool for money in the pubs in Whitby, had paid off. He had what the locals where he grew up called 'form.'

His potential opponent, in his early twenties, enthusiastically sprang up out of his chair and checked his trousers for a 10p piece. Dean looked at his young, fresh face.

"Do I know you?" he enquired.

"I don't think so. Suffolk born and bred. Are you from around these parts?"

"No, I've only been here once before. Last week, in fact," Dean confirmed.

"Well, that will be a no then, sir, you don't know me." The young man slid the 10p into one of four slots and the balls came flying out ready to be assembled.

Dean took a swig of his drink and chose his cue from the six in the rack. It was not a difficult choice as only three had tips, and one of them was tiny.

"Do you want to break?" Dean thought he would offer.

"Yep, I'll break, thanks," the man replied as he finished racking up the balls in the customary order forming their starting positions. He grabbed the only other serviceable cue and approached the table. After chalking the tip, he smashed the balls apart.

He potted a stripe off the break, and his girlfriend sat up and clapped ferociously. Dean thought it was a bit early for cheerleading; it was only one ball. He smiled at her, but she was too busy admiring her boyfriend as if he was a knight in shining armour.

After potting another couple of balls, both of which were greeted with cheers from the adoring fan, the young man missed, allowing Dean in. The spots were not in a great position, but Dean had a pot on. It was a difficult pot, but it was at least an opportunity. Dean managed to sink it and move a few other balls in the process. He was then able to manoeuver around the table, plotting a path from ball to ball before slotting home the black.

He looked at the man to see if he would like another game.

"One–nil to me," the man claimed. Dean gaped at him, and then looked at his girlfriend who was already on cheerleading duties.

"Did we win? Did we win?"

"So I'm guessing you have a local rule. And I guess I have just broken it." Dean laughed as he leant on his cue.

"That's right, you have. You must nominate the pocket you put the black in, everyone knows that."

It was obvious which pocket Dean had intended to pot the black ball into; it had been hovering over the lip of the right-hand corner pocket, but it was not worth the argument.

"Rules are rules," he said, accepting his punishment. "One–nil to you." There was more clapping from the girlfriend, which Dean didn't acknowledge as it was getting a bit annoying. "Before we start, are there any other rules I should know about? Two shots for a foul, I guess, and white ball behind the line. Only one shot on the black…"

"No, just remember to nominate your pocket on the black. Schoolboy error."

Dean nodded.

"Right you are. Mugs away, then."

Dean put an old style 10p piece in the slot. The man had left the coin on the side of the table as if to reserve the next game, which seemed excessive as no one else looked like they wanted to play, but Dean had no coins on him and was grateful for it. To his surprise, the out-of-date coin worked in the middle slot, and the noise unique to pool tables rang out as the balls made their way through the labyrinth of wooden tunnels.

Dean racked up and broke the balls open, potting two stripes before clearing up, being sure to nominate the black into the far corner.

This time, there was no clapping and no steward's enquiry. The man simply said, "One–one, well played. Should we have a decider?"

Dean looked at the empty glasses on the table.

"You paid for the game, so let me buy you both a drink first. What would you and your good lady like?"

"I'll have a Pippin." Dean was quite pleased the man didn't reply, "What do they have?" If David had to go through his beer speech again, they might miss last orders. "And Betty will have a gin and tonic, thanks."

While the man reset the table, Dean headed to the bar where David was now on the bottom shelf of his glass cleaning marathon. After ordering the drinks and signing the chit, Dean picked up the gin and tonic. David offered to bring the beers over as they needed to settle and would require a top-up, and he wasn't going to let a sub-standard pint go into general circulation on his watch. Dean let him have his way and headed back to the pool table.

After the break when nothing went down, Dean mopped up without his opponent getting another look in. He named the pocket for the black, apologising as he did so.

"Sorry, think you just caught me on a good day."

Dean offered his hand for a handshake; the young man smiled and gave his congratulations.

"Care to join us?" he asked. Dean nodded and moved a stool from where he had been sitting before the pool games.

"So, what brings you two love birds here, then?"

"It's our first weekend away. Sort of a honeymoon, I guess. We got married last week. This is my lovely wife, Betty."

The young man took her hand in his and squeezed it tightly. He had not said, "This is my wife," many times yet. It all still seemed new and special.

"Well, congratulations to you both." Dean held his glass slightly higher to salute the newlyweds. "So pleased to meet you, Betty. I don't think I got your name, sir?"

"It's Albert. Albert and Elizabeth Greening."

Dean knew he'd seen the young man before, but not as a twenty-something. More as a sixty-something. He looked into their eyes before quizzing them.

"Have you ever been to Beachy Head, guys?"

"No, I don't think so. Why, is it nice?"

Dean was not surprised with their answer. They hadn't been there yet, but they would in about forty years or so.

"One day you will, and you'll be doing someone a great favour by being there." Dean smiled warmly at them both as if he had a secret he wasn't going to tell.

"If you say so. And what's your name, if you don't mind me asking?"

Albert was still holding Betty's hand tightly and she was gazing at him. They were so in love, and Dean knew that they would be for a very long time.

"It's Dean. Dean Harrison. Pleased to meet you both."

So Dean had already met them both before when he encountered them on Beachy Head, but it was so long ago that it hadn't happened yet. He would shake Albert's hand again, technically for the first time, in forty years or so. He then stood up to kiss Betty on both cheeks.

"Well, I know you are going to have an amazing life together." Dean said this with great authority. He took a moment to visualise them on top of Beachy Head when he'd been at his lowest ebb. He hardly knew them, but he owed them a lot; he would not be here if it hadn't been for them.

"Another drink, Albert, Betty?" Dean did not wait for an answer. It was the least he could do. He got up and headed for the bar mid-way through the offer.

After Dean arrived back at the table armed with another round of drinks on a tray, Albert said, "Thank you, Dean. So, are you married, then? What have we got to look forward to? Any advice?"

Dean thought about Sarah and Jodie and how much he loved and missed them.

"Yes, I'm married to Sarah, and we have a teenage daughter,

Jodie. If you want advice, I would say always appreciate what you have and never stop loving each other, not even for a second. When you think only about yourself, you allow gaps and cracks to appear that break up everything holding you all together."

Dean was welling up inside and his voice was struggling to maintain a steady tone. His emotions were getting the better of him.

"Just live each day like it's the first day you met. Otherwise you'll never know where it all went wrong. Before you know it, you'll be playing catch up and trying to find a way to put things right."

Dean felt like he was getting more out of this advice than Albert and Betty.

"We'll always be in love, won't we, Betty?" They looked into each other's eyes and kissed.

Ding-ding.

"Last orders at the bar," David proudly announced to a more or less empty room.

"One for the road, Albert?" Dean could do with another.

"No, Dean. We have loved your company, but it's getting quite late and we have a big day tomorrow. We are going to tell our parents we've just got married."

"Oh, good luck with that. I'm sure it will be fine."

Dean thought he'd leave too. He now knew what this visit was all about – not funfairs, but self-reflection.

"I think I'll hit the sack too after this one. Next time, maybe. Look after each other, you two." Dean knew they would. "See you around," he added. He meant to say, "See you in forty years or so," but he didn't want to mess with their heads too much.

"Bye, Dean, it was so nice to meet you," Betty said. She smiled and gave him a wave as she and Albert were leaving the bar, hand in hand. Dean smiled and waved back at them. His thoughts more than ever were about Sarah and Jodie and how he was going to get them back. They were so important to him, but he could not see a clear path to reset the world.

He had another gulp of his beer, then he remembered Beachy Head. *How did they know that I would be there?*

"Albert! Betty!" he shouted. "Can you do me a favour?"

Albert and Betty turned and headed back to him.

"Wait there, I need a pen." Dean asked David for a pen

before returning to the table. He took a beer mat and ripped off one side, leaving a white area to write on.

"If you are still together in forty years or so, can you be somewhere for me? I have a feeling there will be someone there who will need your help."

Dean wrote on the beer mat:

Albert & Betty
Beachy Head
11 May 2017 – 8pm
I might need you there.
Dean Harrison, Room 119 x

Albert looked a bit confused as he read the message out loud to Betty. "Beachy Head, the 11th of May, 2017, 8pm. OK, Dean Harrison, if we are still alive, that's a deal." He laughed and gave the beer mat to Betty, who placed it carefully into her handbag.

"See you in forty-three years," she said, giving Dean a kiss before heading out of the bar.

Chapter 18 – The Sound of the Sea

On his way past Reception, Dean could hear the faint sounds of singing. He vaguely recognised the song, a sea shanty, 'Liverpool Lou', which took him back to his childhood. His dad used to sing it with his mates in the pub after fishing.

What now? he thought. As if the last couple of hours hadn't been weird enough, 'Liverpool Lou' in the heart of Suffolk? He was miles from the sea.

He walked over to Mrs McCauley. "What's going on downstairs?" he asked.

"There is a wedding reception, Mr Harrison. I'm sure they won't mind if you pop in if you're after a late drink." She pointed to the stairs with a glint in her eye as if she was not telling him the full story.

"I might just do that, Mrs McCauley. Sure it will be OK?"

Mrs McCauley, busy doing her never-ending paperwork, just nodded.

As Dean headed down the stairs, he could hear the guitars and singing getting louder. He opened the door and was confronted by a large hall with wooden floors and a stage at the far end where most of the singing was emanating from.

He looked around. People were sitting chatting and joining in the celebrations. 'Liverpool Lou' was long gone now, and the fisherman's choir had moved on to a rendition of 'Oh Shenandoah', a slow American folk tune which seemed to have been adopted by fishermen throughout the world. The term 'choir' was probably a bit of an exaggeration for the six people accompanied by an accordion and a couple of guitars, but the sign at their feet proudly proclaimed *The Marske Fisherman's Choir.*

The room felt familiar to Dean, but he couldn't put his finger on why. He headed to the bar, joining in a little bit on the chorus. The bar was quite packed, but he managed to catch David's eye.

"Another Pippin, sir? I thought you had gone to bed."

Dean gave him the thumbs up.

"So did I, David. One for the road, though. I heard the party so thought I'd have a look. Mrs McCauley said it would be OK."

David expertly poured Dean a pint and gave him another slip to sign to his room.

"Have a good night, sir. Do you know anyone here?" David asked.

"No, I don't think so. I've not been here before, David."

"Well, you never know who you might bump into. Thanks, Mr Harrison."

David smiled as if he knew a secret and was dying to tell Dean, but wasn't allowed.

Dean took his drink and sat at the back of the room, trying not to get in the way, doing his best to look inconspicuous. It didn't work. A tall man in a grey suit that was a bit too flarey for the modern day and age sat next to him.

"Hello, are you having a good time?" The man's tie was wider at the bottom than his beer glass.

"Yes, thanks. I've just got here really," Dean replied a bit abruptly. His inconspicuous act obviously needed some work.

'Oh Shenandoah' finished to a polite round of applause. Then the leader of the choir asked for some hush over the microphone.

"Sh, sh, sh, sh," the room obeyed instantly.

"We all know why we are here tonight. So please be upstanding and raise a glass to the newlyweds, Sam and Rosie."

"Sam and Rosie."

Everyone stood and raised their glasses as the happy couple entered from behind the stage. Dean went light-headed and slumped back into his chair. His eyes blurred and he gave his head a shake to try and clear it, watching his dad, Sam, take the microphone from the choir leader.

Sam looked about twenty years old, and Dean's mum, Rosie, even younger. Dean felt like he had been transported into the family album, which seemed to come out every Sunday after dinner, especially when Dean had a new girlfriend. It's said a picture paints a thousand words, and Dean's mum seemed to have a thousand words for every picture to redress the balance. Dean realised that was why he'd recognised this place. It was the backdrop of all the pictures he had endured every Sunday. The room was in black and white then, but it was in full Technicolor right now.

Dean was still in shock, but he managed to get back to his feet as his dad, with his mother on his arm, started addressing the wedding guests.

"On behalf of my wife and I…" Sam paused and accepted the mandatory round of applause. "…I would like to thank everyone for coming and hope you all have a great night. We'll be doing the rounds and hope to speak to you all before the night's over."

He paused again to give his new wife a kiss, which got a spontaneous cheer along with a few northern jibes.

"Put her down, Sam, the ink's not dry on your certificate yet."

Sam kissed Rosie again, just because he could.

"OK, I need a drink. Enjoy the Marske Fisherman's Choir, and please join in. They have done this for free as long as I pick up their bar bill, and the more they sing, the less they'll drink. I need a second mortgage already before I've even got a first one."

Sam gave the mic back to the choir leader and took his wife by the hand and headed off to the bar, followed by an army of well-wishers.

"The next one is 'Grimsby Lads', with Mick on lead. Come on, you all know the chorus."

Wearing the choir's customary knitted blue jumper, Mick shuffled forward from the pack and took the mic, starting the next song full of enthusiasm.

"They sailed in the cold and the grey light of morning…"

They were off again, with everyone joining in for good measure on the chorus.

"So are you on the bride's side or the groom's side?"

Dean had forgotten about his new friend who had been sitting quietly, listening to the speech. He looked at the man and smiled before answering.

"A bit of both really." He looked over to his future mum and dad, who were getting lots of attention at the bar.

"Oh, you know them both. Are you from round here?" The man took off his jacket and got more comfortable.

"It depends what you mean by 'here'," said Dean. Was he in Suffolk or Whitby? His brain had given up on the working stuff out stuff.

"Whitby, of course."

"Well, I used to live here a few years back." Looking at the decor and his mum and dad's age, it was more like a lot of years forward, but his brain wasn't in the mood to work all that out, either.

"What, back in the sixties?"

Was Dean really back in 1974? Of course he was! He was at his mother and father's wedding. He'd seen all the pictures and heard all the stories.

"Sorry, I've not introduced myself. Terrance Hawthorn."

Dean looked at the man – the teacher who had never thought much of him. Or wouldn't in the future.

"Pleased to meet you, sir. My name's Dean."

"No need for 'sir', Terry will do. Do you want a beer, Dean?"

Dean could not remember drinking the beer David had served him, but there was none left in the glass, so he must have sunk it on autopilot. He looked over to the bar, where his mum and dad were talking to guests. Dean didn't fancy a conversation with them just yet, so replied, "Yes, I would love one, Terry. You do not know how much I need one right now."

The choir was on top form, but it was wasted on Dean. He could only stare at his mum and dad. His dad was dead now, and there was so much Dean would have loved to have said to him before the Alzheimer's kicked in. He never went up north to see his mum anymore, except for family weddings or funerals. He couldn't even remember the last time he'd spoken to her on the phone.

When I get out of this mess, I am going to see my mam, he thought. She meant so much to him, but even though he'd needed her more and more over the last couple of years, he'd typically seen her less and less. It was bothering Dean. He had just tried jumping off a cliff and ending it all rather than phoning his mum, who would probably have given him a cup of tea and made everything alright again.

"I got you Crafty Dog Pippin. That's what your glass said. Is that OK, Dean?"

Dean would have drunk sand right now. His mind was doing somersaults.

"Yes, that's great, Terrance." Dean took a couple of large swigs of his beer which reduced it by half.

"It's Terry, Dean. I don't really like Terrance, but I prefer it to sir."

Dean had once thought that if he called Mr Hawthorn anything but sir, he would get a week's detention, but his former (or was it future?) teacher looked so young and normal, Dean thought he would comply.

"OK, Terry. Anyway, are you here for the bride or groom?"

"A bit of both too. Mainly the groom, though. I used to go fishing with Sam; we used to fish off the harbour wall for whiting. We were best mates as kids."

Dean looked over to Sam, his dad.

"He never said he knew you, Terry."

Dean thought about all the times he'd moaned to his dad about Mr Hawthorn giving him a hard time at school. Looking back, he realised his dad would always agree with Mr Hawthorn's point of view. Dean thought they probably went for a beer together to discuss how to sort him out.

"So what do you do, Terry? Let me guess – you've been to university and you're going to be a teacher at the school up the road." If knowledge is power, being in the past when he came from the future certainly gave Dean an advantage.

"Yes, is it that obvious? Was it my accent? Have I lost the northern twang, or was it the suit?"

"No, it's the tie, Terry. You don't go to Oxford University and then get a job back up north unless you became a teacher."

"Oh, very clever. Spot on." Terry raised his glass, which was more or less still full, to Dean. Dean finished his beer in two more gulps.

"One more, Terry?"

Terry nodded, trying to catch up by taking a couple of gulps himself.

Dean couldn't face his mum and dad quite yet; he was still gathering information. On the way to the bar, his mind gave him a quick recap: it was 1974; he was at his parents' wedding; he was talking to a teacher who gave him grief when he was at school. Oh, and he'd just met a couple in the bar and given them a note to tell them to save his life in forty-three years' time.

After being served and returning to his seat, Dean handed Terry his glass.

"Right, Terry, I'd better go and mingle. I'm sure you'll make an amazing teacher, and remember, no matter how much your students get you down, never give up on them. They will always appreciate it in the end. I promise."

Dean clicked his glass against Terry's then surveyed the room for his next move.

Chapter 19 – Singing With The Choir

Dean moved nearer the front of the room, noticing a few aunties and uncles who looked forty years younger. He nodded and smiled at a couple of people he knew without getting the same greetings back. After all, how could they know him? He didn't exist yet.

He moved to a seat nearer the choir, who were about to sing their next song. A growing crowd of enthusiastic wannabe choir members had gathered, and Dean joined them, sitting at the end of the table while his mum and dad led the chorus.

His mother gave him a polite smile. He had not seen her smile like that since he was a kid.

"OK, this next one is 'Liverpool Judies'. It's about a wind that used to blow the sailors back to Liverpool after they'd been trading all round the world, and will be sung by Little Jon. Come on, Little Jon, you're on."

Another blue knitted jumper with a large man inside barged its way to the front and took the mic.

"*From Liverpool to Frisco a rovin' I went, for to stay in that country was my good intent. But girls and strong whiskey like other damn fools, oh I soon got transported back to Liverpool, singing roll, roll, roll…*"

Everyone joined in the chorus, eyes fixated on Little Jon as hardly any of them knew the verses and they were relying on him to get them to the next bit they knew.

Dean looked at his dad, who was one of the few singing every word with gusto.

"Come on, Sam, give me a hand," called Little Jon. Sam joined Jon singing the rest of the song, and everyone who hadn't been joining in now did. It felt like the whole room had got smaller as everyone moved two tables forward en masse. Even Dean sang along with the chorus; he didn't really know this one, but sea shanties are the perfect songs for a drinking session – they always have loads of verses with a chorus at the end of each. Although Dean hadn't known the song when it started, he more or less knew it by the time it finished.

"*And it's row, row bullies, row, them Liverpool Judies have got us innn*

Towwwww."

Little Jon held Sam's hand in the air. "Ladies and gentlemen, Mr Sam Harrison." The crowd, who were already cheering, upped the decibel level with a couple of whistles to boot. Sam took a well-rehearsed bow and clapped back at the crowd, and then turned and applauded the choir.

"OK, that's it for now, folks. We need to double our bar bill for you, Sam. See you all at the bar; we'll be back on in twenty minutes. God bless."

The Marske Fisherman's Choir left the stage and headed off to the bar as one, all wearing navy blue knitted jumpers and most sporting fine beards and carrying song sheets to help them remember the words for the next set.

Dean could see his mum, Rosie, pointing him out to his dad, Sam. They started walking across to him, and Dean took a larger than normal gulp of beer, frantically trying to come up with some kind of back story as to why he was here.

"We saw you singing. You're very good," said Rosie.

"Erm, thank you, Rosie. It is Rosie, isn't it?" Dean was doing his best not to drop the M bomb. He'd called this woman 'Mam' since forever, so Rosie wasn't the most natural thing in the world to say, even though she was over twenty years his junior right now.

"Yes, it's Rosie, and this is my husband, Sam."

"I know," Dean replied immediately. "Pleased to meet you, Sam."

Dean held out his hand; Sam took it in one hand, encased it in the other and squeezed it tight.

"Another drink?"

Dean nodded. "Yes please, Sam, that would be great. It's…"

His dad stopped him.

"Crafty Dog Pippin, it says on your glass."

Sam winked at Dean and headed off to the bar, leaving him alone with his mum.

"So what brings you in here? I don't think Sam or I know you. That's not to say you're not welcome – everyone is welcome where we're from."

Dean loved hearing her voice again and was a bit dazed, just staring at her. He received a gaze back as if to say, "I've asked you a question and it would be polite if you would answer right now."

"Oh sorry, Rosie, I was just passing and I heard the singing. I hope you don't mind."

"Of course not. Like I say, everyone is welcome around here. We never turn anyone away, do we, Sam?"

Sam had returned with two pints, one of which he gave to Dean.

"There you go, son. So, what's your name and what the hell are you doing at our wedding?" The same question Rosie had asked a second ago was now delivered in man speak with all the velvety cushioned edges taken off it.

"Oh, sorry, it's Dean, and I was just telling Rosie I was walking past and heard the singing. I used to live in Whitby and go fishing when I was a kid, and I remember singing some of these songs in the pub with my dad."

"Who's your dad, then? I might know him if he's a fisherman; I've just had a boat built. What's your dad's boat called? Have you got any younger brothers I might know?"

Dean worked through the questions one by one, thinking about the next question while fumbling through the first.

"No brothers, and you won't know my dad. I was born in Whitby, but we moved to Welnetham in Suffolk when I was a kid. But we used to come here on holiday and get someone to take us out fishing all week, so no, he didn't have a boat."

Dean was looking at his mother, who had an uncanny knack of knowing when he was lying. Her lie detector was clearly not turned on, or maybe it wouldn't develop until she'd been lied to a few times by her son. Either way, she seemed to believe his every word.

"How come you have a northern accent, then, Dean? You don't sound like a Suffolk man."

"My mother was from North Yorkshire somewhere, so I guess I kept it up from her." Dean took a big gulp from his glass; his back story was starting to unravel.

"OK. Anyway, you're here now, Dean, and we are glad. What do you do for a living?" asked Rosie, trying to get him off the hook.

"I'm a trader in London for a big trading firm." Dean thought he would resort to the truth for a while. Even though technically he'd lost his job, at least he would be able to cope with an interrogation from his dad.

"So you're a trader from Whitby, who'd have thought? There

you go, Sam – you want a name for your boat. How about *The Whitby Trader*?"

Sam looked at Rosie and then at Dean.

"Do you know what, Rosie, that's better than anything I've come up with, and I have been trying for weeks. We launch her in a week, Dean, if you want a run out?"

Traditionally, women named and launched boats as it was considered unlucky if men did it, and the name Rosie had just suggested was perfect. And on their wedding day, too.

"*The Whitby Trader* it is, then. Well done, Rosie, and thank you, Dean." Sam tapped Dean on the shoulder as he said, "*The Whitby Trader*," out loud as if to test the name.

"*The Whitby Trader*." There were some mumblings of agreement from the rest of the table.

"Can I get you both a drink for your big day?" Dean had resorted to drinking as fast as possible so as to avoid further questions. Sam, who was still testing the new name of his boat, nodded.

"Just an orange juice for me, Dean," Rosie added as Dean headed bar-ward.

"Having a good time, sir?" David asked as Dean ordered the drinks at the bar. "Have you bumped into any old friends?"

Dean put the three drinks into a carrying triangle.

"Yes I have, David, and I think you knew I was going to, didn't you?"

"Just here to serve, sir. Enjoy your night, it might be your last."

David turned and walked away with a tear forming in his eye, which did not go unnoticed. Dean had been having such a good night seeing his mum and dad. He had even enjoyed seeing Terrance Hawthorn, so why did David have to say that? Dean looked at David, who had his head down like a naughty schoolboy who had said too much and dropped his mates in it.

"OK, here we go. One beer for you, Da…" Dean corrected himself instantly, "Sorry, *Sam*, and Rosie, orange juice for you." He handed the drinks over and raised a glass in the way of a small toast. "To Sam and Rosie, I hope everything you wish for in life comes true."

"It has started well, Dean." Rosie held her hand to her tummy.

That's why she is drinking orange juice, Dean thought.

"Rosie, everyone thinks you've had vodka in it all night," Sam said. "I have already sneakily had to replace four drinks bought for you with straight orange juices – the plants near the bar will be pissed. What with that and the choir's bar tab…"

"Once a Yorkshireman, always a Yorkshireman, Sam, you tight arse," Rosie said as she gave her new husband a hug.

"It's called being careful up here, right?" said Dean, and Sam laughed.

Dean looked at his mother's tummy, which she was rubbing with affection.

"Sam, what do you think of Dean?"

"He's OK, love, but a bit old for you."

Rosie gave Sam a tap on his arm.

"No, what about the name, if it's a boy?"

Sam looked at Dean. "Do you like your name, Dean?" he enquired.

"Well, it's never done me any harm. It's better than Kevin or Trevor." Dean tried playing it cool. It didn't work.

"I'll think about it, Rosie, I'll think about it."

As they clinked glasses, a blue mass was heading back to the stage from the bar. The choir quickly got into position, then the leader announced, "We're back, and to kick us off, Mick is going to sing a song about his lovely wife, 'Whip Jamboree'."

"*Whip Jamboree, Whip Jamboree, oh ya pig-tailed sailor hang down behind…*"

Dean knew this one. Before long, he had his dad's arm around his shoulders as Sam recruited others to join in the chorus.

"*Oh Jenny, get your oatcakes done…*"

The song finished and they all held the last note as long as possible.

The night was coming to a close. Sam took the mic – there was enough time left for one more drunken speech, thanking everyone from Aunty Sue who had made and decorated the cake to the cleaners who would have to clean this mess up tomorrow.

"I have one more announcement to make," he said. "My wife has come up with a name for the boat." Everyone looked up expectantly. "She will be called *The Whitby Trader* in honour of Dean, my new best friend. OK, let's have a big round of applause for the Marske Fisherman's Choir, who are now going to play us out with a local favourite, 'Whitby Whaler'."

Everyone cheered as Sam joined his wife on the two seats that had been placed facing the stage for the happy couple.

"Anyone seen Little Jon? It's his song."

"I think he's being ill in the toilets, mate," said a voice from the crowd.

"Anything else you want, Sam? We've lost the lead for that one."

Sam looked at Rosie.

"It's Rosie's favourite, Jim."

Dean walked across the dancefloor and whispered to Jim, the choir leader.

"I know it, guys, if you'll help me out on the chorus."

"What's your name, son?" Jim enquired

"Dean. It's Dean," he replied, frantically trying to remember how the song started.

"Rosie, lucky for you we have a stand in to save the day. Let's have a big cheer for Chris and Bill on the guitars. The room upped the decibel levels as the guitarists took their bows. So to sing us out we have a our newest member Dean…and we're the Marske Fisherman's Choir. Here is 'Whitby Whaler', and let's hear you all join in. Off you go, Dean."

The music started. Dean looked at Rosie and gave her a smile. "This is for the best couple in the world, Sam and Rosie." He cleared his throat and began. Everyone hung on Dean's verses, which he was just about remembering from years gone by, then joined in to sing the chorus.

Could things get any better? Dean was looking at his mum and dad, who were very happy and beginning their life together, and he wanted to thank whoever it was who'd made this possible. Then he thought about Sarah and Jodie, knowing at this moment he was a little baby in his mother's tummy, not even part of this world yet. And he had nearly thrown it all away.

Dean sang the penultimate verse and turned to the choir, who were backing him brilliantly, along with everyone else in the room. Giving the choir a wink, he prepared for the final verse. All he had to do was remember the first line, and the rest would take care of itself.

Giving the choir a last appreciative nod, he turned to face the front again.

Oh my God!

Less than a foot away, staring straight at Dean, was the man with the cane who had pursued him so relentlessly at the fairground. The man took off his fedora; he was bald, and Dean could see the skin on his head doing its best to cover up the bones beneath it. The jagged bones looked like they were starting to win that battle.

The man's eyes were a piercing blue and were on about the same level as Dean's, even though Dean was on the stage. Everyone else in the room was carrying on as normal, the choir coming to the end of the chorus before Dean's big finish for his mum.

"Not now," he said under his breath, looking at his mother and father, who seemed very proud of him right then. "Please, not now."

The chorus ended and the guitar introduced the last verse. The man was still staring at Dean, then he reached into his pocket and took out his battered leather-bound book.

The guitar rolled through the verse and looped back round to give Dean a second chance. Dean looked straight back at the bald figure as if he was glued to the spot. Could nobody else see him?

The man, once again all in black, waved his hand across the book, and the pages transformed to order. Dean Harrison, his date of birth and a calendar of June 2017 appeared on the page, a black mark on Friday 16 June. The man raised his cane above his head. David behind the bar covered his face as the cane was retracted to striking point.

"Mam, Dad," said Dean under his breath as he started to cry. Sam got up from his seat, walking straight through the mysterious figure to climb on stage and stand at Dean's side.

"You're not on your own, son. We're all with you, whenever you need a hand."

The guitar looped around again, and Dean and his dad sang the start of the next verse. Dean joined in slowly at first, and then with more gusto.

If I'm going to die, then singing to my mam with my dad is how I will do it, he thought. *What will be, will be.*

Everyone in the hall belted out the chorus as if their lives depended on it; Dean's life probably did. Rosie joined him and Sam on stage – a couple whom Dean had only met hours ago were standing by him in his hour of need. Then Terry joined them, followed by everyone in the room. The choir did three choruses to milk a good ending, with every guest singing as loudly and tunefully as their vocal chords allowed. The one exception was the uninvited guest in black, his cane, filled with menace, held behind his shoulder. He stood where he had been all along, about a foot from Dean's face, staring at him.

The song came to an end and Sam and Rosie gave Dean a big hug, thanking him for a great night. Then there was a click of the man's bony fingers; the room froze. Everyone was still as if the room had been paused; only Dean and the man continued to move.

Dean blinked a couple of times and felt a shiver work its way through his body. He looked at the man, the poised cane, weighing his options.

This is it, he thought.

All of a sudden, David ran past all the paused figure to get between Dean and the man.

"Please, sir, give him one more chance. Please, sir."

The man looked at David, then at Dean and his parents. He slowly lowered the cane, allowing it to stroke Dean lightly on the face on its way down. He then consulted his book again, shaking his head a couple of times as if he was trying to fit in a doctor's appointment.

He looked up at Dean and David, who were standing side by side. With a bony finger, he slid the black mark from 16 June to the 18th. He put his hat back on his head and tipped it towards Dean before leaving, clicking his fingers as he went to un-pause the room.

"What was that about, David?" David obviously knew more than he was letting on. "Have I been given a second chance?"

David looked at Dean. "I can't tell you, Dean, you have to work things out for yourself. All we can do is guide you."

As David started to walk away, Dean asked, "Who is he, David? What's going on? Please help me."

David turned back and looked at Dean.

"You're safe for today, Dean…"

"Today? But he moved the date to mid-June, so I've got another month. It's only May…"

Dean's voice trailed off at the sad look on David's face.

"It is only May, isn't it, David?"

"I can't tell you, Dean, but I can tell you, he's not made his mind up on you yet. I've only seen that look on his face once before, and he usually decides one way or the other. You're testing him, that's for sure."

"But what…"

"I've said enough. If I say much more, you don't stand a chance. There is only one person who can prove to him what he wants. Good luck, Dean."

As David left for the bar, Dean said goodbye to all the guests then looked at his mother.

"I had a great night, thank you, Rosie." He gave her a hug and kissed the top of her head.

"Thank you for coming in. We've loved it too, haven't we?" Rosie reached out for Sam, who was saying goodbye to the final guests on their way out.

"Yes, and thanks for the last song, Dean, even though you needed some help." Sam gave him a playful punch on the arm.

"You don't know how much you helped, Sam." Dean said this like he meant it. He *did* mean it. If his dad had not come to help him, he was sure that he would not be here right now.

"No problem, Deano. Do you know what, Rosie? If it's a boy, he can be called Dean if I'm allowed to call him Deano. Deal?"

"Deal," Rosie said as she rubbed her tummy again.

"Well, lovely to have met you both, and have a great life together with little Dean – if it's a boy. And don't be too hard on him, especially if he breaks the glass ship on the mantelpiece when he's a kid or wants to move to London and chase his dreams. Never stop someone chasing their dreams."

"OK, Dean. Glass ship on the mantelpiece."

Dean just smiled at his mother's face, which was looking quite bewildered, and gave her a loving look that can only come from a son. Then Dean's smile broke out into a laugh. He knew he would still get in trouble when the ship got smashed, but maybe he'd only get grounded for a week instead of two.

"Take care, Dean. Will we see you again?" asked Rosie.

"I can guarantee it, Rosie."

Dean started to leave the room, turning at the door to get a last look at his mum and dad, who were standing arm in arm, waving at him. Then he opened the door and was again in the hotel. He turned and looked at the room behind him out of curiosity – it was nothing but a storage cupboard full of stationery.

Dean headed upstairs to Room 119 to get some well-earned sleep.

Chapter 20 – Don't Be Scared Of Clowns, Jodie

Jodie could hear a shuffling noise in her room. She squinted her eyes and looked up at the alarm clock.

"Mum, it's only three o'clock in the morning."

There was no answer. Jodie turned and saw a plump figure looking at the chess pieces on the board.

"Oh my God, who are you?" Jodie pulled the covers up to her chest as if they were armour that would protect her.

"So you've given up on your dad, I see."

She recognised the voice and turned on the lamp.

"It's you, isn't it?"

"If you mean the *Nasty Clown*, Jodie, then yes. I don't think I'm that nasty, do you?" The clown was wearing a black and white harlequin outfit with chess pieces on the squares. There was no colour on his face today – he was going for the 'neutral clown' look, all black and white with three black teardrops of decreasing size under his right eye.

"No, I guess you're not. And no, I haven't given up on my dad. I never will. And you *were* quite nasty last time."

Jodie released her grasp on her protective covers. The clown hadn't actually been that nasty last time; he'd just said some nasty things, like the fact her dad was going to leave. Which was more the truth than nastiness, as it turned out.

"You have reset the board. It looks like you have given up to me," the clown said, gesturing at the chess pieces with an opening palm.

"I just thought my dad needed a break. I'm sick of seeing him get beaten." Jodie sat up in her bed. "Anyway, it's impossible for the whites to win, even the computer says so. I've tried everything."

Jodie got out of bed and walked over to the chessboard.

"I though the computer said there was 0.01% of a chance. That's not impossible, Jodie, that's just nearly impossible."

How can the clown know what the chances were? Jodie thought. She then remembered she was in a dream. Anything is possible in a dream.

"Well, I've been trying with Kyle, and it's impossible as far as we are concerned." Jodie followed this up with a knowing nod like her dad would do, an additional full stop to an already powerful statement.

"Oh, so you *have* given up then. What was it your dad said again?" The clown left an intentional pause. "Oh, that was it: *'There is always a way, Jodie. When someone has got nowhere to run, it's better to go down fighting, no matter how futile the fight'*. Is that going down fighting, Jodie? Your dad needs you right now – you know this, don't you?"

Jodie nodded her head. She did know that her dad winning this game was important; she just didn't know why. But deep inside her, she felt like her dad's life depended on it, and she would do everything she could to fix it.

"But I've tried my hardest. I've tried everything." Jodie looked at the clown, tears filling her eyes. "Can you help me? I don't know what to do."

"I can't help you, Jodie, I can only guide you and your dad. However, I can remind you of what Kyle said."

"Yes, anything. I know there is a way, I just can't see it. What did he say? I can't remember him saying anything that would help."

"It's not what he said, Jodie, it's what he meant." He gave her a comforting tilt of his head as if to try and prove he was on her dad's side. "White gets beaten time after time. They're under too much pressure from the beginning."

"How does that help?"

The clown looked at the pieces on the board and more or less blanked her. Jodie knew she was on her own; she had to work this one out for herself.

"White gets beaten time after time," Jodie said under her breath. "They're under too much pressure." She looked up at the ceiling, thinking, then said it again, looking for inspiration. "Time after time. Time and pressure."

Jodie looked at the clown, who gave her a wry smile. He could see the penny dropping in front of his eyes.

"Time and pressure, that's it! Black will always win as they have time to think and all the key pieces. We have to bring in another element to the game. I've got to put them on the clock, haven't I?"

She looked at the clown again to make sure she was heading in the right direction.

"And what will that create, Jodie?" The clown was teasing the last piece out of her like Columbo about to unmask a murderer.

"Pressure!" They said this together.

"Thank you so much." Jodie gave the clown a hug, and he hugged her back.

"Good luck, Jodie, your dad is depending on you. Should I reset the board for tomorrow?"

They both looked at the board. In Jodie's head, the white pieces already looked more aggressive and up for the fight.

"Yes please," she said. "What's your name?"

"Benjie, Jodie, I am Benjie the clown. Pleased to meet you." Benjie gave an extravagant Shakespearian bow, flourishing a pretend hat as he did so. Then he waved his hand across the top of the board and the pieces reset to their positions, ready to resume their battle tomorrow.

"Night, Jodie, good luck." The clown waved his hand in front of Jodie's face and she slowly closed her eyes. The alarm clock still said 3am.

In the morning, Sarah let Jodie have a sleep in. She was normally up by now, but it was a Saturday and Sarah thought she could do with a break. She had been thinking about her dad and his chess game too much and not sleeping.

When Sarah eventually opened the curtains in Jodie's room and the light crept across the floor, Jodie opened her eyes and squinted.

"What time is it, Mum?"

"Eleven o'clock, Jodie. You never sleep in this long, and I thought you were going to give the chess thing a rest," her mother said, looking over to the reset chessboard.

"Oh, that wasn't me."

"Jodie, remember this is a new start. We have to be strong, and lying is not a good start." Sarah plumped a couple of cushions on Jodie's sofa bed. They didn't need plumping, but they always got a plump anyway every time Sarah was in the vicinity.

"But, Mum, it was the clown. It really wasn't me. I…"

Sarah stopped her in her tracks.

"I don't want to hear it, Jodie! Clowns, for God's sake. It's a new start and we've got to be honest with each other, remember?"

Jodie thought about the clown then looked at her mum, realising that Sarah was not ready for the truth right now, regardless of whether it were true or not. She then looked at the board, all set up to continue her game with her dad.

"You're right, Mum. I was going to have one more go before I went to bed last night, but I'll leave it for now."

But Jodie wouldn't leave it; she knew her dad was depending on her. She also knew that she needed an opponent. Then she remembered what the clown had said last night.

"*Time and pressure.*"

She had to put Kyle on the clock; put Kyle under pressure.

Chapter 21 – Don't Pay the Ferryman

Dean woke up in Room 119 of Welnetham Hall, his head a little delicate. It wasn't every day he got to have a drink with his parents before he had even been born, so going to bed early the previous night had not been an option. His mind was frantically trying to put all the pieces of the last two weeks together, but it was like doing a jigsaw with no picture on the box. Dean more or less had all the sides done, but he didn't know where to start with the middle.

It was a sunny summer's day, so after a shower and a shave, he got ready to go out for a walk. He gave Mrs McCauley a smile as he went past reception. She was the only receptionist he had seen, so she must work every hour of the day.

He left the hotel and took a right turn out of the gates. He'd not been this way yet, so he thought he would have an explore and see where he ended up. He might find a town or village to get a bite to eat as he'd missed breakfast at the hotel.

It was a good day for thinking, and Dean was thinking it was going to be a good day. Well at least he was still here. He had visions of the tall man in black with his silver-topped cane raised above his head, ready to strike Dean. He also thought how the man with the cane had looked confused. The man's mood had changed just before he consulted his old book, resetting whatever was inside it, then tilting his hat to Dean and walking out. Dean's thoughts rattled around his head, bouncing off each other one after the other, none of them confirming or denying anything. Nothing and at the same time everything seemed connected, but the angular pieces were still refusing to form into a picture.

Dean ambled along, not really paying attention to anything but his thoughts, until his concentration was broken by the sound of a river flowing ahead. The air was getting colder as a damp mist started to form, pushed towards him by the flowing water. He could feel wetness on his brow and his arms. It felt similar to a fret rolling in from the North Sea in Whitby Harbour, but different too. He was nowhere near the sea, and this mist felt warmer and more welcoming. Dean was drawn to it.

He went over a stile in a wooden fence and made his way into a wooded area which ran along the riverbank. The sound of the water got louder and the mist seemed to get thicker and hotter, as if the river itself was giving off steam like a hot spring. He could see the riverbank through the trees, and the path he was following was more of a downtrodden track in the undergrowth.

It was darker now, although it must have only been 1pm at the latest. The mist had dampened out most of the light and there was a dusk-like feeling to the surroundings. Dean could hear a dog barking and snarling ahead, but he kept walking.

In an opening in the trees ahead, an old lady was attempting to restrain her dog, put him back on the lead and keep him quiet. She gave him a treat out of a belt bag she had around her waist which seemed to do the trick, but although the dog was now silent, he still looked disturbed by something across the river.

"Is he OK? He seems a bit angry."

The old lady looked at Dean.

"What are you doing down here? You shouldn't have come down here!"

"I thought I'd come for a walk. It was a nice day, and…"

"Dean, we can only guide you and try to point you in the right direction. The more you know and the deeper you get, the harder it will be to get you back."

Dean looked at her; she had tears forming in her eyes. Dean did not even know her, so why was she so bothered about him? He thought better of saying, "How the fuck do you know I'm called Dean?" Far too much weird stuff had passed under the bridge now for him to pick up on small details like that.

Instead, he settled on, "What do you mean, guide me?" while trying to sneak a peek through the gap in the trees. The dog was still looking agitated and uncomfortable; Dean got the impression that he was only keeping quiet out of loyalty to the old lady. If he had been on his own, he would be going berserk.

"You don't need to see this, Dean. If you know too much, he won't allow you to go back."

Dean had had enough of being told what to do. There were too many missing pieces in his jigsaw; if he could get a few more pieces in the middle and attach them to the border, the whole thing might click into place. He respectfully moved the lady to one side and looked through the gap in the trees.

The tall man was on the other side of the river, his silver-topped stick sparkling in what little light it could find to sparkle in, and there was a group of about twenty people with him. Men and women, all the men dressed in black suits and the ladies in black dresses, stood in a line. None of them were talking; their eyes were trained on the river upstream.

The silver-topped cane man glanced over to Dean's side of the river and looked surprised to see Dean there. He opened his book and had a quick look, as if checking his diary for an appointment he had pencilled in for later. Then he closed his book and placed it back into his pocket. He was no longer wearing his customary hat; he had more of a black cloak with a hood on. He nodded at Dean in acknowledgement.

"Who are they?" Dean looked at the old lady, who was bribing her dog with another keep-quiet biscuit. She had a resigned look on her face.

"I told you, Dean, there will be no way back now he knows what you've seen. It will make things harder for you."

"Won't let me back where?" Dean enquired. The lady ignored the question.

"Dean, all the pieces are there for you. We have chosen you because we believe in you, and we don't get to choose many. You are one of the lucky ones who earn the right for a second chance, but you're in too deep now you've seen this much. I think you may now be beyond our guidance."

The lady turned and started to walk away, but the dog forced her back by looking upstream and growling. There was the sound of oars disturbing the water as if a team of rowers were speeding through it. This was not a team, though; it was one set of oars slicing and thumping through the river, creating a powerful bow wave before another rhythmic plunging carried through the dense fog.

The lady looked over to the group on the far side of the river. The people in black lined up as the ferry became visible through the fog. It was a long boat with a flattened space in the middle to carry twenty or thirty people at a time. A large muscular man with long blond hair dressed in a red toga was at the back, powering the boat forward, punching the oar into the river and pulling it through before effortlessly dismissing the water. The bow lifted out of the water with each row, then crashed down again, creating waves either side of the keel.

As the boat got nearer to the far bank, the people in the line walked past the cloaked man, who had put down his silver cane. Each presented a coin to him as he brought their heads into his chest and hugged them, lightly tilting their heads backward, putting his hand onto their jaws and opening up their mouths. Inside each mouth, he placed the coin on their tongues as payment for the journey they were embarking upon, gesturing for them to wait for the ferry which was nearing the jetty.

"What's going on?" Dean whispered to the old lady. Her dog had stopped barking; he had lost all of his courage and was letting out a frightened whimper, moving behind his owner's legs for cover.

The Ferryman made a final adjusting oar stroke on the port side of the ferry. The boat turned back upstream to order and settled broadside of the riverbank, adjacent to the jetty.

"Not now, Dean, keep quiet. If you think the man you have already met is scary, I promise you don't want to meet the guy on the boat anytime soon. Even your friend over there is wary of him."

Dean looked on; he thought being quiet was probably a good idea right now. The air felt like it could be cut with a knife. There was a smell of nothingness and emptiness, as if evil was all around. Everyone was respectfully still and silent.

The Ferryman looked over to Dean and the old lady. She bowed.

"Dean, get down now! Bow!"

Dean bowed as commanded. He lifted his head slightly to see the Ferryman's piercing blue eyes aimed straight at him.

Everyone in the queue was also bowing. They had their payment in their mouths ready for the Ferryman and were waiting to be beckoned forward onto the boat.

The Ferryman pointed to Dean and spoke in an ancient language that Dean had never heard before. He was talking to the cloaked man, who had now picked up his customary silver cane. He took his book out of his cloak and seemed to be bargaining with the Ferryman in a tongue that was as old as the planet itself. The words had edges to them and echoed with great power; the ground shook and the river rippled as the words were exchanged between them.

Dean felt cold as the Ferryman looked over to him. The Ferryman's blue eyes gazed deep into his soul; he wasn't looking at Dean, he was looking inside him, and Dean knew it. He could feel his brain burning. His heart was thumping as if to escape from his numb body.

The Ferryman raised his open hand at Dean and slowly closed it into a fist. Dean could feel his neck getting tighter and tighter as the Ferryman's hand closed in. He was on all fours, struggling for air, contorting his head upwards to try and find some much needed oxygen.

The silver cane was lightly brought down onto the Ferryman's arm as if to remind him of the rules and who did what job around here. The Ferryman looked at the silver cane and lowered it before staring over at Dean. There was a seat for Dean on his boat, but maybe not today. Dean felt as if he had just wriggled off the hook like fish sometimes did when he used to go fishing with his dad.

The Ferryman made a parting comment which shook the ground more than anything that had been said before. He then kicked the wooden walkway which extended from the centre of the boat to the jetty for the waiting people to get on board.

Dean was lying on the ground, panting and trying to catch his breath. The old lady had stood up and was watching the people walking onto the ferry like robots, one after the other, taking their seats until the boat was full.

Dean managed to stand up next to her.

"You're right, I wish I hadn't seen that. Who is he?"

With one powerful stroke of the oar, the Ferryman started back upstream, disappearing into the mist with the passengers looking straight ahead, not talking. Far from looking scared, they seemed content with the fate that had been bestowed upon them.

"He is Charon, the Ferryman. For your sake, I hope you won't see him for a while. But that's up to you, Dean. You need to find your own way." She paused. "If you do see him soon, you'll need this." The old lady held out an ancient coin with a gargoyle on one side.

"What is it?" Dean asked, taking the coin into the palm of his hand.

"It's a danake."

Dean looked at the coin, turning it over to show an anchor on the other side.

"A danake? Am I going on that boat?" The old lady looked away. "Am I?" he asked again.

"Dean, we have all been trying to guide you, but at some point you have to help yourself." She turned, pulling the lead of her dog. "Come on, Oscar."

"Thank you. I mean it, thank you. I didn't even get your name."

"Molly. I'm called Molly. How much do you want to change, Dean? If you do, you'd better start proving it. There are lots of people who love you, but you have to give him a sign that you love them back. Otherwise what's the point? I fear you've seen far too much. Nobody has ever seen this much and been allowed back."

"Back to where?" Dean asked again.

"Keep the coin safe, Dean, you may need it very soon. God be with you." Molly put her hand on his arm as she moved past him before disappearing into the woods.

The fog lifted as quickly as it had descended in the first place, and the river looked tranquil and calm as if nature was pretending the last hour had not happened. Unfortunately for Dean, it had.

Chapter 22 – Time and Pressure

Jodie was tucking into her late breakfast. Her mum was sitting opposite, looking over the top of her skinny latte and trying not to think too much. They had more or less agreed last night that today would be a day off from thinking and sulking. Today was about healing and moving on together.

"Mum, I'm going out for a ride on my bike."

Sarah looked at her daughter and laughed.

"Your bike? Do you even know where your bike is?" Jodie had hardly ridden her bike since she got it last Christmas.

"Yes, of course I do. I might go for a ride with Kyle." Jodie looked down at her food, not wanting to engage in a conversation about the whys and wherefores of her sudden interest in cycling.

"You really like Kyle, don't you, Jodie?" Sarah smiled a 'my daughter is growing up' smile.

"Mum, he's just a mate!" Jodie looked up from her food and gave Sarah a full on stare of the 'whatever' variety. Sarah saw this and backed off.

"Enjoy your bike ride then, Jodie, but I need you back here for four o'clock."

"OK, Mum, I will be."

Jodie finished her breakfast and ran upstairs to her room. She texted Kyle, *I'll be at yours in an hour. BE IN* with an emoji pointing at the reader, indicating the *BE IN* part of the sentence was an order, not a request. She then put on some black cycling shorts and a Castelli top with its trademark scorpion which had hardly seen the light of day, grabbed a rucksack from the wardrobe, and looked into a storage container under the bed.

"It's here somewhere," she said as she rummaged around the boxes inside the storage container. In the third box, she found a chess clock with a rocking paddle on either side for the players to stop their clock and start their opponent's. Jodie tried to turn it on, but the batteries were dead.

"Batteries, batteries," she muttered. Surveying the room for likely candidates, she spied the clock on the wall, took it down and pilfered the batteries from the back, leaving the clock on her bed.

"Bingo!" she said as she put them in the chess clock and it lit up.

If getting ready was an Olympic event, Jodie would be a gold medal contender. As she whizzed past her mother in the kitchen and straight into the adjoining garage, Sarah shouted, "If your dad was here, he'd be saying, 'All the gear and no idea', Jodie. When was the last time you rode that bike?"

Jodie popped her head back into the kitchen with all the attitude of a stroppy teenager.

"Well, he's not here, is he?" she said, giving her mum a silent stare that spoke volumes.

Jodie's bike was behind her dad's. They used to go cycling together when she first got her bike, but not so much anymore. She took a deep breath before moving her dad's bike to one side with great care to reveal her racer. It was not a normal girl's bike; it was a ladies' Cannondale SuperSix EVO Carbon all in black, thanks to Dean's failed attempt to push his daughter into becoming a keen cyclist. Jodie needed it today as Kyle lived about five miles away.

Her phone buzzed in the pocket in the back of her cycling top. The text read, *OK, Miss Pushy Pants, I'll be in, x LOL.* His emoji of choice was of a cross-armed gangster with shades on. Jodie smiled.

She put on her cycling cleats and put her trainers into her rucksack before going inside to see her mother, her feet clicking on the kitchen tiles, walking like she was on ice skates.

"Love you, Mum. Off to Kyle's. I'll be back before four, promise."

Her mother looked her up and down. "OK, Jodie, love you too."

Jodie put the rucksack on her back and fastened her helmet before pressing the button to open the garage door. Once the door was up enough to allow her through, she set off. Within two strokes, she'd hooked her cleats into the pedals and shot away. She was on a mission and it showed.

Jodie got to the bottom of Kyle's road, rode up to his door out of breath and rang the bell. He opened the door and laughed as he let her and her bike in.

"What on earth are you wearing, Jodie?"

"Back off, Kyle. I told my mum that I was going out for a bike ride with you, so I had to make an effort to convince her. She's sick of the chess thing." Jodie placed her bike against the hallway wall.

"I'm sick of this chess thing, too. I know it's for your dad, but we've tried everything and failed. What more can we do?" Kyle took Jodie's helmet from her and put it in the cloakroom.

"You wouldn't believe me if I told you, Kyle," she said, peeling off her cycling gloves.

"Try me! I'm all ears."

Jodie looked at him once before kneeling down to tear off the Velcro strap on her cycling shoes. As she stood back up, she gave him a second look before kicking off both of her shoes. *Here goes nothing*, she thought.

"I had a dream last night. And in the dream, someone told me how whites can win. It was actually something you said to me."

Kyle took Jodie's shoes and placed them in the cloakroom with the helmet.

"How, Jodie? We know it's not possible, we've tried. A dream isn't going to help. I think you have issues." He gave her a big smile, then continued, having got no response to the 'you have issues' comment. "OK, so let's recap. You were told in a dream – let's pretend for one second that is true. What's your masterplan? And what was it I said? And who told you in your dream?" Kyle looked at her, cutting her some slack. "I'm still all ears." The smile that followed this was award-winning.

Jodie took a deep breath. She was going to need it to answer all three questions that Kyle had just lined up for her.

"One, I can't really tell you my masterplan, I've got to show you. Two, if it works, I'll tell you who told me, and three, I'll tell you what you said after I've beaten you."

She took his award-winning smile and raised it. This smile did not require a response; they both knew she'd won the persuasive smiling competition.

"OK, you have got me intrigued, Jodie. Let's see what you've got, then." Kyle headed into the kitchen and Jodie followed. His chessboard was ready, the pieces set up in the position where Jodie and her dad had left the game.

"Kyle, how did you remember the positions?" Jodie eyed up

the board and then him.

"I took a picture last time I was round your house." He felt proud of himself as he showed Jodie the picture on his phone. "It's not just you who this has been bothering, Jodie. I've been trying all week to get you an answer."

He looked down, a little embarrassed. She tilted her head to the side as she looked at him.

"That's so sweet, Kyle."

"Sweet?" He raised his tone, trying to regain a foothold in the conversation which was getting a bit too lovey-dovey for his liking. "It's only because I like chess, Jodie. Sweet!" The last sweet was accompanied by a shake of the head.

"Chivalrous, then. Or…"

Kyle cut her off with a 'quit while you're ahead' raise of his eyebrows accompanied by a point of his finger. Besides, he knew it was sweet. He liked Jodie a lot, but didn't want to say it out loud because then she'd know and he would turn into a gibbering wreck.

"Right, who's who, then?" he said as the pause in the conversation was getting too long and he couldn't hold his 'quit while you're ahead' eyebrows forever.

"You're me, and I'm my dad. Oh wait, there's something I forgot."

Jodie ran into the hallway and got her rucksack, taking out the chess timer.

"How many moves does it normally take you to win?"

"Erm, I'd say about twenty-five to thirty, maybe forty if white gets ultra-defensive." Kyle was guessing, but as he'd been trying for a week or so now, he was not far off.

"I agree. Let's say thirty moves each, then, and ten seconds a move. That's five minutes each on the timer."

Jodie was good at maths; Kyle had not even started to work it out by the time the chess clock was set.

"Black and white at five minutes each, a ten-minute game. If your time runs out, you lose. Blitz chess rules, OK?"

She had her serious head on. She could hear the clown repeating the words over and over in her head.

"Time and pressure. It's all about time and pressure."

"Ten seconds a move? Jodie, are you sure? That's not long, especially in the pickle you're in." Kyle laughed, wondering how he'd been talked into this. If this was Jodie's masterplan, her dream must have been a nightmare.

"You're right, Kyle, what was I thinking? Let's go with five seconds a move, two minutes and thirty seconds each, five-minute game. Don't let your timer run out."

"OK, good luck. You're going to need it, Jodie."

They sat down either side of the chessboard and stared at each other, their hands hovering over their timers ready for the first move to trigger the frenzy that was about to ensue.

"Whose go is it again?" Kyle knew it was his turn. The question was more of a defence mechanism; an attempt to lighten the mood, which had got very edgy. This game felt like it meant more than all the other games they had attempted put together. Kyle's palms were sweating.

Jodie wasn't going to give him a way out. The clown was speaking in her head again.

"*He's under pressure already. Don't let him off the hook.*"

Her eyes were glued to the chessboard. She was like a cobra coiled in a basket, ready to strike.

Kyle had not seen Jodie like this before. It was like she was in a trance; nothing mattered other than this game. This made Kyle sweat even more, but it was his go and this was going to be a mad five minutes. He must play it correctly for Jodie's sake. There were to be no favours; he must play to win, and if he did win, so be it. But that was the thing – the word 'if'. Every other game he'd known he would win. That 'if' was planting doubt in his mind even before they had started.

"OK, here we go, Jodie." Kyle made his first move and immediately plunged the timing paddle to Jodie's side. The digital display showed two minutes thirty seconds; her timer had started recording history. Jodie responded with only two seconds lost; Kyle did likewise.

It was frantic, an adrenaline pumping game of fight or flight, not like a normal chess game. No studying, no strategies; they were enemies playing on the edge. Playing by instinct.

But Jodie had a masterplan and was calmly putting it into action. She was making big sacrifices – rooks and knights were being offered up as lambs. Kyle was winning; he could taste blood. His attacking became more and more erratic, and he was accepting the gifts that Jodie appeared to be bestowing upon him. Why wouldn't he? He had no time to ask her why she was throwing the game; they were on the clock, the paddle was bouncing from player to player, and the time was evaporating with each turn.

His chess pieces were circling around Jodie's like a school of hungry sharks that were taking turns to go in for the kill, Distracted by this, Kyle didn't notice that one solitary white pawn was making its way up the board, trying to be as inconspicuous as possible. Jodie's masterplan was working. Kyle could have taken the pawn numerous times, but he was on the main course now. He had no time for starters and hors d'oeuvres.

Jodie was ahead on the clock. She was taking no time at all over her moves, setting trap after trap as her own pieces fell down, and fall down they did. She had a knight, a bishop and a rook of her main pieces left; her queen had just fallen, slain by Kyle's rook. Jodie could have saved her queen a little longer, but instead she managed to get her pawn one more step up the board, and it was the queen that made this possible. She was in on the plan. She died with dignity, trying not to look up at the pawn and give the game away.

Ahead, the lone pawn could now see the opposing king. The black king, with all the excitement ahead of him, was looking exposed. All of his loyal protectors had been drawn into the feeding frenzy at the opposite end of the board.

Kyle's timer was down to seventeen seconds and Jodie still had twenty-three to play with. Jodie knew Kyle's next choice was pivotal; the game could now go either way. The black knight had a choice of placing Jodie's king into check, which would more or less be game over, or making sure by diving into the corner and taking the white rook to humiliate the white kingdom and win in style. Jodie was hoping for the latter as she moved her pawn one more step forward – one away from a confrontation with the black king. Kyle was running out of time and this brought pressure on him to end the game. He knew that taking the rook in the corner would make the white king easier to pin down. He did not care about the pawn's crusade against his king; he opted to take the rook and pressed the paddle down with his timer on twelve seconds. This left him three moves from victory.

Jodie moved her bishop through the gap left by the knight to the right-hand side of the board, a move that looked like a desperate attempt to save him from impending doom. It was as if the bishop was deserting his white king in his hour of need. Kyle, with twelve seconds on the clock and two moves from victory, knew the pressure was off. He looked at Jodie. She had so nearly done it. He took the first move and pressed the timer with five seconds left to play. One move from victory.

Jodie smiled back at Kyle. Ten…nine…eight – her timer seemed to be in slow motion.

"There is always a way, Kyle. When someone has got nowhere to run, it's better to go down fighting, no matter how futile the fight."

She moved her pawn slowly forward so it was diagonally opposite the king. The pawn looked dwarfed by the black king, and the king looked down as though a little kid was tugging at his coat tails. But the pawn was being protected on the diagonal by the apparently fleeing white bishop.

Five…four…

"Time and pressure, Kyle. Check…"

Three…two…

"…Mate." She pressed the plunger with one remaining second proudly displaying.

They both leant back from the board as if they had done twelve rounds in a boxing ring. Kyle looked over to her.

"Jodie, what the hell has just happened? You are a genius."

Jodie cast a gaze back in his direction, catching her breath. It felt like she had not taken a breath the whole game.

"I thought I was winning by a mile. I could pick and choose when I wanted to win, and of all things to get done by a bloody pawn."

"You took your eye off the ball, Kyle. You were enjoying the battle and not thinking about the war." If Sarah had been there, she would have said that Jodie sounded just like her dad. It was as good as any Deanism she had ever heard.

"So who gave you that tactic? You didn't think that up all on your own."

Jodie smiled.

"You wouldn't believe me if I told you, Kyle."

"A promise is a promise. You said…"

She stopped him in his tracks.

"You really want to know?"

Kyle looked at her like a puppy dog who was about to get a treat, with his head slightly to one side and forehead furrowed.

"OK, turn off the charm, I'll tell you. A clown visited me in my dream and said it was all about time and pressure."

Jodie looked at Kyle, expecting a snide remark about her being a loony or something.

"A clown? Next time you see him, congratulate him on some great advice." Kyle started to reset the chessboard.

"OK, I will. Thanks, Kyle, I really do owe you. If you ever need me, I'll be there."

Jodie got home and put her bike in the garage. "I'm back, Mum," she announced as she walked in through the kitchen.

Her head in her hands, Sarah was sitting at the kitchen table, sobbing her heart out.

"Mum! What is it? What's the matter?"

"Oh, Jodie, it's your dad." Sarah lifted a tear-streaked face and looked at her daughter. "He's had an accident. Uncle Jack has just phoned – your dad's in intensive care…"

Chapter 23 – Dying To Get Home

Dean was in his room. He'd given up on making sense of it all and was finishing packing his case ready for the short walk to the train station. Another weird weekend in Room 119 – would it be his last? Nothing would surprise Dean now; he had to be ready for anything.

He closed his case and walked out, having another quick look into the room before closing the door and making his way to reception to hand in his key.

"Bye, Mrs McCauley, have a nice week."

She looked over her glasses at him.

"Not planning on returning, sir? That 'bye' seemed very definite."

Dean had a feeling that the decision to return might be out of his hands. He remembered Molly saying that he had seen too much and that nobody who had seen that much had ever been allowed back. He didn't know where 'back' was, but he had a feeling it wasn't back to Welnetham Hall. He wasn't scared, more relieved that things were getting a little clearer and coming to a conclusion. He'd had enough cloak and dagger and just wanted to front up to whatever stood in his way.

"Yes, it may be bye for good, Mrs McCauley. I've got a feeling that wherever I am going next, back here may not be written in my stars, as lovely as it is."

She took his key and placed it back into the hidden cupboard, which didn't seem to be hiding as well as it used to, probably because he knew it was there.

"Did you enjoy the wedding on Friday night, Dean? Did you meet a few old friends?" She looked over her glasses again, knowing this would strike a chord with Dean.

"Yes, Mrs McCauley, but you knew that already, didn't you."

"We are here to guide you, Dean, but you're not making it easy. How much do you value your life, and how much are you willing to do about putting it right? How much do you care for Sarah, Jodie, and more importantly, yourself? You hit rock bottom,

Dean, but we believe in you. But do you believe in yourself anymore? Well…"

She left the sentence hanging, allowing it to drift into Dean's subconscious before marking his leaving time and closing the hotel register.

"Good day, Dean. I really hope I do see you again. You've come this far, so why get off now?"

Dean had questions queuing up in his mind. Get off what?

"I would love nothing more than to see Sarah and Jodie. They are my world. I would do anything for them." He meant this. "I have been an idiot the last couple of years, taking everything for granted, looking after myself, not really acknowledging anyone in my circle, even the ones closest to me. If they still care about me, I'd be amazed, but I am going to keep trying, Mrs McCauley, I promise you that." He looked into the centre of her eyes, letting his guard down and showing emotions that had been building up for weeks.

"I'm glad to hear it, and quite frankly, it's about time. I hope it's not too late for you, Dean. Take care."

Mrs McCauley disappeared behind her curtain, leaving Dean with his thoughts. Not mixed-up jigsaw puzzle thoughts, just thoughts about Jodie and Sarah. When did it all go wrong? When did he become a self-centred prick?

A tear rolled down Dean's face. He was going to get back and put things right. Enough holidays in Welnetham Weirdo Hall; back to the real world. Was that what Molly had meant by getting back? Back to looking after those who meant the world to him? Life was not all about Dean; it was about the people around him.

Dean stepped outside to walk to the station. The rain was just starting, and again the sky seemed to be darker than it should be – it was only 5.30pm. Dean did not do umbrellas; he would rather get wet than suffer the indignity of carrying one. He got his wish; he was getting wet.

The wind was driving the rain into his face, and he was doing his best to shelter from it. Then out of nowhere he heard a familiar sound – click, click, click. He turned round to see the tall man in black wearing his fedora, marching on with purpose, the silver cane rhythmically beating out its tune on the pavement about fifty metres behind him. Dean sped up. *Not again*, he thought. He had realised the error of his ways and had a clear picture of how to fix things. It was all worked out in his mind – he knew where 'back' was, and he was heading in the right direction. This was the last thing he needed.

"Give me a break," he whispered. He didn't want to join the others on the ferry; he didn't want to spend the coin Molly had given to him. He sped up some more, the latest speeding up turning into a light jog.

Dean could see the train station ahead. Although he was running, he didn't seem to be getting any further away from his pursuer. He knew from the encounter at the fairground that the man had the ability not to lose ground without any effort; he seemed to be able to catch Dean up at will while maintaining his regular gait.

The train was already in the station. Dean could see the station clock, and there were still fifteen minutes before the train left. Just then, the clock's minute hand started speeding up; it was behaving like a second hand. Dean turned to look at the man, who had stopped, his bony finger extended, pointing at the clock.

He wanted Dean to miss the train.

Dean ran up the stairs of the station. The clock was not his friend right now; the fifteen minutes had turned into two, and they weren't in the mood for slowing down. As he ran into the station, he turned. The cane was clicking again and the man was closer than ever, reaching the stairs Dean had just negotiated.

Dean elected not to get into the first carriage as the man would catch him there. He saw the guard in the doorway of the last carriage, beckoning him to go that way. Dean was running awkwardly, his bag weighing him down on one side. The platform clock was under the same spell as the one outside the station, the minute hand visibly moving between 5.59 and 6pm.

The guard looked at the clock and shrugged. He blew a loud shriek on his whistle – rules are rules. But these did not seem like station rules; these were the rules of life and death.

Dean threw his case onto the platform as it was slowing him down too much. It burst open, his clothes going everywhere. He was close to the door now; he sprinted with all he had and the guard helped him in. The door closed and the train started to move out of the platform.

Dean, soaking wet, leaned against the train door in the corridor, panting heavily. The guard was looking at his watch.

"That was a close one, Dean, but you're not out of the woods yet."

Five carriages away, a tall man had got on and was slowly walking towards them.

Dean was still out of breath. "What now?" he managed to say in between gulping for air.

Further down the train, the man was passing carriage four.

The guard put his hand on Dean's shoulder. "He has to know you're worth sending back, and you've seen so much."

"What more can I show him? I'm spent."

The guard looked at Dean.

"We can only guide you, Dean, but if you're spent and ready to go, you're as good as dead already."

"Dead? Am I dead?"

The guard put both hands on Dean's shoulders and peered into his eyes.

"You don't look dead to me, Dean, but you are about to meet up with your destiny. You'll know soon, right enough. How much do you want to be not dead? Have you done enough to convince him? That is the question."

The man, complete with hat and stick, was now three carriages away. He wasn't in a rush. Dean had nowhere to go, and the man knew it.

"Listen, the last couple of years I've sort of lost my way. I want to put things right. I would do anything for Sarah and Jodie; I just want a chance to prove it."

The guard took his watch out of his pocket.

"Excuse me, Dean, I have a train to run."

The rain was still beating down. All Dean could see through the windows were rain droplets obscuring the view. It was a miserable day to die.

The man in black was opening the door to his part of the corridor. This was the end. The man stood at one end of the corridor with Dean in a wet crumpled heap at the other. Dean stood up proudly and faced his nemesis, like they were two gunslingers ready to do battle. If it was the end, there was going to be some dignity about it. Dean wasn't going to cower in the corner; that's not the way he was made.

The train started to slow, and the guard made his way to the door and lowered the window. The tall figure came towards Dean.

Dean stood, chest puffed out ready for whatever was next.

Just then, the guard announced, "The next stop is Cockfield Station. Cockfield Station, the next stop."

Dean turned and looked at the guard.

"I thought we didn't stop here. Disused, you said."

The guard put his head down. He couldn't bring himself to look at Dean.

"It's got a use today, sir."

Dean looked up at the man with the stick who was halfway along the corridor. The train stopped and the door opened. Dean acknowledged the man with a bow of his head. He thought he owed him that at least; he'd given Dean a break when Dean had been with his mum and dad. Dean hadn't worked out why the man had done that, but he was grateful nevertheless.

Dean turned. The train had stopped for a reason – was it a good time to get off?

The guard muttered, "Are you sure, Dean?" as he got out. Dean ignored him and stepped off the train. What could be worse than being in there with Mr Scary?

The man in black wiped the window with the sleeve of his overcoat. He shook his head at Dean in disappointment.

The rain was worse than ever. A rumble of thunder clattered in the distance. The guard stood at the door, looking at the station clock and then at his pocket watch which were both perfectly synchronised, every tick of the second hand passing into history. It was ten minutes past the hour. Dean assumed the train must be leaving at fifteen minutes past.

The guard peered again at his watch and said, "Dean, are you sure you want to get off, sir?" The tone of his voice said much more than the words themselves. It was as if the guard was trying not to give too much away, but would welcome Dean back on the train in a heartbeat.

"Yes, I'm sure."

The guard looked at the man with the cane as if to seek approval before taking a newspaper from the tray in the corridor. He got a slow deliberate nod in return as if the tall man was intrigued to see where this was heading.

"Something to read on your journey, sir." As the guard said this, a bolt of lightning crackled through the air and struck Dean in the back, forcing him to his knees. The guard threw the paper to where Dean had fallen, alone on the station. The rain was pouring off his brow; his chest was thumping with pain from the lightning strike; he was struggling for breath. As the paper landed in front of him, Dean held his hands to his neck and threw his head back to try and get more air into his gasping lungs.

The man with the silver-topped cane tilted his hat forward and looked down on Dean from the train. He pointed his cane at the paper and weaved it in a circular motion. The pages of the paper turned, one after the other.

The guard was still looking at his watch, which now said fourteen minutes past six. He moved his focus to Dean and then back to his watch, which was eating up the seconds before departure.

Lightning again struck Dean, in the chest this time. It was louder and more violent than the first strike. His body went into shock for a second or two, contorting as the lightning made its way through it. He was now on his hands and his knees and in excruciating pain.

This must be the end.

Dean looked down at the newspaper. The man in black withdrew his stick.

The newspaper had settled on the obituary page. Dean read:

Dean Harrison, 42, City Trader,
Loving husband of Sarah Harrison and proud father of Jodie,
Died after a long, hard fight following a car accident.
The boy from the North did well. God bless you, Dean.
Sarah and Jodie
Love you always x

Dean looked up at the guard, who was closing the door. The man in black took off his hat and held it to his chest. He looked sad, as if to say, "I tried my best for you, but you did not see what was in front of your very eyes."

The guard looked at his watch and shook his head before reluctantly blowing his whistle with a loud shriek.

Part Three – Dean and Sarah

Chapter 24 – Back to Life

A month after they'd discovered that Dean had lain for two days unconscious in his smashed up car on an old farm track, Sarah and Jodie were approaching the Intensive Care Unit as the alarms were going off. Doctors and nurses streamed past them as Jack, Dean's friend from work, came towards them.

"Jack, is it Dean? What's happened?" Sarah asked anxiously.

Jack hugged her and said, "You'd better go in, Sarah. This doesn't look good. Jodie, come with me." Jack grabbed Jodie's hand and led her towards an adjacent room. Jodie looked over her shoulder to her mum.

"Mum, will Dad be OK?"

"I don't know, Jodie."

Tears started to run down Sarah's face. She could see through the window of the emergency unit that Dean's gown had been ripped off. Then she heard a shout of, "Clear," and a loud thump. Dean's body contorted upwards as the shockwave fired through it.

Dean was knocked to the ground. The last lightning strike was the worst yet. He could see the train easing away from the station, the man in black and the guard looking on solemnly. He raised himself up and staggered to his feet, shuffling forward to catch the door of the next carriage which was getting further and further away. He tried running, but his body was having none of it. It was like he was wading through treacle.

"Not like this," he said. "Not today, not like this." He managed to gather his limbs and muster some type of running action. His arms were doing their best to propel him forward, but no power was being transferred to his legs.

The second carriage had gone past. He reached for the door of the next one, but his hand slipped. The train was gaining speed, and if anything, Dean was slowing down.

Then his limbs started to respond. He managed to gain some control over his body, and all of a sudden he was running next to the train. His heart rate felt like it was going through the roof and he was struggling for air. Another lightning bolt forced him back onto the platform. He fell; he had nothing left in his body to give. If the train left him behind, he would be paying the Ferryman a visit.

Dean lay flat on the cold, wet station platform. The last carriage was approaching, and with it the last door of hope. He had to get back on the train, but his energy was fading fast.

With everything he had, he managed to get to his feet. It was now or never.

Sarah moved into the back of the ICU. *Beeeeeeep* – the monitor was still flat-lining. The doctors were shaking their heads.

"He's gone." The blind panic turned into organised chaos, then levelled off at reality. One doctor opened Dean's eyes and shone a torch to look for any reaction or last signs of hope. Then he looked over to Sarah.

"I'm so sorry, Sarah, we did what we could."

Sarah crumpled in the corner of the room, her knees hugged into her chest. No sound came from her other than a gasp for air from time to time to fill her lungs; she was crying too much to speak.

"Time of death 6.16pm, Sunday 18 June 2017." The doctor covered Dean's face with the bed sheet and made his way over to help Sarah to her feet.

Sarah broke her silence. "Dean, please, no." She raced to the side of the bed. The doctor in charge held the others back.

"It's OK, leave this to me." He looked at her. "Sarah, I can give you two minutes, then we have to tidy him up. After that, you can come back in. Two minutes. That OK?"

"Thank you, Darren, thanks." Sarah knew Darren from medical school days, before she had given up her career to have Jodie.

Darren turned around as he was leaving. "Sarah, I'm really sorry we couldn't save him."

Sarah acknowledged this with a hand gesture and a nod, then hugged Dean's empty body as reality took a big bite into her life.

"Dean, I love you so much. We can't live without you."

Dean looked up from the platform to the sky.

"Sarah?" he said out loud. "Sarah, was that you?"

He felt adrenalin flowing into his arms and legs. "Sarah!" he shouted again as the end of the train eased past him. With his new kick of energy, Dean managed to stand and limped after the disappearing train, his limp turning into a jog, his jog into a run, and his run into a sprint.

The last carriage had now passed him. This was his life in a nutshell. *Do I want to live or do I want to die?*

Dean was flat out, sprinting for his life. He let out another "Sarah!" as he caught up with the door and fumbled for the handle. He was struggling; at the pace he was running, he could not get a good enough hold on the silver T-shaped door handle. He tried and failed a second time.

The train was matching his pace, but it was speeding up and he was on the limit. He would only get one more chance before they were out of sync and the train would be gone. He again reached out with his right hand to twist the silver door handle. As he did, the door flew open from the inside and a silver-topped cane was held out.

Dean grabbed the cane and was pulled through the doorway into the last carriage. The man in black's hat had come off with the effort he'd expended to pull Dean in.

Dean lay in a soaking heap on the floor, leaning against the back of the train. The guard was working his way over to join them.

"Dean, Dean, are you OK?" Dean looked at the guard, then up the silver cane at the mysterious man's thin face and bald head. He was showing no emotion.

"Thank you," Dean said. "I won't let you down, I promise."

The man put on his hat and retrieved his book from his inside pocket. He was looking confused as if he was fighting with himself to come to a decision. Dean got the impression that it would not be plain sailing yet and he might have another couple of things to prove. This was about giving him a second chance, and he was a long way from being out of the woods. But at least he was still in the woods.

The man again consulted his book, his face morphing with his dilemma, and Dean could do nothing but honour whatever decision he made. Moving his hand across Dean's life calendar, he leant his head to one side and smiled at Dean, who was still in a foetal position near the train door. He slid the date marker to the right, just as he had done at Dean's mum and dad's wedding, before performing the now customary tilt of his hat with his bony fingertips.

Sarah was pleading with her dead husband.

"Not now, Dean, think about Jodie."

Darren peered in and decided to give her some more time.

"Dean, we have got so much to live for. We love you and need you. You are everything to us."

The faintest of lines appeared on the heart monitor. It was not even enough to trigger a sound. Then another bouncing line. It was still very faint, but was strong enough to register the softest of beeps.

"And do you know how many people will miss you, Dean?"

Beep...

Sarah heard that one. She looked up at the monitor. It was faint, but a heartbeat was there.

"Help!" she yelled. "He's alive, Darren. Please come quickly!"

"Sarah, are you OK?" Darren rushed back into the ICU as the monitor beeped again. "It's probably picked up your heartbeat, Sarah..."

"The monitor's on his other hand, Darren." Sarah stood back to prove her innocence.

Beep...Beep...Beep...

The beeps got stronger and the line more prominent. "Jesus Christ," Darren shouted as he punched the red button and sounded the alarm. Within seconds, the room was again flooded with uniforms. "Let's get some air in him now. How long was he gone for?"

"Five minutes?"

"Christ, we have a pulse and he's breathing."

The curtain was flung open as more staff entered.

"Get him on oxygen. If he was out that long, his brain will be starved." Darren looked at Sarah. She already knew this, so he wasn't telling her anything new. Sarah respectfully left the room and watched from behind the glass partition as the medical staff worked on Dean's recovering body.

After a few minutes or so, Dean's heart rate was back to normal and he was breathing unaided. Darren looked through the glass to Sarah and handed the reins over to another doctor.

"He's yours, Brian."

He then walked out to try and explain the inexplicable.

"Right, I don't know what has gone on. You know it doesn't work like this, Sarah."

Sarah wiped the dampness of her earlier tears from her face with the sleeve of her jumper.

"I know, Darren. I just think Dean didn't want to go yet. He's a fighter, you know. Thank you."

"Don't thank me yet. Five minutes he was gone, Sarah. Five minutes. He might…well, you know..."

"I know, Darren, but he is back and I'm just thankful for that at the moment. After that, whatever will be, will be. Miracles do happen."

He gave her a hug.

"Well, for your sake, I hope you're right. We'll get him cleaned up and then you can see him. Is Jodie with you?"

Sarah's tone changed. She wasn't going to take any crap and Darren knew it.

"Darren, don't even think about stopping her seeing her dad. She saw the alarms; she needs to see he's OK, otherwise she'll have nightmares. She's been dreaming about clowns and stuff ever since he left."

Darren squeezed her arm. "Clowns? Well, she has to see him if she's seeing clowns. How can medicine argue with clowns?" He patted her arm again. "Go and tell her he's OK for now, but you know I can't promise anything, Sarah. But his heart rate is stronger than it's been all week. Give us ten minutes; I need to check him over."

Sarah opened the family room door and gave Jack and Jodie a hug. She was crying.

"Ooooh, that was close, Jodie. He's OK for now, but we nearly lost him."

Jack moved back to allow Sarah and Jodie to chat.

"Sarah, I'll give you some time. Thank God he's still with us. I'll visit again tomorrow, same time."

Jodie and Sarah both hugged him. "Thanks, Jack," they said in unison, although Jodie's thanks had an 'Uncle' before the 'Jack'. Then Sarah led Jodie to the ICU which had a calmness about it now. She looked at Darren for approval, which she got.

Sarah and Jodie sat down next to Dean and held a hand each. Jodie gave her dad a kiss.

"I love you, Dad, I knew you wouldn't leave us."

"Jodie, your dad is still very ill. He was gone for five minutes. We have to wait and see – is that a deal?"

Jodie smiled. "He'll be OK, Mum, he's my dad. Anyway, I know how he can win our chess game. I don't know why that matters, but it does."

Sarah looked at Jodie. Everybody needs to believe in something, and that something for Jodie was a chess game. After what had just happened, who was Sarah to make up the rules? The rule book had just been thrown out of the window.

Chapter 25 – Answers

Dean was awoken by the guard. "Liverpool Street in five minutes, Dean, you nodded off."

"Thanks. Wow, you won't believe the dream I've just had!"

The guard shook his head.

"It was no dream. He is letting you stay a while longer to weigh you up. We thought you were gone, but you seem to have him confused. I think he's planning a test for you; when he's confused, he normally has a test. Be ready, Dean."

Dean, who was now a little more awake, felt his clothes. They were soaking.

"A test? Hasn't he tested me enough?"

The guard smiled his normal smile, which Dean had not seen earlier in the journey.

"He'll have tested you enough when he's sure you want to go back. You're a fighter, Dean, I'll give you that, but he's got to feel it deep inside you. He's very fair, but it's his job."

The guard's words would have confused Dean last week, but the jagged pieces in his jigsaw were more jigsaw-shaped now and were starting to slot together. There were just a few more to go, and fewer pieces left meant the picture was getting clearer.

The guard left Dean with his trademark happy smile, heading for the door to open it for the other passengers on the train. "Liverpool Street Station. All change." Dean looked for his case and then remembered that it had been sacrificed earlier, his clothes scattered all over Welnetham Station. He checked his pocket for his keys and phone. Luckily they were both there, along with the coin he had been given by Molly. Then he left the train and headed home. It had been a long day and his bed didn't have to call him twice.

After a good night's sleep, Dean woke up with thoughts flying around his head. If he was getting a second chance, or even a second chance at a second chance, he needed to be prepared. All through his life he'd known that knowledge was power, and nothing was any different wherever he was now.

His mind offered him a recap. He clearly wasn't in the normal world. Everyone seemed to know his name. He had rung Sarah loads of times and she was never in. He had met a clown, a Ferryman, not to mention the silver stick crusader who seemed to be alternately trying to kill him and save him whenever they met. Dean actually quite liked how the man in black went about his business, though, and felt they had mutual respect.

In addition to this, he had met a couple forty years younger than they should be; he had ridden on a train line that did not exist anymore; he had met his mum and dad before he had even been born, and had managed to get his dad's boat named after him. Maybe he had even named himself. In order to solve this conundrum, he would need to have as much knowledge as possible.

He remembered what Molly had said on the riverbank: "*He's called Sharon.*" Dean typed *Sharon Wiki* into Google; it was not a very good first attempt. After disregarding the origins of the name Sharon, Sharon Osbourne, Sharon Stone and Sharon Watts from *EastEnders*, he gave up when he learned that Sharon is a town in York County, South Carolina. He needed a different approach.

He tried *Sharon Wiki ferryman.* Bingo! That did the trick. Top of the search was *Charon (mythology) – Wikipedia.*

"Charon, not Sharon. How was I to know, Molly?"

Dean clicked on the link and read the text out loud to himself.

Oh my God, he thought, *so Charon transported the souls of the newly dead into the underworld. And anyone who could not pay the fee had to wander the shores of the Rivers Styx and Acheron for a hundred years.*

He stood up and checked his trousers, locating the large coin. Looking at the gargoyle on the coin and then back at the Wiki page, he clicked on 'danake'. He was sure Molly had called the coin a danake.

The picture on the page was identical to his coin, complete with the anchor on the back. So this coin was an all-expenses-paid pass to a place Dean didn't want to visit anytime soon. He had avoided the ferry once and death at least twice; he now had to concentrate on proving to the man in black that it would be a good idea to let him go back to the real world. The world of Sarah and

Jodie. It was comforting knowing where 'back' was all of a sudden.

He then typed in 'the Grim Reaper'. Who else could the man following, judging and testing him, be? Google didn't let him down. The picture accompanying the text speculating about The Grim Reaper's role in mythology was of a skeletal figure with a scythe, not a tall, thin man with a silver cane, but Dean guessed that anyone who had seen him had probably never lived to correct Wikipedia. But it sounded like his man.

He needed to go back to the hotel as that was where all the proper answers were. Picking up his phone, he called Mrs McCauley to book in for next weekend.

"Welnetham Hall, how can I help?"

"Hello, Mrs McCauley, can I book in for this Friday?"

"Of course, Mr Harrison, I'm glad you're coming back. We would love to see you; we thought that your visits were all over."

"I'm glad they're not. Can I have my normal room?"

There was a pause and a rustling of paper on the other end of the line.

"I'm sorry, Mr Harrison, but that room is taken. Someone else is in need of Room 119 that week."

"But I always have that room. Can they not be moved?" Dean enquired.

"It's not all about you, Dean, we do have other guests in need of our services." Mrs McCauley was very matter of fact, and Dean knew the lady was not for turning.

"Have you got any other rooms?"

"Of course we have other rooms. We're a hotel, that's what we do. Room 117 is free. It is next door to 119 and is a fine room. I'm sure you will find it acceptable. You don't need 119 anymore."

Dean felt that he was not getting the full picture, but reluctantly accepted the alternative.

"OK, that's fine. I'll be there at the usual time."

"You're all booked in. It will be lovely to see you again, Mr Harrison, good day."

With that, she hung up.

Dean thought about ringing Sarah and Jodie, but knew that it would be fruitless. There was probably very little connection between where he was and where they were, let alone a good mobile signal. He wanted more than anything to get back to the real world and put things right; he missed them so much. He was a fighter, though, and was now armed with the knowledge Wikipedia had provided him. Whatever the fight brought with it, he finally felt like he was in control of his own destiny.

Sarah was getting ready to visit Dean in the hospital when the phone rang.

"Sarah, it's Jack."

Sarah had her phone balanced between her neck and shoulder, and was slipping on her shoes as she replied.

"Jack, what's up? Are you OK?"

Jack was always OK. The question was more "Is Dean OK?" Jack seemed to be at the hospital more than she was. He had been a rock to her since she'd found out about Dean's accident.

"Yep, I'm fine. A couple of the boys from work want to visit Dean this afternoon. Is that OK?"

"Yes, that's fine, Jack. That's nice of them. Which boys?"

Jack paused.

"Martin and Oliver…"

"Oliver? I thought he hated Dean. You told me…"

Jack stopped her.

"Leopards can change their spots, Sarah. I think he's feeling a bit shit about what happened."

"Well, so he should be. Dean wouldn't be in hospital if it wasn't for that prick." Sarah went on the attack. "He's a floppy-haired upper-class dick, Jack."

"I know, Sarah, but he begged me. I think he needs to get a few things off his chest. He really means it, too – don't you, Oliver?"

"Hi, Mrs Harrison, and you're right, I am a prick." Oliver was obviously sitting next to Jack in the car, and it dawned on Sarah that the phone call was on loudspeaker.

"OK, I suppose that will be fine, Jack."

Dean had tubes coming out of his mouth and was still wired up to multiple machines, but everyone seemed to be amazed with his remarkable recovery over the last few weeks. His heart monitor was strumming a constant beat and his breathing was stable. However, although that was good, Dean had not shown any other signs of life. There was no REM; no movement or acknowledgment of any kind.

He was allowed visitors as the doctors thought that voice recognition could be the kick that he needed to get him out of a coma. And Oliver might just strike the right nerve.

Jack led the boys straight to Dean's bed, then left them to it and headed off to the café for a coffee for them all. Oliver sat next to Dean and bowed his head, then looked at Martin.

"Martin, I'm so sorry for what happened. It's all my fault."

Martin could see that Oliver was hurting inside, but also knew that he was right. It *was* his fault.

"It's not me you need to be telling, Ollie." He pointed at Dean.

"I know, I know." Oliver held Dean's hand. "I know you won't believe me, Dean, but I am so sorry. I bet you would not have crashed your car if it hadn't been for me. If I could take it all back, I would."

Martin walked round to Oliver's side of the bed and placed his hand on his friend's shoulder. "The car crash is not your fault, Ollie, but maybe think next time, yeah?" Martin was not good in hospitals. He looked at Dean. "We are all rooting for you, Dean," was the best he could come up with.

Jack arrived with three coffees. "Here you go, boys." He could see the redness of Oliver's eyes. "Have you said sorry yet, Oliver, you floppy-haired upper-class dick?" That was Jack's new favourite saying.

Oliver took a coffee from Jack. "Leave it, Jack," he said, "I feel like shit enough already. Do you think he will be OK?"

"He's pulled through before and he'd been dead for five minutes then, so we know he's a fighter. I don't think he's ready to go just yet, Oliver. Listen, what you did was wrong, but a lot of water has gone under the bridge since then, so don't beat yourself up about. Isn't that right, Yorkie?" Jack patted Dean's hand.

"Thanks, Jack. Dean, you just make sure you pull through, OK?" Oliver vacated his chair for Jack and looked over to the next bed. There was an old man in the bed, all rigged up to machines like Dean. Oliver asked the lady sitting by the old man's side if he could borrow the empty chair on the other side of his bed. She said nothing, but nodded before looking back at her husband, lovingly stroking his hand.

Jack had just sat down as Sarah walked in and headed straight for him. Like a well-rehearsed dance move they had been practising, Jack immediately gave up his seat and Sarah slid into it.

"Any news, Jack?"

"Nothing, Sarah. He's not even batted an eyelid, not even when that floppy-haired dick was speaking to him."

Jack smiled at Oliver; Oliver cast an 'Is this going to last all day?' look in Jack's general direction, and got a gaze which said, "More like all week."

"Hello, Mrs Harrison, I'm sorry about Dean, I really am."

Sarah looked at Oliver, who did look sorry. All the confident edge that Dean had described had gone, and anyway, it was not a day for fighting.

"It's OK, Oliver, what's done is done. Hi, Martin."

"Hi, Mrs Harrison. I think Dean looks well."

Oliver gave Martin a kick under the table. Dean didn't look well at all, but Martin felt like he had to say something and that was the best his brain could come up with under pressure.

"Yes, he's never looked better, Martin." Sarah smiled at Martin, letting him get away with his crass comment. Oliver might not have got the same response if he had said it.

"Right, you two, let's give Sarah a bit of time with her husband." Jack gave Sarah a kiss and said he would be back tomorrow evening. "Martin, Flopsey, come on. Mr Falconer will be wondering where you two are."

As they walked out, Oliver and Martin turned and said, "Bye, Mrs Harrison," as if they had rehearsed it for school assembly.

Chapter 26 – I'm Not a Nurse, I'm a Doctor

Sarah spent the rest of the afternoon with Dean, reminiscing about how they had first met.

"Remember, Dean? I had just qualified from med school and was working in A and E down the corridor from here. It was tiring being a junior doctor, and I was near the end of a twelve-hour shift when you walked in. Well, more like hobbled in."

Dean, in his alternative world, had fallen asleep on the sofa in his apartment. As clear as a bell, he could hear every word Sarah was saying. As she spoke, his dreams joined in and took him back to his younger years…

Dean let out a whimpered "Awww!" as he hobbled into the hospital using Jack as his crutch. They had been playing a charity match against other trading companies, each donating £1,000 to a kids' charity for the privilege, at Upton Park, then the home of West Ham United, and were both in full Middlesbrough kit. As Dean sorted the kit for the team and was a lifelong Boro fan, it was the same strip for every match.

Sarah was looking at her watch when they arrived in their football kits and attempted to walk over to the seating area in the waiting room. Jack got up to book Dean in at reception as Dean was struggling to sit, let alone stand.

"I think it's broken, Jack," Dean said as Jack wandered off.

After a ten minute wait, Sarah grabbed Dean's paperwork. "Dean Harrison," she called. Dean looked up when he heard the call, and that was the first time he ever saw Sarah. She had blonde hair tied up in a ponytail and was wearing a white coat with a stethoscope hanging from her shoulders. Dean tried getting up, but as soon as the weight hit his leg, he fell. Jack caught him.

"Do you need a wheelchair, Mr Harrison?" Sarah enquired impatiently.

"No, I'll be fine. Jack, give me a hand."

Dean and Jack followed the white coat down the corridor into a curtained off area. Sarah went through the formalities of identification to make sure she had the right Dean Harrison.

"So, let me guess – you fell off your bike," she said sarcastically.

"No, it was football."

"Really? I would never have guessed." Sarah looked up and down Dean's Middlesbrough kit, and Dean smiled as the penny dropped. "So, Mr Harrison, do you want to tell me what happened?"

"Well, we were on the attack, but 2–1 down. Jack put me through down the right wing…"

Sarah held her hand up to stop him.

"Do you watch *Match of the Day*, Mr Harrison?" she asked while kneeling down to look at his leg.

"Yes, I never miss it."

She smiled. "So you understand the concept of highlights?" She paused before adding, "I don't need the full match details, just the point when your leg smashed into another solid object would be a good start. And, for that matter, a good end, too."

"I was getting to that! So, Jack put me through down the wing and the full back wiped me out. Caught my left leg about half way up on the side."

"OK, Mr Harrison, does this hurt?" Sarah pressed on his shin.

"No."

"Does this hurt?" She pressed around his ankle.

"No."

Sarah looked up at him. "Do you know how much time I spend in here due to sports injuries, Mr Harrison?" she snapped. "I bet this hurts, though, doesn't it?" She pressed the side of his leg, and Dean's head flew back with the sharp pain.

"Yes, Nurse, it does. If you knew it would hurt, why did you do it?"

"You're lucky I did it before you called me a nurse. I'm a doctor. OK, you need an X-ray, Mr Harrison. I think you're the lucky owner of a fractured fibular. Take this around the corner. If you're lucky, I might not be on duty when you get back."

"Thank you, Doctor," said Jack.

"Are you trying to get me into trouble, Jack? Thanks, Doctor, and sorry about the nurse thing. I should have known by the stethoscope thing round your neck."

She pointed to her name badge. "You might have known by this." Dean looked at the name badge: Dr Sarah Summers.

"Sorry, Sarah." Dean gave her a North Yorkshire smile and a glint appeared in his eye. "I can call you Sarah, can't I?"

Sarah looked at him.

"No, you can call me Dr Summers, although I finish in an hour so you will probably not get the chance to call me anything. Good luck, Mr Harrison, and Jack, look after him. We wouldn't want him to fall, would we?"

Dean gave Jack a stare which said, "How come you get Jack and I get Mr Harrison?"

Around the corner, there was a queue of people sitting patiently, waiting for an X-ray. Dean and Jack sat at the back in the only two seats left together.

"Well, what do you think?" Dean asked. Jack looked at him.

"I think it's broken, Yorkie."

"No, not about my leg, about the doctor. Doctor Sarah."

Jack laughed. "Yorkie, you do take the biscuit. Do you really think you have a chance with her? She is way out of your league – she is beautiful, she has brains and she takes no shit."

"Give me one good reason why not."

"I've already given you a few, but here are some more. One, she is gorgeous, so I'd be very surprised if she's single and available…"

Dean stopped him. "She didn't have a ring on. I checked."

"Can I carry on?" Jack got permission with a rolling hand signal. "Two, she's got brains, so she won't fall for your bullshit. Even though you're good at bullshitting, she'll see through it. And lastly, she hates you. I thought she made that quite clear."

"Yeah, but apart from that?" They both laughed before Dean added, "She is lovely, though. My type of girl. The fact she takes no shit is a bonus – in another world, maybe."

Dean was called after an hour and had his X-ray handed to him in a brown folder. With the evidence, he was sent back to A and E where he handed it in and waited for an assessment.

A deep voice sounded. "Mr Harrison?" It was a doctor, but not the one Dean had been hoping for. Dean looked at the doctor's name badge: Dr Darren Squires.

"Follow me, Mr Harrison," Dr Squires said, taking the brown envelope from the tray on reception.

Dr Summers appeared from around the corner in jeans and tee shirt, having had a shower before getting changed. "I'll take this one before I go, if you like, Darren. It's getting busy in there and I know the history."

"Thanks, Sarah, you're a star. I know how much you like football injuries. Good luck, Mr Harrison, you're going to need it."

Dr Squires winked at Dean as he passed the X-ray folder to Sarah.

"Take a seat. Let's have a look at the damage, shall we?" Sarah attached the two X-rays onto the viewer and flicked the light on. "Here it is." With a pencil, she pointed out the break to Dean. "It's not actually that bad, but it's a fractured fibular as I expected. It needs to be in plaster for four weeks, I would say. It's not a supporting bone, so it should be OK, Dean."

"Thanks. Hey, you called me Dean." If Dean were a puppy dog, he'd have been chasing his tail. Sarah looked across the room at Jack as if it had been an error. They both knew it hadn't been.

"Officially I'm off duty…"

Dean was good at spotting opportunities, and he spotted one now.

"Well, if you're off duty, maybe I can have your number. And when I'm all fixed up, I'll take you out for dinner to say thanks." Dean's blue eyes looked bluer all of a sudden and were aimed directly at Sarah's. She seemed to welcome the attention, but tried to give nothing away.

"Jack, is he always like this?" The question did not require an answer. It was more to buy time as Sarah thought on her feet. "I'll tell you what, my dad owns a couple of racehorses. One of them, a two-year-old filly, is called Baby Doctor – I know, and yes, he did name her after me. She will be running in the next few months or so, not sure where yet. I expect I'll be there for her first race. If you happen to be at the racecourse, wherever and whenever it is, pop by and say hello."

Sarah gave Dean a wink which said, "If you want me, you're going to have to do a lot better than 'What's your number?'" Her head tilted to one side, she smiled.

"Deal. Baby Doctor. Sarah, I'll see you there."

Sarah filled in the paperwork and put it back in the brown file.

"Right, back to the waiting room. They will call you to put you in plaster. It's been nice meeting you, Jack." She extended a handshake to Jack. "And, Mr Harrison, make sure you keep the weight off that leg."

Sarah walked out of the room, shaking her head and wondering if she had really just been chatted up by an A and E patient. Dean had some balls, she had to give him that, and he was sort of northern cute. She smiled. Maybe he would show up, maybe he wouldn't.

Let's see how much he wants dinner with me.

Sarah gave Dr Darren Squires a wave. "That one is done, Darren, broken fib." She handed him the file. "Right, I'm knackered. I'm off home – my bed is shouting for me. See you tomorrow."

"Why the hell did we become doctors again? We never get any sleep."

She patted him on the back.

"'Cos we love it, Darren, and we save lives." Sarah turned and left the hospital, hoping autopilot would last long enough to allow her to get into her car and find her way home.

Dean was back at work within two weeks, on crutches with his leg still in plaster. He was quite junior then and Dexter Falconer hardly knew who he was. Maybe Mr Falconer would notice him now he had a big white plaster of Paris 'pot' on the bottom of his leg.

Dean took the opportunity while he was lame to learn. He studied all the e-learning and Excel spreadsheets he could as if he was studying for an exam, but there was no exam. He was studying to get noticed. If he put his razor-sharp mind into predicting the future, the people who mattered might give him credit.

Every Monday, Dean would pick up a *Racing Post* and painstakingly look through the declarations for a horse called Baby Doctor. He had very little to go on, but at least he had the filly's name and age.

Three months after he'd broken his leg, Dean's learning had paid off and he was a junior trader. He had been recommended by some of the big dogs on the upper floors whom he had given a few trading trends to. Every Monday, his *Racing Post* under his arm, he was greeted with a "Hi, Dean" from the receptionist – that hadn't happened when he'd been on the first floor. Now he would get into the lift and press floor three – he was going in the right direction.

His first job of every Monday was not to look at trades or trends, though; it was to look for Dr Summers's dad's racehorse. Jack often asked why Dean didn't just send her some flowers. But, although Dean knew very little about Sarah, he did know that she had set the terms of the agreement. If he met her any other way, it would be breaking her rules.

One particular Monday, he got to his office, which was moderate at best, and had a coffee delivered by the adorable Kylie, the secretary he shared with five other traders on this floor. He had a sip and looked through the flat race declarations.

Baby Doctor, a two-year-old filly owned by Mr G R Summers, would be running the following Monday, a week today, in the 7.45pm at Windsor.

Dean had another slurp of his coffee and picked up the phone to ring Jack.

"Jack, she wasn't lying. She does exist."

"Yorkie, who wasn't lying and who exists?"

"Dr Sarah wasn't lying. The racehorse does exist."

"Oh, I forgot it was Monday."

"Baby Doctor, owned by Mr G R Summers, is running next Monday night at Windsor. Can you square it with your wife so that you can go with me?"

"If I must. I hope it's all worth it, Yorkie. I'm sure our lass will be fine – for some reason she likes you. God knows why."

Chapter 27 – An Evening at the Races

The following Monday arrived. Dean, leaving nothing to chance, wore a dark blue bespoke Brioni suit with Edward Green 890 Last Shelton shoes, and he left his tie on, which was normally the first thing to be discarded when he left the office. Jack's tie was already off by the time they hit the lift in the office.

They arrived at Windsor and headed for the boat which would take them directly to the racecourse in good time for the first race at 5.45pm. Once they were on the boat, it was no surprise when Jack went to the bar for a couple of cans of beer. The journey was only twenty minutes long, but he had an official pass from his wife and was going to make the most of it.

"Here you go, Yorkie, and good luck on your quest."

They clinked cans.

Dean was bothered about meeting Sarah again. What would he say? Remember me? Dean was not normally stuck for words, but he was not normally under this much pressure, either. Absence is supposed to make the heart grow fonder, and Dean had been thinking about Sarah more or less every day since they'd met briefly in the hospital. But what if she didn't even remember him? After all, he had not been in touch since.

The boat meandered up to Windsor Racecourse entrance. Following the gathering crowds, Dean was wishing that he had left his jacket behind. It was a hot afternoon, but he would probably need it for the dress code in the posh end where the owners gathered. He just hoped Jack would be allowed in wearing his usual 'I have not made an effort' attire.

Dean took out his wallet. "I'll get this, Jack. I owe you that at least. Two tickets for the Club Enclosure, please."

"That's fifty-four pounds, sir."

Dean paid, and he and Jack moved through security and on to the course. Then Dean bought a couple of race cards and handed one to Jack.

"OK, what now, Yorkie? You've got me here, so what next?" Jack enquired.

"How about you get us a drink and we have a bet on the first race. I've not really got a plan; just going to play it by ear. She might not even be here."

Jack took a quick look at the race card.

"Yep, Domino in the first. Richard Hannon and Richard Hughes always win the first race at Windsor." Jack said this with some authority. He knew far more about horses than Dean did. He got back from the bar just as Domino was waltzing her way through the last furlong.

"Told you, Yorkie, follow Uncle Jack and you won't go far wrong."

They won three of the next four races, Dean following Jack's tips. Jack was on fire and he knew it. In between races, they walked around everywhere, Dean's eyes like a hawk's, looking out for a particularly beautiful girl in amongst a crowd of beautiful girls.

The day was slowly morphing into evening. After their last winner, Dean looked at the race card. Baby Doctor, owned by Mr G R Summers, was running in the next race.

"Another beer, Yorkie?" Jack was having a ball. He'd already called his wife twice to brag about his winnings.

"No, Jack. I've covered every yard of this racecourse. If she's going to be anywhere as an owner, she'll be in the parade ring, no doubt telling the jockey what to do."

Jack headed off to the parade ring with Dean, who was nervous but full of optimism. He was walking more quickly than normal and Jack was struggling to keep up, but Dean was not for slowing down. He had a date with destiny.

They saw the jockeys leaving their changing room. Jack took a quick look at Baby Doctor's colours and the jockey's name.

"Make sure you give her a good ride, Shamus," he said.

"I always do my best, sir," replied the jockey in an Irish accent, raising his whip to his head in a salute.

"Jack, what the hell do you know about riding horses?" asked Dean. "I'm surprised he didn't tell you to F-off. He's a jockey, so I think he knows what he's doing."

"I was just saying, Yorkie. Thought it might help."

"Well it didn't."

Dean shook his head and headed to the parade ring in speedy mode. The parade ring was full of the well-to-do doing their best to be…well…well-to-do. The small stand around the parade ring was packed as the sun was making a last ditch effort to shine before packing up for the day.

All of a sudden, it seemed to be shining a lot more brightly for Dean. Jack caught up with him just as he spied Sarah in the middle of the parade ring. Wearing an amazing white AllSaints dress which emphasised her fabulous figure, the dying sun lighting up her blonde hair, she stood out. Dean, who was very rarely overawed, was overawed. She looked amazing, and everyone knew it apart from Sarah. She did not have a clue, which made her even more attractive to Dean.

Dean assumed it was her mother and father who were with her. Sarah looked like her mother so it was not a hard assumption to make.

"Jack, can you see her?" Dean had a sparkle in his eye; he'd been waiting and hoping for this moment, and he was not disappointed. But in a way, Dean loved her look at the hospital in jeans and tee shirt as much as he loved her all dressed up at the races. He didn't love her clothes; he just loved her, and he had known it from the first moment they'd met.

"Well, Yorkie, this is what you're here for." Jack gave Dean a playful nudge.

Sarah was sharing a joke with the jockey, whom she towered over thanks to some silver high heels that were doing their best to make indentations in the pristine lawns. Without really trying, she was the centre of attention. If she laughed, everyone laughed; if she smiled, they smiled. Dean looked on. She was mesmerising not just to him but to everyone in her company.

Dean was doing his best to stand out from the crowd, but the crowd was huge and Sarah wasn't expecting him. She was far too happy in horse owner mode. The parade ring was a ring of hope – every horse still stood a chance, and all the owners were equals. All the horses were going to be on the starting line up, so there was no pecking order. They all had earned their right to be there, win or lose.

Dean had hoped to meet Sarah today, but had not really planned how. Waving to her from afar was definitely not the way forward. He had to come up with another plan to speak to her, and he was good at plans.

"Jack, let's go and have a bet and watch the race."

"Are you giving up, Yorkie?" Jack enquired.

"No, Jack, don't be stupid. I have an idea."

They headed off to the tarter stalls and put £50 each way on Baby Doctor at 20–1 before returning to the grandstand to watch the race.

It was a six-furlong race and the horses were already at the start, so it would only be another minute or so before they saw which of the owners would enter the winners' circle. Jack was feeling like another successful call to his wife was in the offing. She was already planning a shopping trip on the back of Jack's successful day.

"And they're off!" the loudspeaker above the grandstand announced.

Baby Doctor missed the break and stumbled out of the stalls like a carthorse. She was at the back and seven lengths tailed off. Being that far back in a sprint was not a good start.

Jack gave Dean a stern stare.

"Well, I didn't say it would win, Jack."

Jack crumpled up his bet and pretended to throw it away, then he nudged Dean.

"Only joking, Yorkie."

Dean whispered, "Come on, Doctor," and it seemed to work. Baby Doctor started to gain ground and cruised up to the horse ahead of her. One by one, she picked off her rivals.

"And now, two furlongs to go, we have Solar Star, Long Time Gone, Kilimanjaro's Uncle, and making late headway, Baby Doctor."

"She's coming, Jack."

Jack was bouncing up and down as though he was the jockey.

"As they enter the final furlong, it's Kilimanjaro's Uncle with the newcomer Baby Doctor giving chase. Three lengths to gain, but she's in no mood for stopping."

Jack let out a cry. "C'mon, Baby, c'mon."

Dean looked over to the right. Sarah and her parents were jumping up and down on the balcony, willing their horse home. Dean didn't need to give their filly any more vocal encouragement as Jack was doing enough for both of them. Baby Doctor was closing with every stride as they approached the finish line. The loudspeaker could only just be heard over the noise of the crowd.

"It's Kilimanjaro's Uncle. Kilimanjaro's Uncle, Baby Doctor, it's on the nod. They flash past the finishing post together."

"Who won? God, that was close. Did she win, Yorkie?"

Dean was not paying attention. He was still looking over to the balcony where Sarah was going crazy with her parents.

"I don't know, Jack…"

"*Photograph! Photograph!*" boomed the loudspeakers, drowning out the cheers and jeers from the spectators. "*The photograph finish is between, in race card order, number two, Baby Doctor, and number seven, Kilimanjaro's Uncle.*"

Jack hugged Dean. "I think she got it. What do you think? That's a thousand pounds for the win, or two hundred for the place." He started doing a dance. Jack could not dance at the best of times, although it never seemed to stop him trying, and he'd not even won yet.

"*And the winner is…*" There was a pause; there always is. "*Number seven, Kilimanjaro's Uncle.*"

"Oh well, Yorkie, still two hundred notes."

Dean grabbed Jack.

"Come with me."

Chapter 28 – The Sting

Dean and Jack hastily made their way to the owners' enclosure, Jack again struggling with Dean's burning pace. With only one race left, Dean hoped that the coast might be clear and they might be able to sneak in.

It wasn't. There were two burly bouncers monitoring the door. Dean knew he would not be able to blag his way past these guys who looked like they were from a professional security firm, not just the biggest blokes in the gym, which seemed to be the bouncer qualification up north. But he needed a way in, and the way in was not in front of his face right now.

Or was it?

Four very drunken gentlemen walked out. They had gold badges on their lapels which were identical to the one Dean had seen on Sarah's dress at the parade ring. Dean followed them as they left. Jack was in tow, just about.

"Hey, guys, did your horse win?"

"He's still running, bloody carthorse," one of the gentlemen replied.

"What's his name?"

A couple of the gentlemen stopped and engaged with Dean.

"Radical Rolla Coaster. He came last, but it didn't spoil our day. We're off into Windsor for a curry to celebrate. He was a winner in our eyes, bloody donkey."

Dean sensed an opportunity.

"You won't be needing your badges, then, will you?"

The two gentlemen unclipped their badges from their jackets.

"Here you go, lads. There is only one race left. Oh, you might need these as well. We have fifteen in our syndicate, but we're only allowed four in the owners' club, so we've been swapping around all day." The men gave Dean and Jack a coloured scarf each. "Radical Rolla Coaster, if they ask, boys. Have a good night."

The two men put on a bit of a drunken jog to catch up with their friends without appearing to go any faster.

Dean clipped the badge to his jacket and donned his new

scarf, handing the other badge and scarf to Jack. "Radical Rolla Coaster, Jack, remember that name."

"I've never owned a horse before, Yorkie."

Dean looked at him.

"You still don't, you muppet. Come on, Jack, try to act cool."

They walked back to the owners' enclosure entrance and showed their newly acquired badges to security. The bouncers knew that the Radical Rolla Coaster lot had been swapping around all day and had been no bother, so they let the latest two in without question.

After climbing three flights of stairs, Dean and Jack turned and walked through an archway into a large room full of the great and the good. It stank of money, housing more designer handbags than Harrods, and every other table had bottles of Dom Pérignon champagne proudly peering over the tops of ice buckets. Dean scanned the room like an FBI agent, looking for his mark.

Most of the crowd was gathered on or near the balcony at the back of the room, overlooking the parade ring as the horses for the last race were beginning to emerge. Dean and Jack headed over to see if Sarah was amongst them. As they made their way across the room, Dean saw a sign on one of the vacant tables. The champagne bottle was upside down in the ice bucket. Dean picked up the sign which said, "Table reserved for the owners of Baby Doctor".

Dean's shoulders dropped. "I've missed her, Jack. They've gone."

"Yorkie, there're a lot more fish in the sea. Being from where you're from, I thought you'd know that."

"I know, Jack, but she was special. I could feel it in here." Dean pointed to his heart.

They slowly continued to the balcony to look at the horses in the parade ring for the last race. There were a lot of horses in the lucky last – at least twenty runners.

"I know what will cheer you up, Yorkie. How about I pick you another winner in the last race?"

"Not really in the mood, Jack."

Jack put a big arm around Dean and hugged the younger man's head into him, tapping the top of Dean's head with his other hand.

"McFly, McFly!"

Even eighties film humour was not working. *He must be down in the dumps*, Jack thought.

Sarah walked into the room with her mother and father, holding the second place trophy they had just been to collect. Her father gestured to the bar staff that another bottle of champagne would be quite welcome right now.

Sarah carefully put the trophy on the table. It was a silver horse – its jockey in the usual jockey pose, driving the horse forward – mounted on a wooden plinth. They were over the moon with how their horse's first run had gone. The trainer had said she was just out for a blow; none of them had expected second, and after that start, too. They might well have a good one on their hands.

Sarah's dad charged up their glasses and proposed a toast. Many others in the room joined in.

"To Baby Doctor!"

"Baby Doctor!"

Dean was too busy falling over his bottom lip on the balcony to hear the toast. Jack wasn't.

"Yorkie, did you hear that?"

Dean lifted his head up.

"Hear what?"

Jack looked over Dean's shoulder into the room. The previously vacant table reserved for Baby Doctor's owners was now occupied.

"Dean, turn round."

Dean spun round, and in an instant, he saw her. She was striking her glass against that of anyone who wanted to say, "Cheers."

Dean pulled himself together and re-entered the room, making a beeline for Sarah's table. He did not have a clue what he was going to say, but he would let his brain deal with that when he got there. He wasn't going to let her out of his sight again.

"Dr Summers, fancy meeting you here."

Sarah gave Dean a quizzical look, then the penny dropped.

"Mr…er…Ha-rri-son." She enunciated the three syllables as her memory dug deep.

"I assume you're off duty, Sarah?" Dean asked.

"Of course, I would never drink on duty." Her mind was fumbling around for his first name. "It's…oh, don't tell me." Then she saw Jack and it came straight back to her. "Dean. It's Dean, isn't it?" Sarah pretended to wipe the sweat from her brow. "I never forget a name. So, what are you doing here, Dean, and how's the leg? Champagne?"

"The leg's fine, and yes please, champagne would be great."

Jack saw there were no more glasses on the table.

"Should I get some glasses?"

"Yes please. Thanks, Jack," said Sarah. Dean thought about picking her up on remembering Jack's name while struggling with his, but thought better of it.

"Well, I was invited by a beautiful girl in a hospital about three months ago to see her horse run for the first time." Dean had a drink from his recently charged flute.

"Oh. Who is she? Is she here?" She smiled at Dean. He loved the way she could twist the conversation to fall in her favour. He might have met his match.

"She is, and she promised me a dinner date if I found her."

Their eyes locked together.

"I think you'll find she said she would be there if you wanted to see her again, that's all." Sarah took a sip of champagne and added, "You'll have to do better than that if you want to take her for dinner."

In true mother style, Sarah's mother intervened.

"Sarah, are you going to introduce me and your father to your friends?"

Sarah had been enjoying the verbal jousting with Dean and knew she was winning, but she thought she'd better give her mother her moment.

"Mum, Dad, this is Dean Harrison, and Jack…Jack…"

Jack sprang to life.

"Oh sorry, Sarah, I'm Jack Smith. Pleasure to meet you all."

"We are pleased to meet you too. How do you know Sarah? She works so hard, we didn't think she had any friends."

Sarah gave her mother a playful nudge.

"I broke my leg and had the pleasure of your daughter fixing it for me, Mrs Summers. Well done with Baby Doctor. We backed her, didn't we, Jack?"

Jack nodded. "We've won in every race but one, and I'm sure this next race will be no exception," he said confidently as he looked out of the window to see that the jockeys, the colour draining from their silks in the impending dusk, were on their mounts, cantering towards the starting gates.

Sarah's dad joined in the conversation. "So, what do you fancy in the next race, then, Dean?" There was only one thing Dean fancied at Windsor right then, and it did not have four legs. He was still looking at Sarah, and she was returning his stare with interest. She could not believe that a throwaway comment three months ago would have brought him here today. She hardly knew him, but he had gone up in her estimation. The spark had combusted and was turning into a flame.

"I'm not sure, Mr Summers. There are twenty-four runners and the favourite is 7–1, so it's wide open. I might leave this race alone; don't think my luck will hold out forever."

"Well that's no fun, Dean," said Sarah. "I'll tell you what: you back the winner of the next and I'll take you up on that dinner date you've been talking about."

Sarah's mother had not seen her daughter like this before. "Oh go on, Dean, that will be fun," she said. "We'll be rooting for you, won't we, George?"

Mr Summers agreed with a firm nod.

Dean looked at Jack for inspiration.

"You're on your own on this one, Yorkie. The stakes are too high for me."

"OK, let me clarify. If I back the winner in the last race, Sarah, you'll let me take you for dinner next weekend?"

He paused, waiting for confirmation.

"Seems like a fair deal to me, Dean," she said through a playful smile. She felt like her knight in shining armour was fighting for her hand; she felt special, and wanted him to win. She gave him a kiss on the cheek. "Good luck, Dean, I really mean it."

Her mother looked on and gave her husband a nudge. "Ooooh, it's so exciting," she said.

The horses had reached the start. *No pressure, then,* Dean thought. Twenty-four horses to choose from and fewer than five minutes to the off. And for added pressure, Jack, Sarah and her parents were all looking at him as he studied what little he knew of the form.

He closed the race card. "OK, here goes, wish me luck." Dean headed off to the tote at the back of the room, placed the bet, took his slip and folded it over a couple of times.

On returning to the table, he said to Mrs Summers, "Sorry, I didn't get your name."

"It's Theresa, Dean."

Half the horses were already loaded in the stalls. Jack was putting his own bet on. Dean took out his slip and gave it to Theresa Summers.

"Theresa, can you look after this for me? You might bring me some luck. God knows, I need it."

Theresa loved being involved. She felt like she was in a romantic novel.

"What did you back, Dean?" Sarah looked at all the horses on the big screen. Why on earth had she set this challenge? She would love to go for a meal with him, but there was no backing out now – she'd set the rules and would have to uphold them.

"Wait and see, Sarah. If it's meant to be, it's meant to be."

Jack got back just as the horses were off. The commentator was struggling to call the race as the field split into two groups. Jack had backed The Dooser, which was getting a few mentions. Sarah's eyes were locked on Dean's, trying to gauge his reaction when the commentator reeled through the names.

The final furlong came; any one of ten horses could win.

"And it's Fallen Angel, Harp Strings and The Dooser as they approach the final furlong, and coming from the back, Sharp Shoes and Jo Fandango, the big outsider. They are deep into the final furlong and it's The Dooser and Jo Fandango neck and neck. And it's…Jo…Fandango…who takes the lucky last at a massive price."

Sarah did not follow the horses greatly, but she didn't like the sound of the words 'massive price'. Even she knew 50–1 was a long shot, and her chances of dinner with Dean were even longer after that result.

"Jack, did you have The Dooser each way?" The way Jack was jumping up and down, he must have done. Everyone gathered round to offer their congratulations, but after the roars and jeers had settled down, they were replaced by a massive sense of anticlimax.

Theresa was thinking that if this was a romantic novel, there's no way it could end like this. But why would Dean have picked Jo Fandango? Its form was 0-0-0-0-0, so only an idiot would have picked it, and from what she had seen, Dean was no idiot.

Sarah's mind was frantically trying to think of a get out clause. "Well, Dean, you win some, you lose some." It hurt her even saying those words.

Dean smiled. "Sarah, can I ask you a question?"

"Of course, Dean." She was hoping for a "Should we go out anyway?" but that would be too easy and not very romantic.

"You said if I backed the winner of this race, you would go to dinner with me next weekend, is that right?"

She looked at him.

"That's right, Dean."

"What number was Jo Fandango?"

"Erm, number seventeen."

"OK, Theresa, did I back number seventeen?"

Theresa fumbled in her bag for the slip and slowly opened it. The whole room was now waiting for Sarah's mother to answer.

Theresa's face broke out into a smile which morphed into a laugh, and then she was in hysterics.

"Mum, what? Did he back it?"

"Yes, he backed it. Oh, you're a clever boy, Dean," Theresa announced, just about pulling herself together. "He's a keeper, Sarah."

Sarah looked at Dean. "It was 50–1, Dean, how the hell did you pick it out?"

"Because he backed every horse in the race."

Sarah started to laugh. "Is that cheating?" she enquired.

"I'm hurt at that comment, Sarah. I would call it a technicality. You said I had to back the winner of the last race for dinner with the most beautiful girl in the world. I backed the winner, so is it a date?"

Sarah didn't care if it was bending the rules.

"Of course it is, Dean."

Sarah's dad shook Dean's hand. "Well played. Not many get one over on our Sarah."

Jack gave Dean a playful punch, then he got a hug from Theresa.

"You make sure you look after her, Dean, she's very special. You're a lucky boy, never forget that."

Sarah was beaming as she gave Dean a hug and whispered into his ear, "You have gone from a walk to a trot, but you are a long way from a canter. You have my attention, Dean, make sure you keep it." She wrote her number on the back of the sign reserving their table, then left with her parents.

"God knows how you do it, Yorkie, but I guess you could say that was a result. How did you pull that one off? She's gorgeous – make sure you don't screw this up."

Dean patted Jack on the back.

"I have no intention of screwing it up, Jack, I'm going to marry her. I have never been in love before, but she makes me go weak at the knees. Anyway, let's get a beer. Boy, do I need one."

Dean woke up in his apartment. He had relived meeting Sarah in his dream as if he had been there again. He loved her so much. More than ever, he needed to get back to her. He felt like she was calling him.

He kissed the picture of Sarah and Jodie. "I'm going to come back, Sarah, I promise you."

Part Four – Bring On The Clowns

Chapter 29 – The Test

It was the night before Dean's next visit to Welnetham Hall, and he was still a bit annoyed that he was not getting his usual room. Room 119 had unlocked many of the answers he needed, and he was puzzled as to why Mrs McCauley would not let him have it, but it was what it was. He would not be getting back to Sarah and Jodie without paying the hotel another visit.

He packed his spare bag then headed to bed for his last sleep before seeking the final pieces to a jigsaw which was more or less complete. He was not out of the woods yet; the man with the stick, Death, The Grim Reaper – whoever he was – had had an uneasy look on his face after he'd saved Dean on the train. Dean's life was still in the balance; Death had not decided which way the coin was going to fall. Dean had more tests to overcome and was fully aware it was going to be a bumpy ride.

He did not have to wait long to find out just how bumpy a ride it was going to be.

The lift to his apartment kicked in – someone was heading up to see him. But nobody had buzzed. His intercom was silent and he had not given permission for a visitor to come up, but still the lift kept coming.

Dean was no longer in the mood for running. He was ready to face his fears, which was just as well as his worst fears were on the other side of the lift cage.

It opened.

Death, complete with his cane, was in the lift. The clown was with him, dressed in the black and white harlequin outfit he had worn when he went to see Jodie. Dean did not flinch.

Death clicked his cane against the wooden floor as he stepped out of the lift and walked straight past Dean as if he wasn't there. Moving into the living area, Death looked up at the flat screens and then out of the window at Old Father Thames.

The clown went to Dean's side. "Are you ready, Dean?"

Dean responded immediately.

"Yes, I'm ready." He didn't know what he was ready for, but armed with information, he was ready for it anyway. He knew he was up against Death, but he also knew that if Death had wanted him dead, he would already be paying the Ferryman. He had to prove something; he did not know what, but Dean was ready for anything.

Death waved his hand and an ancient stone table appeared in the middle of the room. It had a checkerboard top with black and white squares. Two stone seats appeared on either side of it.

"Chess?" Dean said. The clown nodded as the pieces appeared and took their usual places on the board in two rows of eight, the pawn soldiers guarding their aristocratic wards either side of the chessboard.

Death consulted his book. With a wave from his cane over the board, all the chess pieces obediently re-ordered themselves into a familiar starting position. The clown gave Dean as much of a clue as he was allowed.

"Remember this board?"

Dean nodded.

"It's my and Jodie's game, isn't it?"

"I hope you can win from your position, Dean. Your life depends on it."

"You're joking, right? She was hammering me that night – why do you think I told her to go to sleep?"

The clown bowed his head. He had no smiley face today; he had a white face with no expression, a single tear painted on his cheek. He looked serious, because the situation was serious.

"Can you think of anyone you would want to give you a hand right now, Dean?"

"Only Jodie – is she here?"

The clown stood, looking at Death who had moved back to the window. Death turned and waved at the clown with his stick twice as if to say, "OK, but hurry up."

"Wait there, Dean, and look at that board. You need the biggest plan you've ever made. I'll be back in a minute." The clown walked into the bedroom.

Death gestured to offer Dean a seat on the white side of the board. Dean checked his pocket for the danake and took it out. Molly had told him to keep the coin safe. If this game went badly, he would need it to pay the Ferryman. After looking at it, he placed it back into his pocket.

Jodie awoke and looked at the clock. It was midnight, but she sensed that she was not alone. She turned over to see Benjie the clown at the end of her bed.

"Are you ready, Jodie? Your dad needs you now."

Jodie was not scared. She had always known that there was a reason for her chess game with Kyle, and she had been expecting a visit.

"Come with me, Jodie. You can only speak to your dad for one minute then he's on his own. Are you scared?"

Jodie looked at Benjie. "No, I'm fine. I'm ready."

Benjie took her by the hand and they went through the door. Jodie was not expecting to see the landing beyond it like she normally did, and she was right. Benjie's leg disappeared as he stepped through the door, followed by his body.

Jodie stopped.

"Wait, wait there, I need something." She turned and ran to the corner of her room to pick up her rucksack. Benjie's arm and hand were still in her room, hanging from what looked like nothing. "OK, now I'm ready." She took his hand and they left through the door.

They appeared in the bedroom of Dean's apartment. Most of Benjie was already there, patiently waiting for the arm which was attached to Jodie to catch up.

Dean was making his way to the chair as instructed.

"Dad!" Dean turned round to see his daughter, in her white patterned pyjamas, holding hands with the clown, her rucksack over her back. Although he wanted to run to Jodie, he waited for permission from Death; he know everything he did would be on Death's terms and any wrong move now could be fatal. He had to show respect.

He received permission by way of a bony finger pointing at him and then on to Jodie.

Dean ran over to his daughter. "Jodie, I have missed you so much." He picked her up and hugged her, smothering her forehead with kisses.

Death made a sign to Benjie who pulled them apart. "Right,

Jodie," he said, "you have one minute. Use it wisely."

Jodie was calmer than her dad, who was a mess right now. She whispered out of earshot of Dean's opponent, "Dad, listen, I worked out how to win from your position months ago."

Her dad stopped her. "Months? We only played a month ago, Jodie."

Jodie looked at him, confused.

"Dad, it's over four months since…" She paused. "Well, it was about five months ago."

Now it was Dean's turn to look confused. "Thirty seconds, Jodie," said Benjie, timing them on his oversized clown watch.

"Dad, listen, I have won playing as white. It's possible, but you have to trust me. It's about time and pressure." She got the clock out of her rucksack. "Right, put him on the clock. You have to give all your pieces away. Play to lose to distract him, but keep your bishop and creep your pawn forward in column D. When he's cleared the way, move your bishop to the side of the board and mate him with the pawn. You got that?" She looked at him. "Dad, have you got that? It's important."

"Jodie, that's madness, giving all your pieces away. How many times have you tried?"

"About two hundred."

"How many times have you won?"

"Does that matter?"

"How many times, Jodie?"

"Once, Dad, only once. But there is always a way, Dad, you told me that."

Dean gave her a hug.

"You get that bossiness from your mother, not me…"

"OK, time's up," Benjie announced. The time had actually been up twenty seconds ago. "It's a clown watch," Benjie said to Death. "It's not always working properly."

The skeletal figure stood up and walked over to them, took out his book and waved his hand across the page. Reading the highlights of what Jodie's life had in store for her, he smiled. Placing his hand on her head to get a deeper look, he closed his eyes. Jodie was not scared. Death looked kind, not evil. He could see she was going to be a doctor just like her mum, but more importantly, the life Death was seeing for Jodie was with Dean still alive. If Dean died, her future could be drastically altered.

Death pulled Jodie's head into his chest and lightly kissed it. He then said some soft words in the language that Dean had heard by the river, but this time without anger. These were not harsh words, but comforting words.

Death took Jodie's hand and placed it in Benjie's, then drew an imaginary line on the floor with his stick. They both understood that was a sign for them to stay there and not interfere. He pointed at Dean and then the chessboard. Jodie had set the clock to two minutes and thirty seconds, the same time that she'd set when she'd beaten Kyle.

"Two minutes thirty, Jodie? That's madness," said her dad. "Time and pressure..."

Death put his finger to his lips. "Shhhhh." The sound resonated around the room as if an enormous wave was crashing down onto a pebbled beach. Then there was silence. Jodie had done what she could. It was now up to her dad.

Death and Dean took their seats at the chess table, Dean thinking that Jodie had never beaten him at chess and now she was telling him to give all his pieces away. It was madness, but if it was going to be his last day on earth, he couldn't think of a better way to go down than trusting his daughter.

"Here goes, Jodie, I hope you're right."

The game started.

In the hospital, Dean's heart monitor was gathering pace and had triggered the alarm. Darren was at Dean's bedside, watching his rapid eye movement. This would normally have been a good sign, showing there was still a mind in there somewhere, but his heart rate was racing, and that was bad.

"Come on, Dean, fight it." Darren put a cool flannel on Dean's head, trying to cool him down. Dean's blood was pumping around his body quicker and quicker – 150 beats per minute now. This wasn't in any of the books that Darren had studied at med school with Sarah. If anything, Dean's heart rate should be getting weaker, not stronger.

Darren was joined by his team, getting ready for the cardiac arrest that looked to be heading their way.

Dean was spending no time on the clock. It was easy to play badly; it took no thought. He had managed to slip his pawn forward three spaces and the bishop's way was clearing, mainly due to the fact that his white pieces were quickly disappearing off the board.

Death was in feeding frenzy mode, just like Kyle had been before him. Rather than going for the win, he was enjoying the feast, turning down opportunities to check the white king in order to wipe out more pieces. Dean was winning on the clock – thirty seconds played twenty, but he could see the end was inevitable.

Dean glanced at Jodie. "Come on, Dad," she said under her breath as she gripped Benjie's hand harder. "He's got him. If Death goes for the rook, my dad's got him."

Death had ten seconds left on the clock and was going in for the kill. Instead of heading to check the king, he opted, like Kyle before him, to take the rook in the corner, thus paving the way for the bishop to do a runner to the other side of the board.

Death moved the black knight back, but it was too late. The gap was there, and the bishop had the little pawn back for him to take down the black king. Dean, his own clock down to four seconds, eased the pawn forward.

"Checkmate." Like his daughter before him, he stopped the timer with two seconds on the clock. Death had been defeated with five unused seconds.

Death looked over to Jodie and gave her a nod of appreciation. Then he stood and held out his hand to Dean. Dean's hair was stuck to his head with sweat from the battle. He shook the tall man's hand. Death was not sweating, but to be honest, he didn't look the sweaty type.

Dean had lived to fight another day.

Jodie ran across to her dad.

"Dad, I'm so proud of you. You did it."

Dean gave her the biggest hug.

"It was all about you, JoJo, I would never have done that on my own. Thank you."

Benjie prised Jodie off her dad.

"I have to take her back, Dean."

"Right, Jodie, I love you and your mum very much. I promise

I'll be back soon."

Benjie the clown walked Jodie into Dean's bedroom where they stepped back into Jodie's.

Death made an annotation in his book, touched the rim of his hat and bade Dean goodnight. He clicked his fingers and he and the chessboard were gone. Dean was left standing alone in his living area.

Chapter 30 – Room 117

Dean was no longer fazed by the fact that only a few people acknowledged Platform 19 at Liverpool Street Station. He knew it didn't exist, but that didn't stop him using it. The train line was no longer in use – he knew this, too, but all of these things were part of the game. Just closing his eyes and waking up at the hotel would not be half as much fun as the journey. It added to the drama of it all.

Dean had his normal chat with the smiley guard, who topped up his knowledge on diesel engines and coupling rods, but didn't once mention what had happened last week at Cockfield Station. That is if it was last week. Jodie had said it was five months since they'd started their game of chess and Dean was still trying to work that one out. It was one more item on his 'not making sense' list.

The train journey flew by, partly because Dean's mind was not taking much of it in. As nothing was real anymore, there seemed to be no point in dwelling on it. The one thing he did notice was a worried and confused looking older man sitting opposite him. The guard spent a lot of time with him, probably telling him all about the line and the disused station of Cockfield which they were currently creeping past.

"Welnetham Station, ladies and gentlemen. Welnetham is the next stop."

The guard opened the door and the old man got off. His case was under his arm as the handle appeared to be broken.

"Excuse me," he said to Dean, "do you know where Welnetham Hall is, please?"

Dean looked at the man, who seemed scared, dazed and confused.

"I have a room booked there, you see."

"I'm going that way myself," Dean replied. "I'll show you. Can I take your case, sir?" Dean took the old man's battered case before he had time to reply. They walked out of the station and made their way up the hill.

"Have you stayed at Welnetham Hall before?" the old man

enquired.

"Yes, I've been a couple of times."

Dean stopped to get a good look at the old man, who had fear in his eyes. "I'm frightened," he said unnecessarily.

"Don't be," replied Dean. "You will be guided to find your own way. It will all be OK."

Dean didn't know this for sure, but the old man seemed to be better for hearing it. They continued up the hill, chatting as they went.

"Well, here we are, sir, nice talking to you." Dean put the old man's case next to the hotel reception and rang the bell. A pleasing *ding* resonated around the open hallway.

Mrs McCauley had her officious head on again, the one Dean had seen on his first visit. He laughed quietly as she went through her routine with the old man. He knew she was a caring pussycat really, but she had to win the early exchanges with people to obtain the higher ground. The old man was putty in her hands by the time she turned and gave him his key.

"Mr Thompson, have a good day. I hope you enjoy your room. It's Room 119, the best we have in the hotel."

Dean looked at Mr Thompson's key with 119 written on it. Still bewildered, Mr Thompson crept up the stairs to his room.

"Hi, Mrs McCauley."

Her face lit up.

"I'm so pleased you're still with us, Dean." She probably knew all about the events on the train station and the chess game. All the people he had met – his guides, as they called themselves – seemed to know exactly what had gone on, even if they hadn't been there personally.

"OK, you're in Room 117 today, Dean. It's the best room in the hotel."

Dean decided not to mention that fact that a few seconds ago, she'd told Mr Thompson that Room 119 was the best in the hotel. He guessed Mrs McCauley thought *every* room was the best room in the hotel.

"I would have preferred Room 119, Mrs McCauley."

She raised her eyes above her glasses and gave him *that* look.

"You no longer need that room, Dean, and you know it. Mr Thompson needs to find his way now. We have picked him, although I personally think it is a very long shot indeed."

She looked back at her book and continued to fill in the register.

"Is the bar open, Mrs McCauley? I might have a quick drink before I go to my room."

Mrs McCauley put down her pen.

"Yes, you will find David in there. If you ask him, he'll get your case for you. It was handed in last week – it appears that you left it on the train platform. Everything was a bit wet, so we have taken the liberty of washing and ironing it for you."

Dean had forgotten about the case that went flying all over the platform after last week's visit.

"You didn't have to do that, Mrs McCauley."

Without looking up, she said, "I know we didn't, but we did."

Dean headed to the bar to get his case and see the barman. David looked about forty years older than the youthful, vibrant David Dean had met last week. He still had a moustache, but his blond locks had turned to grey. Wrinkles, nooks and crannies covered his face, giving him character. He was cleaning glasses as usual.

"Hello, Dean." David offered his hand; Dean shook it.

"Hi, David. I didn't get much chance to thank you for last week." He gave David's hand an extra two shakes and gripped it a little harder.

"I'm just glad you're still here, Dean. I think you have him confused. Well done on the chess game, by the way. Benjie told me all about it. That game has earned you a lot of respect. You're not in the clear yet, though, so keep on your guard."

"Can I have a drink, David? God, I need one."

David poured him a pint.

"On the house, sir, it's our pleasure."

"Oh, I nearly forgot – you have my case, I believe?"

"I'll just go and get it for you, Dean."

Jodie was having a bite to eat with her mum before Sarah headed off for night time visiting.

"Mum?"

Sarah looked up.

"Yes, Jodie, what's up?"

Jodie took a deep breath.

"Right, I know you're not going to believe me, but will you let me at least finish?"

Her mother sighed.

"Jodie, we've been through this. If it's about clowns, chess or both, you have to stop it. Your dad is seriously ill in hospital and I need you to be there for him, not just making up stories."

Sarah threw her knife and fork down onto her plate. She'd lost her appetite.

"Don't you believe me, Mum?"

"Jodie, put yourself in my position. I'm trying to be there for your dad and be there for you. I don't think I can cope with this bullshit anymore, and I know that's swearing."

"But, Mum, I think Dad is going to come back."

Sarah gave Jodie a stern look. Jodie had had enough – she was going to say what she had to say.

"Right, Mum, LISTEN. The clown took me to Dad's house last night just after midnight and he played this man in black at chess. I told Dad what to do and he did it brilliantly. It was all about time and pressure. We put him on the clock – two minutes, thirty seconds each, and Dad won with two seconds to spare on his clock, and the man in black had five seconds left…"

Her mother grabbed her bag and keys. "You're unbelievable, Jodie, you really are." She started to cry.

"I knew you wouldn't believe me, Mum, you never do!"

"Jodie, enough! I love you, but can you just think about things, please? This isn't a game; chess is not going to bring your dad back."

Sarah hugged Jodie more through duty than love then headed off to the car, tears flowing down her cheeks.

Dean entered his room, which was a carbon copy of Room 119. *Best room in the hotel,* he thought, laughing. *Well that's because they are all the same, aren't they, Mrs McCauley?* He had more or less the same view as he did from Room 119 – nothing but fields, and nothing going on. He lay on his bed, and before long was asleep.

When Dean awoke, coloured lights were reflecting through

the window and dancing on the ceiling. He ran over to the window and there was his old friend the funfair, the Big Top of the circus as its centrepiece.

Hearing noises coming from next door, Dean rushed to put on his shoes and checked he had his Ferryman coin in his pocket. Anything could happen now, and he needed to be prepared for more than anything. If he did end up queuing for the ferry, he did not fancy suffering a hundred years of turmoil just for not having his fare.

He heard the door slam next door and the footsteps of Mr Thompson leaving the room. Dean finished lacing up his shoes, grabbed his key and opened the door, slipping through and closing it behind him in one movement like he'd been rehearsing it for weeks. Right now, Dean's mind was slick. Everything was sharp; everything he did had a purpose.

Mr Thompson was turning down the stairs. Dean followed, keeping his distance. Mr Thompson left the hotel and took time to orientate himself, getting his bearings and working out where the noise and lights were coming from. He then headed off through the darkening gloom, back down the hill towards the funfair.

Dean didn't want to scare the old man as he'd looked scared enough at the station. He gave Mr Thompson a head start, letting him get a good way down the road. Dean then left the hotel entrance and followed, keeping his distance.

Mr Thompson turned on to the track in much the same way as Dean had done a couple of weeks ago. Or was it a few months ago? His 'not making sense' list gave his mind a nudge as he followed Mr Thompson quietly. He saw the old man approach the fork in the road. The silver cane, complete with its owner, came tapping its usual rhythm up the hill from the other direction.

Mr Thompson approached the turn off for the track ahead of Death, passing the apologetic signpost which was again doing its best to corral people into where the fun was happening. The silver cane made the turn off a few seconds before Dean did, and Death stopped and raised his cane to tip the brim of his hat upwards to acknowledge him. Dean could see in Death's eyes that he was no longer was holding his interest; Death had a new target in his crosshairs. He was catching Mr Thompson without really trying – he was good at that.

Dean followed at a watching brief. He saw when Mr

Thompson noticed he was being followed, and much the same as Dean had done before him, he sped up, frantically looking over his shoulder. Death floated across the ground, and again the crowd parted under his control as if he was a magnet with the same polarity as the people. Meanwhile, Mr Thompson was bumping into just about everything and everyone as he fumbled his way forward.

Dean could not really see them anymore now as they were working their way through far too much human traffic. They passed the stall where Dean had thrown the cuddly toys behind him and headed off through the gap between that and the next stall. Dean got a good sight of Mr Thompson who was deciding which way to go, looking left and right, even more confused than he'd been earlier.

Death was like the lion and Mr Thompson was the gazelle. The lion was relentless, and the feeble legs of Mr Thompson were failing him. He had no run left in him and the lion was going in for the kill.

Dean thought how he himself had fought all the way through every test, and Mr Thompson was giving up at the first hurdle. The old man was now in the clearing, looking for a way out.

"Open the door," Dean said under his breath.

Dean made his way around the stall. Mr Thompson was still in the clearing.

"The door, behind you. Open the fucking door!" Dean whispered, urging the old man into a decision.

Mr Thompson made one last attempt to get away and staggered around the corner. Death gave Dean a regretful look before following Mr Thompson, raising his cane as he did so. Dean could see the shadow of the lion taking down his prey. The old man crumpled into the corner, then both the shadows evaporated into the tent's canvas.

Dean bowed his head. He guessed Mr Thompson had gone.

Chapter 31 – Bobo

Dean looked at the familiar door across the clearing – a door that had once saved his life. Hoping an old friend would be behind it – a friend he owed a big thank you or two – he pulled the door open and walked in. He was not disappointed.

Without turning round, Benjie the clown watched Dean entering the room in one of the angled mirrors on his dressing table.

"Hello, Dean, no Mr Thompson?"

Dean shook his head and lowered it at the same time.

"Shame." The clown stopped putting on his makeup and they shared a few seconds of silence in respect. Dean was not sure exactly what was going to happen next for Mr Thompson, but he guessed from the silence that it would not be a good thing.

Benjie broke the silence and tried lightening the mood.

"Dean, well played in the chess game."

Dean moved closer to get a better look at the clown's face in one of the other two mirrors.

"Well, I think Jodie deserves all the credit."

The clown raised his eyebrows, and he had a lot of eyebrows to raise with the face he had chosen today.

"It wasn't about you winning, Dean."

Dean looked confused and a bit hurt. He'd gone through the mill in that chess game.

Benjie laughed. "He could have beaten you whenever he wanted to, Dean. He has been on this earth since the beginning of time. He just about invented the game of chess."

"What was it about, then?" The clown turned and looked at him, and Dean added, "I know, you can only guide me. I get it." Dean remembered Jodie telling him what to do and he'd doubted her, but in the end he'd trusted her and gone with her tactics. "It was about *trust*, wasn't it? It was about me believing in the ones I love and trusting them."

Benjie smiled.

"There is hope for you yet, Dean. You listened to her and

trusted her judgment. Do you think you would have done that before you started on your journey?"

Dean looked up and pictured some thoughts in his mind to help answer that question. He had always been telling Jodie what to do, or telling her to be quiet as he was talking to her mum. He couldn't find one single memory where he had listened to her and trusted her.

Was I really that bad? he thought.

"No, you weren't that bad, Dean. You just lost your way and ended up a bit of prick, to be honest."

Dean started to agree, and then it dawned on him.

"How did you know I was thinking that?"

"Of course I know what you're thinking. We all do – we're in your head. We are all just visitors trying to help you find your way, whichever way that is. You have got further than most get. It doesn't stop us trying to help, though." Benjie continued applying his colourful makeup in the mirror. "You have had the bumpiest ride of anyone by far. We've nearly lost you more times than I want to mention." He started on his lips with red greasepaint. "You have him confused, and I've never seen him like this, Dean. Keep your coin handy until you know for definite. You might still need it. My guess is that he has another test up his sleeve before he will allow you back, but to be honest, you have us all stumped on this one." More red paint was liberally applied to his clown face. "Be ready for anything."

Dean looked back at the door.

"What happened to Mr Thompson?"

"Dean, we get to choose a few who we think have a chance, but they have to have the will deep inside them to return and prove to him they want to go back. Mr Thompson was a long shot. He's been very ill. He could have come through this door like you did and fought his way out, but I guess he had no fight left in him."

Dean again looked at the door. "What will happen to him?"

"He will be given a danake coin and will take a ride on the ferry with Charon up the River Styx, but he'll be OK. He was ready, Dean. It was Mr Thompson's time."

Dean looked at the floor. That could have been his fate. Maybe it still would be.

The clown tried lightening the mood for a second time. "What do you think?" He stood up wearing red braces, red trousers and a yellow jacket with a check running through it. He had a big flower on the lapel.

"You look great."

Benjie had a full figure bordering on fat, but he had fat in all the right places. As far as the clown was concerned, fat is funny. People laughed more if the fat guy got a custard pie in the face. Dean was normal size, neither short and fat nor tall and skinny. He wasn't clown material.

"Does anyone really fall for the old 'smell the flower' trick?" Dean asked. The clown looked hurt.

"I can't believe you would ask such a thing! A clown needs a stooge and a stooge needs a clown. There's a team. The stooge smells the flower – that's how it works."

Dean looked around. "But I've only ever seen you. Who is the Morecambe to your Wise, the Little to your Large, the Cannon to your Ball, the Vic to your Bob?"

The clown turned his happy smile upside down.

"He died a few years ago, Dean, and for the record, he was the Bobo to my Benjie. I've performed on my own since." Benjie pointed out a picture slotted into the side of one of the mirrors showing a tall, thin figure and a much younger version of himself all clowned up before a performance. "Twenty-five years together, and never one cross word."

Dean could see he had upset the clown. "I'm sorry, Benjie – can I call you Benjie?"

"You can call me Benjie, that's my name. I would like that, Dean." Benjie seemed to perk up a bit. "We have some very special guests coming to see the show tonight."

"Special guests? Who is coming to see you, Benjie?"

"Not me, Dean, you. Who would you like to see more than anybody in the world right now?"

Dean looked at him.

"You know what I'm thinking, so you know who."

"Would you like to see them, Dean?"

"Of course I would! You know that I would do anything to see them right now."

Benjie saw an opportunity. "OK, we need to get you ready." He opened the door to his late partner's wardrobe and rifled through the outfits. "I'm sure we'll find something in here that will fit."

"Hang on, whoa, I know I said anything, but you want me to dress as a clown?"

"Do you want to see Sarah and Jodie?" said Benjie, looking over his shoulder at Dean. Dean laughed.

"Well of course."

"Then yes, I want you to be a clown. This one." Benjie pulled an outfit from the wardrobe. It was the opposite outfit to his own – yellow trousers, red jacket.

"I don't even know how to…er…clown."

"Know how to clown? Does that actually mean anything? I am a performer, Dean. Us clowns perform, we don't *clown*."

Benjie's attitude changed. He blubbed uncontrollably, sobbing and crying real tears. This went on longer than Dean might have expected, so he moved across to Benjie and caught his reflection in the mirror. He hadn't meant to hurt the clown's feelings.

"Sorry, I didn't mean it," he said, putting an arm around Benjie's shoulders.

"Ha, ha, ha, got you! See, we perform. Now do you think you can do as you're told and perform, Dean?" Benjie held up the outfit.

"Are Sarah and Jodie definitely going to be there?"

"Clown's honour."

It was a better offer than anything else Dean had, but he knew Sarah and Jodie hated clowns. The last time he'd talked to Jodie about clowns, he'd said he was going to sort one of them out, and in this very room, he had pinned Benjie against the wall.

"OK, you're on," Dean said with as much enthusiasm as he could drum up.

Benjie had a bounce to his step as he threw the outfit at Dean. "Put this on, then I'll do your makeup and talk you through our old routine."

Dean took the outfit and went behind the dressing screen to get changed.

"How did Bobo die?" he called over to the clown who was preparing the makeup for his face.

"He died of Alzheimer's. I'm eighty-six and we were partners in life as well as on the stage. I really miss him, Dean."

Dean was struggling with getting the cross right on the back of the yellow braces.

"What do you mean you're eighty-six? And how can he be

dead? Aren't you all…"

Dean stopped. It was a bit inappropriate to ask people if they were already dead.

"Oh, it doesn't matter. Sorry. I bet you had fun performing with him."

The clown looked over to the screen.

"When I go, I'm hoping we can perform again. He performed with me here for a while as one of the guides before he passed."

Caught up in reminiscing, Benjie was inadvertently saying too much, but Dean wasn't really trying to work things out right now. He was far too nervous about seeing Sarah and Jodie, and making his clown debut in front of what sounded like a growing crowd beyond the stage door.

Chapter 32 – Four Minutes, Fifty-three Seconds

Sarah arrived at the hospital in good time for visiting. She gave the receptionist a wave – for the last five months it had been just like she was working here again. It seemed she was spending more time in the hospital than at home. Jodie was fine with it as it was for her dad, and anyway, Sarah was still pissed off with Jodie. Clowns, chess and now strangers in black. It was too much.

If Dean did not regain consciousness soon, and that was looking less and less likely, then who knew what might be around the corner? Darren had already phoned to say that something had happened last night that he needed to speak to her about. This conversation could be good or bad news. Good news would be signs of recovery, but if it was bad, it could be that Dean was showing no more signs of life and a decision had to be made. Sarah was dreading the latter. Making a decision to end her husband's life, even if it was the right decision, did not sit comfortably with Sarah.

She headed out of the lift and on to the ward, her mind spinning with possibilities. Darren was sitting on Dean's bed, looking at his charts.

"You have a fighter, Sarah, I'll give him that. I'm not sure he's ready to go yet."

"Why, what's happened, Darren?"

"He went into REM last night, eyes all over the place, so we can safely say his brain is active. He was dreaming like a good 'un, but it's whatever he was dreaming about that worries me." Sarah looked puzzled. "Look at the heart rate, through the roof. He should be dead, Sarah. I don't know how he's hanging on."

"May I?" Darren handed the charts over for her to look at. "Wow, his heart rate touched two hundred and forty beats per minute. When did this happen, Darren?"

"Just after midnight last night, then it went back to normal as quickly as it had started."

Sarah looked at the chart again.

"How long did it go on for, Darren? How long from when his heart rate started to climb until it started to drop?"

"Just under five minutes."

"How much under, Darren? Let me guess – seven seconds."

Darren looked like he had seen a ghost.

"Yes, but how the hell did you know that? It was exactly four minutes, fifty-three seconds from the first beat up to the first beat down. I made a note. What's going on, Sarah?"

"I can't explain right now, Darren." Sarah put a comforting hand on Darren's shoulder as she got up and gave Dean a kiss. "I love you, Dean, but I need to go."

She headed out of the ward as quickly as she'd come in, then, remembering her manners, she turned to address Dean's doctor.

"Darren, thank you so much. I think Dean may be coming back. I don't know why I didn't listen to what my daughter was trying to tell me. She deserves an apology from her mother right now, so I need to go."

Sarah got back to her car and phoned Jodie. The call went to voicemail, which was to be expected. Jodie was in a teenage strop. Sarah drove home as quickly as the speed limit would allow her and headed upstairs before she'd even taken her coat off.

"Jodie, are you asleep?"

Jodie pulled the covers in tightly and rolled further into the corner.

"Yes," she barked.

"Jodie, I'm so sorry. I believe you now. Your dad's heart rate was irregular last night, and do you know how long for?"

Jodie turned one eye in her mother's direction.

"Four minutes and fifty-three seconds, I would guess."

"Now I can't explain any of this, but wherever you were last night seems to have affected your dad, so if you helped him win, you probably saved his life."

Jodie sat up. "I knew it, Mum! It was too real and meant too much."

"How did he look?"

"He looked great, Mum. It was amazing seeing him. He said he loved us both very much and would be back soon."

Sarah hugged her daughter, crying. "I hope so, Jodie, I really hope so," she said, wiping the tears from her face.

"He'll be OK, Mum."

"But how do you know, Jodie?"

Jodie turned her head, looking at her mother face to face.

"Because he promised, Mum. He promised me he was coming back, and I believe him cos he's my dad."

They hugged for a while longer. Whatever had happened last night had injected hope into the situation. Dean was fighting, and if that was the case, the least they could do was fight with him.

"He said I was just like you because I was bossy." Jodie and Sarah shared a laugh, and it had been a while since they had had time to laugh. It had been all about crying in the last few months.

"Am I bossy, Jodie?" Her daughter's silence answered the question. Sarah added, "I really hope he comes back to us, JoJo."

"He will, Mum, he will. He said so."

Benjie was going through his routine while doing Dean's makeup. Dean was in his new clothes, but he had not put his long red clown shoes on yet, and wasn't really looking forward to it. They looked five sizes too big; it would be like walking on planks. He looked the part, though – his makeup was just about there. It looked like he was going to be the sad face clown to complement Benjie's happy face.

"So, have you got that, Dean? Let me test you. Step one?"

"You run on and look for me. I have not arrived yet," Dean replied. "Yep, got that."

Benjie continued through the routine. "I say that you're really nervous and ask the crowd if they would like to see Bobo's new car." Dean nodded. "Then you make your big entrance in Chug Chug."

"Got that."

"Then you press buttons one, two, three and four in order while you're driving along so various bits fall off the car. You got that?"

"Yep, I've got that. What do I press to make the car go?"

The clown laughed at him. "Dean, you pedal it."

"Of course I do! What was I thinking? OK, got that too."

Benjie went through the rest of the routine and got Dean to recite it back to him a few times while he finished his makeup and hair.

"Right, what do you think?"

Dean looked in the mirror.

"You do know after all this that I won't be happy if Sarah and Jodie aren't there, don't you?"

The clown gave him a tap on the back.

"Yes, but I will be, Dean. Is that not enough?"

"I suppose so. How long before we are on?"

Benjie looked at his clown watch.

"Ten minutes, and remember to have fun. When did you last have fun, Dean?"

Dean couldn't remember when his life had last had proper fun in it. It had got far too serious for fun; maybe it was about time he put that right. He didn't reply to the clown; the question did not require an answer. It required some realisation with a side order of self-examination.

In the Big Top, the circus was in full swing. The trapeze artists had just finished their routine, and before them the blindfolded knife thrower had completed his performance, much to the relief of his assistant who would live to see another day. There wasn't really an interval at the circus; it was time for the clowns to keep everyone entertained so the sets could be changed. This was their big moment.

Benjie and Dean were in the entrance to the circus ring.

"Dean, from this moment you are Bobo the Clown, and before we go on, we have to honour the age old clown tradition."

Dean had got this far. If he was going to be a clown, he was going to do it properly.

"OK, I'm Bobo. What's the tradition?"

Benjie leant forward. "We always smell each other's flowers. It's been done for years and pays homage to all the clowns who have come before us." Benjie was primed in the 'smell my flower' position. "Bobo, do you want to smell my lovely flower?"

Reluctantly, Dean took up the offer and got a faceful of water.

"OK, your turn. Would you like to smell my flower, Benjie?"

Benjie gave him an 'are you stupid?' look before ordering him into his car.

"It's not a tradition at all, is it, Benjie?"

"Of course not. Thought it might get rid of your nerves." He laughed at Bobo, soaking wet in a clown car. "Good luck, Dean."

"Benjie, I'm Bobo. No more Dean."

The ringmaster was in the centre of the ring which was covered in sand. She was wearing the tightest of tight white ski trousers and red tails and was holding a cone-shaped amplifier for effect. The crowd's eyes followed her every move and listened to her every word. There was an expectant hush of excitement, a quiet buzz of anticipation.

"As we head for the end of the show, Bobo and Benjie are going to paint their boat. Would you like to see them, boys and girls?" The noise went through the roof – the unmistakable high-pitched cheer of hundreds of kids. Having this many kids hanging on to her every word, the ringmaster milked it for everything it had.

"Are you sure, boys and girls?" A louder shriek bounced off all sides of the Big Top.

"Bobo and Benjie might come out and see you if you shout for them really loudly, kids. Are you ready? After three, shout for Bobo. One, two, three…"

Bobo's name was screamed from all angles. *No pressure there, then*, Dean thought. His clown debut was getting worse by the minute. Trying to remember his routine, he looked over to Benjie who was doing a few stretches like a total pro. Benjie gave Dean the thumbs up.

"OK, boys and girls, and what about his best friend, Benjie? One, two, three…"

Benjie received an even louder scream. That was his cue. The ringmaster had whipped the crowd into a frenzy – what could possibly go wrong? The distinctive *Dut dut, dera dera, dut dut, da da…Dut dut, dera dera, dut dut, da da* clown music started, and Dean, now in Bobo mode, got the nod from Benjie.

Benjie walked on stage carrying two overly large paint pots around his neck on a yoke. He was heading for the boat on the other side of the circus ring, shuffling through the dusting of sawdust on the floor. Every so often, he dipped his finger into the pots to show they contained paint – one tin of red, one tin of yellow.

As he got nearer the crowd, he started spinning, faster and faster. The paint pots were raised up until eventually they were horizontal, but not a drop was spilled. The crowd cheered and gasped all at the same time.

Benjie came out of his spin and put the pots down near the

boat, staggering and dizzy. He cupped his hand to his mouth and shouted, "Bobo…Bo…bo."

"Bobo…Bo…bo…" echoed the crowd.

Dean started to pedal Bobo's car, thinking *what on earth am I doing?* But seeing as he was there, he would give it his best shot. As he came through the archway onto the circle, the sound wave hit him. The kids were screaming and shouting his name.

Benjie had told Dean that his Bobo character was the idiot. In clowning, there is always a boss and always an idiot. "Think Laurel and Hardy," he'd said. The trick was for the crowd not to hate the boss, but they had to love the idiot.

Dean was struggling to pedal the car along the dusting of sand and sawdust under the wheels. It didn't help that the wheels were not actually round, more hexagonal. All the while, he was waving to the crowd. He'd forgotten all about whether Sarah and Jodie were there; he was too busy trying not to let Benjie down.

Benjie was shouting, "Hurry up, Bobo, c'mon, Bobo, hurry up." That was the cue for Dean to press button one on his car. There was a big explosion and the doors blew off sideways. Dean had not been expecting such a big explosion and nearly jumped out of his seat, standing up for a brief second while still pedalling. The crowd roared and screamed with laughter.

Sarah and Jodie were about three rows back from the circle.

"Why didn't you join in shouting for Bobo, Jodie?"

The stare Sarah got back would have melted ice.

"Really, Mum?" Jodie said, and they both laughed.

Jodie was the first to notice. "Mum, there's Dad."

"Where, Jodie, where?" Her mum was looking all around the crowd. Jodie pointed at the ring.

"There, Mum, he's in the car. He's Bobo."

Sarah followed the direction of Jodie's pointing finger and finally saw him. She shouted, "Dean!" but her voice was drowned out by the crowd.

"Mum, he looks so stupid."

Sarah started laughing.

"I think that's the whole point, Jodie."

Chapter 33 – That's Not Clowning, That's Performing

Dean pressed button two and the car bonnet blew off. Again Dean stood up, but this time on purpose. *It worked last time*, he thought.

Benjie ran over to the car and asked for a lift. Dean pointed to the standing plate at the back of the car and Benjie hopped on. After another couple of pedals, Dean pressed button three and the boot blew off, launching Benjie off the back of the car as planned.

Dean pedalled on towards the boat. When he got there, he pressed button four. What was left of the car exploded, leaving Dean in the chassis, soot all over his face and hair. The door of the car was still in his hand, so he opened it and stood up, dropping it onto the floor.

"Ben…jeeee!" he shouted, looking back to see Benjie under the car boot in the middle of the circus ring. Dean took off his little bowler hat and replaced it with a big white one from a prop box behind the boat. It had a red cross on the front and a blue flashing light on the top, and the music changed to an ambulance siren. Dean grabbed a first aid handcart and ran off to save his mate, Benjie.

He removed the car boot and examined Benjie with an enormous stethoscope. The drum beat in the background indicated his heart was fine. Dean then took a large thermometer out of the cart. He was not sure which end of Benjie to place it in, so he asked the crowd for help, pointing to Benjie's big bum which was sticking in the air.

When he said, "Bum," there was a big cheer. "Or face?" There was silence. "Bum?" A massive cheer.

Dean took a big swing as he went to put the thermometer in Benjie's bum. Benjie jumped up as the thermometer hit him, and Dean dropped it. Benjie swung a punch at Dean's head. As he did so, Dean bent down to pick up the thermometer and he missed. Benjie then went to kick Dean's bum just as Dean stood back up, and again he missed. It was slapstick of the highest order.

Benjie and Dean eventually made their way over to paint the

boat, putting on some big white overalls. The music changed to the *Vision On* gallery theme. Benjie had a big yellow pot, Dean had a big red one, and they both had an enormous paintbrushes. Things were going well.

Dean started painting the bottom of the boat and Benjie climbed up the ladder, painting it higher up. Benjie bounced the ladder every time he needed to move it along the boat, which got a big round of applause. The crowd was eating out of their hands right now. Dean then clumsily knocked the ladder over with his big brush, leaving Benjie dangling from the boat holding his paint pot.

"Bobo, ladder!"

Dean picked up the ladder and saved Benjie. While the crowd applauded, he put his brush under his arm and took a bow, knocking the ladder over again and leaving Benjie dangling. Dean looked like he had been Bobo for years.

They were nearing their big finale, and Dean started to look out for Sarah and Jodie in the crowd.

"Three rows back under area D," Benjie said under his breath. "OK, Dean, let's finish this off with a bang."

Benjie gave Dean a wink. There was a drumroll, and the crowd took a huge collective intake of breath. The spotlight was illuminating a large red and yellow cannon at the far end of the circle, opposite the newly painted boat. It had a human-sized barrel.

Dean in the character of Bobo looked at the cannon. "No, no, no, Benjie, not after the last time."

"It's fixed, Bobo, I fixed it myself…"

"Not after last time, Benjie, no, no, no!"

Dean tried to run away; Benjie pulled him back by his braces.

"Ladies and gentlemen, boys and girls, do you want to see Bobo fly?"

Of course they did. There was a huge cheer and clapping.

"I don't want to fly again, Benjie, after last time." Dean's bottom lip started to quiver.

"I promise it's fixed, Bobo."

Benjie passed Dean a crash helmet. "You might need this, Bobo, after last time, remember?"

Dean strapped on his helmet. It had *BANG* written on the top.

"Ladies and gentlemen, boys and girls, do you want to see

Bobo fly?"

"Yes," echoed around the arena. His legs quivering, Dean climbed the stepladder slowly, each step accompanied by a beat from a snare drum. If the ringmaster had been milking it earlier, Dean was pasteurising it and turning it into cheese. Occasionally he took half a step downwards, to loud boos until he replaced his foot on the rung above.

Dean got into the cannon feet first, his head protruding and his BANG helmet in full view.

"OK, Bobo, you're in," said Benjie.

"Yes, I'm in, Benjie." Dean gave a thumbs up. Benjie looked at the crowd.

"Do you think we are aiming high enough?"

"Lower, lower, Benjie," Dean shouted, trying to get out of the cannon. Benjie kicked away the stepladder to stop him.

"Should we go higher, boys and girls?"

There was a deafening cheer of "Higher" from the frantic crowd.

"OK, let's go higher, Bobo."

Benjie turned the big wheel on the side of the cannon, accompanied by a cranky ratchet sound, raising the cannon by about 45 degrees. He then looked at the crowd on all sides of the circle.

"OK, boys and girls, should we go higher?"

"Higher! Higher!"

"OK, Bobo, let's go higher."

Dean, still looking out of his cannon, shouted, "Lower, lower, lower!"

"So Bobo wants to go lower, boys and girls." He pointed to Dean in the cannon. "And Benjie," he pointed to himself, "wants Bobo to go higher. But it's not up to me." Benjie pointed to the crowd. "It's only fair, Bobo, if these lovely boys and girls get to choose. Do you think that's fair, Bobo?"

Dean nodded.

"OK, the boys and girls can choose." Benjie added, "Lower, lower, lower," but got no takers from the crowd. "OK, boys and girls, this is your time to shine. If you want Bobo to go higher, scream and make some noise."

If the Big Top had not been chained down, the roof would have blown off. Bobo's fate was sealed right there and then.

Benjie wound the wheel one turn and moved the angle even higher. He looked at the crowd and pointed upward, asking them if he should turn the wheel again. He got a cheer, so raised the cannon to the limit.

Benjie came to the front of the cannon and looked up at Dean. "Are you OK up there, Bobo?" Dean gave him the thumbs up. "OK, boys and girls, Bobo is going to fly through the air at over a million miles an hour, land on our new boat and raise the Benjie and Bobo flag. Well, we hope so anyway. Wave at Bobo as you might never see him again."

Dean waved at the crowd before lowering himself deeper into the cannon. While Benjie was buying some time playing up to the audience, Dean had to sneak out of the cannon, put in a clown dummy, then run under the seating area to a secret entrance on the far side of the boat. As Dean was making his way under the crowd, he could see Benjie through a gap in the seating. Benjie was in his element; he had been born to do this, and if nothing else, Dean had made an old clown very happy today. For that he was proud.

He continued on to the boat and lay there, blacking up his face for explosive effect, and waited.

Benjie lit an oversized match on an oversized matchbox and made his way to the cannon. He lit the fuse, which fizzed and spluttered slowly towards the back of the cannon. He then started the countdown with the crowd.

"Ten…nine…eight…seven…" the crowd all joined in, "…six…five…four…" anticipation oozed from all around the Big Top, "…three…two…one…"

BANG! The cannon exploded and its wheels fell off. At the same time, a clown-like figure was powering through the air, not quite at a million miles an hour, but flying nevertheless. The dummy did its job perfectly and landed next to Dean in the bottom of the boat. That was Dean's prompt. He took a flag in his mouth and shimmied up the mast. First one, then two, then the whole of the crowd spotted that Bobo had survived.

"Bobo! Bobo!" they chanted as Benjie started a rhythmic clapping. "Bobo! Bobo!"

Dean climbed higher and higher, then took the flag out of his mouth and attached it to the mast. He pulled the tether on the flag, which was a pair of enormous clown's bloomers with Benjie on one leg and Bobo on the other.

Dean jumped off the mast onto a crash mat hidden in the bottom of the boat. The crowd were on their feet, cheering and clapping, some of them still chanting the name of their new hero: "Bobo, Bobo!"

Dean got out of the back of the boat and ran to Benjie and gave him a big hug. Benjie, forever the performer, made him line up and do the proper bows to all sides of the circus ring. The cheering had not yet abated; the spectators were still on their feet.

Then Benjie and Dean shouted, "Water fight!" and ran to the ambulance cart for two buckets of water each. Benjie threw his at Dean, soaking him again. Dean returned the compliment. The crowd was in stitches.

"Does anybody else want a water fight?" Benjie asked the audience. They grabbed another bucket each and walked in opposite directions, accompanied by the 'you're getting crept up on' music of pantomimes, pretending to throw the water into the audience. They circled the first few rows, and the spectators cowered backwards.

Three quarters of the way round, Dean spotted Sarah and Jodie. He shouted, "Benjie, are you ready? One…two…three…" In perfect synchronisation, they threw their buckets' contents into the crowd. Expecting to get drenched, everyone sank their heads into their shoulders as they were showered in silver and blue tinsel.

Dean looked at Sarah and Jodie, who were laughing. "I love you both. I'll see you soon, I promise." He gave them both a wave and blew them two kisses.

The ringmaster announced, "OK, ladies and gentlemen, give it up one more time for Bobo…" Dean took a bow "…and Benjie." Benjie took a bow. Then they both bowed together, hand in hand as they received a standing ovation from all sides of the circus ring. They ran off through the entrance to the ring before heading back to the dressing room. As they entered, Benjie gave Dean a big pat on the back.

"Dean, that was not clowning, that was performing. I'm very proud of you."

Dean had his hands on his knees, exhausted.

"Benjie, I have not had that much fun since…"

It dawned on Dean that it was so long ago he couldn't remember.

Chapter 34 – Breakfast at Epiphany's

The people were long gone from the Big Top. Benjie and Dean, still in their clown attire less their wet jackets, were sharing a drink from Benjie's hip flask.

"That was one hell of a performance," said Benjie. "Even my Bobo would have been impressed. Your timing was fabulous."

They were sitting on the front row of the Big Top. The place looked different with no crowd; the paint and colours had lost their gloss. There were no lights to make them dance. Everything was still and calm; the benches were all vacant, apart for the one they were occupying.

"Not many get to see this, Dean."

Dean looked at his surroundings. "What, an empty circus?"

Benjie hit Dean on the arm with his hip flask.

"No, you idiot, to see themselves crawling out of a hole and heading back to the real world. Very few make it. I think he's going to let you back, you know."

Dean stared at him. "Really?" After seeing Sarah and Jodie tonight, he wanted nothing more than to hold them both right now.

"He was watching, you know. At the back. Didn't you see him? He was there at the end."

"Where? Err, no, I never saw him. Why? "

"He wants to make sure that if he gives you a second chance, you mean it. It won't have gone unnoticed what you did for me, and more importantly, how much it meant to you to see Sarah and Jodie."

Dean gestured, asking to have another sip from the clown's hip flask. Benjie obliged.

"Hope you're right, Benjie."

"He's firm, but fair, Dean, but he has to be sure. You're very close, though, I can feel it. Whatever happens, you have passed all the tests given to you so far. Courage in the fairground the first visit; compassion with your mum and dad; determination on the train station; trust with Jodie in your chess game; and today you proved you can still have fun." Benjie took the flask from Dean and had a swig before handing it back. "I will never forget tonight, Dean. You made an old clown very happy before he goes."

Dean looked at him.

"Before he goes where?"

Before Benjie could answer, Death's silver cane caught what little light there was and cast a reflection in their direction. Death, Mr Thompson under his arm, was at the far end of the circus tent and starting to make his way across the ring. Benjie took back his hipflask and hid it in one of his overly large clown's pockets.

"I shouldn't really be drinking on duty."

Jodie again had a sleep in; it seemed the norm nowadays. It was Saturday morning, or what was left of the morning, and she was recalling bits and pieces about last night. Not only the conversation with her mum and how Sarah now believed her about the clown, but also her visit to the circus to see her dad. She decided she wouldn't push the subject unless her mother brought it up.

She put on some jeans and a tee shirt and headed downstairs for breakfast. Her mother had not been up long, either; last night had taken it out of her emotionally and physically.

"Hi, Jodie, did you sleep well?" she asked.

Jodie more or less managed to answer through a muffled yawn. "Yes, Mum." The yawn continued. "Did you?"

Sarah was at the toaster, trying not to look at the bread as the toaster always seemed to take longer to toast it if she watched it.

"I didn't sleep great, Jodie, to be fair."

Pop! The toast announced it was ready.

"Strawberry jam or marmalade, JoJo?" Sarah asked.

"Is it that silver marmalade or the orange one?"

Sarah had started opening the jar before she'd answered.

"The silver one. I know you don't like the orange one." She buttered the toast, smothered an ample amount of Silver Shred marmalade over Jodie's and passed it over to her. Jodie poured fresh orange juice into a glass from the jug in the middle of the table.

"Mum?"

"Yes, Jodie."

"You know I used to say I didn't like clowns?"

"Yes." Sarah cuddled her oversized coffee mug and took a welcoming sip, her eyes wide open and peering over the rim.

"Well, I had a dream last night, and before you stop me, you were even in it, Mum."

"Go on."

"We were in a circus. Benjie and Bobo the clowns came on. They were so funny."

Jodie looked at her mother for a reaction before carrying on. Sarah's eyes started to well up.

"What happened next, Jodie?"

"Well, Benjie was my clown – the one who has been coming to see me about chess and to help my dad – and Bobo was Dad. He was laughing and joking, and he even got fired out of a big cannon into a boat they were painting." Jodie had a smile on her face as her mind relived the performance. "And do you know what the best bit was, Mum?"

Her mother put her coffee down, her eyes full of tears.

"Was it when he threw the bucket of glitter over us at the end, Jodie?" Sarah grabbed her handbag from the kitchen worktop and fumbled around for her keys.

"Did you dream it too, Mum?"

Keys located, her mother answered, "Yes, every bit, JoJo. I thought it was my dream until you started describing it. I think your dad might be coming back to us."

"He said he would – did you hear him? He said he's coming back."

Sarah gave her daughter the biggest of hugs then went into organisation mode. "Right, I think we need to get to the hospital. JoJo, you've got five minutes to get ready. Off you go."

Sarah grabbed a tissue and wiped the tears from her face, then walked into the downstairs bathroom and looked in the mirror. How could she have had the exact same dream as her daughter? It did not make sense, but not everything had to make sense. As a doctor, Sarah knew that Dean had died and for no medical reason had come back to life. That didn't make sense, nor did Jodie's dreams and the chess game. Maybe it was about time to roll with it rather than picking the bones out of the logic.

Still looking in the mirror, she took a deep breath and said,

"You're nearly back, Dean, don't let us down now. Keep believing." If something magical was going on, then it couldn't hurt to say out loud that they were rooting for him, and it felt like he was close after their shared dream last night.

Jodie shouted, "Ready, Mum."

Sarah had one last look in the mirror as if it was a conduit to Dean's consciousness. "Come on, Dean, she needs you. Christ, *I* need you." When Dean didn't appear in the mirror and answer her, she took a deep breath and headed off to the car with Jodie.

Mr Thompson was more relieved than anything. He was standing more upright and walking more strongly than before, and he did not look scared anymore. He looked like all the suffering and pain he had endured had been taken away. The resigned look on his face was there voluntarily, like he'd had a shot of reality and was happy with his lot.

Death, his cane at his side, towered over Mr Thompson. He had a comforting arm around Mr Thompson's shoulders, not to restrain the old man, but to show that he was there to ensure Mr Thompson got a safe passage to wherever he was heading. Compassionately, he was watching the old man's every step.

They approached Benjie and Dean. Mr Thompson looked at Benjie, and then stared at Dean.

"May I?" he said, asking confirmation from his bodyguard. Death gave him a friendly stare back, granting permission.

Mr Thompson walked to the perimeter of the circus ring and Dean felt obliged to go to meet him. He stood up and walked forward.

"It's Dean, isn't it?"

"Yes, Mr Thompson, it is Dean. Pleased to meet you. Can I help you?"

"Do you know what, Dean? Yes, I think you can."

Dean took a deep breath. This seemed important.

"When you get back, you might see my wife, Harriet. If you do see her, I need you to tell her something for me." Mr Thompson seemed calm and composed.

"How will I know who she is?"

Mr Thompson looked back at his bodyguard and smiled.

Dean could have sworn that he nearly got a comforting smile back, which was not really in Death's job description.

"You'll just know, Dean. I need you to tell her that I will wait for her forever. She will then say that she doesn't believe you. I must warn you she can get a bit feisty, so ask her if she still has our 1962 penny in her bag. Her father gave it to us on our wedding day."

"OK, wait forever, 1962 penny – I've got that."

Mr Thompson continued, "Once she does believe you, tell her that for the first time for over five years, I am in no pain. Then tell her that I have been saving ever since I was diagnosed. She thinks it's all gone on the horses." He laughed. "She's given me so much grief about betting, but I've saved over fifty grand. So tell her she does not have to worry."

Dean was silent, making sure he remembered what he was being told.

"She needs to look in the black box under the bed in the spare room. All the details are in there, and some cash for the funeral."

Dean repeated the salient facts back to him.

"So, Harriet, 1962 penny from her dad, you were in no pain, and you have a secret stash in a black box under the bed."

Mr Thompson nodded. "Thank you, Dean, it means a lot." As he started to walk back to join his bodyguard, Benjie the clown came over to them.

"Mr Thompson, sorry you didn't make it back. You're going to need this for your journey." Benjie took a danake out of one of his deep clown pockets and gave it to Mr Thompson. The old man did not question Benjie or even look at the coin. It was as if it made perfect sense to him. He placed the coin in his pocket and thanked Benjie before heading back to Death's side.

Death took out his ancient book and waved his hand across it to check on Dean's fate.

"Sir, I think you know he is ready," said Benjie. "If you give him a second chance, he will not let you down. He would do anything for his wife and daughter. You could see this evening how much they mean to him."

Death still looked undecided. Benjie brought Dean into the conversation.

"You would do anything for them, right, Dean?"

Dean eyeballed Death to show he meant what he was about to

say.

"I would die for them, sir, so if that's what it takes, then so be it. I am willing to respect your decision, but I have made mistakes. If given another chance, I will always put Sarah and Jodie first, I promise."

Death looked at Dean and then at Benjie before slamming his book closed with a loud clapping sound.

Chapter 35 – Light at the End of the Tunnel

Dean's world went pitch black. He couldn't hear nor see anything. There was just emptiness. The circus had long gone, as had his guide, Benjie. He was all alone, standing in a black room, a blanket of darkness allowing nothing in and nothing out.

Dean blinked three or four times to try and find some light.

"Hello, is anybody there?"

His voice disappeared into the distance before echoing back to him with interest. "*Hello, is anybody there?*"

It can't end like this, he thought. If he was meant to die, Death would have put him in line for the ferry with Mr Thompson and the others. If Death wanted to take him, he could, so what was the point to this darkness? There had to be a point – there was always a point. Dean needed to think, and think fast.

He turned around and shouted, "Hello!" Again the sound travelled away before returning, so loud Dean had to put his hands over his ears. He then made a quarter turn to the right. "Hello!" he shouted once more. His voice disappeared into the distance, but this time it did not bounce back to him. He tried the opposite way and again got an echo. He turned back 180 degrees. "Hello!" No response.

"This way, then," he said quietly.

Dean walked slowly with the default defence mechanism for pitch darkness of his hands held out in front of him in case he hit something solid. Standing in the same place would not get him anywhere, and if his voice had not returned from this direction then there must be nothing for it to bounce off.

"Hello, world," Dean said, adjusting his position every time he started to get an echo. The only problem was, although he was moving forward, was he moving deeper in or creeping out? He could only hope that his starting point was as deep as he could be, so he must be on his way out.

Sarah parked the car, Jodie got a parking ticket, then they made their way into the hospital and on to Dean's ward. Sarah saw Darren sitting at the desk opposite the ward.

"Any change, Darren?"

Darren looked down at Jodie as if to say, "Not in front of her." Sarah cut his look short.

"Jodie knows more about what's going on than you and I, Darren, so you can talk in front of her."

Jodie appreciated her mother's backing and stood close to her side.

"Well, Sarah, we have had a couple of good signs, but there is no pattern. His brain appears to be active, but it's nearly five months now since the car crash. We need a bit more than a few signs."

"What does that mean, Darren?"

Darren again looked at Jodie. "I think we have about another week before the hospital authorities will want to make a decision on him, so if you have anything up your sleeve to get him out of this coma, then now would be a good time. Sorry, Sarah, but he was dead for over five minutes. People just don't come out of that, and my bosses all know it. If he does come round then God knows what state he'll be in."

Jodie took a deep breath to force away the tears. Her mum had stuck up for her to allow her to hear this, so the least she could do was to stay strong.

"Can I see him?" Jodie said to Darren.

"Of course you can, Jodie." He then took Sarah to one side. "Do you want a coffee, Sarah?"

As Darren took Sarah for a coffee in the circular reception room, Jodie headed for her dad's ward. Sitting by his side in a blue tub chair, she could see four other patients in the ward, all of them wired up just like her dad. She held his hand.

"Dad, I know you're in there. Right, you have to listen." She stood up and whispered in his ear, "The doctors are going to turn your life support off. You have to show them something and come back like you promised."

Jodie saw Dean's eyes flicker behind his eyelids.

"I love you, Dad," she said.

Dean was still weaving his way through the contours of his own mind, trying to find a way out, following his shouts. For all he knew, he could be going round and round in circles, but it was better than standing still.

"Hello?" He made another slight adjustment and again headed for the echoless gap.

"Hello?" The echo bounced back.

"*I love you, Dad.*"

Dean stopped.

"Jodie? Jodie, is that you?"

The echo came back. "*Jodie? Jodie, is that you?*"

Dean made a slight adjustment to the right and continued to walk.

"*The doctors are going to turn your life support off…come back…*"

A light appeared on Dean's left-hand side and he stopped to look. A memory was replaying: he was perched on the top of Beachy Head, about to jump. He saw Albert and Betty, Albert looking at the beermat Dean had given him before folding it back into his pocket. The Welnetham Hall black and gold business card spun round and round in front of his face; he could hear Albert's words.

"*Give these people a ring. They are good at dealing with people like you…book into Room 119…*"

Dean continued to walk forward, feeling energised. This *must* be the way.

Another cloud of light appeared on his right-hand side this time. He was on the train as it passed Cockfield Station on his first visit.

"*…closed down in 1961, sir, not stopped here since…*"

"Jodie, is that you?"

Jodie shouted for her mother who joined her at Dean's bedside.

"Dad's eyes, Mum. I started talking to him and his eyes went mad."

Jodie looked frightened, unsure of what to do next.

"Keep doing whatever you're doing, Jodie. Keep him engaged,

don't lose him."

"This way, Dad," Jodie shouted.

Jodie's voice was louder "*This way, Dad.*"; he must be getting closer. Dean continued walking confidently, moving quickly forward. The darkness now had some light bleeding into it.

A plume of smoke appeared on his left. This time, Death was chasing Dean through the funfair. The teddy bears went flying, then Dean was in the clearing, opening Benjie's changing room door. Dean watched himself go through, heard the clown talking to him.

"*Did Jodie tell you about me, Dean?…told her you would leave…*"

"*I had…nasty dream about a clown…*"

He shouted, "I am coming back, Jodie. Which way?" The echo returned to him.

OK, think, think. Which way? He turned to face the memory cloud.

"Jodie! Sarah!"

"*Dad, we're here for you.*"

Dean walked through the cloud. As he left it behind him, another cloud appeared. This time he was playing pool with a young Albert, then sitting down to chat with him and Betty. Dean could see himself taking the beermat from the table and ripping off one side, leaving a white area for him to write on.

"*If you are still together in forty years or so, can you be somewhere for me? I have a feeling there will be someone there who will need your help.*"

The beermat spun in front of his face, much as the Welnetham Hall business card had.

Albert & Betty
Beachy Head
11 May 2017 – 8pm
I might need you there.
Dean Harrison, Room 119 x

Dean's face was twitching, his mouth contorting and his head flicking slightly to the side as if he was fighting against something or someone. Sarah and Jodie could hear the occasional sound. His heart rate had doubled while they had been sitting there.

Sarah moved to Dean's ear. "Do you mind, Jodie?"

"No, Mum, I just want my dad back. Is he coming back?"

They both looked at Darren, who was standing behind them.

"Look, I don't know, but keeping him active and engaged seems like a good thing to do. We have seen almost nothing for five months." He shrugged his shoulders at Sarah. "Your call."

Dean's heart rate was approaching 160 beats a minute.

"While we have him, we need to keep him," Sarah said. "Dean, it's Sarah. Please come back to us. We love you."

"Jodie, which way?"

"*Please come back to us.*"

"Sarah? Sarah, is that you?" Dean marched forward with more purpose. "Sarah, Jodie, I'm coming back."

Another memory cloud was forming. Molly was walking her dog by the river, and Dean saw the crowd of people queuing for the ferry. Then he saw Charon pointing at him, contorting his fingers. Everyone was bowing, and Dean felt the same pain as he'd felt that day. He fell to his knees. His throat was narrowing and he was struggling to gasp for air.

This was not like the other hazy dream bubbles; it had menace. It felt real. Dean knew he had to get past it.

He turned to the right and shouted, "Sarah, which way?"

His shout tumbled back towards him. He tried to the left. Again the echo returned.

He had to face his fears and go through this nightmare. This memory had black thunder clouds pluming around the edges, mini sparks of lightning fizzing and releasing crackles of energy.

Dean got to his feet and shouted through the cloud, "Sarah." He waited. A faint sound struggled to penetrate the sinister clouds in between them.

"*Dean, this way. We believe in you, please come back.*"

Dean could hear Molly's voice as Charon continued to tighten his grip on his life.

"*He is Charon, the Ferryman…I hope you won't see him for a while…You need to find your own way.*"

Dean got to his feet. He could hear the faint voice of Sarah shouting him. He looked at Charon, then at the cloud.

"Sarah, Jodie, I'm coming home."

Dean ran towards the black clouds. As he entered, he was more or less sprinting. He could hear claps of thunder all around him and felt electricity sparks hitting his arms and legs, but he kept running. This cloud was deeper than any other he had been through; he was running across the River Styx.

Then Charon the Ferryman grabbed Dean's arm as he sped past. Charon could feel the danake calling him from Dean's pocket. With no apparent effort, he knocked Dean to the floor of the ferry with one powerful swipe of his hand. Dean's feet flew into the air.

Dean lay flat out on the floorboards of the ferry. Charon stood over him, looking disappointed he hadn't put up more of a fight. The Ferryman pulled back his fist and took aim to finish Dean off once and for all and claim his danake. Dean was helpless, waiting for the inevitable.

Dean's heart rate was off the scale. Sarah was shaking him in his hospital bed.

"Dean, please come back to us." She was crying; she knew this was make or break. They would either get him back now or it would be the end.

Jodie was hugging her mother. "Please, Dad, come home," she added.

Darren tried to step in. "Sarah, it's too much."

Dean, lying on the bottom of the ferry waiting for the strike from Charon, heard Sarah first.

"*Dean, please come back to us.*"

And then Jodie.

"*Please, Dad, come home.*"

He moved out of the way just as Charon's fist delivered the punch. The boat nearly capsized with the power delivered by the punch, and Dean saw an opportunity. He jumped into the water, scrambling to the river bank.

Charon jumped off the ferry into the shallows and followed Dean, making his way to the sandy shore where Dean was lying exhausted. *This is it*, Dean thought, *this is the end.* Charon towered over Dean about two or three feet away.

Death walked up behind Dean and pointed with his stick to the river. Charon bowed his head – he had no power off the water. It was not his patch. Death shook his head and waved his finger, telling the Ferryman off like he was a naughty boy. Charon respectfully nodded to Death. He knew the rules. He would have to collect his coin another time.

With renewed energy, Dean got to his feet and continued to run through the nightmare. As he passed the queue of waiting dead either side of him, they reached out as if drawn to one of the living. He ran and ran until, exhausted again, he fell into the darkness on the other side of the nightmare.

He turned to see the nightmare behind him, the people boarding the ferry. *Where next?* he wondered.

"Sarah! Jodie!"

"*Dean, this way.*"

He could hear them properly now; they were louder and clearer.

"I'll be there soon, Sarah," he shouted. He then took a deep breath and walked ahead into even more darkness.

The next memory was the circus with Benjie. Dean stopped and watched himself as Bobo, laughing as he arrived in the car before painting the boat and being shot from the cannon. Dean took a moment to critique himself.

"Not bad, even if I say so myself."

He smiled. How the hell had Benjie talked him into that? He shook his head.

He then saw himself sitting on the bench in the Big Top with Benjie, having a drink from Benjie's hipflask. He moved closer so his nose was just about touching the outer cloud of the memory.

"*Not many get to see this, Dean.*"

"*What, an empty circus?*"

"*No, you idiot, to see themselves crawling out of a hole and heading back to the real world.*" Dean looked at Benjie's face as they chatted. Benjie could not stop looking at Dean; he was clearly in Dean's corner.

"*He wants to make sure that if he gives you a second chance, you mean it.*"

Death and Mr Thompson entered the ring. Once again, Dean watched the speech Benjie gave on his behalf.

"*Sir, I think you know he is ready…*"

He then saw himself address Death.

"*I would die for them, sir, so if that's what it takes, then so be it. I am willing to respect your decision, but I have made mistakes. If given another chance, I will always put Sarah and Jodie first, I promise.*"

The cloud faded away and a white dot appeared in the distance. He heard his last words echo over and over as they faded.

"*I would die for them, sir…*"

"*…respect your decision…*"

"*…always put Sarah and Jodie first, I promise…*"

"*…I would die for them, sir, so if that's what it takes, then so be it…*"

The cloud vanished along with the echo.

In the hospital, Dean's heart rate had stabilised at 85 beats per minute and his breathing was regular. There were no more sudden movements and his eyes were doing what they should be doing and remaining quite still. Sarah and Jodie were talking quietly, calmly. They could sense something had changed, but were not entirely sure what.

All of a sudden, Dean's face twitched and he let out an audible groan.

Sarah leant up to Dean's ear. "I love you, Dean Harrison, always have, always will."

"I love you too, Sarah."

"Did you hear that?" Sarah asked. Jodie and Darren nodded.

"Say it again, Mum."

"What? What did I say? I don't know what I said, Jodie."

"That 'I love you, Dean Harrison' thing, Mum."

"I love you, Dean Harrison."

"I love you too, Sarah." First one and then the other eye forced its way open before closing again as light hit retinas that had been in darkness for five months.

Dean tried again, this time really slowly. He could see blurred faces looking at him; he had to blink a few times to readjust his eyes.

"Where am I?"

Sarah gave him a kiss.

"You're home, Dean, exactly where you should be. I love you

so, so much."

Dean looked at Jodie. "Hi, JoJo, thanks for the chess tips."

Jodie hugged her dad then took the opportunity of giving her mother an 'I told you so' look in typical smug teenager style.

"Dean, I don't know if you remember me. My name's Darren. I've been looking after you for five months now. It's lovely to see you are back with us, but we can't take things too quickly."

"Five months? Really?"

Sarah was stroking his hand. "Last time I saw you, Dean, was at Jodie's school. I was horrible to you. It's all my fault."

Dean gripped her hand tightly.

"Sarah, I have been an idiot, I know that now. I have the best wife and daughter I could ever wish for, but somehow work became more important. Work will *never* be more important than you two."

Darren interrupted before Sarah could reply.

"Dean, you need to rest now. We will monitor you, but you need time. I don't know how you have come back from where you have come back from. To be honest, there are some things that have happened that none of us can comprehend."

Dean looked at Sarah and Jodie. "He's right, isn't he?" They both agreed. "I'm frightened, Sarah. What if I go to sleep and don't wake up here? I couldn't live without you both – you know that, don't you?"

"Dean, we're just so happy you are back with us. You won't be going anywhere. Jodie and I won't let you."

Sarah gave him a kiss. Jodie followed.

"Night-night, Dean, sweet dreams." Sarah hugged Dean like there was no tomorrow. There would be a tomorrow, though, and Dean would be in it. "Look after him, Darren."

Darren looked at Sarah.

"I've had five months' practice, Sarah. I'm sure I can look after him a bit longer."

"Thank you, Darren, you're a star."

"I know." Darren smiled. "Now, Dean, get some rest. We have some catching up to do. You are what we call in medical terms 'a miracle'."

Chapter 36 – Home Is Where The Heart Is

Although Dean tried telling Sarah, Jodie and Darren what he knew over the next couple of weeks, he kept most of it to himself. It was not so much that he thought no one would believe him, more that some things just didn't need to be said. They were his thoughts, he'd seen some strange things, and he didn't fancy a visit to the loony bin. Besides, had it really happened? No one knew, least of all Dean.

Sarah and Jodie visited every day. As soon as Dean was able to sit up, Jodie beat him at chess, and Dean had only won one game since. Once he had regained some strength, he started building up the muscles up in his arms and legs, and before long he was walking naturally. All the physical symptoms of his accident had gone, and his mind was as sharp as ever. He even started looking at the trading trends again, giving the doctors and nurses tips on making a few quid. He was very rarely off the mark.

A month or so after Dean had come round, everything was normal. In fact, everything was on the hunky end of dory, and there was no need to keep him in hospital any longer.

Darren entered the room. "I've just phoned Sarah. She's coming to take you home. I'm so proud of you, Dean. Sarah said I was a star when you came around, but there is only one star in this room and that's you. Enjoy your second chance; you have earned it."

Dean stood up and put out his hand, and Darren shook it.

"Thank you, Darren, Sarah said how much you did for me. I really, really appreciate it."

"She was a good doctor, you know, Dean. We are always on the lookout for good doctors here."

Dean looked at Darren.

"Sarah always talks about coming back; she only hasn't because of me. That will change, Darren, I promise you."

"Well, I think it's about time you got out of your PJs, Dean. Sarah has put some clothes in your wardrobe."

Dean got dressed, and before long he had Jodie running up to him. "Dad, you're coming home. I can't wait!"

Sarah was right behind her daughter.

"Dean Harrison, I believe you're coming home today. Are you ready?" There were smiles all over the ward. The nurses formed a line ready for hugs and kisses before he left, and Sarah had brought some flowers and chocolates for Dean to give them. Which he did, along with a special hug from his heart.

Dean asked Sarah for the car keys as they entered the car park.

"Dean, you're not allowed to drive until you have been assessed. Darren told you – head injury and all that."

"What happened to my car after the accident?"

Sarah looked at him.

"Dean, we have a lot of catching up to do. I never liked the Porsche anyway. Bit of a hairdresser's car."

Jodie sniggered.

"Did I write it off? It was the fox's fault."

Sarah gave him a hug. "Dean, sometimes there is no one to blame but yourself. Remember that."

Dean knew she was right, but there were a lot of gaps in his memory. He remembered more from the other life he had been leading; real life was still a blur.

"OK, driving is probably not a good idea anyway. I love you both to bits. I can't wait to get home."

They drove the thirty-minute journey home that Sarah had been making every day to see Dean since his crash.

"Jack and Holly have been amazing. They've kept Jodie company and Jack's been every day to see you."

"I know, he told me." Dean smiled. He loved Jack, but his friend was not the best visitor. He would sit and talk bollocks for hours on end. Dean didn't mind, though; listening to a load of bollocks was what he needed right now to catch up on the world. Good friends had shown they were good friends when he needed them, and Dean welcomed Jack and all that came with him.

It was bin day. Sarah gave the bin men a wave as she passed the wagon; they often came up the drive and got the bins when Sarah forgot to put them out, which at least deserved a wave.

Sarah parked at the side of the road as the drive was full of the welcoming committee's cars. Sarah's mother and father were there, as were Jack and Holly. Sarah headed for the boot to take out the cases, and Jodie opened her dad's door. Dean looked at the house that he had last seen over six months ago now.

"Thanks, JoJo."

Further up the road, one of the bin men was struggling with a heavy bin. The driver jumped out to help, not waiting to check whether he had engaged the parking brake properly. As he grabbed the other handle of the heavy bin, the wagon started to roll down the hill, the driver and bin men in hot pursuit.

Jodie left Dean's side as his family and friends greeted him and went to help her mum with the bags. They were so busy looking at Dean, thinking how happy they were to have him back, they didn't notice the driverless bin truck gaining speed and careering down the road. The driver had given up on the fruitless chase; he had his hands on his knees, watching on in horror.

As Sarah and Jodie started to cross the road with the bags, Dean saw the truck getting closer and closer. "Sarah, Jodie, watch out!" They stopped in the road, not knowing what he meant. What did they have to watch out for? The truck was twenty feet away and getting closer by the second.

Life went into slow motion. Dean heard his own voice in his head: "*I would die for them, sir, so if that's what it takes, then so be it..*" He mustered up all his energy and started to run towards them.

The truck was hurtling closer and closer. Dean's run turned into a sprint. He arrived at speed and pushed Sarah and Jodie to the safety of the pavement, then took the full force of the out of control truck. The truck had no sympathy for Dean's trials of the last few months, its back wheels running over him for good measure. After dismissing Dean's body, it smashed into a lamppost to bring itself to a halt.

Dean looked over to Sarah and Jodie, who had got to their feet and were screaming on the pavement. The waiting guests were running from the house. Dean's vision blurred; he was struggling to breathe; his eyes were drifting in and out of focus. Sarah and Jodie were running to him. His dying thought was that they were safe. He closed his eyes and they were gone.

Dean's eyes flickered; he was in so much pain. He tried to open them to see Sarah and Jodie one more time, but Death appeared on the side of the road and clicked his bony fingers. Sarah, Jodie and everything around them paused instantly – the steam billowing out of the bin lorry; the large bin man in his florescent jacket; Dean's reception committee.

Dean's pain subsided. He looked at Death and peeled himself out of his mangled body. Standing over himself, he gazed down at his corpse. He'd looked better. One of his legs was pointing in a direction that nobody's leg should be pointing in. His face was bruised and bloody. Dean pulled an 'ouch' face, thinking that had to hurt, then he remembered that it had indeed hurt.

He felt his ribs. There was no pain now; it had all gone. He'd left the pain in his mangled body.

Dean took a last look at the body that had served him so well over the years. It deserved some respect at least. Then he addressed Death.

"Thank you. They mean so much to me. If you allowed me back for that, then I am eternally grateful."

Death gave him a smile, and Death *never* smiled, then pointed his stick to the other side of the road. Dean's guides were lined up: the train guard, Mrs McCauley, David the barman, Molly with her dog, and of course, Benjie the clown. To the left of him was Betty, but no Albert. Dean asked Death's permission to thank them and say goodbye. Death gestured with his cane and a flick of his head in their direction that it was OK.

Dean could see Sarah and Jodie in suspended animation. Before speaking to his guides, he walked over to them. Their faces were frozen in sheer horror at what had just unfolded in front of their eyes. He cupped Sarah's face before kissing them both. Dean was crying; he could see a tear suspended halfway down Sarah's face. He mopped it up with his finger, rolling the tear back up her face into her eye.

He licked his finger and tasted the salty tear. "I love you, Sarah, always have, always will. And you, young lady, I will be watching over you. God help you when you get a boyfriend."

He took his time – he had lots of it – and looked at his guides.

As he approached them, Benjie the clown let out a single clap, and by the time he reached them, they were all clapping and cheering. Dean did not think what had happened deserved such joviality.

The clown met him in the middle of the road.

"Dean, only five or six have ever got back on our watch. We are so proud of you."

Dean looked at him.

"Proud of me? Well it might have escaped your attention, but I didn't last long. At least they are safe." He looked over to Sarah and Jodie still in mid scream. "And I suppose they will get used to me not being around."

The other guides came over. Dean gave Mrs McCauley and Molly a hug, the train guard shook his hand, as did David, and they all wished him good luck. Then he approached Betty.

"Thanks, Betty."

She smiled. "What for, Dean?"

Dean embraced her.

"You know what for. By the way, where's Albert?"

Betty looked at Death; he shook his head.

"He's not with us all the time, Dean, but say hello for me if you see him."

Dean had seen the shake of Death's head and thought better of pursuing this line of questioning.

"OK, Betty, I will. So, am I missing something?"

The clown let out a laugh, and the other guides all joined in.

"You think you're back, don't you?" Dean raised his eyebrows and gave the clown a 'what type of question is that?' look. "Dean, this was your final test. If he allowed you back, would you do what you said you would do? Remember, you promised him."

Dean looked at the clown and then at Death.

"I said I would die for Sarah and Jodie."

"You certainly proved that you would, don't you think?" The clown shook Dean's hand. "Well done, Dean."

The guides let out a joint 'he's finally got it' laugh. Then they disappeared one by one, waving and smiling at Dean as they evaporated into thin air. Molly's dog Oscar even let out a bark as he disappeared, which Dean took as his way of saying goodbye. This left just Dean, the clown and Death.

"Dean, do you remember when we were chatting in the circus?" asked Benjie. "I said that you'd made an old clown very happy before he goes."

"Yes, I remember. So where are you going? You didn't answer me?"

"When we agree to become guides, we see quite a few things. It's all about whether to live or die – you get that, right?"

Dean did get that. Benjie continued, "Once we agree to work for Death, he tells how long we have left. We can't do this forever."

Dean looked at Benjie. He was starting to fade like the other guides before him.

"And how long have you got, Benjie?" Dean could hardly see him.

"On 2 November 2017 at 3.20am, I will get to see Bobo again, so don't worry about me." As Benjie faded out of sight, he left a faint voice. "Take care, Dean, and say hello to Jodie from me." Then he was gone.

Dean turned to face Death. *OK, what next?* he thought.

Death held out his hand, his fingers moving back and forth as if he wanted payment.

"Oh, the coin. I guess I won't be needing it for a while." Death smiled again, which was unnerving. Two smiles in a day – he must have been after some kind of record.

Dean took his danake from his pocket and placed it into Death's hand. Death put it in his jacket, at the same time retrieving the ancient book. He waved his hand over the book. Looking at the black mark against Dean's calendar, he pressed his finger on it and the mark turned green before disappearing altogether.

Death was about to close his book when he looked at Dean and smiled again. Dean was alone with Death, and Death seemed to be enjoying their time together. He waved his hand across his book once more, shuffling the pages back and forth until he found what he was looking for.

The page was entitled *Hugo Hodgkinson*, which was not a name Dean recognised. Death flicked to November and showed Dean a black mark on the first, Jamaica, 10.26am. Then Death slowly closed the book with an almost impish smile, as if to say, "You accidently saw that. It wasn't my fault that you were looking."

Dean nodded and made a mental note to himself: *Hugo Hodgkinson, 1 November, 10.26 am, Jamaica.*

Then Death slammed the book shut and disappeared, leaving

just Dean and the road.

Part Five – The Whitby Trader

Chapter 37 – Penny For Your Thoughts, My Dear

"Did you hear that?" Sarah asked. Jodie and Darren nodded.

"Say it again, Mum."

"What? What did I say? I don't know what I said, Jodie."

"That 'I love you, Dean Harrison' thing, Mum."

"I love you, Dean Harrison."

"I love you too, Sarah." First one and then the other eye forced its way open before closing again as light hit retinas that had been in darkness for five months.

Dean tried again, this time really slowly. He could see blurred faces looking at him; he had to blink a few times to readjust his eyes.

"Where am I?"

Sarah gave him a kiss.

"You're home, Dean, exactly where you should be. I love you so, so much."

Dean looked at Jodie. "Hi, JoJo, thanks for the chess tips."

Jodie hugged her dad then took the opportunity of giving her mother an 'I told you so' look in typical smug teenager style.

Alarms suddenly shrieked from the bed next to Dean's. Darren left Dean's bedside immediately while hospital staff appeared from all angles, pulling a curtain around the bed. But not before Dean had got a sight of the man lying on the bed.

It was Mr Thompson.

An elderly woman was ushered away, screaming and crying, and Dean listened with his wife and daughter to the frantic efforts of the medical staff to save the old man. The panic continued for five or six minutes, then there was silence.

Doctors and nurses appeared from behind the curtain, their heads held low, taking off rubber gloves and discarding them in the bins. They had lost another one – they had good days and bad days in the medical world, and today they'd had both. The high of Dean coming out of his coma was counteracted by the stark reality of the job they did. They were hurt because Mr Thompson was gone.

Darren was the last out. Dean spoke to him.

"Darren, don't worry. Mr Thompson had had enough. He wanted to go."

Darren looked at him.

"OK, Dean, one, how did you know he was called Mr Thompson, and two, how do you know he was ready to go?"

Dean was annoyed with himself for speaking without thinking. He would have to tread more carefully or Darren would have him taken off to have his head examined, and he'd had enough of that to last him a lifetime.

"I must have heard you call him Mr Thompson when I was in my coma." That was the best he could come up with, but Darren seemed to buy it, even though it didn't explain the Mr Thompson being ready to go bit. That was going to be a tricky one; Dean would struggle to get away with it. Luckily, Darren was too busy to question him further. He went off to see Mrs Thompson in the family room.

"What happened to you, Dean?" Sarah asked. "How could you possibly know that he was ready to go? Was it because the same thing happened to you?"

Dean looked at Sarah, confused.

"You died, just like Mr Thompson. It was five minutes – five minutes, Dean, then your heart started again on its own."

Dean immediately thought of Cockfield Station.

"Did they zap me with the…er…zappers?"

"Yes, five or six times at least."

Dean remembered the lightning knocking him to his knees and the further blows after that.

"I thought so. Come here, Jodie, give me a hug."

As Jodie ran over to him, a tearful Mrs Thompson appeared from the family room. She was a frail old lady with grey hair, wearing a long skirt and a light blue cardigan. Darren had allowed her to sit with her husband before his body was taken away to the morgue, and she disappeared behind the curtain, weeping and wailing.

Dean looked at her as she passed, trying to work out how he could speak to such a distressed woman. She must have really loved him, and he knew Mr Thompson had loved her.

After thirty minutes or so, Darren came back and told Sarah and Jodie that Dean needed some rest. Dean was nodding in and out of consciousness due to the ordeal he had been through, but he was trying to stay awake to fulfil his promise to Mr Thompson.

"Is Mrs Thompson still there with him?" Dean asked Sarah, looking towards the curtain around the next bed.

"Yes, and his daughters are there, too, by the looks of things. It's so sad, Dean."

Dean hadn't seen them arrive; he must have nodded off. Now he could hear them all talking behind the curtain. There was the odd trembling cry from the mother and her daughters as reality hit home that Mr Thompson had gone from their lives.

"Sarah, can you do me a favour?" Dean asked. "I have something I need to tell Mrs Thompson about her husband."

Sarah was so pleased to see Dean back, more than he could imagine, but it didn't stop her throwing a 'seriously?' stare in his direction.

"Dean, you have just come out of a coma after five months, they have just lost their father and husband. Do you think that's a good idea?"

"I know it seems odd, Sarah, but you'll see why. Please get Mrs Thompson for me." He paused and looked at Sarah. "She's called Harriet."

"How do you know she's called Harriet?"

"I can't explain right now, but I have a message for her."

"OK, Dean, but what if she is not called Harriet?"

"What if she *is*?"

Sarah looked at the curtain. She could hear the sobbing and might just be about to make a fool of herself. Even worse, she was going to interrupt their grieving with some gobbledygook from her husband, maybe making them feel even worse, if that were possible. She gave Dean a 'you'd better be right, Mister' look. Dean had missed those looks; he had forgotten how much he loved them.

Sarah, trusting her husband fully, walked over to Mr Thompson's curtain. She could see the mother and her two daughters hugging.

"We'll get through this, Mum," one of the daughters was saying. "We will find the money for the funeral and the house, don't worry. It will be a struggle, but we'll all pull together."

Mrs Thompson started weeping again. Sarah coughed. They turned to look at her. Mrs Thompson wiped away her tears, pulled her cardigan down and stood up a bit straighter.

"Can I help you, dear?"

Sarah was a very confident woman, but she felt the pressure of what she was about to do. Her heart said, "Let them grieve"; her mind said, "Dean knew her name; he must know something."

"I am sorry, Mrs Thompson, but my husband thinks he knows you. He would like a quick word."

"I don't think I do know him, dear, you must be mistaken. I see he has woken up, though. I'm very pleased for you."

Mrs Thompson looked at her husband lying on the bed with no life left to give.

"You're very lucky still to have him, dear."

Sarah felt awful.

"I am very sorry to have bothered you, Mrs Thompson – it's Harriet, isn't it? My husband said you were called Harriet."

"How did he know I'm called Harriet?"

Sarah looked at Mrs Thompson. "I really don't know, I promise. He said he has a message for you."

Mrs Thompson followed Sarah to Dean's bedside. Her daughters came too, not looking best pleased with Sarah's interruption.

"Your name, sir? You seem to know mine?"

Dean smiled.

"Hello, Mrs Thompson, I'm Dean Harrison."

She did not change her facial expression.

"Your wife tells me you're a friend of my husband's. Does he owe you money? He seems to have lost everything we had since he's been ill, gambling it all away."

One of her daughters put her hand on her mother's shoulder.

"Mum, this is not the time or place."

Mrs Thompson folded her arms; she meant business. Dean was going to have to come up with something good.

"I met him yesterday and he told me to tell you that he was in no pain and would wait for you forever."

Dean did his best to sit up a little.

"I don't believe any of this hocus pocus! My husband was lying right here yesterday, Mr Harrison, and if it hasn't escaped your attention, so were you." She shook her head in sheer disgust. "And as for you, dear…"

Sarah lowered her head and looked at Dean. Mrs Thompson

went to walk back to her husband and her daughters followed, giving Dean and Sarah the same look their mother had.

Dean sat up a little more.

"Harriet, he said you were a bit feisty and wouldn't believe me." Mrs Thompson stopped. Her husband had always used the word 'feisty' whenever she was in a mood. It was like their ceasefire keyword.

"Have you still got the 1962 penny in your bag that your dad gave you on your wedding day?"

Mrs Thompson turned around with a startled look on her face. She looked in her bag and took out the coin, then slowly walked towards Dean and took his hand.

"What did he say?"

"OK, let me get this right." Dean looked into Mrs Thompson's eyes. "Right, it's the first time he has not been in pain for five years. He also said he will wait for you forever. He is OK, and you don't have to worry." She gripped his hand tighter. Dean continued, "Oh, and he's been saving for the five years he's been ill. All the details are in a black box under the bed in the spare room."

Mrs Thompson smiled at Dean. "I knew he wouldn't leave us with nothing. Thank you, Dean – did he say anything else?"

"Only that you thought he was betting on the horses all that time."

She thanked him again and gave Sarah a hug.

"I'm so pleased he has no pain now. He's been in a lot of pain. Thank you for passing the message on."

Mrs Thompson went back behind the curtain followed by her daughters. Sarah eyed Dean up for an explanation.

"Another time, Sarah, I promise."

Just then, Mr Thompson appeared at the end of the bed dressed in a black suit ready for the ferry. By his side was Death, who tilted his head and tipped his hat in Dean's direction. Mr Thompson mouthed, "Thank you," to Dean as he and Death followed the rest of his family behind the curtain. Dean assumed this was Mr Thompson's last wish coming true.

"I'm so proud of you, Dean," said Sarah. "Now get some rest. Jodie and I will be back tomorrow."

"What if I don't wake up again?" Dean said anxiously through a yawn.

"You will, Dean. I'm never letting you go again."

Chapter 38 – Sixty-two Million Reasons to Get Better

Over the next couple of weeks, Dean got better and better. Sarah visited every day, usually with Jodie in tow. They all knew something strange had gone on while Dean had been in a coma, but now he was on the mend, it would all come out in good time. So the elephant could stay in the room as long as he sat in the corner and promised not to cause a fuss.

Jack also visited every day without fail and talked about anything but work. He and Dean talked about the car crash and the night in the strip club, and Dean even told Jack a little bit about Beachy Head, but nothing was said about work. Dean knew Jack was keeping something back, and the day eventually came when he had had enough. Today was the day that was going to change.

Jack turned up with another bowl of fruit for Dean, already talking as he walked in.

"Make sure you eat your fruit, Yorkie, you need strength, remember?"

By this time, Dean had been moved to a normal ward.

"Hi, Jack. Put it on the side with the rest." There was more fruit on Dean's table than he could eat in a week. "Right, I think they are going to let me go home next week. I've been doing physio every day and they are pleased with my progress. They say the word 'miracle' a lot, so I guess I've been very lucky."

Jack sat down.

"Dean, you were a right mess. I can't believe you're still here."

"So, Jack, I know you have been avoiding the subject, but…"

"I have brought you a crossword book…"

"Jack, cut the bullshit."

Jack took the crossword book out of a plastic bag. "It's not bullshit, look."

"Jack, you have been in every day since I woke up, and Sarah tells me you have been every day since my accident. I'm sure Dexter won't be happy about you having all that time off work, especially for me. He must hate me. So, what the fuck is going on?"

Jack thumbed through the crossword book.

"It has quiz words in it as well. Remember when we used to do those at work, Yorkie, back in the day, eh?"

"Jack, you've left work, haven't you? Did they fire you?"

Jack threw the crossword book onto the table.

"I took a pay-off, Yorkie. You lost a lot of money; there had to be casualties. And to be honest, it's the best thing I ever did." Jack gave Dean a smile; he meant it. "Holly and I have enough money, and Dexter made sure I was OK."

Dean put his head down. "Sorry, Jack. How many others?"

"It was all voluntary, Yorkie. No one was made to go. It was mainly the dinosaurs like me and you. No one blames you, Dean. Oliver more or less took the rap, admitting he spiked your drink and didn't pass on that call, but at the end of the day, it was your trade and it was not authorised."

Dean shook his head.

"It *was* authorised, Jack, you know that, although that doesn't excuse what happened. I got in too deep, took my eye off the ball. How is that prick Oliver, anyway?"

"Yorkie, you're still deep in the shit, you know. Dexter has settled on a hundred million, but you lost more than that. That's the best I could do for you."

"Wow, a hundred million."

"Actually, just over sixty-two million now." Dean gave Jack a confused look. "Your apartment went for twelve million. I know it was worth more than that, but we had to get them off your back, Yorkie."

Dean did the maths in a heartbeat.

"So what about the other twenty-six million that has disappeared from the debt? Are they after the house?"

Jack laughed.

"Even Dexter wouldn't do that. I think he wants you back to work it off."

"What, like going out for a meal and offering to do the washing up?"

"Fucking lot of washing up, that, Yorkie."

They both laughed.

"So sixty-two million off the debt. I must have a guardian angel."

"I wouldn't call them angels. Trading is probably the most

cut-throat business there is, but when one of our own gets fucked over, we can still find a heart beating somewhere deep inside our titanium bodies." Jack paused. "You can thank your best mate Oliver for that – twenty-five per cent of everyone's bonus is going on your debt. He's slipped into your office as top dog and is on a mission to pay off your debt. The rest of the lads all agreed, but they have been dining out on your bonuses for about fifteen years, Yorkie, so they owed you that much."

Dean let out another "Wow" then added, "Can you thank them, Jack, and how much does Sarah know?"

Jack's eyes refocused on Dean's.

"She knows the lot. I didn't think it was a good time to try and wing this one, Yorkie."

"Good. No more secrets – that's how I got into this mess. Bloody Barcelona!"

"Oh, I told her about that, too, and showed her my credit card bill. Holly went fucking mad with me so I think we all learned a lesson on that one…"

"You told your Holly? I bet she went bonkers. I've got a lot of making up to do, haven't I?"

Jack grinned at Dean.

"I don't think you can be blamed for Barcelona, Yorkie. That was a joint effort."

"Thank them, though, Jack – sixty-two million. Christ! Tell the boys to keep their bonuses, they have done more than enough, and thank Oliver, will you? Tell him I'm OK with it. It's my problem and I'll deal with it. Can you do me another favour, though, Jack?" Dean grabbed the puzzle book and took a pen from the table. "I need a portfolio put together on this guy. Please find out what you can…" Dean wrote the name Hugo Hodgkinson on the puzzle book "…and keep it quiet in the office." Dean stopped. "Sorry, I forgot you don't have an office. You sure you're going to be OK?"

Jack nodded and looked at the name.

"Hugo Hodgkinson? I've heard of him. Don't know where from, though." Jack thought about asking why Dean wanted to know but thought better of going through with the question. He would find out what he could either way; maybe not knowing right now was a good thing.

"OK, Yorkie, I'd better get back to my life of leisure." Jack stood up and gave Dean a handshake that morphed into a man hug. "Look after yourself, Yorkie," Jack whispered into Dean's ear as the man hug lasted a little longer than they were both anticipating, It eventually gave way to a more manly punch on the shoulder.

"Bye, Jack, and thanks for everything."

It was a clear autumn day, not a cloud in the sky. Sarah and Jodie left for the hospital with an empty case ready to put Dean's things in and a big bouquet of flowers for the ward staff. He was coming home today, two weeks after he'd woken up and a lot earlier than anyone had expected. Sarah and Jodie were playing music in the car, both joining in with Robbie Williams's 'Angels'.

They arrived at the hospital with a bounce in their step as they made their way to the ward.

"Come on, Jodie, it's home time."

"I can't wait to get Dad home, Mum."

Sarah stopped in the corridor and gave Jodie a big hug.

"Me too, Jodie, me too."

Dean was dressed already in jeans and a tee shirt that Sarah had brought in for him last night. Jodie ran over to her dad who stood up to greet her and receive her hugs.

Sarah joined in the team hug. "Are you ready to come home, Mr Harrison?"

"Thank you so much, you two, I could not have done this without you. You mean the world to me." As Darren entered the room, Dean added, "Thanks, Darren."

Dean held out his hand and shook Darren's with a proper northern grip, putting his left hand on top of their clasped hands.

"Thanks, Dean, and you think about what I said." Darren looked in Sarah's direction and added a knowing nod.

"I will, Darren."

Sarah gave Darren a kiss on his cheek. "What was that about?"

"Just a little agreement I have with Dean." Darren winked at Dean, who nodded back at him.

"Boys will be boys! Seriously, what are you two up to?"

Darren and Dean looked at each other.

"Nothing for nosey, Sarah," Dean said to break the silence.

Sarah, not wanting to pursue her line of enquiries, gave the flowers to Darren. "These are for the nurses. I was going to get some fruit, but there was none left in the shop. Jack had bought it all."

Dean thanked Darren again and gave the nurses at the main desk a hug.

"OK, I'm ready."

Dean, Sarah and Jodie left the ward, Dean walking backwards and waving as they made their way out of the door.

As they arrived at the car, Dean got in the front and Jodie put his case in the boot. Sarah sat in the driving seat and put her hand on Dean's knee. "So glad you came back to us, Dean."

She looked more beautiful than ever.

"Is it bin day today, Sarah?"

"I was expecting something a bit more romantic, Dean, but as you asked, yes, it is bin day."

As they entered the street, Dean could see the bin wagon at the top of the street. The drive of the house he hadn't seen for nearly six months was more or less full of a welcoming committee. Sarah went to park on the side of the road.

"Sarah, can you squeeze it on the drive?"

Sarah looked at Dean.

"There is no room."

"Please, Sarah. You can squeeze onto the drive for me, please."

"OK, Parker, but you're going to be a nightmare to drive around. On the drive it is."

She squeezed past Jack's car to the back of the drive. The bin wagon had already passed their house. Dean watched it and made sure that it was out of sight before he could relax. They were in the clear.

They entered through the kitchen to a chorus of, "Surprise! Welcome home!" The kitchen was full of Dean's family and friends. Sarah's mother and father rushed over to him.

"Welcome back, Dean."

Dean embraced Sarah's mother and shook her dad's hand before making his way around the room. Some of the girls from the gym were there, as well as Jack and a couple of the boys from work, including Martin and Oliver.

Doreen was next in line. "Hi, Doreen." Dean gave her a hug; Sarah had mentioned how Doreen had been there for her.

"Glad you're OK, Dean. Kyle has got something to ask you."

Doreen shuffled Kyle in front of Dean. He looked like he wanted to be anywhere else in the world than standing in front of Jodie's dad right now.

"Kyle!" Doreen prompted.

In the background, Jodie mouthed the words, "Sorry, Kyle."

"Mr Harrison, Jodie and I have been playing this mad game of chess, and…er…"

"I know, Kyle, she said she couldn't have done it without you, and it meant so much to her. And me."

"Well, she said…err…"

"She said what, Kyle?"

Doreen was just about to let out another "Kyle!" prompt when he finally plucked up some courage.

"I was wondering if you would mind me taking Jodie to the Christmas prom?"

Dean looked at Jodie.

"Well, Kyle, I cannot think of anyone I would rather she went to the dance with. But I want you here on time and back on time, and…"

Jodie rolled her eyes, wondering what the last 'and' would be.

"…make sure you give her the time of her life. She deserves it, Kyle. Is that OK?"

"Of course, Mr Harrison, I promise."

Doreen allowed Kyle to shuffle back out of the limelight, and Dean made his way to Oliver and Martin who were outside on the patio area.

"Oliver, I have been meaning to have a word." Oliver took a gulp of air, expecting the worst. "Jack told me what you and the guys have done at work. I really appreciate your help. And yours, Martin."

Oliver flicked his hair to the side.

"It's the least we could do, Dean. I'm really sorry. I mean it, you know." All of the cockiness had gone from Oliver. He was still on the 'he's a dick' register in Dean's head, but maybe a bit lower down it than he had been before the accident.

"Well, Oliver, I'm still here so no damage done, eh?"

Dean moved back into the house to find Sarah with the girls

from the gym, helping to offer food round to the guests.

"So glad you're back, Dean, I thought I had lost you."

"You'll never lose me again, Sarah. I love you to pieces, and thanks for the welcoming committee. It means a lot."

The guests left one by one. Respecting that Dean was still not well, they didn't want to tire him out. Jack and Holly were the last to leave after washing up and putting the kitchen back together.

"Bye, Yorkie, we'll be off. I've put some fruit in the fridge – you need your five a day."

Dean shook his head at Holly. "He hasn't, has he?"

She gave him a kiss. "Of course not, Dean, he's joking with you."

Jack and Holly left, leaving Dean with his loving family.

"Well, you don't know how hard a journey it's been to get back. I love you both and will never let you get away from me again. I don't know how I can ever repay your support."

Sarah recognised an opportunity to ask the question that had been bugging her since they'd left the hospital.

"You could start by telling me what you and Darren have been talking about."

Dean laughed.

"Oh, that. We were talking about whether you wanted to go back to medicine. The hospital is always on the lookout for good doctors, and you're a good doctor."

Sarah pondered over the statement.

"Dean, we have many things to sort out before that, but yes, I have been spending a lot of time in the hospital and it has crossed my mind."

She looked over to Jodie and then back at Dean, trying to gauge their reactions.

"Well if it's what you want, why not think about it?"

"We have other things to sort out before that, Dean," Sarah repeated.

"It will all be OK, Sarah. Jack told me all about Dexter and everything." Dean followed this with a long, drawn out yawn. "I'm goosed, girls, looking forward to a proper bed."

He gave his wife and daughter a kiss then headed upstairs for the best night's sleep he'd had in what seemed like forever.

Chapter 39 – Reality Bites Back

A weekend at home gave Dean the time to confront a large dose of reality. £62 million was a lot of money to find. His first step had to be to get all the facts and figures and see the depth of the shit he was in. Dean had Dexter's private number in his phone book at home – he didn't really want the indignity of going through his PA – so he took the bull by the horns and called.

"Dexter Falconer."

Dean took a deep breath, long enough for Dexter to say, "Dexter Falconer," again.

"Dexter, it's Dean."

"Oh Dean, I heard you'd pulled through. We've been so worried – how are you?"

Dean thought he would cut the niceties off before they started.

"Dexter, you know why I've called. What's the damage? How bad is it?"

"Well, Dean, some of the boys have chipped in, so it's sixty-two million at the moment. I capped it at a hundred million and Jack asked for your flat to be thrown in. I have also frozen any interest until the end of the year. I can't do any fairer than that."

"Dex, really? You authorised the trade."

There was an uneasy gap in the conversation. Dean could imagine Dexter squirming around in his chair.

"I can't remember authorising anything. You must be mistaken."

Dean thought better of having a row.

"So what are my options, Dexter?"

"You could always come back and work here on a reasonable salary, and pay it off by forgoing your bonuses. We would welcome you back, Dean – you have more talent in your little finger than most of the guys here put together."

Dean knew that going back was not an option, especially for the ten to fifteen years it would take to pay off that sort of money. He thought long and hard about his next response, which in his mind was, "*Thanks for the kind offer, Dex. How about you go fuck yourself?*"

It came out as, "Dexter, I'm not well enough to work yet, and besides, I'm enjoying spending some time with Sarah and Jodie…"

"Staying at home with Sarah and your kid won't pay your bills. Or your debts, for that matter. There are people I could sell this debt to, Dean, you know that as well as anyone."

"Alright, Dexter, you don't need to call in the Rottweilers yet. How about fifty million by the end of this year and we are square?"

Dexter again paused, but Dean knew he wasn't squirming this time. He was thinking, and he was in control.

"OK, Dean, fifty million by 31 December. All of it, mind, otherwise you come to work for me on my terms and the debt goes up with interest to a hundred million again."

"That's hardly fair, Dex."

"Life isn't fair, Dean. It wasn't fair when you were fucking around with my money, either, was it?"

Dean knew he had a shit hand and Dexter had a pair of kings, but there were a few cards in the deck that might fall his way. Perhaps one of them was Hugo Hodgkinson, whoever he was. Death had given him Hodgkinson's name for a reason, although it would have been easier to give him the winner of the 2.30 at Kempton Park. Was Hugo going to be his ace?

"OK, fifty million by the end of the year, Dexter."

"And if not, a hundred million and you working for me until you have paid it all off."

Dean took a deep breath, looked at the picture on the wall of Jodie and Sarah, and said, "OK, Dexter, you are on."

"Good, Dean. You have my word…"

Dean jumped all over this statement.

"I'd rather have it in writing, Dexter. Your memory doesn't appear to be as good as it once was – I think we established that earlier."

"Very well, I'll get it drawn up in writing. Good luck, Dean, see you in January."

Dean put the phone down and picked it up again in the same movement.

"Jack, any news on Hugo Hodgkinson?"

There was a sizzling sound in the background. He could hardly hear Jack.

"Wait there, Yorkie, I'll just turn the bacon off." The sizzling stopped. "What you after?"

"Any news on Hugo Hodgkinson?"

"Yorkie, where the hell did you pluck his name from?" Before Dean could answer, Jack continued, "I'll just have this bacon sandwich and I'll be round yours in half an hour."

The sizzling started again.

"OK, Jack, see you soon."

Dean went to the bathroom and splashed his face with water. "Fifty million, Dean." He took a deep breath and had a staring competition with himself. "Fifty million." He blinked and lost the staring competition. Or maybe it was a draw.

"Dean, we're home." Sarah more or less sang this like Maria from *The Sound of Music* as she entered the house. Jodie headed upstairs as Dean had a last look in the mirror.

"OK, Dean, no more secrets." He went into the kitchen to tell Sarah about his call with Dexter.

"Fifty million, Dean?"

"As long as it's before the end of December."

"And a hundred million if not. Dean, how the hell are we going to find that sort of money?"

There was a knock at the back door.

"Hugo Hodgkinson, Sarah, that's how. Hugo Hodgkinson."

"Dean, have you gone mad? Who the fuck is Hugo Hodgkinson? And why is he going to give us fifty million pounds?"

"I do not have a God's earthly clue who he is, Sarah. But I think we're just about to find out."

Jack walked in carrying a black folder embossed with *Falconer International Trading* under his arm. Oliver Steadman-Fisher was with him. Dean looked at Oliver and then back at Jack.

"Don't worry about him, Yorkie. I needed to dig deeper into your man Hugo, and Oliver has helped me. You'll keep schtum, won't you, Floppy Mop?"

"If you stop calling me Floppy Mop, Jack."

Jack put the folder on the kitchen top. "OK, Floppy Mop."

"Enough, you two, enough. So who is our friend Hugo, then?"

Sarah put the kettle on; she sensed it was business time.

"Coffee, Jack, Oliver?" She posed the question while getting mugs out of the drawer. "Dean, do you want another?"

They all nodded.

Once everyone was sitting on the bar stools around the breakfast bar, Oliver asked, "Me or you, Jack?"

Jack pushed the file in Oliver's direction.

"You found it all out, Ollie, so off you go."

Oliver opened the folder. "Where the hell did you find the name of this guy, Dean?" he asked.

"Believe me, Oliver, you don't want to meet my source any time soon. Let's have it, then. We are bursting with anticipation here."

"You do pick them, Dean. Of all the lowlifes on the planet, you couldn't have got much lower than this man." Oliver looked up for a reaction. There was none. "Hugo Hodgkinson, born 7 May 1955, majored in Statistics at Harvard, made his first million by the age of twenty-one."

"Impressive. How?"

"That's the interesting thing, Dean. He was a venture capitalist. He had no money, and basically acted as a broker for one small family-run company without them asking, promising them huge investment. He then approached a venture capitalist company, also without being asked, and told them about this amazing opportunity."

Dean looked at Oliver.

"This isn't going to end nicely, is it?"

"He then drew both companies into big contract agreements which neither of them could keep and walked away with over a million dollars for allegedly sorting it all out by stopping the deal going through. The small company's shares went through the basement, so guess who bought them all?" Oliver didn't need an answer. "Yep, Hodgkinson took a company worth thirty to forty million, screwed it over until it was on its knees and bought it for the million he'd just made for the privilege. He then trashed that company for all it had, sold all its assets, the buildings, the machinery – well, everything, really. He laid off all the staff, some of whom had worked there for thirty years, and closed the whole thing down. No pay-offs, no pensions. He just ripped the heart out of a company that never wanted to be involved in the first place. The papers called it a 'Targeted Massacre'. Hodgkinson walked away with – well, no one's sure. Fifteen to twenty million dollars was the best guess."

"At twenty-one? Wow, I don't like him already."

Jack held up his hand. "There is more, Dean. Ollie, carry on."

Oliver shuffled in his seat like he was just getting comfortable. "With that one in the bag, Hodgkinson did the same to any company which would bite. He was ruthless, with no care for the history of or people who worked for these firms. Having upped sticks from the US, he now lives in Jamaica with his two sons. He is the billionaire owner of a telecommunications and media company, Astra Zing, and is about to strike a deal with a large communications company in the US, Howell Media." Everyone in the room was listening. Oliver continued, "The market does not see this as a good move for Howell Media – its shares are already through the floor. The talk is that Hodgkinson has something on this company and is threatening the owners."

Dean's interest sparked. He stood up. "What are their shares now, Oliver?"

"Whose, Astra Zing's?"

"No, Howell Media's. What are they trading at?"

Oliver turned the page. "The US price this morning was $9.36. Before people got wind of the so-called merger, they were over $27 and that was only a month ago. They were $43 at the turn of the year and thought to be massively under-priced. But the company might not even survive if Hodgkinson gets his way."

"How have the shareholders ever agreed to this?"

"Hodgkinson has bought the CEO and the board and promised them big pay-offs, so the shareholders have trusted the board and their recommendations." Oliver added, "Idiots."

"That's what we are looking for, Jack. When is the deal being signed?"

Oliver went back to his notes. "It looks like next week, in Jamaica. Wednesday 1 November. The guys at Howell's know they are getting screwed over, but the CEO and shareholders have all agreed so I guess it will take place."

"What time on Wednesday?"

Oliver, who took pride in his research, gave Dean a stare.

"Bloody hell, Dean, I don't know. I thought I did well working out it was Wednesday."

"Oliver, I need to know what time that meeting will be on Wednesday. Exactly, not estimated."

"OK, Dean, I'm on it."

Oliver walked over to the patio doors and made a phone call. He was already on "Hello" as he opened them and walked outside.

"You're being a bit harsh on the kid, Yorkie. Are you going to tell us what's going on?"

Sarah, who was sitting next to Jack, put her elbows on the breakfast bar and placed her chin into the palms of her hands.

"Let's just say I have some inside information. If that meeting to sign over the company hasn't happened by 10.26am, Jamaica time, then it will not happen at all."

They both looked at him in anticipation, waiting for him to carry on. He didn't.

Oliver walked back into the room. "OK, 10.45am. The meeting is at 10.45am, which is 4.45pm in the UK. Is that good or bad?"

Dean walked around with his coffee and took a sip. "It's very good, Oliver. OK, plan, plan, plan. Oliver, you mentioned the two sons. Are they big Dad supporters?"

Oliver again opened his folder. His research was thorough, Dean had to give him that.

"Not really, Dean. The older son, Robert, is against the deal. He thinks that enough is enough, and rather than crush opposition, he and his dad should work with them to their mutual benefit. Nice bloke, by all accounts."

"And the younger one?"

"He's a pro-surfer, and not a very good one. He's not into business stuff; he just likes spending the money he doesn't earn on a playboy lifestyle. I wouldn't mind a job like that."

"You've got the hair for it." Jack couldn't resist. Oliver took it on the chin; he was too busy looking for a reaction from Dean.

"So, what's this all about, Dean?" he demanded.

"Let's just say I have had a tip that the deal won't happen. Jack, what would be your forecast if it fell through on the day?"

Jack stood up, as he always did when he was asked a question. "It looks like that company is worth a damn sight more than where it is trading now, right, Oliver?"

Oliver looked at the last accounts published in his folder.

"It has more in assets than where it is valued now, but – and it's a big but – we know that if Hodgkinson gets hold of it, he will strip all those assets and eventually the company will go out of business. He only wants Howell's subscribers – customers Zing doesn't have. He couldn't give a shit about the company." Oliver took a breath. "So who would be stupid enough to invest in them right now?"

"Us, that's who," said Dean. "Jack, do you trust me?"

"Of course I do, Dean."

"Oliver, are you in?"

Oliver again consulted the figures and then turned to Dean.

"It's the most stupid trade I have ever seen, Dean, but I was once told in a classroom that sometimes you have to trust intuition. Let's hope you're right. I'm in." Dean patted Oliver on the back. Maybe worms could turn.

Sarah gave Dean a trusting 'I'm with you' smile and Dean took a deep breath. He needed her support more than anything right now.

"I know what I'm doing. We'll only get one crack at this. Are we done?"

The silence filled the room more than any noise could have.

"Right, that's sorted, then. Thanks, Jack." He left a pause. "Oliver."

Over the next week, Dean, Jack and Oliver grabbed as much money as they could get their hands on and watched the market like a hawk, choosing when to make their move. Each person involved would give 25% of their profits to pay Dexter off, then keep the other 75%.

Dean was getting nervous – his last insider deal hadn't gone that well. For all he knew, he could have had a few bad dreams when he was in a coma. But Hugo Hodgkinson really existed; he couldn't have dreamt that.

Dean spoke with Sarah, who had full faith in him, and they transferred all their savings to his trading account. Then he suggested selling the house.

"Dean, listen, I believe in you, but the house – it's everything we have. What if you're wrong?"

"I'm not wrong, Sarah, but perhaps the house is a step too far."

"How much have we got?"

Dean looked at the account: £1.8 million.

"Where did that four hundred thousand come from?" asked Sarah. Dean looked uncomfortable.

"I cashed in the timeshare. I don't like the South of France anyway."

Sarah could see the spark in Dean's eyes. He had one chance to sort things out and he wasn't going to let it go by.

"We've haven't used it for longer than a week in the last two or three years anyway," she said. "Even bloody Dexter's been more than us. At twenty-five thousand a year for twenty-five years, it was more of an expensive status symbol than anything else. So, should I have a word with my dad? I know he's got money put aside for me."

"No, Sarah, what am I thinking? This is madness. I'll just go back and work for Dexter. At least then we won't need to worry."

Sarah put her fingers in the way to stop him closing the MacBook.

"The Dean Harrison I fell in love with would stop at nothing if he wanted something. Remember Baby Doctor?" She gave him a kiss on the neck. "I'll call my dad. It's my call, Dean, not yours."

Sarah came back into the room after finishing her call.

"Right, Dad's in."

Dean tilted his head her way.

"What do you mean, your dad's in? I lost millions on my last trade – I'm surprised he'll touch anything I've suggested with a bargepole."

"You know how bored he gets. He had some money put away for an old nag, and he thought with your 25/75% deal he might just get a thoroughbred this time. Dad knows you were stitched up."

"I love your dad. Still surprised, though. Does your mother know?"

Sarah laughed.

"Are you mad? Of course not. He's transferring four hundred thousand as we speak."

"He's crazy, your dad. Rich, but crazy. He'll get it back, though. You know what, Sarah? He should tell your mam. I'm sick of secrets – remember Barcelona? He doesn't want to end up like me."

She stood behind her husband and placed her arms around him.

"I know he will get it back, Dean, and I'm sure he'll tell my mum in good time. Dad always does; he just pretends he's in charge. Anyway, she knows he's got money put aside for a horse."

Dean looked at the online account as Sarah's dad's money bolstered it up. "We have £2.2 million, give or take a few quid. Let's hope it's enough, Sarah."

"And all the others – Jack, Oliver, and Martin's in now, you said – when are they transferring in?"

Dean looked at his watch.

"The deadline is five pm tomorrow; it's the big day on Wednesday." As he said this, he saw £400,000 come in from Jack. Not long afterwards £75,000 arrived from Oliver, and Martin had stumped up £25,000.

At 5.05, Dean looked at the account. Staring back at him was £2,700,000.00.

Just before he put his MacBook away, Dean asked Sarah, "Have you heard of Sweet Dreams Nursing Home for Alzheimer's?" He typed the name into a Google search as he said it.

"No, was that where your dad was?"

Dean laughed bitterly.

"There was nothing sweet or dreamy about where my dad was."

Sarah shrugged her shoulders. "No, then. Why?"

"Remember I told you there was a couple on the top of Beachy Head who stopped me jumping?"

"Yes, Albert and…"

"Betty."

"That's right, Betty. Why?"

"Well it's been bugging me ever since I got back. I saw the bus up there, a battered old minibus, but couldn't remember the name on it. It's just come to me. It was Sweet Dreams, definitely Sweet Dreams. I can see the logo now, all in blue." Google did what Google does. "Have you seen this, Sarah? It's on the same road as the hospital."

"If you're right about Hodgkinson, you can buy them a new minibus."

Dean closed the laptop.

"Do you know what, Sarah? If all goes well, I might just do that."

Chapter 40 – Sweet Dreams Are Made Of This

Sarah and Dean were woken up with breakfast in bed by Jodie, who wasn't going to be appearing on *MasterChef* anytime soon. Something trying its best to look like scrambled eggs on toast sat on the tray next to two very strong coffees that could have made a spoon stand up on its own. It was the thought that counted, thank God, as it took a lot of thought to imagine it tasting any worse than it actually did.

All three of them sat on the bed, chatting.

"Seen much of Kyle, JoJo?"

Dean got a dig in the ribs from Sarah.

"Daaaaad."

He pulled Jodie in for an unwanted hug. "Well, just asking. He'd better look after you. You're very special."

Another dig in the ribs from Sarah changed Dean's line of questioning.

"Jodie, your mum and I are going to see a special friend today. He looked after me after I saw you at school that day."

"OK, Dad. Are you enjoying your breakfast?"

Dean looked at the half-eaten breakfast and made a big effort to have another mouthful. "Lovely, Jodie. Where did you learn to cook, from your mother?"

He got another bigger dig in the ribs.

Jodie laughed. "You deserved that one, Dad."

When Jodie had left for school, Dean and Sarah had another coffee downstairs to wash away the taste of the last one. Dean thought of Betty on her own when he'd met his guides for the last time on the roadside on Bad Bin Day. "*Say hello for me if you see him,*" she'd said. He guessed that meant Albert was still in this world, and if he was still here, he would be in Sweet Dreams.

"OK, let's go. Sweet Dreams, here we come."

Sarah drove the route she knew so well. Sweet Dreams was more or less next door to the hospital, and as they parked in the large driveway, Dean could see the minibus a couple of bays down.

"There it is," Dean said as he got out of the car. Holding Sarah's hand, he walked across to it. "They do need a new one."

"One step at a time, Dean," she replied.

Sweet Dreams Nursing Home was a Georgian building with a big driveway set back from the road. It had gargoyles up in the eaves and two large doors which were already open onto a grand black and white checkerboard tiled area.

They walked into the reception, Dean in the front, Sarah following behind him. Dean approached a woman in a blue nurse's outfit sitting behind the desk.

"Can I help you, sir?"

Dean thought for a second.

"Well yes, we have come to see Albert and Betty."

The nurse looked up at him.

"Are you family?"

"We're old family friends."

She looked in the visitors' book.

"They are not expecting any visitors, Mr…?"

"Harrison. Dean Harrison."

"I'm sorry, Mr Harrison, but if you're not booked in, I can't let you in."

"But I need to see him, please."

"Sorry, sir. Maybe if you contact a family member and book in as a visitor."

"I only want to see him for a minute."

Sarah could see Dean getting agitated and grabbed his arm.

"Come on, Dean, she's not going to change her mind."

Dean took a look at the door to the side of reception.

"Do I need to call security, sir?" the nurse asked sternly.

Dean backed off.

"OK, OK, I'll go."

As Dean and Sarah turned to go, a man with black hair and a thick well-groomed beard appeared from the door at the side of the reception. He was wearing a white coat and carrying a clipboard.

"What was all that about?" he asked the receptionist.

"Mr Harrison here has come to see Betty and Albert. I told him that he needed to be booked in. He isn't family."

The doctor stroked his black beard and twisted his head to the side.

"Dean Harrison?"

The nurse looked at him.

"Yes, Doctor, do you know him?"

"Sort of..." The doctor turned to Dean. "It is you, Dean, isn't it? Thank you for the donation."

Dean's mind flicked back to Beachy Head. He vaguely remembered a man walking up the hill to collect Betty and Albert. He also remembered putting money under the wiper blades of the bus.

"No problem, I hope it helped."

"What donation?" said Sarah. Before Dean could answer, the doctor introduced himself.

"I'm Dr Rhodes. I run this place, and your husband made a donation last time we met."

"Hi, well, I'm Dean, as you know already, and this is my wife, Sarah."

The man gave Sarah a nod.

"Pleased to meet you. So, you have come to see Betty and Albert?"

"Well, we wanted to, yes."

"OK, I think you'd better come with me."

As Dr Rhodes walked towards the back of the reception area, Dean turned to the nurse behind the desk.

"Sorry about earlier, I just need to see them. I owe my life to them."

She accepted his apology in her own way.

"Only doing my job, Mr Harrison."

Dean shrugged his shoulders and mouthed, "Sorry," again as he followed Dr Rhodes.

The doctor took them through the double doors and into his office.

"Take a seat. Coffee?"

"No thanks, we're OK. Are Betty and Albert both here, then?"

The doctor smiled.

"They have been here for about five years now. Betty has Alzheimer's really badly; her mind is elsewhere – well, you saw her on the cliff, Dean. Albert has good days and bad days. Today's a good day. I'm sure he'd love to see you; I'm sure they both would."

Dean stood up. "Can we see them now, please, Dr Rhodes? I've got some big thank yous to dish out."

"They have been telling me since they got here that they had to be on Beachy Head on 11 May to save Dean Harrison. They also told me how they knew you would be there."

Dean remembered giving them the beermat in Welnetham Hall on his second visit.

"You're not the first, you know, Dean."

"The first to what?"

"You stayed in Room 119, didn't you?"

Dean gave Sarah a glance to see if she was keeping up. The more Dr Rhodes said, the more explaining he would have to do.

"How do you know? Who else has been here?"

"Two others I know of, and you make it three, so glad you made it back. I think I need to show you something." Dr Rhodes stood up too. "Dean, do you believe in miracles?" Before Dean could answer, the doctor opened the door. "Follow me."

Sarah grabbed Dean's hand.

"Dean, Welnetham Hall? Room 119? What the hell is going on?"

"Sarah, I don't know. I thought I might have dreamt it until now."

The doctor opened the door to the common room. Dean could see lots of wheelchairs and patients in the room, some looking better than others. Some were playing cards and draughts, others were vacant and obviously in a more advanced state of Alzheimer's.

Sarah then broke free of Dean's hand and ran to an old man in a wheelchair. "Dean, it's him. It's Benjie the clown. He's here."

"Oh my God."

Sarah was giving the old man a hug. "Dean, it's Benjie. Jodie said he helped her win the chess game. He showed her what to do. Thank you, Benjie, thank you."

Benjie showed no reaction apart from a slight curling of his mouth upward.

"That's his happy face, Sarah." Dean held Benjie's hand. "Thank you, Benjie, I couldn't have asked for a better guide."

Dean started to cry. Sarah gave him a hug.

"He was a good clown, Dean. Hey, you weren't so bad yourself."

Dr Rhodes joined them. "This is Benjamin Grimaldi. Do you know him, Dean?"

Dean wiped away a tear.

"Know him? We are practically partners. We once did an act together."

"He was apparently a very good clown back in the day."

"He was the best, Dr Rhodes, and still is."

"We used to have Robert, Benjamin's partner, here as well. Benjamin called him Bobo. Robert sadly left us a few years ago; they used to have the place in stitches. Benjamin went downhill soon after Robert died, I'm afraid. He never really reacts to anything now."

As the words came out, a tear formed in Benjie's eye. It slowly weaved its way down his wrinkled face. He moved his head towards Dean and smiled.

"Sarah, I'll only be a minute. Stay here with Benjie."

Dean walked to the other side of the room, which opened out to overlook the gardens. The doctor went with him.

"I don't really know what goes on, Dean. Sometimes it feels like they are elsewhere while they are in this state. Let me introduce you to some of our patients."

Dean laughed.

"No need, Dr Rhodes. This is David, and he is the best barman in the land." Dean went down on his knees to shake David's hand. "Hi, David. Not only is he the best barman, Dr Rhodes, he also saved my life." Dean then turned to his right. "And this is Molly and her dog, Oscar." The dog was sitting loyally at her feet.

"He has not moved since she slipped into her trance. He only goes out when we feed him. We have a 'no dogs' policy, but we make an exception with him."

"Hi, Oscar." The dog came out from under Molly's chair, wagging his tail and jumping all over Dean as Dean stroked him. "Have you been looking after your mam for me?"

Dr Rhodes looked on in astonishment.

"How do you know them, Dean? They have been here for years, nowhere else."

"OK, Dr Rhodes…"

"You can call me James."

"OK, James, what if…" Dean paused, looking for the right words. "Try to clear your mind for a second. What if while their minds are no longer in a fit state for this world, they are guiding people who need help in another place?"

Dean looked for a reaction. James murmured, "Welnetham Hall," and Dean nodded and smiled.

"They are my guides, James. They guided me back to my wife and daughter. They pointed the way and helped me grasp a second chance." He gave Molly a kiss on the head. "Have you got a big man here who likes trains? I don't know his name, but he knows everything about locomotives and train lines."

James shook his head, trying to make sense of it all.

"That will be Bill. This way."

The smiley guard, dressed in his black jacket complete with his pocket watch, was sitting in a chair across the room.

"He has ten outfits and they are all the same," said Dr Rhodes. "His family say he has to be dressed this way every day, complete with pocket watch so he's never late."

Dean smiled.

"He's the best train guard I have ever met. He saved my life too." Dean shook Bill's hand. "I'm honoured to have travelled with you, Bill."

Dean turned to James. "And Mrs McCauley?" he asked. James pointed to the corner of the room.

"The staff are scared stiff of her. Used to call her a battle-axe."

"She's a little pussycat when you get to know her." Dean ran over to her. "Hi, Mrs McCauley, how's things?" Mrs McCauley moved her head slightly and gave Dean a smile. "I've made it back. Thank you so much."

Dean looked over to Sarah and asked her to come across to him. One by one, he introduced her to each of his guides. They were making their way back to Benjie when Dean said, "James, we actually came to see Albert and Betty."

James pointed to the patio doors. A couple in wheelchairs were sitting outside, hand in hand.

"They sit out there together all the time. Never apart."

Dean held Sarah's hand as they followed the doctor.

"Sarah, I want you to meet a very special couple. I met them a long, long time ago. Before I was born."

James and Sarah gave each other a 'he's gone a bit mad' look, but they both ran with it for now.

Dean walked out into the garden with its well-manicured

lawns and stopped in front of the couple. Betty had a vacant stare, as if her mind was elsewhere. Dean knew exactly where it was. He'd been there. Albert was asleep, holding her hand.

"Betty." Her expression morphed into a smile. She didn't look at Dean, but he took it as acknowledgment. "Sarah, this is Betty. She's a very good friend of mine."

"Hello, Betty."

"And this young fellow is Albert. Albert?" Dean shook the man's shoulder lightly to awaken him. Albert's eyes slowly opened and he saw Dean in front of him.

"Dean, is that you?"

Salty water was filling Dean's eyes again.

"Yes, Albert, I made it back and I can't thank you enough." Dean wiped the tear from his cheek.

"I knew you'd get back. Betty told me you would get back." He looked lovingly at his wife. "She told me you'd make it. She comes to see me in my dreams; she said you were a fighter." Looking up, Albert added, "You must be Sarah."

"Pleased to meet you, Albert."

James spoke. "I told them, Albert, that since you have been here, you've been pestering me to take you to Beachy Head. You were quite specific about the date and the time, weren't you?"

Albert chuckled. "That's Dean's fault. He made us promise all those years ago – remember, Dean? We had just got married. You haven't changed a bit."

Dean knew this one would take some explaining, too. James and Sarah gave each other another look.

Dean shook Albert's hand and gave Betty a kiss. "Well, it's all well and good making a promise, but you lived up to it."

Albert laughed again.

"That was Betty's fault. She kept saying through the years, 'Remember that nice man who beat you at pool? We promised to be there for him.' I couldn't have lived with myself if we hadn't been." He took Betty's hand and kissed it.

As Dean and Sarah turned to leave, Albert called them back.

"Hey, Dean, I won't need this anymore." He took a battered folded beermat out of his pocket. It could barely stop itself from falling apart as he carefully unfolded it and gave it to Dean.

Sarah took it from Dean and read the message out loud.

"Albert & Betty
Beachy Head
11 May 2017 – 8pm
I might need you there.
Dean Harrison, Room 119 x"

She looked at Dean. "This is really old."

Albert replied, "We have been holding that promise for over forty years, Sarah. We are so glad we were there to help."

She carefully put the beermat into her pocket and gave Albert and Betty a kiss before heading back inside with Dean and James. Stopping in the middle of the room, she looked at her husband.

"I don't pretend to know what went on, Dean, but that beermat is really old, so can you answer one thing? How is the message in your handwriting?"

"Sarah, I will tell you everything one day, but some things are better left where they are, at least for now." He gave her a kiss, then turned to James Rhodes. "You have a very special place here, James. Whatever you are doing, keep doing it."

The doctor shook Dean's and Sarah's hands.

"We will do what we can, Dean. Days like today make it all worthwhile."

Dean took a last look around the room at every one of the patients before leaving Sweet Dreams Nursing Home with Sarah and going home.

Chapter 41 – Bulls On The Rampage

Dean opened one eye the next morning to see Sarah was not in bed beside him. The unmistakable aroma of breakfast was making its way up the stairs, accompanied by Sarah singing along to BBC Radio Two. Dean got up, had a shower and put on a suit – making millions in his pyjamas did not seem right, somehow.

Dean's confidence was born from seeing his guides at Sweet Dreams the day before, confirming that Room 119 had not been a dream after all. And if it was not a dream, then Death had showed him Hugo Hodgkinson's name for a reason. The only gamble was that the reason was to give Dean a fighting chance in Second Chance Saloon.

No one did a better breakfast than Dean's wife, and today's breakfast was no exception. Dean finished everything that was in front of him then switched on the news and the trading board in his office. He homed in on Howell Media's share price, which had gone down even further overnight. As 10.30am in Jamaica was 4.30pm in the UK, there was no need to be trigger happy. It was a waiting game, and Dean was waiting.

The shares were trading at $8.76. Dean switched the view to cover the week. The price had been tumbling all week, and the month and six month views were not much better. It looked like a flight of stairs dropping down to the basement. Nobody in their right mind would touch them with a bargepole, let alone two and a half million bargepoles.

The one thing bugging Dean was why the shareholders had agreed to merge with Astra Zing. He decided to ring Jack.

"Can't talk now, Yorkie."

Dean was taken aback by this.

"You'd better have a good reason why, Jack."

Jack laughed.

"I have. I'm in your kitchen."

Dean walked back into the kitchen to see Jack eying up the pans on the hob.

"Do you want breakfast, Jack? There's loads left." Sarah

always cooked too much on the off chance a passing army might need feeding. Today Sarah's 'just in case' was Jack's gain.

"I'd love one, Sarah, if it's not too much trouble."

"Nothing is too much bother for you, Jack." She accompanied that comment with a smile that would have melted butter.

"Have you seen the price, Yorkie?" A slice of sausage disappeared from Jack's plate into his mouth before he added a mumbled, "Are we going to pile in straight away?"

"Jack, it will go down further."

"So, what's the angle? What's going to stop us buying all of those shares and our friend Hugo still taking the company to the cleaners?" Jack carefully mopped up the baked beans and egg yolk residue with some fried bread.

"Let's just say I know that deal won't be signed by Hodgkinson. You've got to trust me on that one. I'm more worried that Howell Media will pull out. Why would the shareholders agree to kill off their own company?"

Jack had left the plate cleaner than if it had just come out of the dishwasher. "Sarah, thank you, I needed that. Well, Dean, Astra Zing is a bit of a Jekyll and Hyde company. If the son does the deal, he's a good man who has turned companies around with mutual benefit to both. Hugo Hodgkinson himself hardly does any deals now, but when he does, he crushes them into the ground. And my sources say Hodgkinson is all over this one. He seems to take pleasure from power; he could not care less about the consequences. He normally buys off the board and the CEO, and they make false promises to the shareholders."

"But how does he get the board on board, if you pardon the pun?"

Jack took a sip from his coffee. "I can't confirm this, but it seems Hodgkinson is in bed with some nasty people. I'm not saying the board members would wake up with a horse's head in their beds, but he would make life very difficult for people who didn't comply."

Dean pondered on this thought.

"He's a first class prick, Yorkie. So what have you got on him? How do you know he won't sign? He doesn't sound like the type to back off."

Dean knew it had to come out sooner or later. If he couldn't trust Sarah and Jack, who could he trust?

"OK, I know you'll think I am mad, but…" He paused. "OK, I'm going to say it. Hugo Hodgkinson will die at 10.26am in Jamaica, and the meeting is at 10.45am. He can't sign if he's dead."

Jack looked at Sarah.

"Did he just say that out loud, Sarah?"

Dean felt verbally naked. He'd put a hand grenade on the kitchen table and pulled the pin out, and was now waiting for the explosion.

"Jack, there has been a lot of weird stuff going on. I don't know where Dean was when he was in hospital, but I know that he met people. I even met them, for real, in a home."

Sarah stood by the side of her husband.

"What, a mental home?" Jack continued before that could be taken the wrong way, "Well, Yorkie, I've put in my and Holly's nest egg for our retirement. Nobody put a gun to my head. I trust you. By the way, when am I going to die?"

Dean laughed. "I don't know about everyone, only two people."

"Who else, Dean?" asked Sarah nervously. "Who else is going to die?"

Dean realised what he had just said. "Oh, it's OK, he wants to go. It's Benjie. His time's up, but he wants to see Bobo, so he's ready. On 2 November at 3.20am, Benjie will leave us."

Sarah let out a big sigh. "Oh, thank God, I thought it was you. I thought you were leaving me again." She gave Dean a hug. "Don't leave me again, Mr Harrison."

As they kissed, Jack looked at them both.

"Yorkie, who the fuck is Benjie and who the fuck is Bobo?"

Sarah and Dean turned and looked at Jack, replying together, "They're clowns."

Sarah gave Dean a playful punch before offering her little finger for a pinkie shake and a perfectly timed "Jinx", then added, "Do keep up, Jack."

"Oh, that's OK, then, it all makes sense now. You know Hugo Hodgkinson is going to die at 10.26am in Jamaica, and the next day Bobo the fucking clown is going to die in England."

"It's Benjie, Jack. Bobo died a few years ago."

Jack carried on his rant. "Are we going to buy four million quid's worth of shares in Billy Smart's fucking Circus when Benjie goes?"

"Stop swearing, Jack, and calm down. You said you trusted me. Don't you?" Dean said this laughingly.

"Well I did before you went loopy – sorry, *fucking* loopy."

"Hang on a minute," said Dean, his serious head back on. "What do you mean, four million quid's worth, Jack?"

"Oh, I forgot to mention. Have you not checked your trading account this morning?"

"No, not yet, why?"

"You were well thought of at work. People trust your judgment, Dean. Some of the other guys heard about the deal and they are in. The older guys are leaving if it comes off. I'm glad I didn't tell them about your clown mates."

"It will be OK, Jack, I have a good informer."

"Does he have a red nose and a honking horn?"

Dean pictured Death in his mind, showing him the old book with Hodgkinson's name in it.

"No, Jack, this guy is no clown. He's as serious as they come."

"OK, Yorkie, they don't need to know about your clown mates. Some of the boys have taken the afternoon off. Sarah, they're coming round about three pm, is that OK?"

Sarah looked at her messy kitchen and then at her watch. It was 1pm already.

"Do I have a choice, Jack?"

Jack pulled his head into his shoulders.

"Not really, Sarah. Sorry."

"Well you'd better give me a hand tidying this lot up, then."

It was 3pm and people were starting to turn up. There was just over £4 million in Dean's trading account. Looking at a spreadsheet of who had paid what, he took a deep breath.

"Jack, are we doing the right thing?"

"The famous Dean Harrison having doubts over a trade? Whatever next."

In a way Jack's words felt reassuring, but normally Dean traded with the company's money. Gambling with real people's money was a different ball game, especially when they were his friends. The fact that so many people were involved was a good thing, but if the trade went belly up, they would not be happy with him, no matter how much they had known the risks beforehand.

Sarah had laid out some nibbles and was offering coffees and fresh orange and apple juice around, but this was not a party. This was work and the champagne was hidden away for now.

Howell Media had slowly been creeping down every hour and was now trading at $5.89. Dean and Jack had been watching it fighting a losing battle in Dean's office. It would occasionally rally, and when it did, Jack was all over buying. Dean knew better; he had the inside track and had to time things to perfection. Jack's trigger finger was not helping, so Dean was relieved when some of the guests arrived and gave Jack something else to think about.

"Jack, go and sort some drinks out for people. You're making me nervous."

"I'm making myself nervous, Dean. I think I need the toilet."

"*Again*, Jack? Sort yourself out, say hello to the guys and tell them where I am."

Dean's eyes never moved from the board where the candle was flickering blue and heading in an upward direction.

Oliver and four of his young colleagues were in the kitchen.

"Hello, Mrs Harrison."

"Hello, Oliver, I like your haircut. You don't look so much of a prick."

Oliver's Army laughed, but the teasing didn't bother Oliver anymore. He had done a lot of growing up in the last six months.

"Thanks, Mrs Harrison. You know Martin, and this is Laura, John and Steven."

"Pleased to meet you all. Help yourselves to some nibbles. Coffee, anyone?"

They all wanted a coffee. The Nespresso stash was going to take a beating today.

Jack joined them in the kitchen. "Hi, guys, this is exciting, isn't it? Now remember, if you want to pull out, now is the time. If it all goes wrong then you have no one to blame but yourselves. Anyone got itchy feet?"

"No, we are all OK. What will be, will be, Jack. Where's Dean?"

Jack pointed to Dean's office. "He's in there. He's not taken his eyes off the trading board for the last hour. It's still dropping, but occasionally flickers the other way."

Dean had a big office, but it looked far from big right now. People were coming and going, a few disappearing into the garden for a nervous fag, others popping out to the kitchen for another coffee or a bite to eat. It was 4pm – 10am in Jamaica. Dean was in the box seat, his eyes trained on the trading candle which had tumbled to $4.60. It seemed like everyone in the trading world was on a different page to the Harrison household and could not get rid of Howell Media shares quickly enough. The company's assets alone were worth ten times what the shares were trading at right now, which only meant one thing – Howell Media was going under.

Jack was getting twitchy again. "Dean, it won't go much lower."

Dean was staring at over £4 million on his laptop with the trade set up ready to buy. He did not flinch, blink or reply. There was no need to reply.

"Fuck, I need another wee."

Dean and Sarah's house had three toilets, and all of them had nervous queues at the moment.

At 4.07pm, the shares went for another tumble to $4.22. The candle was red and the price was falling. Dean's eyes were still not blinking, staring at the screen as if nobody else was in the room.

A shout of, "Dean, make the fucking deal," was followed by, "He knows what he is doing, back the fuck off."

At 4.11pm the shares hit $4.03.

"He'll put it on now."

Dean had not spoken for over thirty minutes; he was in the zone. Then he broke his silence.

"OK, just a bit longer."

Jack walked back in just as the candle turned blue and shot up to $12.

"Fucking hell, Dean," was followed by a team, "Shhhhh!"

Jack looked at Dean. "I can't fucking stand this," he said and walked out again.

At 4.15pm, the candle turned red and went down as quickly as it had flown up. It was back to $5.76.

"OK, just a bit longer. That was its last flip, like a fish dying in the bottom of my dad's boat. They always give a last flip when they are on their way out."

Everyone was listening; there were no more shouts. Dean looked at his watch, it was 4.24pm and thirty seconds. The candle was red and flying down; it hit $3.00, then $2.50. The company was more or less worthless, but still Dean did not make the trade.

Dean now had his watch in front of his face – five, four, three, two. On one, he hit Buy. The price was $1.56.

The confirmation appeared on the centre of the screen. "Right, we are on, boys and girls. Say a prayer, cross your fingers, touch some wood, stand on one leg, salute a magpie – do whatever you think might help. There is no turning back now."

The price tipped down to $1.34, and then something happened. The candle flickered blue, and then red, then blue, blue, blue – $1.30 became $2.30; $2.30 became $7.30, and it kept going up. There were no more red lights; the Bulls had taken control and were running riot.

"Fucking hell, Dean, you called a Bull Run." Being at the start of a Bull Run was what traders' dreams were made of.

Dean took a deep breath, which felt like the first breath he had taken for hours.

"It won't turn back now. Look at him go."

The price was already up to $23.60, and if Dean took his eyes off it for a second, it had gone up a couple of dollars more by the time he looked back.

"What makes something turn like that?" one of the traders in the room asked.

Dean turned on the TV on the other wall and went to see Sarah in the kitchen. She was with Jack.

"We got $1.56, Jack. Sarah, can I have a coffee, please?"

Sarah gave Dean a kiss. "I assume that's good, Dean," she said. Jack answered for him as Dean was catching his breath.

"Good, Sarah? Your husband's…can I swear?"

Sarah patted him on the back. "You've been swearing like a trooper all day, I don't think you need permission now."

"Have I?" Bemused by the thought of it, Jack continued. "OK, your husband is a fucking star, clowns or no clowns." He started to dance. "It just needs to turn now, Yorkie."

"It already has, Jack. We have what we call a…Sarah, can I swear?"

Sarah had an 'if you can't beat them, join them' look all over her face. "You may as well, Dean, every other fucker has been."

Sarah always had been able to make Dean laugh, and at that moment he realised why.

"OK, Jack, are you sitting comfortably? We have a fucking Bull Run."

Jack's face straightened out, then he looked over to the office where everyone was cheering and shouting. There was even some singing.

Oliver ran out. "Jack, Jack, it's running – $38."

Martin popped his head round the door. "It's $41, actually."

Jack picked Dean up and carried him back to the office. The gathered traders jumped all over him.

"OK, guys, OK. Calm down," he said, getting up from the bottom of the pile. "Even running Bulls get tired. Let me see what's going on."

Dean had one eye on the board and another on *Sky News*. The shares were trading at $65 and still climbing.

"Right, quiet!" There was silence; a flicker of red lit up the trading candle. "What is it I say about trading, Oliver?" Dean asked.

"It's about when you get in and when you get out," Oliver answered. With that one statement, the atmosphere again became tense. The Bull was getting tired as more and more Bears got in its way.

Dean looked at the figure on his spreadsheet. "OK, that will do. That's covered Dexter, no need to be greedy."

The candle was still more blue than red and had a last burst just before Dean sold the shares as quickly as he'd bought them.

"OK, sold at $72.43. It was still climbing, but it's about done. Who cares about a few extra bucks?" He punched the figures into the spreadsheet. "OK, scores on the doors, boys and girls – £4.15 million placed at $1.78 and sold at $72.43…that's 164 million, 414 thousand, 606 pounds and 74 pence."

There was a big cheer. Dean added with a grin, "Oh, and less the twenty-five per cent to help bail me out with Dexter – thank you all for that. Our shared profit is just over £123 million. You can see your individual amounts on this spreadsheet. Enjoy your lives."

Another big cheer went up.

Dean walked back into the kitchen. "I think they will want some champagne, Sarah." Sarah already had the glasses out and was waiting for the nod. Dean walked out onto the lawn and took a seat near the patio, exhausted. As Jack joined him, they heard the first of many champagne corks flying for the sky with the customary pop.

"It all feels a bit wrong, Jack. Someone just lost their life and we took advantage of it. It doesn't seem right to celebrate."

Jack looked back at the kitchen where a couple more pops were greeted with a cheer.

"Hugo Hodgkinson was a dick, Yorkie, and everyone's time is up at some point."

"Yes, but I know where he is heading next and who he is going to meet along the way. And no one really deserves that, no matter how much of a dick he was. Has it been on the news yet?"

Jack thought better than to question Dean about what he meant. "No, not yet, but Jamaica news is not UK news. It might be on Bloomberg later. It's probably best they don't know what went on. I'm sure they will find out in the next couple of days. Anyway, it's not your fault. Whoever told you must have had their reasons."

Dean lifted his head. "You're right, Jack. Let's have a drink and then get rid of this lot. I feel like I have been given a chance of sorting my life out. I've got well over the fifty million needed for Dexter, and I reckon he will lose half of his staff. They probably don't need to work there anymore."

"Dexter's alright, but he's greedy. He stitched you up, Yorkie, don't forget that. And you are one of the reasons his company is what it is today. He deserves everything coming his way."

"Thanks, Jack, for being there for Sarah, Jodie and me."

Jack gave Dean a hug.

"Come on, Yorkie, there's some champers in there with your name on it."

Chapter 42 – The Jigsaw is Complete

After the other traders had left, Jack and Dean entered the office. The trading board was still showing Howell Media; the price had stabilised at $55, so getting out of the trade at over $70 had been a result.

Dean changed the TV channel to Bloomberg. A breaking news banner was at the bottom of the screen.

Billionaire Hugo Hodgkinson has died in a helicopter crash. The presenter declared that the pictures were just in from the scene. Mr Hodgkinson had been piloting his helicopter to sign a deal with Howell Media. He never made it to the meeting, his helicopter hitting some overhead cables while attempting to land at a hotel in Jamaica. The presenter added that Mr Hodgkinson had died instantly. Howell Media's shares had tumbled to just over a dollar and the deal had been seen as a bad thing by the markets. As news of the helicopter crash filtered through, the markets knew that the deal was off and the shares recovered to a year's high before stabilising at around $50.

Dean and Jack watched and listened to the news anchor.

"In a statement, Mr Hodgkinson's son Robert has asked that the family have time to grieve over what was a terrible accident. It is thought at this early stage that pilot error was to blame; the weather was fine and the helicopter had just been serviced."

The presenter had some more breaking news delivered into his earpiece.

"And now we can go live to the crash scene and our reporter, Kenton Shaw. Kenton?'

"It's still early, but what we know is that Mr Hodgkinson apparently had a falling out with his son before climbing into his helicopter and making the five minute journey to the Sea Breeze Hotel. You can see the crash site behind me. Mr Hodgkinson had been going to seal a merger deal with Howell Media. There had been lots of rumblings in the markets about this deal – it was thought that Astra Zing was going to get the better of it, with the customer base of Howell Media being the main motivation behind the acquisition."

As the camera zoomed in on the crash site, Dean saw him.

"Pass me the remote, Jack." He rewound the images on the TV and paused it. "Can you see him?"

"It's just a tangled wreck, Yorkie. See who?"

A dark figure was walking into the crash site, his silver-topped cane tapping on the wreckage. Dean un-paused the picture as the camera zoomed in deeper. The reporter was saying that the fire crews had put out the fire and confirmed that Mr Hodgkinson had died at the scene. Dean watched the ambulance staff taking a body bag away, Death walking alongside the stretcher trolley.

"Sorry, Jack, I thought I saw someone."

Sarah walked into the office. "Are you OK, you two?"

Dean took a last look at the screen before turning the TV off with the remote.

"Yes, fine thanks, Sarah."

She handed them a glass of bubbly each. "Well done to you both. I guess we are in the clear with Dexter, now, Dean? Can we get on with our lives?" She gave him a kiss. "I'm so proud of you both. You won't have to work again, Jack, and can retire for good."

Jack gave her a hug.

"I won't, thanks to Dean and you, Sarah. You can buy back your timeshare now, Yorkie."

"Jack, I will transfer your funds tomorrow. Have you given me your bank details?"

"I emailed them earlier, Yorkie. Thanks again – I won't pretend to know what happened, but I'm glad it did."

It was 8pm when Jodie entered the kitchen.

"I went round Kyle's after school. His mum just dropped me off. Dad, did everything go OK?"

"It could hardly have gone better, JoJo, now give your dad a kiss."

"I knew it would be OK. Benjie told me."

Dean thought about what Benjie had told him in the circus tent. "It's the second tomorrow, isn't it?"

Sarah knew where this was heading. Benjie was going to die in the night and Dean knew it. He even knew the time.

"Yes, it is, Dean."

The mood dropped.

"Hey, it's OK, he told me he was ready to go, and he's going to see Bobo again. He's looking forward to it. No sad faces, he wouldn't want that." Dean raised his glass. "To Benjie, the best clown I have ever had the pleasure of knowing."

"To Benjie," chorused Sarah and Jodie.

Dean felt like the jigsaw in his head was complete. He knew why he had been given a second chance and had taken it with both hands. He had a good life, he loved his wife and daughter, and some things were worth fighting for. The final piece was Death giving him the chance to climb back onto the ladder he'd fallen from so spectacularly six months earlier. Now he could make a difference for the good of the world. And he knew the very first thing he was going to do.

Dean Googled minibus companies and placed an order.

"I love you, Dean Harrison," Sarah said when she saw the screen of his laptop.

"I love you too, Sarah. You'd better phone your dad and tell him the good news."

"He was the first person I phoned. He's already looking at the *Racing Post* for his new horse."

Dean looked at her beautiful face. "The new Baby Doctor?"

Sarah smiled. "He's thinking about calling it Whitby Trader."

Dean had thoughtfulness etched all over his face. Sarah gave him a playful nudge.

"What? What is it, Dean? You're thinking, and I don't like it when you think."

"I *am* thinking, Sarah. Darren said what a good doctor you were. Have you thought any more about going back? Would you like to?"

Sarah's face lit up.

"You know I would, but I'm going to enjoy a bit of time off first."

"You should, Sarah. You sorted out my leg, remember?"

"We'll see, Dean."

"Anyway, it's been a long day. Maybe we should have an early night."

"Good idea, Dean, your wife needs taking to bed."

They ran up the stairs together like naughty kids bunking off school.

It was 3am. Jodie was woken by a tap on the shoulder. She turned to see Benjie, complete with a black and white happy face, dressed all in black with white pompom buttons down his front.

Jodie sat up on the bed, yawning.

"Thanks for looking after my dad, Benjie."

Benjie gave her a hug.

"I want you to come with me, Jodie."

"Do I need to get ready?"

"No, you're fine as you are. Now let's go and get your mum and dad."

Jodie walked into her parents' bedroom. "Mum." She shook Sarah's shoulder. "Mum!"

Sarah opened one eye and looked at the bedside clock.

"Jodie, it's the middle of the night."

Jodie shook her again to make sure her other eye opened.

"We have a visitor, Mum."

Light was bleeding in from the landing, illuminating a clown-shaped silhouette.

"Benjie?"

"Hi, Sarah, thanks for coming to see me the other day." He bowed his head in appreciation before continuing. "I would be honoured if you and Dean would accompany me and Jodie. I would like you to see me off, if that's OK?"

Sarah remembered she was naked and pulled the covers up to her neck.

"Dean, Dean, wake up. It's Benjie."

Dean woke up and saw Benjie in the doorway.

"Benjie, we weren't expecting you. Sorry, can we help?"

"I can see you weren't expecting me." Benjie smiled and looked at Jodie. "Shall we give them a minute to get ready, Jodie?"

Jodie gave her mum and dad a 'have you two been at it?' look and rolled her eyes at them. She could think of nothing more disgusting.

"I think you might need some clothes on. Come on, Benjie, we'll wait outside."

Dean and Sarah were ready in seconds.

"Sorry, Benjie. Are you OK?" asked Dean.

"Do I look OK?"

Dean looked him up and down. "You've never looked better, Benjie, and the happy face suits you. I've always liked your happy face."

"Today is a happy day, I don't want any tears." Benjie looked at Jodie. "Especially from you, young lady. I am going to see Bobo again."

As they followed Benjie into the bathroom, the room transformed into the riverbank near the Ferryman's jetty. Dean recognised the place instantly, and did not want Sarah and Jodie to experience what he had gone through. The atmosphere was different today, though – no mist; no angry water; just a serene calmness.

Dean looked at his watch; it was a minute or so before 3:15am.

Benjie said, "They will be here in a minute," and from behind the reeds came David the barman, followed by Molly and her dog, Oscar. Then came Bill the train guard and Mrs McCauley, as well as Betty and Albert. Dean guessed Albert must have been having a bad day if he was in this world. They all looked resplendent, dressed in black.

As they walked past, saying hello to Dean and his family, a couple of them stopped for a kiss.

"Jodie, we are all proud of you for the chess game," said Mrs McCauley.

As the guides formed a line by the riverbank, Benjie gave Dean and his family a smile.

"I wanted you to be here. There are only a few we manage to get back, so he allows us to have guests when we go. It's a sort of perk of the job."

Dean was fully aware of who 'he' was. Although he respected Death, he wasn't really looking forward to seeing him again.

"It's all fine, Dean, you're no longer on his radar. We get a special send-off – no need for cloak and daggers with us. He's thanking us for our help, and when we need to go, he makes sure everything is fine."

Just then, Death appeared through the reeds and shook hands with the other guides, taking his place at the end of the line. Benjie looked at his fellow guides and friends, all waiting patiently to say goodbye to him.

"Well, here goes. Thanks for sharing this moment with me."

He gave Sarah a hug. "Thank you, Benjie. Thanks for getting him back to me."

Benjie wiped a tear from her face. "Sarah, I'm ready to go. Happy thoughts, please. Smile – I'm a clown; I like smiles. And you, young lady, we are all very proud of you. Make sure you have a nice life. We will all be looking out for you – we might even visit you from time to time."

Jodie threw her arms around his big frame. "I love you, Benjie."

Benjie uncoupled her hands from around his waist.

"I know you do. Make sure you look after your mum and dad, Jodie."

"Are you going to be OK, Benjie?" Tears flowed from her watery eyes. She started to speak again, but before she could, Benjie put his finger to her lips.

"Happy thoughts, remember? I haven't brought you here to go all weepy on me. And you, Dean, thanks for the journey. I can't thank you enough for your performance in the Big Top – you make a great clown."

Benjie took a black flower out of his lapel and gave it to Sarah, who instantly drew it in and hugged it.

"Dean, you made a sad old clown into a happy old clown. You are without doubt the second best Bobo I have ever met."

Benjie gave Dean a wink, then looked over to the line. The guides had formed a guard of honour, their hands clasped ready for Benjie to do his final walk.

"I'd better go."

As Benjie walked past his fellow guides, they stopped him for hugs, kisses and handshakes along the way. Death made a circular gesture with his cane to beckon Charon, but there was no crashing of waves this time, just the unmistakable sound of an oar lightly disturbing water. In the distance, the ferry was making haste across the water – with a passenger. A clown-shaped passenger, dressed exactly opposite to Benjie. Where Benjie wore black, the other clown wore white, and where Benjie wore white, the other clown wore black.

Benjie's face lit up. "Bobo!" he shouted. "It's Bobo."

Everyone cheered as Charon wheeled the boat astern to shore

up on the jetty. There were no histrionics, even from the Ferryman. Charon looked like it was his day off from being Mr Scary.

Benjie stepped onto the boat and hugged his long-time partner. As quickly as the ferry had arrived, it left again, with Bobo and Benjie heading for whatever was next. They turned and waved to the special guests who were there to witness it.

As the boat disappeared, there was a click of Death's fingers and Jodie and her parents were tucked up in their beds again.

Dean opened one eye. He was naked with his adoring wife hugging him.

"Good luck, Benjie," he whispered before rolling onto his side to sleep.

Chapter 43 – Enjoy Every Second

The next morning, Dean was first up. He wandered downstairs to sort out breakfast for his girls.

A black rose stood in the middle of a vase on the kitchen worktop. He took it out and smelt its beautiful scent before replacing it. Putting a capsule into the coffee machine, he set it off to make its unmistakable coffee producing noise.

Today was going to be a good day. Dean went to his office and checked his emails, finding a receipt from the minibus company and a picture. He'd asked for the Sweet Dreams logo to be put on the side of the new bus and he smiled to himself when he saw it. It was nice to be doing something good, and to be honest, if the home's old bus had not made it to Beachy Head, he might not even be here.

The phone rang. Before the man on the other end could speak, Dean said, "Is that Dr Rhodes – James?"

"Yes, Dean, it is. I have some sad news…"

"No you haven't, James, you have some happy news."

"Have I?"

"Yes, James. Benjie has gone, I know, but he got a good send off, and he's back with Bobo. He's very happy, I assure you."

There was a pause before James answered.

"Is there any point in me asking how you know this?"

"You can ask, but I won't tell you. James, will you be at the home this afternoon? Sarah and I were thinking of popping over. We have a surprise for you."

"Of course, Dean, I'll be in all afternoon."

"OK, we'll see you about one pm-ish. Have a good day, James."

Dean put the phone down and returned to the kitchen, taking his espresso from the coffee machine and replacing it with an empty cup as he could hear murmurings from upstairs. Sarah appeared, looking as lovely as ever. She was greeted with a kiss and a coffee.

"Thanks, Dean. Who was that on the phone?"

Dean sat next to her on the breakfast bar.

"That was James Rhodes from Sweet Dreams. Hey, I have something to show you."

Dean ran and got his Mac from the office. "Look," he said proudly.

"Very nice. How did you get the logo on it?"

"Well, I asked them to pinch the logo from the home's website and put it on both sides of the bus."

Sarah gave him a sarcastic 'my hero' look. "You're so clever, Dean."

"I said we would pop over this afternoon. And we are giving James this, if that's OK?" Dean showed Sarah a cheque he'd written out for £500,000.

"Of course it's OK, Dean, that place is something special. Did he mention Benjie?"

Dean looked down. "Yes, that's why he rang. I told him Benjie was fine with it and..." He paused. "Was I the only one, Sarah?"

Just then, Jodie appeared.

"No, Mum and I were there too, Dad. Weren't we, Mum?"

Sarah smiled at Dean.

"You're not crazy, Dean, unless we all are. We were all there."

"Thank God for that. And are you both OK about it?"

"I'm OK with it, although I liked Benjie visiting. I'm going to miss him."

"We all are, Jodie, he was a nice man." Sarah gave her daughter a kiss on her head before adding, "Right, what time is the big surprise going to arrive at the home, Dean?"

Dean looked at his watch, more as an automatic reaction than to confirm when the minibus would be arriving. He would even look at his watch if someone asked when someone's birthday was.

"I said about one pm. I have to transfer some money to make some people very happy this morning, including my old friend, Dexter. I'd love to see the look on his face when he gets the mail."

"Dean, no gloating. Show some class, please."

Dean transferred the £50 million to Dexter with a lovely email thanking him for all his help over the years and wishing him luck in the future. Dean wrote this email with a grimace on his face as he knew Dexter had stitched him up good and proper, but Sarah was right. It was the classy thing to do.

After paying everyone off, Dean was left with over £30 million. He and Sarah could do anything they wanted, but that didn't seem right. It wasn't blood money, but it felt a bit like it was. Both he and Sarah would make a list of worthy causes that could benefit; they only wanted enough to get by.

Sarah had put on some makeup and a nice purple and white polka dot dress.

"Come on then, Dean, let's go."

They arrived at Sweet Dreams at 1pm and did the visiting rounds of all the guests before asking the staff to bring Dean's guides out to the front of the home. James Rhodes stood at the front of the guides.

"We thought that your old bus looked a bit battered and bruised, James, so Sarah, Jodie and I decided you needed a new one."

As the words came out of Dean's mouth, a brand new bus in the Sweet Dreams colours made its way into the drive. The driver handed the keys to Dean, who in turn handed them over to James.

"You can't give us this, Dean, you just can't."

Dean asked Sarah for the cheque she had in her handbag.

"Oh, and this is to keep her in fuel."

James looked at him.

"No, you can't. Really, Dean, you can't."

Sarah caught James's eye.

"You know how much this place and these people mean to Dean," she said. The doctor stood motionless, looking at the bus and then the cheque. All of his staff gathered around him.

Dean took Sarah by the hand.

"Come on, let's go." They waved at James Rhodes and made their way home.

Over the next eight weeks, the world still revolved as normal, but there were some changes. Dexter lost over half of his senior staff, and a couple of notable junior ones. Dean had set up a small trading company from a new office he had constructed in his back garden, and Oliver, Martin and Jack had all joined him. They were not being greedy, just sensible, and were doing very well out of it.

It was the end of term, and tonight was the Christmas prom at Jodie's school. Jack, Oliver and Martin were having a beer in the kitchen, talking about the day's trading. It had been another good day. Dean's mother had come down from the north for Christmas – Dean remembered how he had hardly spoken to her for years before his accident, and he was putting right as many wrongs as he could. She was sitting in the conservatory, looking through old photographs.

"Hi, Mam, are you OK?"

"Sarah told me all about your car crash, Dean, and Beachy Head. She asked me to come down to see you, but I thought…you know, after not seeing each other for all these years, you wouldn't want to see me then…" Rosie was fighting back the tears. "You should have rung me before you got so low."

"I was a mess, Mam. Things all went wrong, but you're right – one phone call would have put it all right. I know that now." He smiled at his mum; she had always been there for him and always would be.

"Anyway, get on with it." Dean looked at the large photo album. "I know you want to show me them."

"You've seen them all, Dean. You haven't seen these ones, though."

Rosie Harrison took out a small photo album and passed it to Dean.

"Your dad and I removed these when you got older and we knew."

"Knew what?" Dean opened the album. There were only five pictures inside.

"We knew that you were special, Dean. Your dad joked that if we left them in and people saw them, they would think I'd had a fling with the mysterious older man at our wedding."

Dean looked at first picture. It was taken at his mum and dad's wedding, and he was singing with his dad. The next showed them all on stage at the end – Mr Hawthorn and all the other guests.

"How long have you known, Mam?" he asked as a tear formed in his eye.

"Your dad and I have always known. We knew even more when you broke that glass ship on the mantelpiece like you said you would." Rosie took Dean in her arms. "We love you, Dean.

We never brought it up much, but we both knew."

"Thanks, Mam. I miss Dad, you know. It was lovely seeing him again."

Rosie took the pictures back and placed them into safekeeping in her bag as Sarah shouted to them both from the kitchen.

"Dean, Rosie, come in here. I've got something to show you."

As Dean walked in, he saw Jodie.

"Jodie, you look amazing." She was in a pink halter-neck dress and black high heels, and her hair was a mass of ringlets down her back.

"Do I scrub up OK, then, Dad?"

"Jodie, you look so grown up. I'm so proud. You look stunning – a beautiful young lady."

Dean's eyes started to well up, but Jack had beaten him to it and was in floods of tears.

"You look lovely, Jodie," Oliver added. He was turning out not to be a prick after all. Maybe he had just needed a dash of reality in his life to realise how it all works.

The doorbell rang.

"Well, are you going to get it, Jodie?" Wiping away a tear, Dean pulled himself together and stood with an arm around Sarah and his mum.

"Hi, Kyle, come in."

Kyle had a suit on with a pink tie to match Jodie's outfit. Doreen was with him.

"Let's have a picture of you two lovebirds," Doreen said, thrusting a camera in their faces. Jodie hated having her picture taken, but was willing to make an exception today.

Dean shook Kyle's hand and pulled him in for a manly hug.

"Make sure you look after her, she is very special. If you don't, I'll…" Dean stopped, "Oh, never mind."

"I know she's special, Mr Harrison. I promise I will."

His little girl was growing up, and Dean was going to enjoy this moment. It was then he noticed the black flower in the back of Jodie's hair.

"I'll never forget Benjie, Dad, he brought you back to me. And don't worry about Kyle – I'll kill him if he doesn't look after me."

Jodie walked off hand in hand with Kyle to the taxi, Dean and Sarah watching her walk away. She turned as Kyle opened the door for her and flicked her hair around her shoulders as she blew a kiss to her parents.

There was a tattoo of a clown's face with *Benjie* written underneath on the back of her shoulder.

"Jodie!" Dean shouted.

"Shit!" Jodie said under her breath. "Come on, Kyle, we need to get out of here." She added a further three or four 'Shits' as they climbed into the taxi.

"Did you know she had that tattoo?" Before Sarah could answer, Dean's question turned into a rant. "I can't believe she's got a tattoo! She's only fifteen. Did you know, Sarah? I wouldn't let her have one and she knows that."

Sarah put her hand to his lips. "Dean, there are more important things in life to worry about. Anyway, it's a mother and daughter thing."

"What! You knew she had it? I can't believe it, Sarah, you let her get a tattoo?"

Sarah lowered the top of her dress. "Dean, you can't have a Benjie without a Bobo." There was a tattoo of a clown on her shoulder with Bobo written underneath. "And you're the *best* Bobo I have ever met," she added.

Dean started to laugh. "I love you, Sarah."

"I know, Mr Harrison. This is your second life. Not many get more than one, so I think you need to chill out a bit, don't you?"

"She's still in trouble when she gets in."

Sarah gave him the smile that had melted his heart all those years ago when they first met, and still did today.

"No, she's not, Dean. We both know she's not."

They waved at Jodie and Kyle as the taxi slipped out of view.

The End

Acknowledgements

Claire Lince (My Wife)	For chess & book cover idea
Alison Jack (Editor)	For turning water into wine
Julia Gibbs (Proofreader)	Made sure wine wasn't corked
Nik (bookbeaver)	For cover art

Readers who I forced to read and contributed;

Martin Gibb	Molly & her dog
Loretta Georgio	Sarah's back story
Phil Lince	For reading & feedback
Jenifer Lince (Mam)	For reading & feedback
Abbie Lince	For reading & feedback
Ian Hutchinson	For reading & feedback
Greg Openshaw	For reading & feedback
Iva Brunning	For reading & feedback
Gary Millward	For reading & feedback
Paul Carter	For reading & feedback
Ian & Diane Vart	For reading it on our holiday
Pierre Roets	For reading and feedback
Marske Fisherman Choir	For allowing their name

Early reviewers;

Michelle Ryles	Twitter - @thebookmagnet
Meggan Turner	Twitter - @MegsTyas

About The Author

Trev Lince originates from Marske-by-the-Sea on the north-east coast of England, but now lives in Darlington with his wife, Claire. Their daughter, Annie, is a very good guitarist and is setting up a band, playing every pub in the north-east that she can. She's so rock and roll, living the dream while her father is approaching his mid-life crisis.

A keen golfer and frustrated Middlesbrough FC fan, Trev gets to as many matches as work and leisure time allow. He writes in what little spare time he has, when not working as an IT Consultant for a major oil company in Surrey.

Room 119 – The Whitby Trader is Trev's first book and he really enjoyed the experience of writing it. Who knows? He may have a few more stories bursting to get out of his head.

He would like to thank you for reading his debut novel.

Made in the USA
San Bernardino, CA
16 June 2018